THE FAVOURITE OF THE HAREM

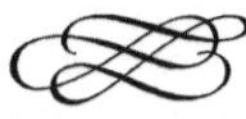

CINDY DAVIES

ODYSSEY
BOOKS

Published by Odyssey Books in 2023
www.odysseybooks.com.au

A catalogue record for this book is available from the National Library of Australia

ISBN: 978-1922311566 (pbk)
ISBN: 978-1922311573 (ebook)

For my husband Harvey, who shares my interest in all things Turkish.

And remembering the kind friends we made when we lived in Zonguldak, Türkiye.

In memory of the people of Türkiye who perished in the earthquake of February 2023.

AUTHOR'S NOTE

The Favourite of the Harem is set in Constantinople (present day Istanbul), Türkiye, in the year 1518. The Turkish Ottoman Empire was expanding, and it was the custom for the sultan's sons to serve as Prince Governors in various parts of the empire.

The imperial palaces were staffed by slaves and eunuchs. All the royal children had mothers who were slaves. These women were captured in the regions around Türkiye: the Balkans, Poland, Lithuania, the Crimea, Russia, and Armenia. They were purchased in the Constantinople slave market, which was near the present-day closed bazaar. In the novel, I relocated it nearer to the harbour to make the scene more dramatic.

As was sometimes the case, the sultan's sons had their own quarters and harems in the Topkapı Palace. At the time of my novel (1518), the imperial harem was, in fact, housed in the Old Palace, not the Topkapı Palace. I decided to set the novel in Topkapı to make it easier for the prince to access his harem. He was also close to the sultan, the seat of power.

The harem was not the lascivious palace of debauchery depicted by some nineteenth-century artists and writers, but a well-organised entity run like a present-day corporation. The novel is a love story, but also examines the intrigues and personal interactions between the inhabitants of Prince Orhan's harem.

Everyone who was brought into the palace, including captured soldiers, female slaves, and eunuchs, had to convert to Islam. The harem was staffed by eunuchs, both African and Caucasian. They all received an education, some worked as servants, and some gave lessons to the women, including reading and writing in Turkish. In a large harem, very few women spent the night with a prince or the sultan. Often a sultan gifted an *odalisque*, a harem woman, in marriage to high-ranking officers of the empire. The odalisques could also request to leave the harem after a given time. Those who remained spent their time studying, embroidering, or learning a musical instrument. Some rose by their own talents to powerful positions in the organisation. Others shared the care of the sultan's or prince's children.

The most powerful person in the imperial harem was the sultan's mother, the Valide Sultan. This was also the case for a prince who had his own harem. The *Kızlar Ağası*, the chief eunuch in charge of the women, worked closely with the sultan or prince's mother. In *The Favourite of the Harem*, this is Abdul, from North Africa.

The sultan's first-born son, the *shezade* (shayzādeh) or crown prince, did not automatically become the next sultan. Whichever son succeeded the sultan, it was the custom, from 1453, that he ordered the executions of his half-brothers. This was a way of avoiding civil war.

Under pressure from the women of the Imperial Harem, fratricide ended in 1603. A system of luxurious imprisonment called 'The Golden Cage' replaced it for extraneous brothers.

Royal and high-ranking women had the title *sultan* after their names; in the novel this is the prince's mother, Emira. Others were called *hatun*, meaning 'lady'. Initially, all new entrants to the harem were called *jariye*, meaning 'slave'.

In 1923, six hundred years of Ottoman rule ended in Türkiye, and the last sultan went into exile. The shrunken empire became a republic. In order to improve literacy rates, its first president, Mustafa

Kemal Atatürk, changed Turkish from Arabic script to Latin script. Thus only a few students of the old Ottoman Turkish can read historical documents written prior to 1928. The former palace at Topkapı is now a museum, housing thousands of Ottoman documents. Yet very few of them relate to the women of the imperial harem. What little information we have about them are comments in letters written by foreign envoys or their wives. There are also letters written by some of the favourite concubines to the reigning sultan.

I lived in Türkiye for two years and learned the language. I've used some Turkish in the novel, followed by an English translation.

I've included a list of characters and titles in the Ottoman Empire, as well as a pronunciation guide and maps to help describe the complex world of the harem. In addition, I've uploaded lots of photographs of the harem and the Topkapı palace buildings on my website: www.cindydavies.com.au

I hope you enjoy reading *The Favourite of the Harem*.

Cindy Davies, Sydney, Australia

LIST OF CHARACTERS

The Sultan of the Ottoman—Father of Prince Orhan. Also known as the pādishah

Prince Orhan—The second son of the Sultan of the Ottoman Empire

Rusalka Maria Ivanova, also called Süreyya Jariye (Süreyya the slave)—A young Russian woman, niece of Bishop Andrei of Slavo

Hafiz Pasha—A general in the Ottoman Army, friend of Prince Orhan

Abdul Agha *(eye-a)*—The chief black eunuch in charge of Prince Orhan's harem

Roshan Kalfa—A servant and Mistress of the House, assistant to Abdul

Perihan Jariye—Süreyya's young Russian-speaking servant

Sami—A child eunuch

Emira Sultan—The prince's mother, who oversees her son's harem

Zeki—A eunuch in the service of Emira Sultan

Galina/Melek—An old school friend of Süreyya's, now in the harem

Davut Hodja—Süreyya's teacher

Zeynep Hatun—Another odalisque and Süreyya's rival

Father Dmitri—A Greek Orthodox priest who lives with his wife Irene in Kyrgios, a Greek village near Constantinople

Oya and Ayşe—Two young women from Poland, who were purchased at the slave market by the prince's mother

Gülbahar—Emira's old friend, who used to run a high-class brothel in the city

Şefika—A high-class prostitute who visits the harem to teach lovemaking

Yusuf Agha—The eunuch in charge of the harem in Edirne, an Ottoman city

Prince Ahmet—Younger half-brother of Prince Orhan

Prince Murad—Older half-brother of Prince Orhan

Bishop Andrei and Aunt Ludmilla—Süreyya's Russian uncle and aunt

Vasily Ljubov—The man Süreyya's uncle wants her to marry

TITLES USED IN THE SIXTEENTH-CENTURY OTTOMAN COURT

Agha (pron. Eye-a)—Honorific title for a high-ranking male

Cariye (pron. Jariyeh)—Slave: used as the suffix to the names of harem servants

Haseki—Chief consort of a prince or the sultan

Hatun—Lady: used as a suffix to an odalisque's name

Hodja (Turkish: Hoca)—Learned man, a teacher

Ikbal—Favourite concubine of a prince or sultan

Imam—Muslim cleric who instructs students in Koranic studies

Kalfa—A servant in charge of a department within the harem

Kızlar Ağası (Kuh z lar I a suh)—The chief eunuch, head of a harem who was in charge of the women

Muezzin—The man who climbs to the top of a minaret and calls the faithful to prayers five times a day

Pasha (Turkish: Paşa)—A title for a prominent statesman or military leader

Pādishah—An alternative title for the sultan

Sultan—This title is also given to a former female consort of the sultan and in formal address to the sultan's children, both male and female

Vizier (Turkish: Vezir)—Title for ministers of the sultan—often only three or four men had this honorific. The grand vizier was the sultan's chief minister

TURKISH PRONUNCIATION GUIDE

Ş ş—sh (as in ship)

Ç ç—ch (as in cherry)

Ğ ğ—Unvocalised: the word *tuğra* is pronounced *turah* in English

I ı—The undotted I, pronounced like *uh* in English. Topkapı palace is *Topkapuh*

Ü ü—Similar to French u (as in *tu*)

Ö ö—Similar to French eu (as in *deux*)

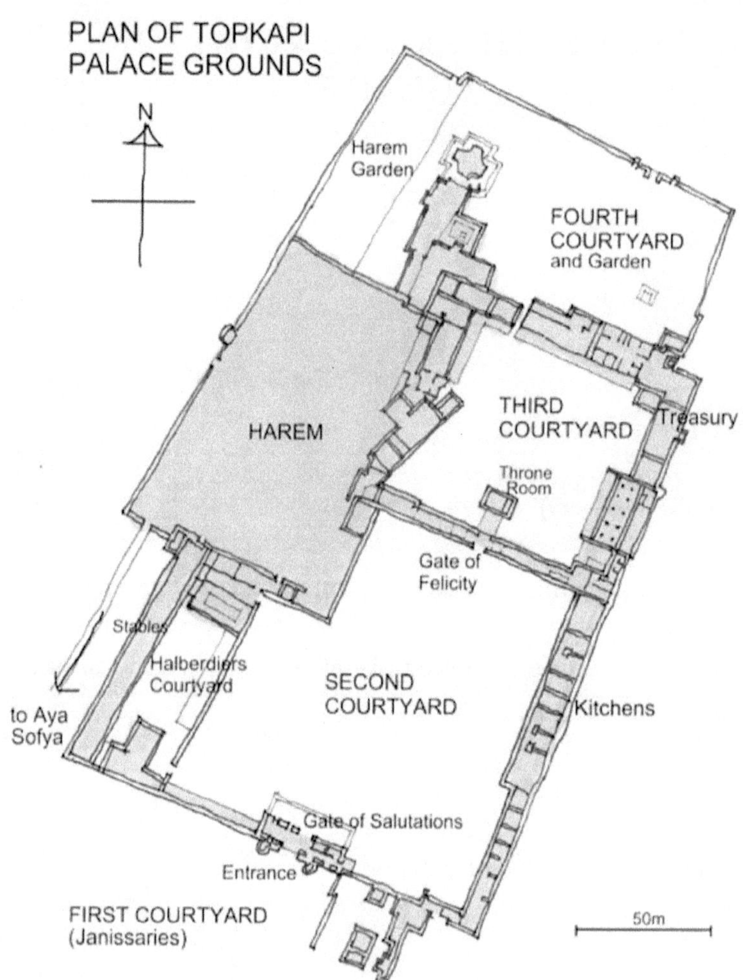

PLAN OF TOPKAPI
PALACE GROUNDS
N
Harem
Garden
FOURTH
COURTYARD
and Garden
HAREM
THIRD
COURTYARD
Treasury
Throne
Room
Gate of
Felicity
Stables
Halberdiers
Courtyard
SECOND
COURTYARD
to Aya
Sofya
Kitchens
Gate of Salutations
Entrance
FIRST COURTYARD
(Janissaries)
50m

PLAN OF 16TH CENTURY CONSTANTINOPLE [ISTANBUL]

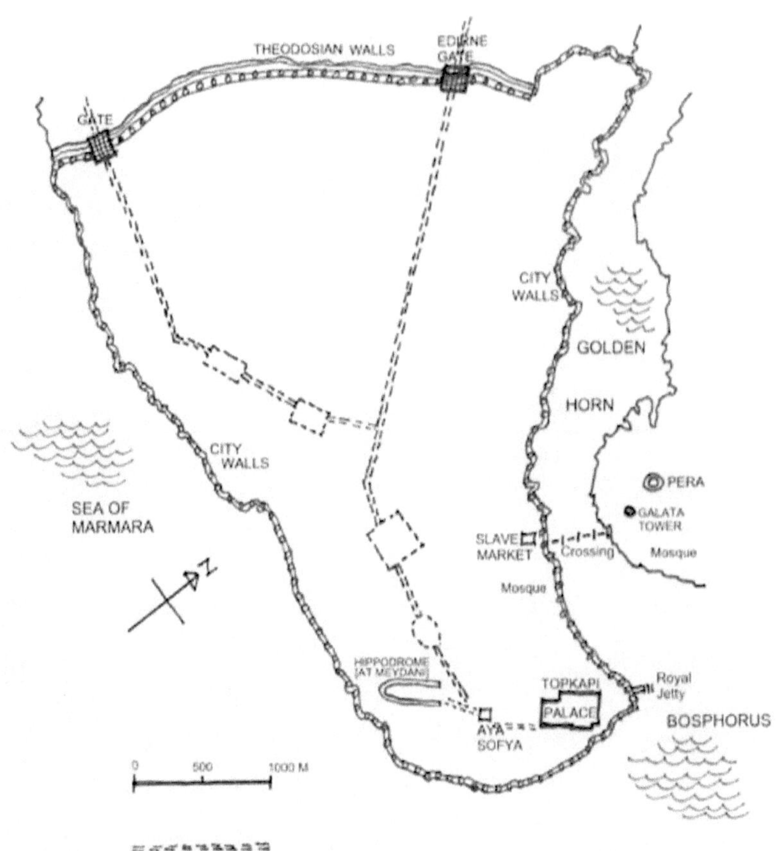

I see only your beauty
when I open my eyes,
I drink only your wine, dear
when I open my lips
To talk with the people,
That seems sinful to me—
When I talk about you, dear
—long, so long is my tale!

— MEVLĀNA JALALUDDIN RUMI, A THIRTEENTH-
CENTURY PERSIAN POET, WHOSE WORK WAS
POPULAR IN THE EARLY OTTOMAN COURT

CHAPTER 1

The sailing ship rolled and lurched. Huddled in a cramped rope cupboard on deck, Rusalka prayed that her life would not end in a watery grave. She had survived the slave-trader's raid on her town in Russia, when the Tartars captured her and she was force-marched for days across the grasslands, a rope around her neck and her hands tied to a stick down her back. At the docks in the Crimean city of Kalla, they separated her from the group and pushed her toward the open deck.

'Keep this beauty away from the others!' a rough voice called. 'She's worth a lot in the slave market.'

On board, they shoved her into the rope store. Rusalka spent the four-day voyage able to stand and sit but scarcely able to move. They let her out only to relieve herself in a stinking bucket on deck. Once a day, a sailor pushed victuals at her through a small hatch. She knew the ship's destination was Constantinople in Türkiye, and the ship's owners would sell his human cargo, including her, as slaves. Unless … *unless* she could escape.

The ship rolled again. With a loud snap, the door of her prison flew open; outside, the rain-soaked deck was momentarily empty, and spray from the churning sea hit her in the face. Rusalka dropped to her knees and crawled out on all fours, kicking the door shut behind her. She moved as quickly as she could toward a wooden box and hunched behind it on the sodden boards. Sailors ran past, yelling and cursing as the vessel plunged forward. No one noticed her crouching figure, as she rubbed her stiff and aching limbs.

A flash of lightning lit up the grey sky. The ship's rail was near, and she crawled toward it, sliding on the drenched deck. The vessel listed toward the shore side. Rusalka grasped the rail and pulled herself up. She crossed herself and whispered, 'Save me, Holy Virgin Mary!' as thunder erupted overhead.

Lightning tore through the sky and illuminated city walls, a mosque … this was her only chance to escape. Rusalka crossed herself once more. At the next thunderclap, she clambered over the side, seizing the damp wood with her fingers. She winced as the wind flung her against the ship, and her weakened arms ached as she clung on. The black water below swirled and slapped the ship. Suddenly the vessel rolled to starboard, and she gripped harder. She looked over her shoulder; it was still too dangerous to jump.

With another lurch, the ship tilted toward the land, and Rusalka saw seaweed floating on the water. Her heart clenched with fear; it was now or never. A gust of wind filled the ship's sails. She uncurled her fingers, felt the vessel heave, and her skirt billowed around her as she plummeted downward.

Prince Orhan grabbed the tiller of the imperial caique, as the waters of his beloved Bosphorus turned ugly. 'Hold steady!' he yelled to the crew above the wind and thunder.

A sailing ship veered past them, its wash threatening to splinter the royal caique against the dock. The bostanji, the armed mariners who rowed the imperial caique, pulled hard on their oars against the current and the wash from the sailing ship. The prince glanced at the other vessel as it tilted sideways, then plunged into the Golden Horn, the channel that led to the city of Constantinople. He ordered the chief bostanji to take over as they steered the caique toward the jetty. On shore, men pulled ropes and dragged the imperial vessel into the safety of the dock.

The sailing ship was still battling its way toward the city. As Orhan leaped up onto the dock, ignoring the helping hands, he paused and watched its progress. His friend Hafız Pasha, a general in the Ottoman army, was waiting for him with six men from the Imperial Guard. They stood to attention at his approach.

'Your highness.' Hafız bowed, then pointed to the struggling ship. 'Do you think it will make it?'

'*Inshallah*—God willing,' Orhan said, looking again at the vessel.

He could see the ship's crew pulling hard on the sail ropes to control it. If they were skilled, it would dock safely in Constantinople —the city he would inherit, along with an empire of cities. If the sailors lost control, then the strong Bosphorus currents would drag it back out to sea.

The prince clicked his fingers, and the Imperial Guard followed. He walked along the shoreline with Hafız, keeping his eyes focused on the sailing ship. As it listed toward the shore, he stopped and narrowed his eyes. Was that a person clinging to the outside of the ship's rail? A flash of lightning lit up a mass of golden hair and a white robe. A woman! The vessel lurched, and her garment billowed as she fell, arms flailing.

Hafız turned to him. '*Allah! Allah!* sire. Did you see it? A woman fell overboard from that ship!' He pointed.

'I saw her! *Mashallah*—God protect her!'

Before anyone could stop him, Prince Orhan flung off his coat and dived into the water. The woman had already disappeared under the swift flowing waves.

～

Water rushed up Rusalka's nose, and its icy cold seeped into her body as she sank. Her heart banged in her chest, and she tried to kick for the surface with legs that were weak from her imprisonment. She fought against the strong current carrying her toward the open sea. She surfaced, lungs bursting, gulped in a breath of air and risked a backward glance. The wind had caught the ship's sails, and it was battling its way up the channel.

She was free! Rusalka could see the shore and the walls of the city. But the current dragged her under again. It was pulling her away from the land, sucking her strength, carrying her further out to sea. She surfaced again and threw her head back, trying to stay above the water, but she was sinking. Two powerful arms pulled her close against a hard chest and everything went black.

She opened her eyes, spluttered, coughed, and looked up at her rescuer. He glanced down at her, his dark eyes concerned as he pulled her toward the shore. A small group of men threshed through the water to help him.

'*Allah!*' he muttered as droplets of salt water from his wet hair fell on her face. '*Janlı!*' he called to the others.

Rusalka understood what he said—*she's alive!* Hadn't she heard those words many times on the Turkish slave ship? She felt other arms taking her and helping her through the shallows, guiding her to sit on a flat rock. Her rescuer shouted orders, then someone threw a warm garment around her shoulders. She sat up straighter and pushed her arms through the long sleeves. The fur-lined coat still had the owner's body heat trapped inside it, along with a musky, masculine smell. She pulled it close to her freezing flesh and let them arrange a scarf over her wet hair; the long ends fell over each shoulder. She coughed again and shivered despite the warm coat.

'Jariye,' someone said in Turkish. Although her own language was Russian, she understood: they knew she was a slave.

Were they her captors, the Turkish slave traders? Had they dived in to drag her back to the ship? The rain had stopped, but the thunder still rumbled. A short, stocky man with black hair and a pock-marked face put his hand under her elbow and helped her to her feet. Still holding her arm, he motioned her to cover the lower part of her face with the scarf.

She raised her eyes. Two men, their baggy pants and orange-coloured kaftans wet from the sea water, stood behind a tall figure. Further away, near the city gate, a group of soldiers stood to attention. An attendant threw a long cloak over the tall man's shoulders. The stranger pulled the fur-lined garment close to his body and fastened it at the neck with a gold clasp. A sudden flash of lightning illuminated him, picking up the gold embroidery woven through his dark cloak. Under it she glimpsed his wet kaftan that still clung to his muscular body. Her rescuer! His damp dark hair framed his face; she moved toward him then lost her footing as the thunder rumbled in the distance.

He caught her around her waist, and pulled her against his chest and the soft fabric of his cloak. She struggled to release herself from his firm hold, but he tightened his grip. She remembered clinging to him in the water and now, weary and defeated, she let him hold her. He bent his head, and his damp beard brushed her cheek.

'Türçe biliyormusun?'

Was he asking if she understood his language? She shook her head but used the word for 'nothing' from her scant Turkish vocabulary: 'Yok!' She met his gaze and saw a glimmer of amusement in his dark eyes as he released his hold on her.

'Do you understand Turkish?' he repeated in her own language. 'Are you Russian?' His accented Russian had an attractive foreign lilt. She nodded.

'You're in Constantinople, Türkiye now,' he said.

'Can you help me return to my country?' she asked.

'First, I need to know your name.'

She hesitated—hadn't he understood her request for help?

'Your name, please,' he repeated.

'Rusalka Maria Ivanova.'

His gaze slid over her body. She pulled the coat closer—he must have felt every part of her when he'd held her in the water.

'Rusalka! The water spirit?' He laughed. 'Truly?'

Rusalka stared at him. How did he know the Russian language or Russian legends? Who was he, this infidel Turk? A high-ranking soldier who had once lived in the Ottoman Crimean lands near the coast? She tried her Turkish again.

'*Sen kimsin?*—Who are you?'

To her alarm, one of the Turkish soldiers stepped forward, his face contorted with anger. '*Sus Jariye!*—Shut up slave!'

Her rescuer waved the soldier away and inclined his head. 'I am Prince Orhan, son of the Ottoman Sultan of Türkiye.' He glanced at his bodyguard. 'Your Turkish is woeful, madam. They're upset because you addressed me in Turkish as if I were a servant,' he said in his perfect Russian. 'Welcome to my country, water spirit. You are mine now—a gift from the sea.'

She stood up straight. A prince! Then he *could* help her—if he chose to.

'Your highness, I'm not a "gift",' she said. 'My uncle is the Bishop of Slavo, in Russia. The Tartars captured me when they raided my town. I would like to go home, or be taken to Pera, in the Christian area of your city.' Rusalka pointed to a gate in the thick wall behind him, unable to control her shaking hand.

'I understand.' He smiled. 'First, let me offer you some refreshment. You're cold. I have sent a servant to tell them to expect you.'

Them? Did he mean the people in Pera? After her 'refreshment', would he grant her freedom and let her go? A surge of hope rose in her chest—and she was starving.

'Thank you.' She bowed her head.

'I have named you *Süreyya*. It means star.'

'But I'm Rusalka.' She looked up at him.

Prince Orhan ignored her, then turned and gave a few terse orders in his own language. 'My soldiers will escort you,' he said.

She backed away when two soldiers stepped forward and stood on either side of her, but when she tried to move away from her escort, her knees buckled. The men took her arms and steered her along the sand. She focused her eyes on the orange uniform and matching conical hat of the soldier who led the way. The long sword that one of them wore brushed against her body as they walked over the uneven ground. Rusalka clenched her fists, trying to quell the sick fear that rose in her throat. Despite his friendly manner and promise to look after her, had the prince put her under arrest?

Rusalka glanced back at him as they led her away. She was still wearing his long coat. His eyes met hers and he smiled, showing his even white teeth. Rusalka straightened her back. She didn't want him to guess how terrified she felt. *Save me, Holy Virgin, I'm a captive again!*

Prince Orhan observed the girl as the soldiers led her away, surprised that she had turned and met his gaze full on. She looked tired but defiant, like a prisoner going to an execution. He felt sorry for her, but curbed the urge to follow to reassure the Russian girl that he wouldn't hurt her. One thing he knew for certain, Rusalka Maria Ivanova wasn't going anywhere—neither to the Christian area of Constantinople or back to her own country. He would look after her and give her a home in the safety of his harem.

Orhan watched until Rusalka's escort disappeared through the palace gates, with the woman between them. She had obviously mistaken the old walls around the palace for the city walls, as they had once been. And she'd risked her life, rather than end up in the slave market. He shivered and pulled his cloak tightly around himself. Flanked by his bodyguards, he strode toward the gate, still thinking about her.

The slave girl knew about the Christian area of the city. Her uncle was a bishop, and the Tartars had captured her in a raid. Maybe her uncle hadn't survived. But if he had, there might be trouble if he came looking for her. The powerful head of the Orthodox Church, His All Holiness the Patriarch of Constantinople, lived in the city as he had done for centuries, not far from the Topkapı Palace. Orhan's father, the sultan, didn't want trouble in Constantinople; Jews and Christians lived in their own separate districts in this Muslim city. The sultan was intent on capturing fresh territories to add to the empire, and trouble from the minorities in Constantinople was a distraction he didn't need.

Orhan remembered the stories about his great-grandfather, Sultan Mehmet II, who had conquered the city of Constantinople in 1453. It had once been one of the grandest Christian cities in the world, but by the time the Ottomans captured it, the city was past its former glory. Mehmet had vowed to rebuild Constantinople as the capital of his new Ottoman Empire. The sultan had renamed it in the Turkish language: *Konstantiniye*, but most people still called it Constantinople. Now it was a thriving multi-ethnic city of which he, Orhan, prince and soldier, was proud.

He thought again of Rusalka's defiant eyes that had met his. Did she think he would bow to her demands? Was she unimpressed by his status, or was it an act? He had once served as Prince Governor in Kalla, in the Ottoman lands of the Crimea. She spoke her own language with a more refined accent than his Russian-born mother, Emira. It was clear she came from a respectable family. The Tartars didn't distinguish between a village girl and a high-born woman, he reflected. They raided towns and villages, grabbed who they could, and then sold the survivors to slave traders who shipped them to Constantinople.

Occasionally, among the masses of slaves, there was someone special, a jewel like her, with blue eyes, the finest fairest skin, and golden hair. Something stirred deep in his body when he remembered holding her close in the churning water. How she had clung to him …

Prince Orhan frowned, trying to shake off the memory. He was cold. He needed to bathe and change his clothes for evening prayers. He had been summoned to an audience with his father, the sultan, the next day. He would order the servants to bring the slave girl, Rusalka, to a reception room in the harem. Orhan shook his head; he had never met a woman who was brave enough to leap off a sailing ship.

Rusalka Maria Ivanova—Süreyya—had piqued his curiosity.

CHAPTER 2

Rusalka's step faltered when the soldiers took her through the gates. She wasn't in a city. She'd expected streets and houses and people peddling their wares, and further up the hill, the sultan's palace of Topkapı. Instead, her bare feet sank into a sandy path. Her escort led her toward a large, deserted garden with flowerbeds full of tulips and other spring flowers. She looked around and saw an ornate, domed pavilion in a corner of the garden and her heart thumped in her chest.

Blessed Mary, Holy Virgin, where am I?

She tried to remember the old maps her father had shown her of the city. With a sinking heart she realised she wasn't in Constantinople, in the city of the Grand Turk. She was inside the sultan's *palace*, with its courtyards, gardens, and kiosks and thick, well-defended walls.

The soldiers released her and motioned her toward some steps that disappeared under the garden. She shivered with cold and fear—were they taking her to the dungeons? Rusalka was tired and frightened. She had been a captive, and she'd thought she was free, but she was wrong. The soldiers took her arms again and said something to their colleague in front. The man turned to her, averting his eyes from her face.

'Yok!' she said, shaking her head at him, using her scant Turkish again.

He made a sign for eating and drinking with his hands and nodded, showing her the steps. She was hungry, and her fighting spirit was dwindling. There was no chance of escape here either, she thought as her escorts nudged her forward. The air in the underground passage was warm after the chill outside, and bright torches flared from brackets in the walls. To her relief, there was no sign of a dungeon. The passage seemed endless, but then she saw sunshine; the storm had passed and she smelled fresh, sweet air. She looked up, and her blood ran cold.

A towering blackamoor, swathed in yellow robes and wearing a white turban, waited at the top of a flight of steps. Next to him stood a small boy in identical garb. The child clapped his hands, and grinned at the older man, who nodded to the soldiers. When she reached him, he took Rusalka by the arm and patted his chest with his large jewelled hand.

'Abdul,' he said and repeated his name, then he pointed to the boy. 'Sami.' He said something to the boy, who scampered ahead of them.

'This way!' Abdul said in accented Russian. He nudged Rusalka along a garden path bordered by pink and white flowers, through a high wooden door, and into a tiled passageway. Sami was waiting for them by another enormous door.

Prince Orhan strode through the palace gates flanked by his armed guard. He hurried to the third courtyard and went straight to the hamam, his personal bathhouse. He smiled, imagining his mother's disapproval and the buzz in the harem when they heard about his dramatic rescue of the slave girl. When they had bathed and dried him, his servants helped him into a black kaftan, threaded through with fine gold. He tied his jewelled belt at his waist and fastened its gold clasp. It was May, but the evenings were still cool, and he shrugged on the sleeveless fur-lined robe a servant held up for him. He slipped his dagger into the scabbard on his waist, pulled on his leather ankle boots, adjusted his small turban, and nodded to a servant to open the door.

He would visit the harem buildings after prayers and ask them to bring the Russian girl to him. Orhan glanced across the courtyard where his father, the sultan—the pādishah—God's shadow on earth, had his own chambers. One day, *inshallah*—God willing—Orhan would be sultan and in charge of this palace. His mother, Emira Sultan, nagged him constantly about fathering an heir, a brave and powerful son. A son needs a courageous mother, he thought. Someone like the Russian girl, who dared to jump from a ship into the Bosphorus and swim to freedom.

It was Abdul's task as chief eunuch in charge of the harem to purchase women at the slave market. But Orhan had found this beauty himself. He sighed; the Russian girl had disturbed his equilibrium.

The heavy wooden door swung open, and Abdul led Rusalka inside. She looked up at the barred windows high above the tiled walls of a wide passage and winced as her bare feet touched the marble floor. The door clanged shut, and the sound echoed around the walls. Had they brought her to the harem? She couldn't stay here. She had to escape again!

She stared at the elaborately tiled walls and marble floors, and shivered in the chilly emptiness. Further down the passage, several young girls peered at her from a doorway. Abdul shooed them away and motioned to a girl in a long white dress and blue vest. She lowered her eyes and stepped forward. Even in the dull light, Rusalka could see that someone had threaded seed pearls on a fine silver chain through the girl's brown hair. Abdul clicked his fingers at her and nodded.

'I'm Perihan Jariye, madam,' she said. 'Abdul Agha called for me because I speak your language. Welcome to Prince Orhan's harem. Sami will wash your feet, then two servants will take you to the bath-house. After that, I will bring you some food.'

The blackamore, Abdul, indicated a foot basin and motioned for Rusalka to sit on a cushioned stone bench and put her feet in the water. He tutted when he saw her cracked nails and the cuts and sores on her soles. Her shoes had lasted barely a week after the Tartar raid, when they forced their captives to walk to the port of Kalla.

The little boy, Sami, knelt and washed her feet in the warm, scented water, then he dried them carefully with a smooth towel. He smiled and chattered in Turkish to her as he worked. Abdul handed her soft leather slippers and Sami helped her put them on. She was shivering now and hugged the prince's coat close to her chest. The flower-decorated tiles that covered the walls of the entrance made her feel cold again. Abdul beckoned to two young women. They were dressed in identical long tunics over pants caught at the ankles with silver thread. Like the first woman, their ebony hair was tied back, and interwoven with seed pearls on silver thread.

Abdul spoke to them, bowed his head, clicked his fingers at Sami, and walked away. The women helped Rusalka to her feet, slipped their arms through hers, and led her through the second door and along another cold passage. They opened a carved door into a large tiled area, where high stained-glass windows cast shards of light across the walls and floor. Rusalka inhaled the warm, rose-scented steam that swirled under a glass dome.

The taller woman introduced herself, 'Sevim Jariye,' then smiled and indicated her companion, 'Sevtap Jariye,' then pointed to Rusalka. 'Süreyya Jariye.'

Rusalka was too tired to correct them. They removed the prince's robe from her and laid it carefully over a rail. When they peeled her wet skirt and bodice from her body, they exchanged glances and tutted, touching the bruises the Tartars had inflicted and the scratches on the inside of her forearms from where she'd clung to the ship's side. Sevim and Sevtap pushed high wooden shoes at her. She put them on and allowed the women to lead her to a marble bench, heated by the steam, where they poured warm water over her body from large ceramic jugs. The two women washed her with a soft cloth, then massaged her hair with scented soap as they untangled the curls. Rusalka closed her eyes and tears seeped from under her eyelids; her pain eased as the water relaxed her aching muscles. But her mind was in turmoil as they led her to a long bench and mimed that she should remove the shoes, and lie down.

Would they let her out of here? Or was the prince going to keep her a prisoner?

She lay on the narrow ceramic table and the young women massaged her with scented oil, then they patted her dry with thick towels. They led her to a warm dressing chamber, where they soothed salve on her scratches and bruises. The servants helped her dress in a long white gown and sleeveless blue vest, then fastened a gold jewelled belt around her waist. She fingered the small rubies and diamonds on the clasp in amazement, and ran her hands over the fine fabric of the gown and vest. She smiled and thanked her helpers as they massaged her feet, then helped her into her slippers.

Sevim and Sevtap clapped their hands and said, '*Çok güzel!*— beautiful!'

When Rusalka repeated the words, they giggled and made a sign for food. She followed them into the corridor, then to another chamber, where Abdul was standing in the centre of a patterned silk carpet. He told her to sit on the low cushioned bench that ran around the walls of the chamber. Perihan, the young girl who spoke Russian, waited, holding a tray in her hands. She wore the same clothes as Rusalka, but the girl's belt was of fine silver with no precious stones. Perihan came forward, smiling, and put the tray down on the table in front of Rusalka. Several silver rings on her small fingers flashed as she moved.

'Welcome to Prince Orhan's harem,' she repeated. 'Did you like our hamam—our Turkish bath?' She laughed. 'There is no bath! Turkish people bathe in running water. They say the prince has a private bath, though.'

She handed Rusalka a glass in a filigree silver holder. 'This is sherbet. You must be thirsty, and hungry too. Please eat.' She pointed to a silver plate of figs, watermelon, and sweet cakes.

Rusalka accepted the drink and took a sip. The sherbet tasted of roses, it was very sweet, and her spirits lifted. She gulped it, feeling as if she was in a dream. She took a cake and a large piece of watermelon and put them in her mouth, not caring what they thought of her. For the past two weeks, she'd eaten only thin gruel and hard bread.

'My name is Perihan Jariye,' the girl reminded her. She ignored Süreyya's busy eating and poured more sherbet for her. 'I live in the prince's harem,' she went on. 'They sent me because I speak your language. Roshan Kalfa, the Lady Steward, says the prince named you *Süreyya*. It means star, and beautiful lady. Roshan Kalfa will greet you tomorrow,' she added.

Rusalka swallowed and stared at the girl, then at the blackamoor and the boy, who stood near the door. How did everyone know about her? It was such a brief time since she'd arrived in the harem.

'This is Abdul,' Perihan continued. 'He's the *Kızlar Ağası*—the Head of the Harem. Can you say that? *Kuh z lar I a suh?*'

Rusalka repeated the strange words, and all three listeners smiled and nodded.

'We address him as *Abdul Agha*—Abdul Ah ga,' she said slowly.

'Abdul Ah ga,' Rusalka repeated.

'Yes, very good.' Perihan nodded. 'He speaks some Russian and many other languages. He's in charge of the women in the harem and all the eunuchs. They come from many countries. Abdul is a eunuch—his manhood has been cut off,' she added in a matter-of-fact voice.

Rusalka listened, feeling dazed.

'And this little boy is Sami,' Perihan continued. 'He was out of breath when he arrived with the message about you.'

Rusalka stopped eating. The food had refreshed her, but she felt slightly sick. 'Can I speak with Prince Orhan now?' she asked.

Perihan bit her lip and shook her head. '*We* cannot ask to speak to the prince,' she said seriously. 'We must wait until he requests *us* to come to him.'

'Us?'

'His harem women and servants. I'm one of them. My name is Perihan *Jariye*: Jar i yea,' she pronounced carefully. 'It means Perihan the slave. Abdul bought me at the slave market two years ago.'

This child is in the prince's harem?

'How old are you?'

'I think I'm thirteen,' the girl answered. 'But I'm a servant. I'm not an odalisque—a harem lady—a … a concubine,' she added.

'You are five years younger than me,' Rusalka began, but Perihan touched her arm, looked at the door, then at Abdul.

Rusalka heard a tapping noise on the marble floor outside. It was coming nearer.

'It's the prince,' Perihan whispered. 'He wears silver-soled shoes to warn us of his approach. You must stand, face the door, and keep your eyes lowered.'

Rusalka wiped her mouth on a napkin and scrambled to her feet, keeping her eyes on the silk carpet. She caught her breath when she heard the prince's seductive voice, speaking his own language. Abdul said something to the other servants, then a few words in a low voice. Someone opened, then closed the door.

'Good evening, water spirit,' the prince said in Russian.

Rusalka looked up; she was alone with her rescuer. A shaft of evening sunlight from the long window left his face half in shadow. He wore a long black kaftan that sat well on his broad shoulders. It was caught at the collar with a gold and diamond brooch in the shape of a crescent. Over the kaftan, also threaded through with gold, was a long sleeveless vest. Rusalka noticed the handle of a jewelled dagger protruding from the scabbard in the gold belt at his waist. His dark hair had dried into a mass of unruly waves, which escaped from under his small black turban. His brown eyes were bright as he appraised her and his lips curved in a smile.

'Come forward and let me look at you,' he said.

She stepped nearer, his musky scent reminding her of their last encounter. He took her hands in his and his eyes, with their long black lashes, met hers.

'You are exquisite,' he whispered. He raised her hands to his lips and kissed her fingers, his eyes holding hers. 'Have my servants treated you well?'

'Yes, sire, but I don't want to stay here.' She tried to keep her voice steady, but his kiss and his warm touch had unsettled her.

He released her hands and put his index finger on her lips. 'Indulge me for a short time, Süreyya Jariye. It is comfortable here. Abdul will take you to your chamber, so you can rest after your ordeal.'

He smiled, turned on his heel and rapped on the inside of the door. It opened immediately and with a last glance over his shoulder, he joined his guards in the passageway. The *click, click* of the silver-soled shoes died away. Perihan returned to the chamber, looking astonished and biting her lip.

'I have never seen the prince so close,' the girl whispered. 'He spoke to Abdul about your accommodation. You won't have to sleep in a dormitory with five others, like me. You will have your own chamber!'

'I've asked Prince Orhan to release me. I think he will ... soon,' Rusalka told her.

She took another gulp of her drink and looked up at Perihan as Abdul returned to the chamber. The girl stared at her and said something to Abdul in Turkish.

He replied in his soft voice, 'Abdul Agha says his highness likes you. He saved you from drowning, so you are his now.'

Rusalka shook her head, trying to dispel the image of the charismatic prince from her mind. 'I am *not* his. My family will come to Constantinople and find me. They'll take me away from here.'

'You are lucky to have such a family. My parents were poor. They sold me to the slave traders.'

Sold by her family! Rusalka stared at her.

'I'm so sorry, Perihan.'

'But I have friends and a comfortable life.' The girl looked surprised. 'The prince will not call me to his bed.' She looked down and blushed. 'I am too young. One day I might become a *kalfa*, a chief servant in charge of dresses or jewels or even the household.'

'How many women are in the harem?'

'About twenty *odalisques*—harem ladies. Prince Orhan has a few favourites, but the rest of us—another twenty—are servants with jobs to do.'

'Twenty! And a *few* favourites?'

'I will never be an odalisque,' Perihan said. 'I'm not pretty enough. I will always be a servant.'

So, the man who had rescued her had twenty women to choose from! Rusalka knew about Muslims' customs. Their religion allowed them four wives and concubines if they could afford them. He was a prince, and she was now just another of his possessions. She clenched her fists. She *did not* want to stay locked up in this luxurious prison.

When Rusalka had finished her meal, Perihan led her up a flight of stone stairs and opened the door to a small chamber. The girl helped Rusalka undress, then pulled a silk shift over her head. She drew back the yellow brocade covers of a small bed. Rusalka sank into it, luxuriating in the scent of the clean linen, the softness of the pillows. It was the first time in months that she'd slept in a bed, she thought as her eyes flickered closed.

Rusalka woke suddenly when she heard a loud *click*. She sat up and clutched her nightgown to her chest. The chamber smelled of the same musky fragrance that had clung to the prince's coat. In the dim light that sputtered from the wall sconces, she saw Prince Orhan standing close to her bed. She threw the covers aside and struggled to her feet. Was he going to ravish her?

'Süreyya!' he whispered. 'Don't be afraid. I won't harm you.'

She took a step back, but he caught her around her waist as he had on the beach, and pulled her against his chest. She pushed against him, but then relaxed into his firm embrace. When his lips met hers, she returned his kiss, then tried to pull away.

'Goodnight, water spirit,' he held her firmly and his lips sought hers again. She yielded to his embrace as his kiss deepened. He smoothed his hands over her buttocks and when he pulled her even closer to his body, she felt his arousal through her shift. He took her arms and placed her hands around his neck and kissed her again.

'I want you now,' he murmured.

Her thoughts were in turmoil, her knees felt weak. If he made love to her, he would discover her terrible secret. She wasn't a virgin. And if he learned that, he would send her to the slave market, and from there to a brothel.

'Please, sire … I am not ready.' She withdrew her arms and looked up, her eyes searching his, hoping he couldn't hear her heart thudding in her chest.

He released her with a sigh. 'Dearest water spirit, you're shaking.' He held her face in his hands and kissed her forehead. 'Now rest.' The prince strode to the door, then paused. He turned and looked at her, his face half in shadow. 'I will not wait long.'

Rusalka stared at him, feeling desperate. She had to escape from the palace before his patience ran out.

He left her bedchamber as quietly as he'd come.

CHAPTER 3

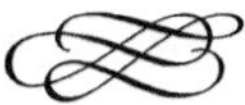

Rusalka woke with a start. A man was pushing open the wooden window shutters of her chamber and sunshine dazzled her eyes. She sat up, blinking in the bright light from the rectangular windows opposite her narrow bed. The dark-skinned, richly dressed man knelt at her side and said something in Turkish. She shrieked and drew the bed covers up to her throat. He said something else that she didn't understand.

'Don't be afraid, Süreyya Jariye, this is Amir. He's a eunuch,' a bright voice said. 'Remember me? I'm Perihan Jariye, and you are Süreyya Jariye—the slave Süreyya. He says he will bring you something to drink before we take you to the hamam,' she translated. 'We are your personal servants. He won't harm you!'

Rusalka stared at the two people at her bedside with wild eyes. A familiar sound filtered through the open window: the Muslim call to prayer. Five times a day it had echoed around the city of Kalla, where the Tartars had held her prisoner.

'Remember you're in Constantinople, in Prince Orhan's living quarters in the Topkapı Palace,' the girl said. 'You slept for a long time. That's the call to midday prayer. We must pray now, but we will return soon.'

Another eunuch came into the chamber and handed her a silver mug, and she sipped the thin yoghurt drink as the servants left quietly. Rusalka got out of bed and walked over to the window.

Below her chamber was a paved courtyard, and beyond that, a waterway. As she watched, a vessel sailed by slowly. The dying sounds of the call to prayer drifted across the water from a small mosque she could see on the opposite bank. She shivered and sat on her bed, trying to make sense of what had happened to her. The prince had come to her chamber! She'd returned his kisses; he would think she was an easy conquest. Another woman for his collection.

When the servants returned, they took her along silent passages, bathed her in the hamam, and swaddled her in thick towels. Then Perihan helped her into silk undergarments, a fresh white gown, and a long sleeveless blue vest. The fabric felt smooth against her skin, and she ran her hands over it.

'Silk and wool, it will keep you warm.' Perihan fastened the gold belt around her new mistress's waist. Once again, Rusalka fingered the small rubies and diamonds on the clasp, feeling as if she was in a dream. Perihan was wearing similar clothes, but like yesterday, she wore a silver belt.

'All of us dress like this until we go to the salon,' she said. 'Then the ladies change into gowns. I must wear a silk tunic and silk pants in the salon, because I'm a servant. Abdul says you can wear a gown.' She nodded.

Rusalka walked back with Perihan to her sun-drenched chamber. The servants had made up her bed into a couch with a yellow velvet cover and matching cushions. An identical long divan ran the length of the wall under the windows. The walls featured a mixture of marble panels interspersed with tiles painted with delicate red tulips.

There were no cupboards, only shelves covered with carved wood, into which a clever designer had cut designs of fruit and flowers. Someone had propped a pearl inlaid tabletop and folded table legs against a wall. Rusalka traced her toe across the pile of the flower-patterned carpet. Only yesterday, slave traders had kept her locked in a rope store on a ship. Rusalka crossed to the window and kneeled on the window seat. Amir had opened the glass and fastened the windows against hooks in the tiles. She looked through the ornate lattice that was fitted between the glass and the outer shutters.

'That's the courtyard of the favourites below us,' Perihan said as she joined her. 'Abdul reserves this chamber and others along the passage for the favourites of the harem.' Perihan smiled at Rusalka. 'The prince ordered that *you* should live here.'

The girl's eyes widened, and she nodded. 'It is the custom that a favourite who has pleased him in his bedchamber should have one.' Perihan blushed. 'Most of the larger chambers are empty, but the prince's mother may gift them to women *she* has chosen for Prince Orhan.'

Rusalka felt nervous again. How soon would the prince wish *her* to please him? Not long, he'd said. She looked down at the paved courtyard where red, yellow, and purple flowering plants spilled out of marble pots. Beyond a low wall, a pool glinted in the midday sun.

Perihan pointed. 'That's the pool where the odalisques can refresh themselves in the hot months.' She pulled Rusalka's sleeve. 'And over there—see the three windows? That's Emira Sultan's chambers. She's the prince's mother, and she has a wonderful view of the Bosphorus waterway.'

'I can see the Bosphorus too, beyond the pool!'

'Yes, and you can see the Golden Horn waterway that leads to the city. Look! Now, do you remember your new name?'

'Süreyya? But I'm Rusalka!'

Perihan tilted her head to one side. 'Everyone is given a new name when they come to the harem. You are Süreyya Jariye now.'

Süreyya Jariye. The words sounded strange. So, she must forget she was Rusalka Maria Ivanova and think of herself as Süreyya the Slave from now on. She was determined to petition the prince for her freedom, so did it matter what they called her?

'You must eat something, Süreyya Jariye,' Perihan said, telling her to sit on the bench seat while she assembled the table. The servant, Amir, arrived with a tray of food and arranged plates of cheese, tomatoes, olives, and sliced cucumbers on the pearl inlaid tabletop. Perihan passed her a basket of warm bread.

Süreyya grabbed a large piece, tore it apart, and ate it hungrily. She looked up at the servant's startled faces and blushed.

'You must be starving,' Perihan said. She put small amounts of the savoury food on Süreyya's plate. 'We must eat slowly and with dignity,' Perihan whispered, and asked the eunuch to leave. 'If you eat too quickly, you may feel sick.'

Süreyya felt ashamed of her impulse to stuff everything into her mouth. 'Where are the other odalisques?'

Perihan hesitated. 'You can't meet them yet. You will need some training first, and everyone must see Doctor Rebeka before they're accepted into the harem.'

'Because?' Süreyya asked, but she'd guessed the answer.

Perihan spoke quietly. 'She will check that no man has ...'

Of course, the examination she dreaded! She'd learned from her fellow captives that only virgins were admitted to the harem, and she was terrified. When they discovered her secret, the prince might think she'd made a fool of him. The blackamore and his servants would bundle her out of the harem immediately. They would doubtless send her to the slave market.

Abdul appeared at the door and said something to Perihan. The young girl's hand flew to her mouth and her eyes widened as she looked at Süreyya.

'The doctor must wait. Prince Orhan's mother, Emira Sultan, has requested to see you immediately.'

Prince Orhan presented himself at the meeting of the Imperial Council in the Imperial Audience Hall. The sultan was already seated on an ornate divan under an elaborate canopy of silk and gold. He beckoned Orhan forward. The prince remained standing during his audience.

After they had discussed a few state matters, his father said, 'My son, you are to travel to Manisa as my envoy.'

Orhan's mind raced—Manisa was at least five days' ride from Constantinople. It was where his older brother, Crown Prince Murad, was Prince Governor.

'Murad is neglecting his duties,' the sultan declared. 'He spends his time hunting instead of governing. We have had many petitions and complaints from our subjects there. We entrust you with a personal letter of rebuke from us. You must stay for at least seven days, then return and report your findings to us personally.'

'Yes, sire.' Orhan bowed.

'You are to leave tomorrow. Take Hafız Pasha with you.' He looked across at the general, who inclined his head. 'And thirty Janissary soldiers. If you have trouble with your brother, send a fast rider with a request for more.' The sultan dismissed his son with a wave of his hand.

Prince Orhan bowed his head and took three steps back. As he left the chamber, the imperial guard, stationed at intervals around the chamber, stood to attention. The door opened silently, and he nodded to the other guards, who stood in the passageway on either side of the door to the audience chamber. Damn his brother; he'd only just come back from a long campaign.

He conferred with Hafız on his way back to his living quarters. The general assured Orhan he would put everything in motion.

'After prayers, I'll come to the first courtyard and speak to the troops,' Orhan said. He raised his eyebrows. 'Then, I must visit my mother.'

The prince climbed the stone steps to his mother's chambers. He guessed Emira Sultan had summoned him because she'd heard about the Russian girl and wanted more information. As he approached her chambers, two eunuchs opened the polished wooden doors for him. Orhan removed his shoes and accepted the leather slippers her eunuch, Zeki, offered him.

Zeki escorted him into his mother's luxurious chamber, where shards of sunlight from the lattice screens on the outside of the windows filtered across the patterned carpets. His mother, Emira, was alone. She had dismissed the three ladies, women of her own age who were her constant companions. The prince's mother stood with her back to one of the long windows, waiting for him with her head bowed.

The prince breathed in the familiar scent of rosewater and a heady perfume from the incense burner set in a corner alcove. He tried to forget he had a million things to do. Orhan bowed his head and raised Emira's hand to his lips. She was still a beautiful woman, he thought, even though a few silver hairs showed through the rich brown. His mother stood on tiptoe and kissed him on either cheek. Then she frowned in mock anger.

'So,' she began, 'my son, *aslanım,* my lion, wishes to destroy my life's work.'

He extended his hands, pretending not to understand.

'You are twenty-four years old. I spent all my life protecting you from harm and now …' She paused. '*Now* I hear that you nearly drowned below my window—saving a runaway slave!'

Emira Sultan turned and pointed to the broad blue expanse of the Bosphorus waterway with her jewelled fingers.

'Forgive me, Mother. I had no choice.'

'I think you did. Diving into the Bosphorus is surely the bostanji's job.' She patted his face. 'Anyway, tell me about the woman you saved. I believe her name is Süreyya?'

'You know her name?'

'Of course.' She clicked her fingers and Zeki reappeared. 'I have sent for her; we can both be better acquainted.'

Orhan stared at his mother and frowned.

'The girl only arrived yesterday afternoon,' he protested.

'I am aware of that. She has had no training, of course, but I thought you might like to hear her story.'

I certainly would, he thought. As usual, his mother's curiosity knew no bounds. She might even have heard of his nocturnal visit to the girl's chamber. He looked hard at Zeki, wondering if the servant had been spying on him. The eunuch stood quietly near the door looking down at the carpet.

'Madam, Süreyya Jariye is here,' he announced, looking as curious as his mistress. Orhan frowned at Zeki as he ushered the Russian slave into Emira's presence. The prince waved a dismissive hand. The eunuch bowed respectfully, and with a last look at the girl he left the chamber.

Süreyya stood with her eyes lowered, waiting for his mother to speak. He stared at her bowed head with its mass of thick blond curls, willing her to look up at him.

'Come closer, girl, and look at me,' Emira Sultan spoke to her in Russian.

Süreyya raised her head, glanced quickly at the prince, blushed, then kept her eyes fixed on his mother. 'You have met my son, of course; he saved your life!'

Süreyya cleared her throat and turned to the prince. 'I am in your debt, sire.'

He inclined his head, marvelling at how striking she looked even in the simple blue and white clothes that all the harem women wore during the day. Orhan remembered the taste of her lips on his, and when her eyes met his briefly, he knew she too recalled their late-night encounter.

'We are all intrigued by your bravery,' his mother addressed her.

'Thank you, your highness,' Süreyya began. 'I thought I was near the city walls. I believed that once I had swum to shore, I could find my way to Pera, the Christian part of your city.'

Orhan suppressed a smile. His mother was temporarily lost for words. Most of the women of his harem gave monosyllabic answers, and kept their eyes lowered when they spoke to Emira Sultan.

'As you see,' his mother said in Turkish, turning to him with pursed lips, 'she does not know how to behave in our presence.'

'There's a certain charm in her honesty,' he replied in the same language.

Emira turned to Süreyya and resumed in Russian. 'I believe you have already asked my son for your freedom,' she said coldly. 'It won't happen. Be grateful that you are here.'

'But …'

'Süreyya Jariye,' Orhan said, aware that his mother had little patience for arguments. 'We will take care of you in the palace. Please tell us about yourself.'

Süreyya looked at Orhan, her hopes of release fading. His brown eyes were kind as they met hers. She was aware of his mother watching him like a bird of prey. Emira Sultan had a strange accent that Süreyya found hard to place—the prince's mother wasn't from her own wealthy region of Russia. She resembled the people from the devastated regions further south that bordered the Tartar Khanate near the Crimea. Her intense, dark eyes slanted upward slightly, and her high cheekbones had a faint blush of colour. Her hair was darker than her son's, but her skin was a lighter olive.

'You told me your name was Rusalka,' Orhan prompted.

'Rusalka Maria Ivanova. I was born in Slavo, northwest of the Tartar Khanate. My father was a merchant. The Tartars sacked and burned our town, and they took the young people prisoner. My parents died several years ago, and I lived with my uncle and aunt.'

'So now you are Süreyya,' Emira interrupted. 'Forget your other name. Forget everything. Only my son and I need to know about your past. None of the women of the harem has a past, only a future— understand?'

'But madam,' Süreyya said, 'my uncle is a bishop of the Russian Orthodox Church. I am an educated woman.'

Emira Sultan glared at her, but before Süreyya could speak again, Orhan held up his hand. 'I'm sure your family will be glad that you are safe here in the harem,' he said.

They would be relieved she was alive, Süreyya thought. But they would be dismayed if they learned she was incarcerated in the harem of an infidel Ottoman prince.

'I want you to remain here where you're safe,' he continued. 'We will not send you to the slave market.' He smiled, stepped forward, and took her hands in his. Orhan's hands were warm and hard, his smell musky and clean.

She heard his mother's sharp intake of breath.

'In Pera,' he said quietly, 'the Christians would treat you as an outcast because you have been in the harem. I will not do that. *I* will give you a home.'

Süreyya felt tears of gratitude welling in her eyes, mingled with a deep sense of dread. Maybe when he found out her secret, that she was no longer a virgin, he too would treat her as an outcast. And his mother, despite speaking Russian with a peasant's accent, was obviously powerful. If she knew her secret, what would *she* do?

Emira's voice cut across her thoughts. 'My son will not be in the harem for the next few weeks. You will begin your training as an odalisque and study the Turkish language and your new religion. Only then will I admit you to the salon.'

'My new religion, madam?'

Emira frowned. 'You will embrace Islam as every recently acquired slave must do,' she said.

The prince squeezed Süreyya's hands and smiled into her eyes before he released her. 'Until we meet again,' he murmured, then moved away and stood next to his mother.

The eunuch, Zeki, appeared at Süreyya's side and led her from the chamber.

'Well, pretty one.' He smirked once he'd closed the door. 'You seemed to have impressed the *prince*, at least!'

Before she could ask him what he meant, he clicked his fingers and two other eunuchs led her away from Emira's chambers.

After the girl had left, Emira turned to her son. 'And I believe you kissed her goodnight?'

'Mother!'

'I know everything that happens in the harem,' she said more sharply than she'd intended. 'Young lion, love is for ordinary people. You are a prince; your duty is to produce heirs with the women in your harem.'

A stubborn expression crossed his face. She remembered it well from when he was a child.

'A prince can find love,' he retorted.

Emira Sultan held her tongue. Two years ago, he had left Nesrin, his pregnant favourite, behind in the Crimea, and visited his troops in Constantinople. The young woman had died in childbirth, along with his firstborn son. He had been devastated. Surely, Emira reasoned, that experience had taught him not to get emotionally involved with an odalisque?

'I know you're thinking of Nesrin,' he said, startling Emira. 'Forget her.'

Since then, her son had elected to go on lengthy campaigns to capture new territories. It wouldn't be long, she knew, before he would be ordered to leave again. Emira Sultan frowned. He was already twenty-four years old and he had no children.

'The pādishah ...' His voice cut across her thoughts.

'Your father, the sultan ...'

'My father seems determined to keep me busy.'

Emira Sultan fingered her diamond necklace. 'I hope this means that the pādishah favours you as his successor,' she said carefully.

'It is dangerous to speculate ...'

'Your older half-brother, Prince Murad, and your younger one, Prince Ahmet, are both incompetent idiots,' she said. 'While they remain in the provinces, you have a chance. This is your opportunity to gain favour with your father. He may choose you to succeed him, over Murad, even though he's the eldest.'

'You know the rules, Mother,' Orhan sighed.

'It's regrettable,' she opined, 'that you must kill your half-brothers to become sultan. However, if your brothers are not in Constantinople upon the death of your father and you are, you have an advantage. The Sword of Osman will be yours.'

She stepped forward and curled her fingers around his wrist.

'I have several suitable women for you. You must produce sons, my darling,' she repeated. 'Each favourite may only produce one son, as I did. You must take many to your bed. Don't sigh, *aslanım*, my lion, you know I speak the truth.'

He walked to the window and stood with his back to her.

'The girl, Süreyya …' Emira chose her words carefully. 'She has powerful connections. If the Tartars didn't kill her uncle, he might come looking for her. It has happened in the past.'

'But by then she may have given birth to my son.' He turned and met her eyes. Her heart ached with pride when she looked at him.

'I am determined she will stay,' he said firmly.

'As you wish, my lion.'

'I'll take my leave, Mother.'

'Won't you take some refreshment?'

He shook his head, kissed her hand, touched it to his forehead and bade her goodbye. Zeki opened the door silently. Emira watched as her son left without a backward glance.

After Orhan had gone, Emira Sultan stood at the window gazing unseeing at the magnificent view. Until yesterday, her son had seemed to prefer a light-skinned beauty with green eyes, called Zeynep. Unfortunately, the girl was extremely stupid.

As for the new slave, Süreyya … there was something about her that made Emira feel uneasy. Admittedly, it took courage to jump overboard from a ship. But how would a woman like that adapt to life in the harem? She clicked her fingers at Zeki, the eunuch, and sent him for Abdul Agha. When the chief eunuch arrived, she told him to organise some training for the reckless new acquisition.

Emira would decide when Süreyya Jariye could enter the harem salon with the others, subject to the doctor's report, of course. Heaven knows what had happened to the girl after her capture. *And if she isn't suitable,* she mused, *I will contact the Russian community in Pera myself. I could remove the girl from the harem before Orhan returns from Manisa.* Emira smiled. *First let's see what Doctor Rebeka finds.*

CHAPTER 4

The heavy door swung open, and Süreyya followed her helpers outside into a warm sunlit garden, which smelled fresh after the cloistered atmosphere of the harem. Perihan and Amir ushered her along paths through a green wonderland of ponds and fountains, where early roses nodded against the high walls. Their heady scent, carried on the spring breeze, enveloped her. Spring had already arrived in this city, she thought, looking at the new leaves on the spindly branches of the trees. It was so different from the filth and degradation of the slave ship.

The hospital for the harem women was a long, low building painted a dazzling white. Instead of carved doors, the hospital doors, open shutters and window frames were black with silver latticework to give privacy to the patients. A door swung open as they approached, and her escorts led her into a cool passageway. The wall tiles were the same as those that covered the harem walls, but their swirls of blue, red, and white flowers were clearly visible in this brighter area.

'This is the infirmary,' Perihan announced. 'We will wait outside.'

She knocked on a door that was opened by a young woman in a plain dark gown. Inside the sparsely furnished chamber, the female assistant helped Süreyya remove her clothes and slip a calico shift over her head. The woman took her arm and led her into another chamber where a middle-aged woman was sitting at a desk. She stood and held out her hand in greeting.

'*Hoş geldiniz*—Welcome.'

Perihan had taught her how to reply, and Süreyya tried out the strange words. '*Hoş bulduk*—I found welcome.'

'I speak a little Russian.' The doctor smiled.

She dismissed the assistant, then stood aside, motioning her patient to sit on a long-cushioned bench against the wall. The doctor walked across the cotton carpet and locked the door.

'Please be comfortable,' she said kindly.

Süreyya tried to relax, relieved that the other woman could speak her language. The doctor patted her hand.

'I am Doctor Rebeka. They gave you name: Süreyya?'

'I was Rusalka. Here I'm Süreyya.'

'Your new name means "star". It is Persian name. Prince Orhan speaks Persian good. Now I ask you question.' She pointed to Süreyya's lap. 'Tell me, has any man go there?'

Süreyya clutched her hands together and looked at the floor.

When she didn't speak, the other woman said gently, 'Let me look.'

She pointed to a high couch covered in thick brocade and a white towel. She helped Süreyya hoist herself up.

'Open legs.'

Süreyya felt as if her entire body was blushing as the doctor examined her gently.

The other woman straightened up, crossed to a table, and poured water from a decorated ceramic jug into a matching basin. She washed her hands, then after she'd dried them, she came over to her patient.

'You are not virgin,' she whispered as their eyes met. 'Did Tartar man do this?'

Süreyya swallowed the tears that were stuck in her throat. The doctor helped her sit up and return to her original seat.

'Tartars?' the other woman repeated. 'This why you jump from ship? You hear they sell you to brothel if they know you not virgin?'

Süreyya nodded. 'My fiancé, Stefan, took my virginity, not the Tartars.'

She poured out the story in her own language, not caring if Doctor Rebeka understood everything. How she'd escaped from her uncle's burning house and how Stefan had helped her. They'd spent the night in a forest ditch. He held her close and begged her to let him have his way. They were to marry soon, he whispered. Of course, she said yes; Stefan had saved her life. The next morning, her fiancé told her to stay where she was, while he went to find food and help. She heard him yell, then silence.

'The Tartars found me. One of them jumped into the ditch.'

Süreyya stifled a sob, and the doctor took her hand.

'Another man touches you?'

'No, he was astride me, but someone pulled him off. They argued in their own language. I saw him make the sign for money. I'd heard they get a good price for virgins!'

'Then …'

'They dragged me out of the ditch, and I saw they had killed Stefan —so much blood!' Süreyya covered her face with her hands. 'They tied my hands behind my back and pushed me in front of them. Then I saw the others, groups of young men and women. They made us walk and walk and walk.'

She dreaded them discovering her lost maidenhood. Other captives on the long trek told her they were bound for Kalla, a port in the Crimea. Once there, slave traders checked them all. They only put virgins on the ship, the others were sold to brothels in Kalla. Süreyya spent a night of terror in a filthy shed with hundreds of others. The ship had to sail quickly, the traders said, and there wasn't time to examine anyone.

'They'll do that in Constantinople,' a woman whispered to her. But before the ship docked in the Turkish port, she had leaped to freedom.

As Süreyya finished her story, Doctor Rebeka took her patient's hand and whispered, 'I can fix, make you virgin again. I sew.' She mimed sewing a stitch and raised two fingers. 'Only two—is enough. First, I check no baby. Come to couch again.'

Both procedures were quick but very painful, despite the herbal potion the doctor dabbed on her skin. Afterward, the other woman helped her down and sat opposite her.

'No baby there, but you will have pain for some days,' the doctor told her.

'Next week,' she went on, 'I will take out stitches. First time you make love, *inshallah*—God willing—with the prince, he will think you virgin. I give you salve for pain, help you heal.' She took Süreyya's hand. 'This our secret. Tell no one about stitches, it is great trouble for you, for *me*, understand?'

Süreyya nodded.

'Servants say Prince Orhan likes you.' The doctor paused. 'In Turkish, you are *gözde*.' She repeated the word slowly: 'Guz-deh. It means you have caught his eye.'

Süreyya stared at the doctor. So, word of the prince's interest in her had even reached the hospital. The older woman patted her hand. Her eyes met Süreyya's as she leaned forward.

'Maybe one day you become *ikbal*, the favourite. If you have son, they call you *haseki*—mother of prince, like Emira Sultan. Then if me, or my husband, have trouble, you can help us; you can talk to prince.'

Süreyya felt a frisson of apprehension. This woman had restored her virginity, but at what cost? Blackmail in the future? Should she be honest with Prince Orhan if she ever got close to him?

'Maybe I'll tell the prince the truth. Stefan and I were engaged ...' she ventured.

The other woman looked aghast. She grabbed Süreyya's hands and squeezed them hard. 'Never! No say, no say I stitch!' she hissed urgently. 'Prince Orhan's mother—she kill *me*, my family, and *you*.' Rebeka drew a finger across her throat. 'Understand?'

Süreyya's body tingled with fear. She vowed she would say nothing. Doctor Rebeka's olive-skinned face relaxed. She helped her patient to her feet and hugged her against her bosom, then held Süreyya at arm's length and nodded.

'I sure you become prince's ikbal—favourite. You young, strong, beautiful. You will heal quickly.'

The doctor touched the gold star at her throat. 'I am Jewish lady; all Jewish people expelled from Spain by king and queen. Sultan give us a home. What I do for you—*dangerous*.' She stared hard at Süreyya, put her finger to her lips, then across her throat again. 'Say nothing, *nothing!* You, me, my family executed! Remember!'

Süreyya nodded and shivered; the other woman's fear was infectious.

Doctor Rebeka's assistant led her to the small chamber where Perihan and the eunuch, Amir, helped her into her clothes. She smoothed them down with shaking hands. Her painful ordeal and her conversation with the doctor had frightened her. She was trapped in the harem, and what was worse, Doctor Rebeka knew her deepest secret. Her bravery of the previous day was a thing of the past; she was Prince Orhan's prisoner. Maybe if she could see the prince again and plead with him, he might release her.

The servants opened the door, and Süreyya stepped out ahead of them into the sunshine. The deserted garden was alive with birdsong and the sound of water splashing from several fountains. They were within sight of the harem when she saw the prince coming out of a building. Two richly dressed guards in flowing red robes followed him at a distance. He strode along the path toward her, then stopped and smiled.

'Süreyya Jariye! Good afternoon.'

Taking her cue from Perihan and Amir, she lowered her head, but not before her eyes had met his briefly. The prince addressed Amir, who replied in his quiet voice.

'Amir tells me he is showing you our beautiful gardens,' Orhan said in Russian.

Please God, the eunuch hasn't told his highness where we've been.

Süreyya looked up at Orhan and their eyes met again. The pain between her legs throbbed despite the salve the doctor had used. She glanced around. 'They are *truly* beautiful, sire.' She managed to smile.

All thoughts of petitioning him for her freedom flew from her head. She just wanted to lie on her bed in her quiet chamber, with him beside her holding her hand. His parting words the previous evening, though, haunted her thoughts: 'I will not wait long.' What if he wished to see her tonight? His next words eased her anxiety.

'I was enjoying the gardens before I leave early on the morrow for Manisa—a provincial capital,' he explained. 'I shall be away for nearly three weeks.' He lowered his voice. 'On my return, Süreyya, I will send for you.'

She stepped back quickly when, with a swift movement, he pulled his dagger from the scabbard at his waist and cut a pink rose from a nearby bush. The blade flashed in the sun as he swiped it down the stem to remove the thorns.

'A blushing rose,' he murmured as he handed it to her, his eyes fixed on hers. 'Until we meet again, water spirit.'

He nodded to her servants, and they jumped aside to let him pass. Süreyya watched him go, clutching the pink rose with both her hands. The sunlight shimmered on the long silver brocade vest he wore over his green satin kaftan. The light breeze ruffled the dark hair that framed his small flat turban. She saw him hesitate, but instead of retracing his steps, he nodded and continued his walk along the deserted paths.

Süreyya stifled the thrill she'd felt on seeing the prince. A sharp jab of pain reminded her of what the doctor had just done. If Doctor Rebeka was telling the truth, Emira could have both her and Rebeka executed for their deception. But surely the prince would intervene? A picture of his mother flashed across her mind. She was sure that no one—not even her son—would contradict an order handed down by Emira. After all, if she were executed, he still had twenty other women to choose from.

Süreyya followed her escort, trying to walk so that no one could guess the pain she felt between her legs. She held the rose carefully in her hands, inhaling its heady scent.

The heavy door of the harem closed behind her and the servants, and she was once again in the cool, shadowy corridor. While Sami helped her into her slippers, she tried to quell the feeling of desperation that rose in her throat. Was any woman granted freedom from this place, especially one who had caught a prince's eye?

'The prince gave you a rose!' Perihan whispered, her eyes wide. 'How strange that we should meet him so unexpectedly.'

Süreyya nodded. From the way he looked at her, she knew that Prince Orhan would not grant her freedom—yet. Maybe she could escape before he returned? But ever since she'd arrived, servants had surrounded her, as she was now: Abdul, Perihan, the little boy … Three others stood waiting for orders. She glanced at the enormous door. She couldn't open that; besides, tall, well-built, black eunuchs stood on either side of it. Süreyya was in a passageway between the interior door into the harem and the outer door that led to the garden. All doors, according to Perihan, were guarded night and day. Maybe there was another way out? A secret passage, like the one she'd come through from the beach. Could she find that again?

'Don't be dismayed, Süreyya Jariye. Three weeks will pass quickly,' the girl said, mistaking Süreyya's sigh. She took the rose and promised to put it in water.

That night, no one entered Süreyya's chamber. A prayer call in the early hours woke her, and she touched the rose near her bed. Its scent still filled her chamber. Süreyya pushed the bedcovers aside and crossed to the window. She opened the glass, fastening the windows on either side of the frame, then reached through the decorated metal screen and pushed aside the outer shutters, as she'd seen the servant do. The sounds of horses and men's voices drifted toward her on the still, cool air, but she couldn't see them from the courtyard. She wished she could see Prince Orhan, maybe for the last time, as he left for his journey to Manisa. The sun was just rising in a blaze of gold and pink, and the waters of the Golden Horn shimmered with the reflected light. A few small caiques floated along on the still surface. She clutched the windowsill and leaned her head on the decorated metal screen. This was her third day in the most luxurious prison in the world. She *had* to escape!

After breakfast, Abdul Agha swept in the door, ready to escort

Süreyya to her first lessons. He clicked his fingers for Perihan to follow them down the stairs. They walked through the now familiar tiled hall, and as they approached the large salon, Abdul paused. Süreyya had never seen inside the chamber before, and she stared at the groups of attractive women breakfasting together.

'Emira Sultan will decide on the day and time you may visit the salon and meet the other slaves and odalisques,' the chief eunuch remarked.

A woman with deep auburn hair and white skin looked up as they paused. She stared at Süreyya, then leaned toward her friends, saying something in a low voice. The other beauties watched Süreyya with the same coldly curious expression.

'Roshan Kalfa, the Lady Steward, will monitor your progress.' Abdul ushered her toward the door of the harem. He seemed unaware of the wave of silent hostility that washed out of the salon doors. 'She will report to me, and I will report to Emira Sultan,' Abdul concluded.

Outside, beyond the second door, the breeze caught Süreyya's scarf, and she shaded her eyes against the bright sunshine. She followed Abdul down a winding path, bordered on one side by the high hedges of the gardens, and on the other by windowless walls.

At the back of her mind, she could still see the hostile and curious expressions on the odalisque's faces. Had they heard that the prince had paid her a late-night visit? She vowed she would escape from the harem before she had to face those menacing women, *and* before the prince returned.

'This is part of the third courtyard,' Abdul told her in his broken Russian, unaware of her secret plans. 'Only the royal family, foreign dignitaries and special members of the household may pass from the second courtyard through the Gate of Felicity.' Abdul pointed to the canopied gate. 'Over there is the Chamber of Holy Relics,' he murmured. 'It contains the mantle, bow, and sword of the Prophet Mohammed, Peace be Upon Him. When you become a Muslim, you will understand the sacredness of these things.'

He pointed out the princes' school, the quarters for the white eunuchs, and in a corner, the chambers where she would study.

'Study well, then you can write to Prince Orhan,' he said with a rare sideways smile.

Süreyya inclined her head. *I have a different reason for learning Turkish. I will need to speak it so that I can find my way through the city after I escape.*

Abdul introduced her to Davut Hodja, her teacher. Like Abdul, he was a eunuch, with a treble voice and soft skin. He was as fair-skinned as Abdul was dark, with kind, pale blue eyes, and he spoke Russian. He smiled when his new pupil responded to his greeting in Turkish.

'Abdul wishes you to have classes for a couple of days each week. Your maid may stay to assist you for a while,' he said. 'After that, you must work hard to understand your lessons.'

Her teacher handed her some scrolls of paper and a leather-covered book. Its blank pages were of the same high quality as the scrolls. He tapped the book and said *'defter'*. He gave her a rectangular ceramic box decorated with blue flowers and Arabic script. In the corner were two ink wells; she opened the metal lid and chose a wooden pen with a metal nib. She spent the morning leaning over her paper and copying the Arabic letters that were used to write the Turkish language, trying to disguise her discomfort and the pain between her legs.

When she made a perfect copy on her scroll, her teacher allowed her to write it in her defter, using a fine pen. He gave her some words to learn: *finjan*: cup, *bardak*: glass, *buyrun*: please help yourself, *çok güzel*; very nice or beautiful. It was going to take her a while to learn enough Turkish to navigate the city. But she had always been a good student *and* she had a motivation to learn quickly. She asked him to tell her the words for *'where is'* and *'where are'* and *'where am I?'* He obliged without comment, and she wondered if he would report her request to Abdul.

'They're very useful words, my teacher,' she said. 'I often get lost in the harem passageways.'

Davut inclined his head. 'Your lessons will finish before midday prayers,' he said. 'After lunch, Imam Mustafa will teach you about the Muslim religion and how to pray. *Aferin*—well done today, Süreyya Jariye. You have worked hard.'

✿

After Süreyya had gone, Davut Hodja put his pens in an orderly line. So, this was the girl the young prince had rescued when she jumped off a slave ship. She was a fast learner and her writing already showed promise.

An odalisque who became the mother of a prince needed an excellent education, Davut reflected. If Prince Orhan favoured this woman and she produced a son who became sultan, then the empire would enter a golden age. Davut Hodja shook his head, remembering the young Emira when she was a student. She had always been erratic and forceful, and now she had a powerful position in her son's harem. He wondered what the prince's mother thought of Süreyya.

✿

Following a week of discomfort, Süreyya returned to the doctor. After she'd removed the stitches, Doctor Rebeka nodded.

'Your torn hymen has healed,' she whispered. 'You are virgin again. The discomfort will end soon, maybe by the time the prince sends for you.'

'But when he … will it hurt?'

'Enough so he believes he is your first lover.' The doctor raised her eyebrows.

✿

During the weeks the prince was away, Süreyya had learned a lot of Turkish and she was beginning to understand fragments of conversations. She had also taken lessons on the etiquette of the harem. In one of her instruction sessions, Roshan Kalfa, the Lady Steward, a small neat young woman, added to Perihan's explanation of the eunuchs, as well as telling her about the hierarchy of the harem.

'The eunuchs are not complete men. Their manhood was removed when they were young boys,' she said with no trace of embarrassment.

'Abdul is a eunuch, of course. He is in charge of all the women in the harem. You must obey him totally and address him as Abdul Agha. He answers directly to Emira Sultan. The only *complete* man who may enter the harem is Prince Orhan, and the sultan, of course, if he chooses.'

Roshan Kalfa adjusted her pink brocade gown and matching skull cap. She asked if Süreyya had any more questions.

'I wish to ask the prince when he will return me to the Christian part of the city and my people,' Süreyya said.

Roshan Kalfa shook her head and sighed. 'We have talked of this before!' She patted Süreyya's hand. 'We all came here as slaves; you are no different. After nine years, and sometimes before, odalisques may request to leave the harem and get married. The prince's mother decides if they can, and chooses a husband for them. But the prince and his father, the sultan, must also give permission. Emira Sultan may choose someone to leave if she is not happy with them. I am a kalfa, a head servant, so I may leave after ten years.'

'But I want to leave now!'

Roshan Kalfa tutted and shook her head. 'You have many advantages: your own chamber, at the prince's request, unlike most of the others. Be thankful for that. You have done a good job cleaning and looking after it.'

'How do I become a favourite?'

The other woman raised her dark eyebrows. 'If Prince Orhan calls you to his bed—and you please him—his mother will send word to Abdul. We will provide you with more servants to wait on you. You are lucky you have Perihan Jariye and Amir some of the time already.'

'And when may I go to the main salon?' Süreyya asked.

'When the prince's mother, Emira Sultan, invites you. Meanwhile, your education here will continue, with Perihan's help.'

Despite admiring the prince, Süreyya kneeled by her bed at night and prayed fervently that she might find a way out of the harem. Every day she sent Perihan on several unnecessary errands, back to the school or the mosque where she took her instructions. As soon as she'd gone, Süreyya left her chamber quietly and explored the maze of narrow tiled passages in the building. Someone always stopped her, a eunuch or a female servant, and asked why she was in a particular passageway. They escorted her back to her own chamber where Perihan waited anxiously. Hopes of escape faded, but she vowed she would keep trying.

Across the courtyard below her window, a path wound past a bathing pool and fountains to a wooded area. Süreyya was sure it led downhill to the beach where Orhan had found her. If she could only discover the path to the water, she could follow the shoreline to the city.

But in the ensuing days, she was hardly ever alone. Someone, it seemed, had instructed Perihan never to leave her side. When she made vacuous requests, Perihan now sent a eunuch servant instead of going herself. She even asked Süreyya to attend prayers with her if they didn't pray in her chamber. Once, when they visited the courtyard to take the air with a few of the other women, Süreyya slipped away from Perihan. She ran like the wind down the paths toward the water, only to find herself in front of a long, high wall. From her chamber window, trees had hidden this barrier. In the distance, she saw two guards hurrying toward her. A eunuch appeared at her side, slightly out of breath, and invited her to take refreshments near the pool. He followed her closely back up the stony path as she brushed away tears of frustration.

At the end of Süreyya's third week in the harem, Perihan arrived after midday prayers babbling excitedly. She was wearing a long cream-coloured silk tunic over pants that were caught at the ankles with silver ties, threaded with diamonds and seed pearls.

'Emira Sultan wishes you to come to the salon this afternoon,' Perihan said. 'Prince Orhan returned last night and he may visit. Remember, he wears shoes with silver soles, so we hear him coming. He doesn't want to surprise us!' The young girl laughed. 'Amir has brought some suitable clothes for you.'

Süreyya stood back as two servants entered, carrying a collection of luxurious clothes. They laid them out on the long divan.

'For me?'

After lunch, Perihan helped Süreyya into a rose-coloured gown. The long sleeves fanned out at the elbow into a bell shape made from thin silk. A gold-embroidered band on the sleeves and hem was sewn with tiny seed pearls, small diamonds, and rubies. Süreyya touched the jewels that decorated the bodice.

Perihan wound a filigree gold belt with a jewelled clasp around Süreyya's waist and helped her into a deeper pink sleeveless garment that reached below her knees.

'I've never owned such a beautiful gown. I thought it would be heavy, but it isn't, it's beautiful.'

The fabric was like the silk her father had imported from China to Russia, but only the very rich in her city had worn such garments.

As Süreyya followed Perihan along the marble passageways, she felt nervous. She had passed the salon several times now and seen the other ladies through the open door. Since the first time she had looked into the large chamber, no one gave her a second glance. They were all busily engaged in their occupations of embroidery and board games. Now Emira Sultan was permitting her to enter. She had expected to be free by now, instead she was still trapped in the harem.

Eunuchs stood on either side of the doors and bowed as they walked in. Several groups of women sat on the wide divans set against the dark gold-coloured walls. Like Süreyya, they were wearing opulent dresses in a variety of colours—bright yellow decorated with amber-coloured stones, vibrant green with gold belts studded with emeralds. Like Perihan, the servants wore tunics and pants. The chamber smelled of rosewater and fresh flowers.

On a platform opposite the door, a small coterie sat around the central figure: Emira Sultan. The older woman wore a deep maroon gown. A heavy diamond necklace complemented her diamond earrings and matching diamond clips emphasised the richness of her dark hair, in which she wore a small diamond tiara. Next to her sat a young woman with waist-length auburn hair. Someone had fastened it with an emerald and diamond clip and arranged it over her left shoulder—the same woman who had stared at Süreyya several weeks ago. Her pale green eyes appraised her rival, and her mouth twitched into a disdainful sneer.

The prince's mother stood up and instructed the younger women to sit at a distance, but allowed her own waiting women to stay. She beckoned Süreyya to come forward. The low buzz of conversation stopped. Inquisitive faces turned to look at her as she stepped onto the low platform with Perihan.

'Emira Sultan, the prince's mother,' Perihan whispered. 'She wants to welcome you.'

Emira's keen eyes held Süreyya's for a moment, and she clicked her fingers at Perihan. The girl's voice shook as she introduced her mistress in Turkish. Emira dismissed her and addressed Süreyya.

'*Hoş geldiniz, salonu, Süreyya Jariye*—welcome to the salon, Süreyya Jariye.' The woman's husky voice had a harsh edge Süreyya remembered from their first meeting.

'*Hoş bulduk, Emira Sultan*—I found welcome, Emira Sultan,' Süreyya replied.

The prince's mother made a slight sound in the back of her throat. 'I'm glad you have learned to pronounce Turkish better since the last time I summoned you,' she remarked in Russian.

Emira didn't dwell on Süreyya's arrival in the harem, but questioned Süreyya again about her family. Her full lips twitched when Süreyya told how her uncle and aunt took her to live with them, after her father and brother had perished in a fire at her father's warehouse.

'So, your father was a merchant?'

'Yes, your highness, my father imported silk and fine cloth. My mother died of grief shortly after his death. My uncle is a bishop of the Russian Orthodox Church,' she reminded Emira.

'They were not a poor family then?' the other woman interrupted.

'No, madam.' Süreyya wondered at the question. Would Emira Sultan prefer she came from peasant stock? Like herself perhaps?

'I will remind you again to forget your family and your former name, forget everything. Only *I* need to know about you. None of the slaves or the odalisques has a past, only a future—understand? And yours is here.'

She fixed Süreyya with a sharp look, as if she knew Süreyya had been hurrying along the deserted passageways in her quest to find a hidden exit and escape. She was sure someone had informed Emira about Süreyya's desperate run through the trees toward the palace wall.

'The doctor tells me you are healthy and suitable,' Emira remarked.

Süreyya swallowed, but before she could answer, she heard a man's voice outside the window and then the *click, click* she'd heard on her first day in the harem.

'Ah.' Emira smiled for the first time. 'My son returned from Manisa last night. He came to see me immediately, of course, and now he is gracing us all with a visit.'

The women in the salon looked expectantly to the door when they, too, heard the silver-soled shoes and the prince's voice.

Emira pointed to a divan on the other side of the chamber. 'Sit over there,' she said to Süreyya, beckoning her young coterie to re-join her.

A ripple of anticipation fanned through the salon. As Süreyya hurried to the distant seat, she heard the silver-shod feet getting nearer, tapping on the marble slabs of the passage outside the salon and echoing off the tiles. She, too, fixed her eyes on the door, and her body tensed as the sound of Prince Orhan's silver slippers halted.

CHAPTER 5

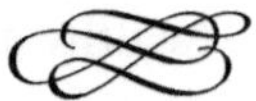

Two servants opened the doors to the salon, the buzz of chatter died, and Süreyya looked up from her distant seat. Prince Orhan stood in the doorway, scanning the salon with his deep-set brown eyes. He had changed into soft leather slippers, and a jewelled gold pendant around his neck caught the filtered sun from the long windows. His dark hair framed his face, and his long silver brocade kaftan emphasised his muscular chest and sat well on his broad shoulders. Around his waist he wore a jewelled leather belt, and Süreyya shivered again when she saw the tip of a dagger protruding from its sheath. Only weeks since, this man's arms had encircled her and carried her to safety, then later had crushed her against him.

Süreyya was still staring at him when Perihan nudged her.

'We must lower our eyes until the prince approaches his mother,' the girl whispered.

Süreyya obeyed, feeling overawed by his masculine presence among his women. She clenched her fists together and forced herself to think clearly. This man was her *jailor*, and every woman in the salon wanted him. He had noticed her, and despite her misgivings she felt a quickening in her body when he smiled directly at her. It was a slow smile that lit up his sun-burnished face.

Süreyya smiled back then looked away. She heard the wooden platform creak as he stepped onto it to greet his waiting mother. Abdul clapped his hands loudly.

'We may watch now.' Perihan whispered.

The prince kissed his mother's hand and put it to his forehead. He acknowledged the group of women around her, who lifted their heads as he greeted them.

Süreyya risked another look in the prince's direction, and was rewarded by a last glance and a smile that hovered around his lips. She pinched her thigh to remind herself that she was here against her will. Did she really want to stay with these fawning sycophants whose sole desire was to be taken to the prince's bed? He had positioned himself directly opposite her, and Süreyya watched as he chatted politely with the other women and his mother. Occasionally he glanced across at her.

From her distant seat, Süreyya saw Emira frown at her. Then she leaned forward and patted her son's knee, indicating the redhead, who was adjusting her long hair. Emira clicked her fingers at Abdul Agha, who stood motionless near her on the platform, his eyes roaming the room. He leaned forward as she spoke to him, straightened up, and stared directly at Süreyya. With his usual fluid dignity, Abdul stepped deftly around the hems of the odalisques' outspread gowns, and descended the platform.

Süreyya looked away quickly. Had Emira seen her smiling at the prince? Would she and Perihan be banished from the salon in disgrace, watched by the beauties surrounding the prince and his mother?

Perihan nudged her. 'Abdul is coming.'

The eunuch walked slowly toward them, and Süreyya was certain he would escort her out of the door. The blackamore arrived at their distant corner. He adjusted his yellow satin robes, bowed his elaborately turbaned head, and cleared his throat.

'Emira Sultan wishes you to join Prince Orhan and the odalisques for coffee, madam,' he addressed Süreyya. Then he glanced at Perihan and nodded. 'And you.'

Perihan scrambled to her feet. 'Such an honour, madam,' she said as Süreyya stood up. They followed Abdul, placing their feet in the indentations he'd made on the carpet.

'You must keep your eyes lowered when approaching the prince,' Perihan whispered. Süreyya obeyed the custom and concentrated on walking sedately across the carpet behind the chief eunuch.

'The redhead next to Emira Sultan is Zeynep,' Perihan told her. 'Many think she will become ikbal—the favourite concubine of his highness.'

The muted chatter from the group died away as they approached, and Süreyya risked a look.

Four women, two young and two about Emira's age, sat on divans near a low octagonal table. The boy, Sami, stood next to the stool Süreyya had recently vacated. He beamed from under his child-sized white satin turban as she approached. Prince Orhan was sitting between his mother and Zeynep, the possible favourite. Zeynep was chattering brightly to him, and he inclined his head toward her with a smile. He didn't look up or try to catch Süreyya's eye when Abdul pointed to a low seat near one of Emira's ladies. Perihan sat on a floor cushion next to her. Emira Sultan said something in Turkish, and the other women laughed quietly behind their hands and looked at Süreyya. The prince's mother snapped her fingers at Perihan and told her to translate.

'She's introducing you as "the runaway",' Perihan said reluctantly.

'Correct,' Emira Sultan remarked in Russian. 'Your daring escape fascinated our little group. It sounded like one of those stories from Baghdad in "The Thousand and One Nights".'

She repeated her comment in rapid Turkish. The other women nodded.

'Except, unlike in the story,' Zeynep countered, '*she* isn't a princess!'

Süreyya guessed that Zeynep's words weren't flattering even before Perihan's translation.

Orhan looked up and his eyes met Süreyya's for a moment. 'Not at present,' he said in Russian. He smiled at her and raised his eyebrows slightly.

Turning to the other women, he repeated his comment in Turkish. A couple of them looked sideways at Süreyya. Emira Sultan tutted and said something to a hovering attendant.

'I have ordered a drink called kahve,' she said. 'The governor of our newly gained territories in the Yemen sent it to the palace. We all love it.'

Süreyya had never heard of the strange new drink—was it hot or cold? She had no idea, but pinched her thigh to remind herself of who she was: an educated woman, not a slave. As Rusalka Ivanova she would have made Stefan, scholar and teacher, a good wife. They had planned to marry soon, and she would have been mistress of her own house. Instead, she was trapped in a harem. *I don't want to sit here*, she thought angrily as the servants set up a circular table. *Is this my future? To do nothing but think of escape and daydream about a Turkish prince?*

'It's the tradition that an odalisque pours a beverage for the prince.' Perihan's voice cut across her thoughts.

Zeynep said something to Emira Sultan and peevishly pointed to her hand. The prince's mother looked across at Süreyya.

'Zeynep suggests you pour the coffee for the prince. She says she's hurt her hand,' Perihan translated.

Emira Sultan glanced at Süreyya. 'You've had no training yet, but it's a simple task. I'm sure you can manage,' she remarked in Russian.

'Madam, I think it better if a servant does it for me,' Süreyya replied, looking around.

Emira Sultan shot her an angry look. 'It is an *honour* for a slave—and one so recently acquired—to pour coffee for my son.'

Süreyya said nothing. Emira had spoken.

'It's very easy,' the prince encouraged.

When the coffee arrived on a gold tray, Süreyya's heart sank. There was no samovar with a small teapot under it, as she'd expected. The tiny cups decorated in flower patterns and gold leaf weren't a problem, but the coffeepot was. Its long gold body and neck were encrusted with precious stones, and it belled out at the bottom then narrowed to a small stand. Chains looped from the lid to the elongated spout and the gold handle. Süreyya thought she could manage it, but when she picked it up using a napkin around the handle, the ornate lid wobbled precariously.

'You must hold it down,' Perihan whispered.

Süreyya put her index finger on the lid and jumped when it burned her skin. Across the table she saw Zeynep whisper to one of her friends. As she walked around the table, the other woman bumped Süreyya's arm. The coffeepot wobbled in her hand and the lid flew off. The gold chains that were supposed to hold it dangled uselessly along its neck. Thick black coffee splashed across the table and over Prince Orhan. The odalisques screamed, and the prince leaped to his feet. In an instant, servants overran the entire area brandishing cloths. Horrified by what she'd done, Süreyya stood up and scrabbled around the table for the lid.

'*Aptal kız!*—Stupid girl!' Zeynep squealed.

'Quiet!' Emira Sultan's voice rang out.

Süreyya glanced at the prince. He ignored the dramatic shrieking of the women and crossed to where Süreyya sat. She stood up, and with his back to his mother and the other women, Orhan took her hand. His felt warm and hard—a soldier's hand.

'Are you hurt, sire?' she asked.

'Of course not, but what about you, Süreyya?' he whispered.

Süreyya shook her head, angry tears stinging her eyes. This was Zeynep's doing—she told her friend to nudge her arm. Maybe someone had tampered with the gold chains that held the lid as well.

'Please, sire, let me leave. I don't want to stay here in the harem,' she implored.

Orhan waved away the servants, who were wiping coffee stains from his kaftan. He squeezed her hand, ignoring her plea, and smiled as he slipped something into her pocket. His hand brushed against her thigh. 'Wear it for me,' he murmured.

The prince returned to his seat next to his mother. Zeynep was still raging furiously in Turkish, but lowered her voice when Orhan sat down. Emira Sultan seemed to agree with her. Süreyya backed away from the table, where servants had restored some order and brought more coffee. Emira Sultan beckoned to Süreyya and touched her arm.

'I will invite you to sit with me again, but only when you have learned more skills. I was obviously mistaken,' she said. 'Now return to your seat.' She pointed to the far end of the salon.

Süreyya walked through the salon, past gaping servants and the odalisques who sat in small groups. Her face burned with embarrassment and pent-up anger. She didn't see Orhan turn to his mother.

'Why did you dismiss her?'

'It's for the best. She needs more training.'

Süreyya resumed her place at the back of the salon. She saw the group on the platform reassemble and continue chatting. The younger women glanced at the prince, then lowered their eyes. The servants brought a fresh pot of coffee. Zeynep picked it up and poured a cup for the prince and his mother. Zeynep and her friend exchange a quick, triumphant glance.

Orhan watched as the Russian girl returned to her distant corner. Süreyya held her head high, but he saw the pink blush that had spread over her pale skin. He imagined her body underneath her gown. At every step she took, he relived the heady sensation of holding her and crushing her firm breasts against his chest. *I will order her brought to my bed tonight.*

Süreyya was still furious with the other women when she sat down next to Perihan. They could forget their stupid customs. She would not stay here—they had no right to keep her! Prince Orhan had found her; he didn't *buy* her in the slave market! She would petition the sultan. She was not a *peasant*. She was from a prestigious family. She had connections.

Glancing around quickly, she slipped the prince's gift from her pocket, and cupped it in her hand. She opened her fingers and stared. A large sapphire set in gold and surrounded by diamonds hung on a thick gold chain. It was the most beautiful gift she'd ever received. Süreyya returned it to her pocket, where she could feel the heaviness of the precious stone against her thigh, remembering his words: 'Wear it for me.'

He can't buy me. She pinched her thigh again. She needed to get away from here, from him and his charismatic presence. Perihan brought her a drink of sherbet in a silver mug, and when she sipped the cool strawberry-flavoured concoction, she felt a little better, but no less determined.

'Someone wants to meet you,' Perihan said.

'To meet *me?*'

'She says her name is Galina Volkov, and she knows you. She's called Melek now.'

Süreyya could hardly believe her ears. Galina Volkov was her oldest friend from home. They had shared the same tutor! Her friend disappeared over two years ago in the last Tartar raid. Süreyya stared at the sophisticated odalisque walking toward her. 'Galina?'

'Rusalka!'

Süreyya embraced her old friend. 'I'm Süreyya now. They changed my name.'

'And I'm Melek!'

'What happened to you?' Süreyya asked. 'We thought you'd run away!'

'I was staying with my cousins in a country village when the Tartars arrived. They killed all the old people and babies, and enslaved everyone else.' Melek's eyes filled with tears. 'They marched me to the coast and kept me locked with hundreds of others in a ship's hold. You were so lucky to escape.'

'But they've imprisoned me here!' Süreyya answered.

Melek glanced around and whispered. 'I heard the prince saved you from drowning. Everyone's talking about it. In the Muslim religion, they believe that if someone saves your life, it was your destiny and theirs. The prince will think you belong to him, and because he saved you, he's responsible for you.'

'Belong? I don't belong to anyone, especially Prince Orhan!'

'Rusalka … Süreyya …' Melek looked around again. 'The prince is powerful, and so is his mother. Don't cross her. Orhan may be the next pādishah—Sultan of the Ottoman Empire. If that happens, she'll be the Valide Sultan, Mother of the Sultan, the most powerful woman in the Ottoman Empire. She's alarmed because Orhan has no sons. His favourite, Nesrin, died in childbirth and their baby son didn't survive. They say the prince was inconsolable. His mother is pushing him to take many women to his bed.'

She related how the prince volunteered to lead the army on a campaign to Baghdad. He had returned recently after being away for two years. Harem gossip held that he hadn't made love to anyone in his harem since he got back.

'If the prince requests you come to his bed, you refuse on pain of death,' Süreyya's friend added. 'But his mother is cultivating Zeynep to become ikbal—the favourite. She doesn't want him to fall in love again, and he doesn't love Zeynep. He hasn't requested her yet, but everyone thinks it will happen soon.'

'How do you know this?'

'Gossip,' Melek said. 'When a prince or the sultan chooses someone, no one knows, but the next day there is more gossip. That's true, isn't it?' she said to Perihan.

Perihan nodded. 'Zeynep hasn't said anything to her friends, so it hasn't happened.'

'When the prince chooses someone, the chief eunuch, Abdul, takes the girl secretly to the prince's chambers.' Melek raised her eyebrows. 'Every visit is entered in the *Book of Couchings* by Abdul—in the event of a conception,' she added. 'If she pleases the prince and there are more visits, she becomes the ikbal and gets her own suite of chambers with servants. If she bears a son and becomes haseki, then she has a lot of power.' Melek smiled and raised her eyebrows.

'But would he take others to his bed?' Süreyya asked.

'Of course! Once a favourite has a son—a prince—it's her job to raise him. She is never called to the prince's bed again. It's the same in the imperial harem of the sultan.'

'Never?'

'No, but she gets beautiful chambers, lots of waiting women, a wet nurse, and she's almost as powerful as his mother! If she has a daughter, then he may take the favourite to his bed again. The royal family do not usually marry. In the community, men can have four wives and concubines if they can afford them, but the prince has a harem.'

Süreyya listened with a sinking heart. How could any woman share the prince with others? She would rather not be chosen.

'Madam, the royal party is leaving.' Perihan nudged her. 'We must stand and bow our heads.'

The three women faced the door. Süreyya bowed her head, but raised her eyes and watched the prince walk to the door and change from his slippers. The double doors opened silently, then closed behind him. The sound of his silver-soled shoes died away and the odalisques sat down on the divans, chattering and laughing in their small groups.

Süreyya looked across at Zeynep. How would she feel if she heard he'd taken Zeynep to his bed? Certainly not indifferent.

'You must learn Turkish quickly,' her old friend said as they sat down. 'You need to know what the others are saying.' She lowered her voice. 'Be careful of Zeynep. She's ambitious—and dangerous.'

Just as the words left her lips, Melek's expression changed, and Süreyya looked up. Zeynep and her friends were walking toward her. She got to her feet as they stopped and surrounded her. Perihan stepped aside when Zeynep put out her hand, her green eyes glittering maliciously.

'He gave you something. He meant it for me.'

'She's got nothing!' Perihan protested.

Zeynep turned and smacked her across the head. 'Shut up, she has.' She looked at Süreyya and raised her eyebrows. 'Show me!'

Süreyya didn't need the words translated. She shook her head, fearful that if she admitted the existence of the gift, Zeynep might drag it from her. The other woman smoothed her long red hair over her left shoulder. She fixed Süreyya with a malicious look.

'I'll be ikbal soon, understand?'

She snapped her fingers at Perihan to translate, then Melek stepped forward.

'Leave Perihan alone, I'll translate.'

'I don't care who *she* is,' Zeynep glared at Süreyya. 'The prince will be mine soon. I want to see what he gave her. Tell her that.' Zeynep's green eyes glittered.

'She has nothing,' Melek repeated after she'd translated Zeynep's words.

'She's a liar!' Zeynep spat. 'I heard they threw her overboard from a slave ship, like rotten meat.'

'I won't translate that.'

'Do it or you'll be sorry.'

Melek reluctantly translated. Süreyya met her rival's eyes defiantly, then turned away. Zeynep lunged at her, grabbed her shoulder, and pulled her around. Her long talons scraped down Süreyya's cheek.

'See if he likes you now, spoiled meat!'

Shaken, Süreyya clapped her hand to her cheek and pushed past the women. She rushed for the door, followed by Perihan and Melek. In the passageway she collided with Abdul; when he saw her bleeding cheek, he hissed through his teeth. He ordered Perihan and Melek to take Süreyya to her chamber, then he turned back and headed for the salon.

'Zeynep Hatun! I wish to speak with you, *now!*'

CHAPTER 6

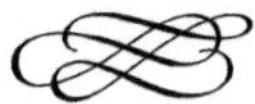

$\mathcal{A}$fter they left the salon, Orhan accompanied his mother to her chambers. 'I'll take my leave, Mother,' he said.

To his surprise, his mother didn't insist that he stay. He was heading for the door when she said, 'The slave, Süreyya, the one who threw coffee over you. What do you think?'

Orhan shrugged. 'She's a possibility, and she didn't "throw coffee". It was an accident.'

'Well, I'm not sure it's worth training her as things stand.'

'What things?'

'There's some trouble in the Christian area of the city. The sultan may want to see you.'

'Does it concern the new slave?'

'It's really not my place to say anything,' his mother replied. She raised her eyebrows and shooed him toward the door.

He hated playing these foolish games. He had enough on his mind with the imperial marine fleet. Now his mother was piling more aggravation on him. He'd left his friend Hafız trying to sort out the problem, and he should be there. Instead, he'd spent the afternoon in the harem. Orhan took a deep breath when he remembered the stricken look on Süreyya's face when she'd spilled the coffee.

I would rather look at her than a boat.

'Just tell me what you mean, Mother.'

'Don't get too fond of her.'

'Right, Mother, thank you, I won't.' He bowed to her and flicked his hand. Her eunuch, Zeki, bowing low, opened the door for him.

Orhan headed for his own chambers as the afternoon prayer call began. He needed to clear his head to discuss matters with Hafız, but he couldn't banish thoughts of Süreyya from his mind. He imagined running his hands through her thick curls and over her warm body—tonight.

He had told Abdul to bring the girl to him this evening and sworn the chief eunuch to secrecy. The Russian girl didn't need training in how to please him, as was the custom. He himself would initiate her into lovemaking. He let his mind wander as he thought of her body again, firm and young. It wasn't just her body, but everything about her that attracted him. She was beautiful, lively, and intelligent. He knew she was determined to leave the harem. He was just as determined she would stay.

'Don't get too fond of her.' His mother's parting words rang in his ears.

It was too late for warnings, he thought. *I want to know more about her, and how it would feel to make love to her.*

His servants had laid out his prayer mat near the mihrab in his own chamber. He washed, and stood quietly facing the holy city, Mecca. He breathed in slowly, trying to ready his thoughts for the prayer ritual.

Perihan and Melek excused themselves when they left the harem, explaining that they had to attend *Asr*—afternoon prayers in the servant's mosque.

'Madam, pray in your own chamber,' Perihan advised, looking at the large cotton pad Süreyya held against her cheek.

She walked alone to her chamber, where two eunuch servants were waiting. Amir had tutted sympathetically when he helped her change into long pants and a tunic. He dressed her wound with a neater dressing, while the other eunuch shook his head when he saw the coffee stains. The outer garment had protected her skin from being burned by the hot liquid. Before he left, Amir showed her the silk prayer rug he had laid out for her near the mihrab, the prayer niche, in the corner of her chamber.

'Prayer time,' he said slowly. 'And gown, for tomorrow.' He pointed to the garment laid out on her divan.

So, someone had told the Mistress of the Robes about the accident with the coffee, Süreyya thought. They had already sent her a fresh gown. Did everyone in the harem know *everything*?

Süreyya clutched the prince's gift in her hand after the eunuch left. Ignoring the prayer mat, she sat on the divan under her window. She opened her palm and gazed at the large sapphire on its gold chain, holding the necklace up to the light. The gemstone caught the sun's rays as it swung on its chain.

He gave me a gift—a beautiful personal gift!

She remembered the look in his eyes and his whispered words: 'Wear it for me.'

On the one hand, she longed to leave the harem, but on the other, her desire for him grew stronger by the day, even by the hour …

Süreyya fastened the necklace around her throat and picked up the jewelled hand mirror next to her bed. The sapphire was almost the same colour as her eyes. The prince had brought it to the harem to give to *her* and no one else. Would he call her to his chambers soon … to his bed? She touched her face where Zeynep had scratched it.

Süreyya lifted the pad and looked at the ugly scratches. Tiny spots of blood oozed from the wounds, and she pressed the patch back in place. Looking like this, she wouldn't be able to visit the salon for a few days. The final phrase of the prayer call jolted her back to reality. She washed quickly and began the prayer ritual, wishing she could petition Allah for help. After she'd stumbled through the still unfamiliar prayers, she lay down, still holding her face, and fell asleep.

A gentle tap on the door startled her awake. When she opened it,

Abdul Agha and another eunuch walked past her into her chamber and closed the door. The second eunuch, whose arms were full of clothes, began to lay them out carefully on the long divan.

'Prince Orhan has sent a request,' Abdul Agha said.

'A request?'

Had someone told him about her argument with Zeynep? Did he want her to return the sapphire?

'He wishes you to come to his chambers tonight. You will need help to get ready.'

'Tonight?'

Abdul inclined his head. 'Yes, madam.'

Süreyya's hand flew to her cheek. 'I can't. My cheek ...'

'You cannot refuse, madam. The prince has requested you.'

Süreyya shook her head. How could she let the prince see her with four scratch marks disfiguring her face. 'You must tell him I'm sick, I cannot come!'

Abdul looked shocked. 'Süreyya Jariye, I repeat, you *cannot* refuse.'

She wanted to see the prince, but on her terms, not like this. Her scratched face looked ugly. He would find her repulsive and send her away. Better that she reject Orhan and make an excuse. But would they force her to go, even if she were unwilling?

'No! Please relay what I have said to Prince Orhan. I cannot come tonight.'

Abdul drew his finger across his throat, and a shudder ran through her body. 'He can order your death for disobedience,' he whispered. 'You have no choice.'

'I'm sure the prince would not harm me, Abdul. He's not a savage,' she answered.

'Death is by drowning for women,' Abdul continued. 'They would tie you in a sack and throw you into the Bosphorus. His grandfather ordered that punishment when an odalisque refused him.'

'He is not his grandfather. Tell him I'll come another night.'

Abdul, still looking shocked, bowed and turned to his assistant, who had finished arranging the nightwear. The man opened the door as Abdul Agha, with a worried backward look, stepped out into the passage.

Before Süreyya could consider what she'd done, another group of people came into the chamber with a tray of food.

'A special meal,' the servant told her in Russian with a smile.

Was this her last meal? Had the prince ordered her execution? She shook her head; that was impossible. Abdul would be still on his way with her message.

When the servants left, she sat at the small table and picked at the food, wishing that Perihan and Melek would return before evening prayers. Maybe someone had ordered them not to come near her. When Prince Orhan received her reply, would he send for Zeynep instead?

Süreyya imagined him kissing Zeynep's lips. She grabbed the mirror and looked at the wound again. He'd chosen her, and she'd refused. With so many women to choose from, she might not get a second chance.

She touched the clothes the servants had left for her. One was a long diaphanous gown of a fine blue silk. Maybe the sight of her in this transparent garment would please him and he wouldn't notice her face. Her throat felt dry when she imagined his hands caressing her body. Süreyya clenched her private parts together when she thought of him touching her there. She shuddered and stroked the transparent shift and the ermine lining of the matching blue satin robe.

'Come!' Orhan turned quickly when someone knocked on the door. He frowned when he saw Abdul—was there a problem? He hadn't expected the agha so soon. He dismissed his servants and beckoned Abdul Agha inside.

'Where is she?' he demanded.

When Abdul hesitated, he repeated the question.

The chief eunuch did his best to explain that the lady was sick. She sent her apologies, but she would come on another night. In answer to the prince's question, no, the lady did not have 'the women's problem.'

'Is she sick in bed?'

'No, your highness.'

'What then?'

'I cannot say.'

Orhan stared at the blackamoor, hardly able to comprehend what he was saying.

The Russian slave had refused him! Süreyya had said no! No woman ever refused him. How dare she?

'Did you explain about our customs?'

'I did, sire. I told her about the punishment. The sacks in the Bosphorus.'

'Not that!'

Allah be praised! Süreyya would think he was a monster.

'I also explained the custom of a prince choosing a favourite,' Abdul Agha clarified.

Orhan took a step toward him. 'Tell me the truth. Why isn't she here?'

'She had an accident; she's hurt her face,' the agha said quickly.

'No matter. Say I *request* her company.' He frowned. 'And assure her I would never order a woman to be thrown into the Bosphorus. And remind her I saved her life.'

Abdul returned to Süreyya with the prince's reply. 'He has sent a second message, a *request*, madam. I must remind you, his highness is an Ottoman prince, Süreyya Jariye. A powerful man.' His serious expression seemed to alarm her. '*You* are a slave. He wishes to remind you he saved your life.' Abdul paused. 'I have a salve that will cover your injury, but it may still be visible.'

Süreyya took Abdul's enormous hand in hers. Why hadn't he suggested that before? Had he been too shocked to think of it?

'Thank you, I will prepare myself.'

Abdul's face crumpled with relief, and Süreyya felt a stab of guilt. She had put Abdul Agha's position, maybe his life, in jeopardy by her actions. But Zeynep had planned this discord, Süreyya thought.

'Thank you, madam.' Abdul touched his fingers to his forehead and his heart. 'Amir will bring the salve. I'll take your message to the prince.'

While Amir and Perihan fussed around her, taking her to the hamam, then dressing her hair, Süreyya's mind was in turmoil. She had already lost her maidenhead to another man. The doctor had removed the stitches. She was pleased at how well Süreyya had healed. But would the prince, experienced as he was in lovemaking, guess her secret? If he did, it might mean certain death, as the doctor had predicted.

The harem and palace were luxurious, but she shuddered when she thought of its dark side. Would any high-ranking official agree to marry her if she had been the prince's favourite? If she had a child, she would be forced to stay here and endure the torture of seeing Prince Orhan with other women. Süreyya longed to be with Orhan, to feel his strong arms around her and lean on his chest. But she yearned for many nights in his bed, not just one.

Scented, swaddled and in secret, Süreyya followed Abdul to Prince Orhan's chambers up a private staircase above the harem. She patted her cheek with her fingertips, where Amir had smoothed the herb potion on her wounded face. She glanced at the leather-bound book in his hands. This must be the *Book of Couchings* that Melek had mentioned. It was Abdul's job to write the date and time of every assignation the prince had with a woman from his harem. It was a record for posterity, to prove the legitimacy of a royal child.

Two armed guards stood on either side of the door to the prince's chambers. Abdul ignored them and tapped on the door; it opened silently to admit them. He said a few words to the eunuchs inside, who helped Süreyya remove her outer cloak. They bowed, and together with Abdul, they left her alone. She waited uncertainly on the thick carpet of the empty chamber. She heard the door click closed behind her, and she fingered the sapphire she wore around her throat. The chamber was silent except for the faint patter of rain on the windowpanes. Süreyya stood with her head bowed until she heard the rustle of silk as the prince walked toward her and stopped. Following Abdul's instructions, she knelt and kissed the hem of his black silk kaftan.

'At last,' he said quietly. He took her arms and raised her slowly to her feet. She kept her gaze lowered until he tipped her chin and whispered, 'Let me look into your beautiful eyes, my water spirit.' He threaded his fingers through her hair and sighed. 'Süreyya,' he breathed as their eyes met. He caressed her back and pulled her closer to him, loosening his kaftan so that she leaned against his warm chest. Her lips parted, and he kissed her, gently at first, then with a primal urgency. She felt a flash of fire engulf her, wound her arms around his neck, and returned his kiss, melting into his body, longing for more.

The prince pulled away. He let the kaftan fall to the floor and now wore only his loose black pants. She gazed up at him, overawed by his dark good looks. His thick hair framed his face in tangles of raven waves that reached below his ears. He removed her silk gown to reveal her sleeveless nightshift beneath it, and ran his hands gently down her bare arms. He touched her cheek and frowned.

'How did this happen?'

'An accident, sire.'

'You are still beautiful,' he murmured quietly. He slid his hands over her breasts. I've dreamed of these,' he whispered.

She shuddered and crumpled against his soft chest hair. He pulled the strings of her blue nightshift, and it slipped to the floor. He bent his head and circled each nipple with his tongue. Then he took her face in his hands and kissed her again. She relaxed into his arms, pushing her hands through his hair, drawing him closer into her. She felt his arousal, knew instinctively what it was. Her body opened in readiness for him, and he swept her up in his powerful arms, carrying her naked and longing to his large divan. He laid her down, loosened his long black pants, letting them fall to the floor, and stepped out of them. In the filtered light, a quiver of excitement ran through her body when she saw his erection.

'My God, I've wanted this ever since I held you in the water,' he murmured. 'Süreyya, I have to tell you …'

He stopped suddenly and turned his head. Someone was banging on the outer door of his chambers. Süreyya gasped with fright and fumbled with the bedsheets to cover her nakedness. In the distance she heard raucous shouts and the clash of steel.

'*Allah Aşkına!*—For the love of God! How dare they?' Orhan exclaimed.

Grabbing a robe, he strode out of the bedchamber. Süreyya heard him open a door and then a voice—a soldier? She pulled the sheet from the bed and wrapped it around her body. The distant clamour sounded like a Tartar raid: the clash of steel, the shouts. She was terrified. Had someone invaded the palace?

Orhan, looking furious and dressed in his kaftan and breeches, came into the bedchamber followed by Abdul Agha.

'I am needed elsewhere,' Orhan said.

'Are we under attack?'

'No.' He shook his head and took her hand. 'Don't be frightened, Süreyya. My bodyguard is outside the door. Some people from the Christian community are in the first courtyard. They're clamouring to see the pādishah. My father has summoned me.'

He nodded to Abdul to wait outside.

After Abdul left the chamber, Orhan pulled her into his arms and kissed her. Her senses reeled, and she longed for more.

'I cannot disobey the sultan. I will send for you tomorrow night, my beloved, my Süreyya.'

He strode from the chamber, and she heard the outer door close behind him.

❧

As he made his way across the courtyard with a servant attempting to throw a fur-lined robe over his indoor clothes, Orhan hit the palm of his left hand with his right fist. The discussions with his brother, Prince Murad in Manisa, had been tense and angry, and now this! Curses on these petty local arguments in Constantinople. How dare anyone interrupt him when he was about to make love to a beautiful woman?

The sultan was waiting for him in the throne room, surrounded by his ministers. The imperial guard stood at intervals around the tiled walls. The chief minister took the prince to one side and related the events of the early evening to him. A group of Muslim clerics wanted to change a Greek church to a mosque, and an uproar had ensued. Orhan glanced at the pādishah, and obeying the custom, waited with bowed head, for the sultan to speak first. Orhan knew these arguments had erupted regularly since the Turks took the city sixty-five years ago. Where possible, his father, like his grandfather and great-grandfather, had tried to use peaceful means to quell such disagreements.

'We must have peace in the city,' the pādishah told his son. 'It is the beating heart of our Ottoman Empire. You speak excellent Greek; I leave you to negotiate with them.'

Orhan drew a deep breath. 'Where are they?'

'We are told that a large group of Christians is waiting for you in the first courtyard. You must go with them to Pera. A couple of my ministers will accompany you, and several guards of course.'

Orhan took his father's hand and kissed it, promising he would be discrete and diplomatic, but he was still furious at the turn of events. He glanced across at his own quarters as he walked under the vast canopy and past the columns that supported the dome of the Gate of Felicity. He was now outside the inner sanctuary of the third court-yard and in the second palace courtyard.

'Are they under control?' he asked one of the guards.

'Yes, sire, they're in the first courtyard. They quietened down when the Janissaries came out of their barracks in large numbers.'

Orhan nodded. 'All right, open the gates. Don't let them come through. I'll go and speak with them.' Was Süreyya back in her chamber now? He would have to wait until tomorrow evening to see her again. *Damn those troublemaking idiots!*

Orhan shook his head and tried to focus his mind. He paused as the imperial bodyguards took their places on either side and in front of him, and the gates swung open. His job was to calm the delegation. He sighed and gave orders for the Janissary soldiers to stay on guard as he walked from the second courtyard to the first, surrounded by the imperial guard. He knew from experience that the negotiations in situations like these would be difficult, quarrelsome, and long.

Perihan was waiting for Süreyya when she returned to her chamber. She helped her undress and put away her clothes. Perihan returned to her dormitory, and Süreyya lay in bed, recalling her brief encounter with the prince.

'I have to tell you …' he'd said.

Tell her what? That he loved her—would he ever say that? Or maybe he wanted to say he'd chosen Zeynep as ikbal—his favourite? Would this hasty meeting be the first and last time he would invite Süreyya to his bed?

Another thought occurred to her as she lay in the dark. Was someone looking for her? Had news of her dramatic rescue reached the Christian district of Pera? Is that what he was about to tell her? Or maybe they were the people in the courtyard?

Süreyya lay on her back and brushed away tears as she faced the truth. No one in Constantinople knew or cared about her. Her family would think she was dead or enslaved somewhere. No one was looking for her—the harem was her life now. She was a slave with no chance of freedom. She touched her lips, bruised from Orhan's urgent kisses. But why would she want to leave now, when the prince had chosen her?

She wanted him to make love to her. Even though every fibre of her being rebelled against being his slave, his concubine, he enthralled her. She had seen his arousal, and she longed for more.

The dawn prayer call echoed around the waking city as Orhan and his escort rode down the steep streets of Galata toward the waters of the Golden Horn. After much discussion in the palace, he had ordered to be taken to the disputed site on the other side of the waterway. Finally, they had reached a satisfactory outcome. The Muslim clerics accepted another piece of land as a gift from the sultan. The church would remain a place of worship for Christians, subject to an extra tithe to the sultan for the privilege.

The imperial caique rocked gently on the water at its mooring place, and Orhan boarded the vessel for the voyage across the Golden Horn to the palace. He stood at the rail and rubbed his hands over his face, staring at the rippling water that reflected the pink and gold streaks of the dawn sky. He thought of Süreyya, remembering her firm, youthful body against his. How close he'd come to making love to her. He vowed nothing would stand in his way tonight.

CHAPTER 7

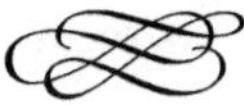

The dawn prayer call woke Süreyya from a sleep full of confused dreams. She got out of bed, opened the wooden shutters, and looked out of the window. The sun was rising, and a long low vessel, its prow embellished with gold, was sailing around the point of the peninsula below the palace.

'Orhan,' she whispered.

She saw him standing in the prow, a long maroon cloak wrapped around his body. He was looking toward the Courtyard of the Favourites. The diamond in his black turban flashed in the morning sun. Was he looking for her? The imperial caique sailed out of sight, and she moved away from the window. The dawn prayer call reminded her she had to get dressed and face the day. Another day, and a hope that the prince would summon her to his bed again that night.

Perihan arrived early to help her bathe and dress. She was brimming with excitement. 'I forgot to tell you! We're going out today with some of the harem ladies. We'll sail along the Bosphorus, in one of the imperial caiques, and then have a picnic!' She clapped her hands.

A trip on the water! Süreyya felt sick.

'Three caiques—think of it! We'll be in a special sitting area surrounded by curtains,' the girl continued.

'Is everyone coming?'

'No, the servant girls have to stay and work. I'm assigned to the mistress of the robes, remember?' Perihan said. 'I help to mend and clean the odalisques' garments. But because I'm your servant too, I can come!'

Süreyya was happy for Perihan, but she wasn't looking forward to getting into a boat. She walked alongside Perihan to take breakfast in the salon. As soon as she entered, the prince's mother beckoned to her.

'I trust you slept well?' Emira said.

'Thank you, yes, Emira Sultan.' Süreyya lowered her eyes. No doubt Abdul had informed her about the previous night's tryst.

'I see your face has healed from your accident.' Emira looked directly at Süreyya. 'I sent some of my salve to Abdul. It appears to have covered the area.'

'Thank you, madam.'

'I'm sure you will enjoy the picnic today,' Emira continued. She didn't invite Süreyya to sit down. 'I've heard you know how to swim—most unusual.' She smiled slightly.

'Yes, madam, I lived near a river as a child. I …'

'Please do not choose to swim in the Bosphorus again; it has very fast flowing currents,' she interrupted. 'Or expect to see my son this morning. There was trouble last night and I believe he has only just returned to the palace. I have seen him of course, but I don't expect him …' She stopped mid-sentence.

The quiet chattering in the chamber died away, and a buzz of anticipation swept through the salon. Süreyya turned toward the door. Like everyone else, she heard the distinctive sound of the silver-soled shoes echoing around the tiled walls of the passage outside.

'Sit over there.' Emira waved her hand at Süreyya.

Two servants opened the double doors, and from her distant seat Süreyya heard Orhan's voice as he changed into leather slippers. All the odalisques stood as he entered. Although she longed to look at him this time, she obeyed the harem rules and kept her eyes lowered.

'Good morning,' the prince greeted the women, who answered in unison.

Süreyya risked raising her eyes. Orhan was looking at her, and he smiled. He pushed back his hair. Perihan told her that the prince didn't often wear his turban in the harem. She blushed, remembering how he'd kissed her, and how she'd clasped his thick hair in her fingers. Orhan's brown eyes searched her face, and he inclined his head slightly. Aware of the jealousy his look might provoke, Süreyya looked down quickly.

'Good morning, my son, *aslanım*, my lion.' Emira's voice reached the far corners of the salon.

Orhan turned his attention to his mother. When he moved from her embrace, he smiled at something she said to him. He glanced again at Süreyya, then sat down next to his mother, a signal for the women to take their seats. Emira Sultan beckoned to Zeynep to join the small group. The redhead put her delicate fingers on Orhan's arm, smoothed her hair, and tipped her head toward his to ask him a question.

'I think the prince likes you,' Perihan whispered, 'but Zeynep likes *him*.' Süreyya risked a look at the raised dais; Zeynep and some of her friends were staring across the salon at her.

Orhan removed Zeynep's hand from his sleeve and glanced again at Süreyya. When he'd watched her before, he was like a stranger in a strange land. Now he knew how her body felt, how soft the skin was under that seductive silk dress, how she smelled, and how she tasted. He vowed to send for her again tonight. And nothing would stop him.

'Excuse me, Mother, ladies. I have work to do.'

He removed his slippers, and a servant helped him pull on his boots. He hurried into the cool passageway where Abdul Agha was talking to another eunuch. Orhan called him to one side and gave instructions for the chief eunuch to bring Süreyya to him again that night. The agha bowed his head in assent.

In her chambers, Süreyya let Perihan help her into a purple fur-lined velvet coat. It matched the tunic and pants Abdul had instructed the women to wear for their picnic.

'It's cold on the water, so the ermine lining will keep you warm,' Perihan commented as she fussed over her. 'You won't need it when we get there.'

Süreyya ran her hands over the beautiful fabric. In each embroidered square, a carefully worked flower had a tiny jewel at its centre: a ruby in a red rose and a diamond in a white one. Süreyya fingered the blue flowers encrusted with small sapphires and green leaves strewn with tiny emeralds. She fastened her pendant around her neck and tucked it deep under her bodice. Perihan fitted small diamond earrings in her ears and arranged a close-fitting shallow hat over her hair. She showed Süreyya how to release the opaque silk fabric and attach it across her face so that only her eyes showed.

'We can see, but no one can see us,' the girl commented.

Perihan pulled on her own elaborate coat. It was in a darker material with a silver thread. She told Süreyya that the mistress of the robes said she was too young to wear clothes embroidered with gems. She showed Süreyya the silver strands that another servant had helped her thread through her long, brown hair.

'I'm so excited, madam. This is my first excursion!'

Several eunuchs ushered the chattering women out of the harem and into the warmth of the walled garden of the fourth courtyard. Abdul Agha was waiting for them. At his signal, they followed him through the high gate of the palace, through a passageway, and down to a small beach. Süreyya's heart clenched—it was the same way she had come only a few weeks since. And this was the beach where Orhan had brought her, after he'd saved her from drowning. Ships with full sails passed by on the way to and from the city. Were they carrying the same miserable human cargo? She looked at the choppy water and shivered. How had she mustered the courage to jump from the slave ship?

Süreyya glanced around, trying to get her bearings. Across the water was a mosque on a hill and a few streets with wooden houses. Davut Hodja, her teacher, had told her Pera was further up the Golden Horn waterway, on the opposite side of the harbour. The palace stood on a peninsula bound by the Golden Horn, the Bosphorus, and the Sea of Marmara. She realised they were now on the very tip of the peninsula, but the waiting boats obscured her view up the Golden Horn that led to the city. If she could only find her way to this beach from the harem, she would be able to get to the metropolis. She dismissed the thought; the only way to leave the harem was to beg Orhan for her freedom.

A snigger interrupted her thoughts, and Süreyya turned around. Three women stood behind her. Like her, they were veiled, but she knew Zeynep's sharp green eyes and sneering voice, even though she couldn't fully understand what she said.

Zeynep clicked her fingers at Perihan to translate.

'Planning to run away, Russian damaged goods? We're in boat number three, just like you,' Zeynep said. 'What a lovely time we'll have together.'

Süreyya felt as if a cloud had obscured the sun. The glittering water and the warm, fresh air seemed tainted. How could she enjoy the day with Zeynep at her elbow, whispering in Turkish and laughing with her friends? Süreyya pulled her shoulders back—she wouldn't allow this woman to spoil it. She took a deep breath and followed Abdul's towering figure.

They picked their way along the sand, past the yellow sun-baked walls of the palace, to where three imperial caiques were moored against a long wooden dock. Huge silver motifs on their prows glittered in the sun. Perihan explained that they were the Ottoman coat of arms, with the sultan's turah, his personal signature, in the centre.

'The sultan and Prince Orhan's caiques are decorated in gold,' she added.

Several eunuchs ushered the first group of laughing women into a silver-roofed square structure on deck. Four silver pillars supported a pelmet of the same metal. Attached to the pillars were heavy red velvet curtains. Someone had tied them back with thick silk ropes.

'We'll sit in a covered area like that, but with the curtains closed,' Perihan said.

Süreyya nodded, overwhelmed by the opulence of their transport.

'I can't wait to sit there with the water rushing past,' Perihan added.

'Will we be able to see outside?'

'A little—I'll show you later,' Perihan said. 'The caique has many bostanji, and they row fast.' She pointed to where the oarsmen sat near the waterline, their oars raised, their eyes lowered. 'We'll fly through the water!'

Süreyya's heart lurched—she'd seen these men in their orange and black uniforms the day Prince Orhan had rescued her. She could hardly bear to look at the swaying vessel. She felt sick again when she thought of stepping onto the deck. As she watched the first caique leave, Süreyya tried to muster the courage she'd had when she jumped off the sailing ship. The voices of the laughing women drifted from behind the closed curtains as the oarsmen steered the boat away from the dock.

Perihan clapped her hands with excitement. 'Come on, it's nearly our turn! Abdul is waiting for us.'

The second vessel took to the water, and the third stood swaying at the dock. Eunuchs, under Abdul's stern directions, helped the women onto the swaying caique. Süreyya's legs shook as she climbed up the wooden steps and on to the deck. She glanced at the covered baskets of food stored in the prow. Perhaps if she could conquer her terrible memories, she might enjoy herself.

Perihan joined her, and they settled down on the plush red velvet bench built around the inside of the covered area. Like the other women, they leaned against the padded backrest and loosened their veils. On a sturdy table in the centre of the seating area, servants had laid out silver dishes of almonds and sweetmeats. Eunuchs splashed lemon-scented cologne on the women's hands from bejewelled flasks.

Süreyya rubbed it into her hands and patted it over her warm face. The servants left, but before they closed the curtains, Abdul appeared and reminded them they must not go outside. He pulled the drapes closed and tied them with the red ropes. They heard the chief bostanji bark an order, and the oars hit the water with a uniform splash. The boat lurched forward, and the other women squealed.

Perihan tapped Süreyya's arm.' We can look through here, madam.'

As the caique gathered speed, she eased the heavy drapes that covered the window spaces to one side and revealed diaphanous silver-threaded curtains behind them. Süreyya clenched her fists together, trying to forget the rope store and how she'd crawled to the side of the slave ship and looked into the dark water.

She had escaped, and a prince had saved her from drowning, she reminded herself. It was a miracle! And now, he wanted her in his bed.

Perihan nudged her and pulled the curtain open further. 'I can see the palace, and those are the prince's chambers.' She pointed. 'Oh madam, he's on the terrace. Look!'

Süreyya narrowed her eyes and saw a figure standing near the terrace wall. Even from a distance, she could see the precious stones on his long vest as they caught the sunlight. The other women murmured, and someone said his name. Zeynep dug Süreyya hard in the ribs and pushed her to one side. Süreyya backed away as the sharp-featured woman pressed her face to the curtain.

'Oh, he's gone!' Zeynep wailed.

'She thought the prince was looking for her,' Perihan muttered.

Zeynep returned to her seat between two of her friends and glared across at Süreyya. 'You know he has a different woman every night,' she said. 'He won't choose you.'

Zeynep's remark rankled, but she didn't know about last night, Süreyya reflected. Maybe the other woman was right; despite his promise, he might not call for her again. She could only hope.

'I've been on the imperial caique many times,' Zeynep's boastful voice cut across her thoughts. 'Tell the Russian trash that!' she said to Perihan, who translated reluctantly.

Süreyya ignored her and gazed through the curtain panel at the mosques and picturesque villages on the shoreline. The air smelled fresh and salty; the sky was clear blue with a few puffy clouds. Perihan pointed out the forests behind the villages and told her that's where the prince went hunting with his friends. The beauty of Orhan's country entranced Süreyya, and she felt more relaxed as the caique churned through the water. Fishermen in white boats stared, then turned their faces away as the imperial caique passed by.

'We'll see Rumeli Castle soon, built by Prince Orhan's great-grandfather,' Perihan told her. 'He built two, one on either side of the Bosphorus.'

Süreyya looked across the water as they neared the impressive fortress. The caique moved closer to the shore, bringing them level with the castle. Its majestic towers rose solidly against the background of the blue sky, with castellated walls that swept down to the water's edge. She imagined Orhan standing on the ramparts looking up and down the waterway, his sharp eyes seeking foreign ships coming into his city.

Zeynep leaned across and grabbed Süreyya's sleeve. She pulled her roughly to her feet, then pushed her toward the closed curtain at the entrance. 'Come with me!'

'No!' Perihan pulled Süreyya's other sleeve. 'Abdul Agha said we mustn't go outside!'

Zeynep's friend dragged Perihan backward, and she fell against the cushions.

'Stop her!' Süreyya shouted at the other women, but they drew their veils across their faces. She fought to get free.

No one moved, and Zeynep tightened her grip on Süreyya's arm. She unhooked the rope and dragged the heavy curtain aside. Süreyya struggled and thrashed, but now Zeynep's friends were behind her, helping Zeynep to bundle her captive out onto the deck.

'Let me go!' Süreyya yelled. She twisted and fought, but two of the women held her arms. A third woman pushed her in the back.

'The prince is mine, rotten meat!' Zeynep hissed and slapped her hard on the face.

Süreyya stumbled, and the bright daylight blinded her for a second.

She glanced over her shoulder. She was close to the low rail, and she struggled harder with Zeynep and her friends. They pulled and pushed her to where a rope covered an open space. The water rushed past as Süreyya fought harder and grappled with the women.

'Help me!' she yelled. 'They're going to kill me!'

Some of the others hurried through the doorway and tried to drag Zeynep and her friends away. Zeynep screamed at them and unhooked the rope. Süreyya fought and kicked, but in the melee, Zeynep pushed her hard in her stomach. She lost her balance, her hat flew off, and she screamed and fell backward into the Bosphorus. Her heavy velvet coat pulled her under the waves.

She tore at the coat as it pulled her deeper into the icy water. Her arm was tangled in a sleeve, and she rolled in the water, trying to release it. She surfaced, gulping for air, the coat still stuck on her arm. A piece of wood floated toward her, and she kicked hard to get to it, still gasping with cold and fear. The object was closer now, a round piece of wood with a hole in the middle. She grabbed it and, hooking her elbow through the centre, she got the coat off her other arm. It snagged on the wooden lifesaver, but with a tremendous effort she tore it free, and it floated away.

Süreyya saw the caique speeding away in the distance. She coughed and choked, but kept her head above water. Eventually, the current eased into a swirling eddy that washed her toward the shore. As she clung to the life-saving wood, she saw the caique turn slowly. A wave slapped against her face, and she shivered with fear and cold. She hooked both arms through the middle of the lifesaver, then kicked hard, letting the eddies carry her toward the land.

The waves swept her close to the walls of Rumeli Castle, then into a calm bay. A straggle of houses lined a steep village street above the bay. At the top was a stone building with a cross on the roof. A church!

The wood of the lifesaver rubbed painfully against her forearms. Her wet hair straggled down her neck and she was shaking uncontrollably, but the water felt warmer. The current had eased.

'You have saved me again, blessed Virgin Mary,' she whispered.

She saw two men wading toward her and she felt sand beneath her feet. She was safe! The men held her arms and helped her on to the beach. Someone threw a large blanket over her. She swayed and stumbled as they helped her out of the water.

CHAPTER 8

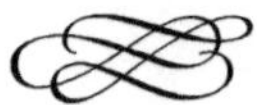

Süreyya's caique returned at high speed to the palace. Abdul Agha and a bevy of servants escorted the weeping women back to the harem. On the return journey, several bostanji had been hastily positioned around the outside deck of the caique. But they saw no trace of the woman who had fallen overboard. Abdul tried to question the hysterical witnesses, but it was impossible. The eunuch servants said they had seen nothing, and they begged Abdul Agha for mercy. The agha was apoplectic with rage; he slapped both men hard across the head and dismissed them. Although he had little proof, and he knew none of the women would talk, he guessed the redhead Zeynep Hatun was involved somehow.

Surely, the Russian girl wouldn't try to kill herself or make a bid for freedom? She knew she was *gözde*—she'd caught the prince's eye. Maybe that wasn't what she wanted. Either way, Abdul knew he was in trouble. Emira Sultan and her son would be furious. He muttered a quiet prayer to Allah that the prince would not order his execution. As for Zeynep, he would make sure she was married off to the oldest, ugliest army officer he could find.

Emira Sultan was angry, but it was nothing compared with Prince Orhan's fury when he learned of the accident. He sent for the agha and demanded an explanation. He scoffed when Abdul told him he'd thrown a life preserver.

'You deserted your post! Why?' Orhan demanded.

'Sire, the call of nature …' Abdul answered.

The prince fingered the dagger at his waist and glared at the eunuch. 'Bring the chief bostanji here, with a map! I'll deal with you later.'

The man arrived, bowing low and looking terrified.

'So, what do you have to say in your defence?' Orhan snapped.

'Sire, my apologies …'

'Did you look for her?'

'Sire, the third caique turned quickly. May I?'

He unrolled a map of the Bosphorus on the prince's table with shaking hands. 'I believe she fell overboard near here.' He pointed to Rumeli Castle. 'The current would have carried her this way, sire.'

'To?' Orhan asked.

'Calmer waters near the castle.'

'So, what are you saying?' Orhan frowned.

'The eddies may have washed her into this bay, sire.' He pointed to the map.

'Did you send anyone to the villages on the shoreline?'

'They are looking now, your highness.'

'And no one looked for her immediately after it happened?'

'Abdul Agha threw a life preserver. When we turned the caique, we expected to find the lady in the water.'

Orhan clenched his fists and thumped the table. 'The sultan should execute you for this!' He glared at the sailor and the trembling man bowed his head. 'And *you* saw nothing?'

'No, sire.' The chief bostanji kept his eyes lowered. 'Another boat left immediately from the palace to search for her.' He shook his head. 'We are waiting for its return.'

Orhan glared at the man and examined the map again. He traced his finger along the shoreline. 'The bay you pointed to—it's near this Greek village, Kyrgios. Could she be there? It's the nearest place to Rumeli Castle.'

'It is possible, sire.'

The prince looked up from the map and snapped out orders. 'Have the boats ready. I will cross the Golden Horn and then ride to Kyrgios. Meet me there with the imperial caique—and bring a palanquin for the lady. Go!'

'At once, your highness.'

Orhan knew his mother would be against the idea, but he didn't care what she, or anyone else, thought. *He* would look for Süreyya, or Allah forbid, her body. He'd bring her back to the palace in the imperial caique, dead or alive. He sighed and examined the map again, trying to quash the thought that thrummed in his brain. Was it an accident, or had she tried to escape?

A servant crept quietly into the chamber and told him that Emira Sultan wished to see him.

The first thing Süreyya saw when she opened her eyes was a crucifix hanging on a plain white wall. She vaguely remembered being put on a donkey and carried half-conscious up a steep street. Süreyya looked around, then pushed herself up on her elbow, dislodging the blanket that someone had placed over her. She was on a divan in a small chamber, and a bright wood fire burned in a grate. The only other furniture was a table and chairs under a window and two plain wooden chairs near the fire. Süreyya swung her legs onto the cotton kilim that covered the stone floor, but when she tried to stand, her legs felt weak, and she sat down again on the divan. She fingered the rough cotton shift she was wearing. She remembered someone helping her out of the water, but nothing after that.

Where was she now?

'Oh!' a voice exclaimed as she tried to stand again.

A middle-aged woman in a plain blouse and brown skirt hurried toward her. She smiled and said something in Turkish.

'*Biraz Türkçe biliyorum,*' Süreyya said—that much she'd learned from her teacher. She swallowed and added in Russian, 'I know a little Turkish.'

Her throat was sore, her voice hoarse and strained. She remembered swallowing a lot of water. And she remembered Zeynep and her friends pushing her off the caique. She grasped the woman's hand.

'They tried to kill me!' she croaked.

The other woman looked concerned and helped her to a chair by the fire, all the while speaking soothingly in a language Süreyya didn't recognise.

'Irene.' The woman pointed to herself and fingered the cross that hung around her neck.

She must be a Christian, maybe a Greek Christian, Süreyya thought, *but here in a village near Constantinople?*

'Your name is Irene?' Süreyya asked. 'Süreyya. I'm Süreyya.' She put her hand on her chest and searched her mind for a Turkish word. '*Neredeyim?* Where am I?'

'Kyrgios.' Irene pointed out the window. 'Kyrgios,' she repeated, then, '*Gel, gel*—Come,' in Turkish.

She put her arm under Süreyya's elbow and pointed to a door. Süreyya's legs buckled, and Irene called out. A young servant girl ran in, and together they helped her across the stone floor and into a steamy chamber at the rear of the house. The girl released her and finished pouring hot water into a small tub. The two women helped Süreyya out of the coarse shift she was wearing and into the bath. Smiling and nodding, they left her.

Süreyya sat in the warm water and tried to remember what had happened. Someone had pushed her in her stomach, and she'd fallen backward and sunk. She'd torn off her jewelled coat. These people had rescued her, but they were Christians. This must be one of the Christian villages on the outskirts of Constantinople that Perihan had told her about. She remembered seeing the church on the hill from the water. Maybe they would help her and let her stay with them.

She closed her eyes, then opened them. Those in the palace must know about the accident. Did Orhan think she was dead? They would surely look for her, but if they found her coat, they might believe she had drowned. She took a long breath as the steam enveloped her. She was alive. And free! But was that what she wanted? If she *was* free, she would never see Orhan again. Then what if they found her? What lies would Zeynep have concocted? Would she say that Süreyya had jumped overboard like before? Tried to escape again?

Irene's maid knocked on the door, interrupting Süreyya's chaotic thoughts. She assisted her out of the bath and wrapped her in a rough towel. The girl helped her dress in the clothes Irene had left for her: a long dark blue skirt and a white blouse decorated with blue flowers. As soon as she opened the door, her hostess ran forward and helped her into a chair at the scrubbed wooden table. Irene put a bowl of soup in front of her and watched her eat, concern on her plain face.

'Papás.' She pointed to her wedding ring, then the crucifix and the window.

Süreyya looked out at the small church, its domed roof surmounted by a cross. *Papás*—was Irene's husband the local priest? As if in answer to her question, she saw a short, bearded man walk out of the church door and make his way down the slope toward the house. The light breeze ruffled his long black gown, and he held on to the flat centre of his black hat. He looked like the priests in her hometown, she thought as he approached. His clothes and serious expression were so familiar that they brought back painful memories of what she had lost.

Orhan's mother was standing near a low table in her chamber when her son arrived. She embraced him and patted his face. She ordered coffee, then dismissed most of the servants.

'What a terrible tragedy,' she whispered, handing him a small cup. 'Do you have any news about the girl?'

Orhan sipped his coffee, then put it down. 'Not yet. They're searching in the water. I want Abdul executed for this.'

Emira Sultan held her son's eyes. 'Let us not be too hasty,' she said firmly. 'I rely on Abdul. He is irreplaceable.'

She beckoned to Zeki, who was waiting as usual in the shadows near her door. He laid a linen-wrapped parcel on the table in front of the prince and his mother.

'The men on the rescue caique found this,' Emira said. 'Abdul thought it better if I broke the news to you.'

Orhan met his mother's eyes again. 'Is it something of hers?' he asked, staring at the package.

Emira Sultan nodded. 'Open it.'

Orhan turned back the damp linen around the parcel and touched the sodden garment inside.

'Abdul says it's the coat she was wearing,' his mother said.

She watched as Orhan stared at the damaged coat in dismay, and her heart ached for her son. Emira was sure the girl hadn't survived in the freezing water; the current was too strong. They would probably find her body washed up on the shoreline somewhere, *if* they found it. Of course, there was another possibility …

'She knew—*knows*—how to swim, darling,' Emira said.

'She might be in Kyrgios,' Orhan answered. 'I'm going to ride there through the forests.'

'Orhan, you are a *royal prince!*' his mother remonstrated. 'You must let the bostanjis and servants search for her.'

'I'm going *myself*. I don't believe she'd dead,' Orhan said firmly. He stood and kissed his mother's hand. 'Please tell the servants to preserve the garment.'

When he'd gone Emira stared into space, thinking. She remembered Kyrgios from boat trips she'd enjoyed in her younger days, with women from the imperial harem. The Greek church on the hill was visible from the water. Maybe the girl saw it and took a chance. She had jumped overboard from a vessel over a month ago and survived. Perhaps she'd attempted to escape that way again. The Russian was raised a Christian and had only begun studying Islam recently. Maybe she believed the Greek Christians would help her.

Emira frowned; was her son about to make a fool of himself? She motioned for Zeki to take the sodden coat to the Mistress of the Robes.

'Tell her to clean the garment. It is ruined, but my son wishes to preserve it,' Emira said.

Zeki shook his head in disbelief and bowed. He left the chamber, carrying the coat across his outstretched arms.

The priest's wife opened the front door for her husband, and Süreyya half rose from her chair. A faint scent of incense wafted into the house with him on the spring breeze, and again Süreyya felt a pang of homesickness. Irene greeted her husband with a torrent of words. He nodded and patted her arm as he looked across at Süreyya with a slight frown. He gathered his robes together, pulled out a chair, and sat down opposite her. To Süreyya's relief, he spoke Russian.

'Welcome, my dear. I'm Father Dmitri, the village priest here in Kyrgios. We're of the Greek Orthodox religion.' He smiled. 'I studied at a Russian Orthodox seminary for two years, so I speak your language,' he added.

Süreyya thought quickly. She cared about Orhan, but this might be a chance to escape from her enslavement and the dangers and intrigues of the harem. Perhaps the priest could help her return to her own country.

'Father Dmitri, I'm called Süreyya now, but my real name is Rusalka Maria Ivanova. My uncle is a bishop in the Orthodox church of Russia. I need your help!'

'So, you're from the palace … and you fell from an imperial caique,' the priest said.

'Yes, but I am there against my will!'

'Everyone saw the boats pass,' the priest answered. 'And when they found you in the water, the villagers knew by your clothes and jewellery where you are from.' He beckoned Irene forward, and she passed Süreyya a handkerchief in which she'd wrapped Süreyya's diamond earrings and sapphire pendant. Süreyya thanked her, replaced the earrings with shaking fingers, and hung the pendant around her neck.

'Are you from the sultan's harem?' the priest asked.

'No, I'm from Prince Orhan's harem.' She touched the priest's arm; she knew now what she wanted. 'Father Dmitri, I come from a devout Christian family,' she said. 'The Tartars captured me, and now I'm a prisoner in the palace. Please don't send me back.'

Father Dmitri translated for his wife, and to Süreyya's surprise, Irene looked alarmed.

'Can you take me to Pera? I might find some Russian people there,' Süreyya urged.

Again, the priest looked at his wife and translated Süreyya's request. Irene smiled sadly at Süreyya and shook her head.

'We cannot do that, my dear.' Father Dmitri paused, his face serious. 'The villagers saw the imperial caique return. They pulled something from the water; they are looking for you—or your body.'

'They found my coat!' she said.

Of course, they would look for her, she thought. Did they think she'd tried to escape? If she returned to the harem, would they punish her?

'You are in the harem, so you belong to the prince,' the priest told her. 'Your uncle is a bishop in Russia, but here in Türkiye, you are a slave.'

He told her that the Greek community was indebted to Prince Orhan, the sultan's son. Only this week, he had saved one of their churches from becoming a mosque. They had no choice but to return her to his protection.

'We must maintain good relations with the Ottoman sultan. He allows us freedom to practise our own religion.'

Süreyya's eyes pricked with tears. 'Please, Father Dmitri!'

He patted her hand. 'I will do what I can to help you.'

'I want you to help me leave the harem!'

The priest sighed. 'Do you know how to write, my dear?'

When she nodded, Father Dmitri turned and said something to his wife.

'You can write an epistle to your family. Imagine how they will feel when they learn you are alive and safe. I will send the letter myself from Constantinople. No one at the palace need know about it.'

Süreyya grasped the priest's hands and thanked him, as Irene put paper, pen, and an inkpot on the table. She wrote quickly, sealed the letter, and handed it to the priest.

'It may take months to arrive, but at least they will know that you are alive,' Father Dmitri repeated. 'I've heard of families who have paid a ransom for the return of their daughters,' he said. 'But be thankful, my dear. You survived the terrible voyage from Kalla. God has protected you and given you a comfortable place to live.'

'But I am not free, and I can no longer follow my religion.' She looked up at him.

Father Dmitri crossed to a plain desk and opened a drawer. 'Take this, to remember our Saviour.' He handed her a small silver cross on a chain. 'But keep it hidden from everyone in the palace,' he warned. He made the sign of the cross on her forehead and murmured a blessing.

Süreyya bowed her head and slipped the cross into the pocket of her skirt. She felt desolate and abandoned, although she understood why the priest wouldn't help her; his community came first.

If only she could speak to Prince Orhan, make him understand *why* she wanted to leave. Again, she feared returning to the harem with its intrigues and jealousies. She was sure Zeynep wouldn't rest until she, Süreyya, was dead. There were plenty of ways Zeynep and her friends could kill her. They might poison her food or bribe a eunuch to put a pillow over her face as she slept.

'My wife thinks you should rest.' Father Dmitri's voice cut across her thoughts. 'You've had a frightening experience.'

Irene took her to a small chamber with a single bed. Alone, Süreyya knelt at the bedside and looked at the crucifix on the wall. She prayed the priest would change his mind and let her stay. Her head ached and her throat was still sore.

But is that what I want? Süreyya knelt on the hard wooden floor. As she gave thanks for being saved, her thoughts were not of God, but of Orhan's embraces. She touched the sapphire pendant around her neck, letting it fall outside the plain blouse, then patted the silver cross in her pocket. When they came for her, and she knew in her heart they would, she must hide the Christian symbol.

As he walked out of the palace, Orhan tortured himself with dismal thoughts. *Inshallah*—God willing—Süreyya was in Kyrgios. Or was she dead? They'd found her coat; would they then find her body floating in the Bosphorus? His mother had warned him to leave others to look for her, but he had to find Süreyya himself. Thoughts of her tormented him. His body had throbbed with longing for her all morning and now he had lost her. He was determined to discover where she was. A nagging doubt troubled him: had she fallen overboard accidentally, or had she tried to escape?

Orhan frowned; the last time he'd loved a woman, he'd lost her. He couldn't bear that pain again. He had vowed he would never allow himself to have feelings for a woman. There were plenty of odalisques to make love to and secure an heir. But Süreyya had bewitched him— he *must* find her. He had to know if she was alive or, he shuddered, dead.

CHAPTER 9

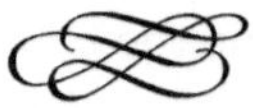

Orhan swung himself into the saddle just as a breathless messenger arrived. The man dismounted, bowed, and informed the prince that the search party had found Süreyya Jariye alive. As the prince had predicted, she was in Kyrgios.

'Allah be praised!' Orhan murmured. Bowing his head, he said a silent prayer of thanks. A dizzy sense of happiness washed over him. He spurred the horse forward onto the forest tracks and galloped along the ridge above the small villages that bordered the Bosphorus. His bodyguard rode ahead until their leader raised his hand and looked over his shoulder.

'Kyrgios, sire.' He pointed down to the small village nestled on the shores of the Bosphorus.

Orhan manoeuvred his sturdy black Turkoman horse, Akkula, down a steep path that led to the Greek village. Through the trees, he saw the simple church on a rise, its yellow stonework reflecting the afternoon sun. Flanked by four of his soldiers, he dismounted. A few parishioners who were leaving the church stopped and stared at him. Orhan led Akkula by his jewelled reins along the stony path in front of the church. He breathed in the fresh country air and the scent of incense that drifted from the open church door. Orhan's heart lifted. Was she really here in this simple village?

'The priest's dwelling, sire.' One of his men pointed to a small wooden house.

Orhan paused. Just beyond the church, he saw Süreyya standing between the priest and a village elder. She wore modest clothes—a long skirt and a blouse embroidered with blue flowers. She had covered her hair and the lower half of her face with a blue scarf. He felt overwhelmed with relief as he clutched Akkula's reins. She was alive! And she looked even more beautiful in these plain clothes than in her harem finery! The sapphire he'd given her hung between her breasts on its gold chain. With an effort, he controlled his impulse to run forward and embrace her.

'*Allah Şükür*—Thank God,' he murmured.

He threw the horse's reins to his bodyguard and strode over to the little group, addressing the priest in his native Greek. The bearded priest inclined his head in greeting. He reminded the prince they had met recently during the discussion to save a church in the city. He introduced the headman of the village, Yannis Poulos. The prince shook hands with both men.

'We sent word as soon as we found the woman in the water, your highness ...' Yannis said. 'The priest and his wife have taken good care of her.'

Orhan turned to the priest. 'Thank you. Father ... ?'

'Dmitri,' the man answered with a smile.

Orhan bowed, then snapped his fingers. One of his bodyguards stepped forward.

'The prince wishes to show his gratitude,' the guard said.

Father Dmitri and Yannis returned his bow, and accepted the purses of coins the soldier gave them. Before they could speak, the soldier said, 'His highness accepts your thanks. And now we will take the woman, and return to the palace.'

The man saluted, stepped back, and nodded to the prince. Two other guards moved forward, ready to seize Süreyya.

'Wait!' Prince Orhan ordered. The men stood back. He walked up to Süreyya and held out his open palms. 'You are not under arrest,' he said. 'I wish you to return to the palace with me.' His dark eyes searched her face, but she didn't move. 'We'll travel back together on the royal caique,' he added.

Would she come with him willingly, or would he have to lift her into the palanquin? Surely she realised she had no choice?

When her eyes welled with tears, he felt as if a hand was squeezing his heart.

'Süreyya, I want you to come with me. Please,' he said quietly.

Süreyya bit her lip. She knew there was no escape from the palace now that she was *gözde*, a woman who had caught the prince's eye. She turned to the priest and his wife and thanked them, telling them to keep her harem clothes. Süreyya brushed away her tears, and the angry thought that Prince Orhan had exchanged her for two pouches of coins.

'My dear,' the priest whispered. 'Accept your destiny with God's grace.'

'Thank you, Father,' she replied.

She allowed the prince to lead her to the palanquin and help her inside. He mounted his horse, and four bostanji raised the palanquin on its poles. They set off down the village street toward the harbour, where the ornate imperial caique swayed against a rough wooden dock.

Everyone had turned out to see the royal prince, with his dark colouring and sturdy figure. The afternoon light flashed on his long, bejewelled robe. Instead of a turban he wore a soft circular leather hat, the fur trim mingling with his own thick dark hair. As he passed, the villagers broke into spontaneous applause.

Süreyya pulled the curtain aside and watched Orhan as he rode alongside her. He sensed her eyes on him, turned his head, and smiled. He dismounted at the small jetty and gave her his hand. She met his gaze, even as a demon in her breast still niggled for her freedom when she stepped on to the caique. Orhan joined her on the divan inside the palanquin, pulled away her scarf, and tossed his leather hat to one side. He held her face and kissed her.

'I thought I'd lost you,' he whispered as he held her close. 'I want to make love to you now, but I can wait.'

Orhan kissed her again, and she relaxed deeper into the silk cushions. With a swift movement, he unsheathed his dagger and cut a lock of her hair with its sharp blade. He put it to his lips, twisted it around his finger, smiled, and slipped it inside his coat.

'Tonight, my darling.' His eyes met hers. 'I will send for you tonight.'

'I'm ready.'

As she looked at his handsome face, thoughts of petitioning for her freedom melted like snow on the mountains.

Two of the prince's guards and Abdul Agha were waiting for them at the royal jetty. Abdul helped Süreyya onto the dock, and she was followed by the prince.

A guard stepped forward and spoke to Orhan. 'Sire, the pādishah wishes to see you on an urgent matter.'

'It's an order I can't ignore,' the prince told Süreyya.

He turned to the agha and told him to take care of her. The eunuch bowed his head and led Süreyya toward the underground passageway into the palace. She turned to say goodbye to the prince, but he was deep in conversation with Hafız Pasha.

His father received him in the formal audience chamber, surrounded by his ministers. Osman Bey, grand vizier and chief minister, turned to the prince and bowed.

'Your highness,' he began, 'a messenger arrived this hour from your half-brother, Prince Ahmet, the Prince Governor of Edirne—our former capital.'

Orhan took the letter scroll and frowned as he scanned the contents. He glanced around the assembled group and at his father. The sultan sat motionless on his divan, his face half in shadow from the canopy above it. The prince turned to the grand vizier, Osman.

'Hafız Pasha has already informed me that my half-brother, Ahmet, may be in trouble, Osman Bey. But this missive is most worrying.'

He knew better than to address his father directly; protocol demanded that he must wait until the sultan spoke to him.

'Yes sire, as the message states, there is an uprising in the province of Rumelia,' the grand vizier said. 'Groups of armed Bulgarians are burning villages in our conquered territories. We fear the royal palace at Edirne may be attacked.'

The sultan rose to his feet. 'Prince Ahmet's troops are holding back the insurgents. He believes they will soon be overrun. You, Orhan, are a better soldier than he. You must go to Edirne and quell the rebellion.' He walked across to his son.

Orhan, like the assembled company, waited with bowed head. 'Sire, it will take three days to organise a full brigade of soldiers,' the prince replied, looking up, 'and another three days to travel to Edirne.'

The pādishah tapped his son's chest sharply. 'Not soon enough. Think like the soldier you are!' he snapped. 'Five hundred troops and supplies must leave tomorrow. We order *you* to follow shortly afterward. Take fifteen hundred more Janissaries—show the conquered subjects what happens when they defy us.' He paused and stared hard into his son's eyes. 'Nothing, *nothing* must delay the preparations for the campaign. Do you understand?'

The sultan clicked his fingers; the audience was over.

Orhan bowed his head again, took three steps backward, then turned and left the chamber. A campaign such as this might last three months, he thought angrily. Months when he would not see Süreyya. But the hard-won conquered territories must not be lost. His father would scoff at a son who wanted to stay in Constantinople because of a woman.

He strode along the marble passageways of the sultan's palace and out into the warm garden. He must give orders immediately for the troops to be readied.

Abdul Agha met him before he could make his way to the soldier's barracks. 'Sire, about Süreyya Jariye—the doctor sent word. She has fallen sick.'

Orhan sighed, remembering his father's parting words. 'First, I must plan the troop deployment,' he told the agha. 'I shall return to the harem as quickly as I can,' he promised.

Süreyya woke from a deep sleep, after dreaming that she was sinking in a dark pool. Drenched in sweat, she staggered to the door and called to the eunuch who stood outside. She heard feet running along the passageways, then everything went black as she collapsed on the floor. She thought she heard the prince's voice, felt muscular arms carrying her upstairs and laying her on a soft mattress. When she opened her eyes, Doctor Rebeka stood at her bedside. Süreyya looked around; she was in the prince's chambers—in his bed!

'I'm burning,' she croaked.

'Drink—this is syrup of pomegranate, rose, and violet,' the doctor said in her accented Russian. 'Reduce fever. Tomorrow evening, *inshallah*, much better.'

The doctor's servant helped Süreyya sit up, and she drank the syrup from a heavy silver beaker.

'Fever will break soon,' the doctor repeated as Süreyya lay back against the pillows.

The other woman wore her usual dark brocade dress with the gold star at her throat. She nodded and patted Süreyya's hand, her brown eyes full of concern. Doctor Rebeka looked across the bed and said something in Turkish.

Süreyya turned her aching head and blinked. Orhan was sitting by her side. He grasped both of her hands. 'Thank God, you're awake!' He touched her face. His voice sounded distant, as if she were dreaming. 'The doctor says you caught a fever from the water.' He laid a cool damp cloth on her forehead. 'I will stay with you until you're well.'

He spoke to the doctor in Turkish. Süreyya heard the doctor reply, '*Bilmiyorum*—I don't know.'

She shivered as an icy wave washed over her body. She began to drift away. *Am I dying?*

~

Süreyya opened her eyes and blinked in the sunlight that flooded the chamber. Orhan was by her side, and he bathed her forehead with the cool cloth. A servant hovered nearby with a silver mug and helped her drink more of the syrup.

'The doctor says she expects the fever to break today,' Orhan said, but his voice seemed far away.

Süreyya drank, then closed her eyes. When she next woke, she heard a prayer call. Large candles cast shadows that flickered on the rich silk wall hangings. Her sheets were cool, and she looked down at her shift. The servants had bathed and changed her while she slept.

Someone had pulled gold-threaded silk curtains around the large bed, but had drawn one side back and secured it with a satin rope. For a few seconds, Süreyya couldn't remember where she was. She stared at the quilted cream satin above her head. It was secured to the bed canopy with rubies, emeralds, and sapphires. She smoothed her hands over the soft cotton sheets and the quilted cover, decorated with pearls, that was tucked around her.

Süreyya felt warm and comfortable. Through an open door to another chamber, she saw a log fire blazing in the grate, and Prince Orhan standing at a table near the window. She remembered she was in his chambers—in his bed! She said his name, closed her eyes, then heard the swish of his long kaftan as he walked across the carpet.

'Süreyya!' He waved away his servants, and she heard the door click quietly behind them.

His soft hair brushed her face as he kissed her cheek gently. He sat by her bed, reached out his hand and stroked her forehead and neck, running his fingers across her lips.

'Let me help you sit up.' He put his arms around her and arranged her pillows to make her comfortable, then held a silver goblet to her lips.

'Drink this, my darling, it's pure water from the pine forest springs outside the city.'

She lay her hand over his and drank slowly. The refreshing mineral water slid down her throat and she smiled at him.

He touched her forehead. 'Your skin feels much cooler.' He placed the goblet on the table next to the bed and returned her smile.

She reached out and took his hand.

'I've been here most of the day, watching you from over there.' He pointed to the wide salon and the table. 'I've been looking at maps and planning ...'

'Planning?' she breathed. 'You must have so much work to do, yet you are here.'

He sat on the bed, took her in his arms, and held her against his chest. 'I worked here, near you. I prayed every minute that you would wake and be well again,' he whispered. He stroked her hair and kissed her eyes. 'Süreyya.' He took her hand. 'I have to leave Constantinople —the day after tomorrow. The sultan has ordered me on a campaign.'

'A campaign? Where? Will you be away for a long time?'

'I'm going to Rumelia near the Bulgarian border. I won't return until autumn.'

'Autumn?' Tears welled in her eyes.

'It will pass, my darling.' He squeezed her hand gently.

'Must you go so soon?' she said.

'You've been sick for two days, Süreyya. Tomorrow is the final day to ready the troops, then we leave early on the following morning. There's unrest in the Bulgarian territories,' he added. 'My half-brother Prince Ahmet needs help.'

He kissed her lips. 'I want you to continue your studies in my language while I'm away. I'll write to you every day, first in Russian, then in Turkish. Davut Hodja is an excellent teacher. Promise me you will study hard.'

'I promise.'

'The doctor says you'll be well enough to watch the march-out parade.' He wiped away her tears with his fingers.

She put her arms around his neck, and he kissed her, holding her gently against his chest. His kiss became more urgent as she relaxed against him.

'Orhan, I'm ready,' she whispered.

He laid her back on the cushions, strode across the salon, and locked the outer door. A flood of desire swept through her when he returned and drew back the bedcovers. He slipped her silk shift over her head, then slowly explored her body with his hands and mouth.

She helped him pull off his kaftan and undergarments, and he joined her on the wide bed. She clasped his naked body against her own. The soft hairs of his chest brushed against her breasts, and she felt his warm breath on her cheek. She grasped his muscled upper arms and pulled him closer.

'Are you sure, Süreyya? Do you feel strong enough?' he asked.

'Yes!'

He entered her, and her mind cleared suddenly. Would he know she wasn't a virgin? He probed gently and pushed himself slowly inside her. Her flesh had healed, but when he pushed a little harder, it gave way and she gasped at the sudden sharp pain.

'My beautiful virgin,' he whispered.

When his mouth found hers again, she lost conscious thought. He kissed her deeply, and she felt him release inside her. He threw his head back and pulled her against him.

'Oh Süreyya, you are wonderful!' he gasped.

He withdrew slowly and kissed her again. He lay on his back close to her, breathing heavily. She closed her eyes, feeling weak but elated.

'Darling Süreyya, how do you feel? I'm sorry if I hurt you.'

She turned to him and stroked his face. 'I'm happy, Orhan.'

She curled against his warm, hard body and fell asleep. *Isha*, the final prayer call of the day, stirred her consciousness and she reached out for him. But she was alone in his bed. Süreyya slept, and when she woke again, she sat up and pulled on her discarded shift. To her surprise, the morning sun-dappled the walls of his bedchamber. She heard someone open the door, and Abdul Agha, a long coat over his arm, came in, treading carefully on the carpet in his yellow satin slippers.

'Good morning, Süreyya Jariye. Are you well enough to walk?'

She nodded, and he helped her to her feet, but when she stood up, her legs felt weak, and she leaned heavily on Abdul's arm.

'Your servants are waiting to bathe and dress you,' he said. 'I will assist you to your own chamber.'

He would organise for breakfast to be sent, he told her. He eased her into the long coat and fastened it over her thin shift. Before she left the bedchamber, she glanced over her shoulder at the bed. To her relief, there was a small dark stain on the white bed linen; doubtless Abdul had seen it and would make the appropriate entry in the *Book of Couchings*.

CHAPTER 10

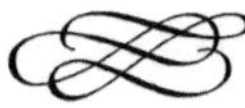

*O*rhan knew he was a day behind with his preparations, and it displeased his father. He leaned on a long board, covered with maps, in the military planning area near the sultan's chambers. Aided by Hafız Pasha and several army officers, he examined the charts of battle strategies his generals presented him.

Süreyya's sickness had distracted him, and after midday prayers and lunch, he excused himself. He sent for the palace goldsmith, then returned to his officers.

'If we plan well, we will defeat the Bulgar insurgents quickly, sire.' Hafız Pasha pointed to places on the map. 'News from the first battalion close to Edirne is good. Together with Ahmet's troops, they have encountered and routed many insurgents. But they need help to retain their gains.'

Orhan concurred with some of Hafız's ideas, but not others. 'We must attack from several sides. We've conquered their country and we intend to remain.' He looked at his colleagues. 'Don't they realise how lucky they are to be ruled by we Ottomans? We have treated them fairly, allowed them some self-government and freedom of religion. Did not my father and I release those prisoners who vowed allegiance to us?'

Everyone nodded. Hafız leaned on the bench, making notes of the deployment positions as Orhan dictated.

'The sultan has entrusted me with this commission. We mustn't fail,' Orhan reminded him.

He ordered copies of the battle plans and dismissed everyone. Once again, his thoughts wandered to Süreyya. They had coupled so naturally, without stifling palace formality. Orhan didn't want the woman he loved to stand before him with a bowed head or kneel at his feet and kiss the hem of his kaftan. He wanted a *wife*, not a concubine—someone intelligent, someone he could talk to, a woman who would be there when he returned from his campaigns. He longed to see her, but he forced himself to concentrate on his work.

The sunset prayer call reminded him it was time to pray, and he had not yet seen Süreyya. The following day he must leave on the campaign. After prayers, he returned to his chambers and summoned Abdul Agha.

'How is Süreyya Jariye?'

'She is well, sire, but still a little tired.'

'Is she well enough to see me?'

'I will arrange it, sire.'

When Orhan walked into his salon from the bed chamber, Süreyya was standing inside the door with her head bowed. He wanted to tell her to forget the custom, but Abdul Agha and several other servants were also there.

As usual, the agha was clutching the *Book of Couchings* under his arm. Orhan knew the eunuch was duty-bound to make an entry of each encounter the prince had with a woman from his harem. But this evening, it irked him that his lovemaking should be reduced to an entry in a book. He had no doubt Abdul had carefully scratched the date and Süreyya's name in the volume yesterday.

'Süreyya Jariye, come forward,' the prince ordered.

Orhan suppressed his irritation with palace protocol when

Süreyya knelt and kissed the hem of his kaftan. He put his fingers under her chin and asked her to stand. He leaned forward and whispered, 'When we're alone, I will not expect you to obey that custom.'

Dismissing the servants, Orhan frowned when he saw the questioning look on Abdul Agha's face. Did the man want to write about the possible coupling here? Now?

'I wish to be alone,' the prince said tersely. He waited until the door closed behind Abdul, then turned to Süreyya and kissed her lips. 'How are you, *sevgilim*—my darling.'

'I'm recovered now, sire,' she said. 'I rested today.'

He took her hand and led her to the bedchamber. 'Let us make love for a last time before I leave,' he said.

Later, she lay in his arms, stroked his chest and face, touching the long battle scar that was partially hidden by his neat beard.

'I must bathe,' he said, moving away slowly from her and giving her a last kiss. She heard him sluicing himself in his private bathing area, then he returned with a white towel wrapped around his waist. Her eyes swept over his body, and she was overwhelmed by feelings of love, mingled with the despair that he was leaving her.

He dropped the towel—he was ready for her again, ready to explore her body even more slowly and tenderly than before. Much later, he left her, and she heard him moving around the salon, then bathing again.

She washed herself using the basin of scented water and the cloth that a servant had left for her. She pulled her shift over her head and slipped her arms into her long robe.

Did he really care for her? And if he loved her, would he ever say the words?

When they made love, he was tender and caring. Yet Süreyya still felt apprehensive. The doctor had promised she would never reveal the secret of Süreyya's lost virginity, but what if she did? What would happen to her if Rebeka decided she needed a favour, and then another and another?

'I have a gift for you.' Orhan's voice broke across her thoughts. He took her hand and led her to the other chamber. From a pocket in his dark green robe, he extracted a small pouch. He tipped out something, placed it in her palm, and closed her fingers. 'You may look now.'

She opened her hand slowly. A crescent brooch in gold, set with diamonds, caught the light. It was a twin of his. Süreyya looked from the heavy jewel in her palm to the prince's smiling face.

'Sire, it's beautiful!'

'Tomorrow, as you know, I will lead my troops in a march-out procession.' He took the brooch from her and put it against her silk robe over her heart. 'Wear it here when you watch me tomorrow, dear one.' He returned the brooch to its pouch and gave it to her. 'In Turkish, we say *güle güle giy*. It means, wear it with smiles,' he said, stroking her face.

'It's exquisite! Thank you, thank you.' She put her arms around his neck and kissed his mouth.

'I pray you will return safely to me!' He returned her kiss, then took a box from a small table. 'This is my half of the circle, and one day, *inshallah*—God willing—we will be joined again, like the circle,' he said.

He folded his arms around her, and she leaned against him. She remembered how she had been desperate to stay in the Greek village. Now, only days later, she felt safe in his embrace. He made her forget the harem with its petty jealousies, and Zeynep and her friends ... but who would protect her once he left? She still didn't understand his language. Once again, she had only Perihan and her old friend Melek to rely on—and *herself*. She knew that she alone must deal with her rival.

He kissed her hair, her eyes, and his lips lingered on hers. He took her face in his hands, his eyes full of love and, as if reading her thoughts, he said, 'While I'm away, I've asked my mother to look after you. Pray for my safe return, Süreyya.'

'Every day, sire,' she said.

'Tomorrow I will not be able to see you clearly.' He smiled. 'But I will search for you with my eyes. *Inshallah,* the brooch will catch the sun and I will know you are there.'

The following morning was sunny and bright, but a cool breeze blew from the water. Süreyya hugged her dark blue fur-lined coat to her body. Abdul Agha stood at the head of the waiting harem women. On a signal from him, and walking in twos, they moved forward. Süreyya followed them, leaning on Perihan's arm. Dr Rebeka had insisted that Süreyya must wear a woollen scarf over her head, and like all the other women, she covered her face so that only her eyes showed.

A group of eunuchs ushered them through the dewy walled garden and onto a deserted pathway. According to Perihan, it led from the third courtyard and alongside the two other courtyards of the palace complex.

At the end of the path, soldiers, eyes lowered, stood on guard at an iron gate. They swung it open and bowed their heads as the women were hurried into coaches with heavy drapes at the windows. Before Süreyya was hustled into a carriage, she felt cobblestones under her feet. She risked a quick look at the outside world at the end of the laneway. In the distance, she saw a horse pulling a cart laden with vegetables and fruit, and heard the shouts of street vendors and children.

Abdul, chivvying the women to hurry, frowned at her. 'Keep your eyes lowered, Süreyya Jariye!'

Perihan pulled her sleeve. 'We're going to Aya Sofia. It used to be a Greek cathedral, but now it's the imperial mosque,' she said. 'When the sultan or the princes leave for a campaign, we always come here to pray that God will protect them and the army.'

Their crowded carriage lurched along on its brief journey. As she climbed out, Süreyya glanced quickly at the ochre-tinted walls of the thousand-year-old building. Close-up, it was much bigger than she'd imagined from the drawings of it her uncle, the bishop, had shown her.

'It's the oldest Christian church in the world,' he'd said. 'And now the infidel Turks use it as a mosque!'

It stood squat and solid and surrounded by a small garden. Süreyya looked up at the domed roof. Her uncle had told her that after they'd conquered the city, the Turks replaced the cross at its apex with the crescent of Islam. As they walked along the garden path, Süreyya touched the stone buttresses that supported the walls and vast dome.

'Stay close to me,' Perihan whispered as the prayer call from the single minaret died away. 'We have to walk up a steep slope to the gallery where the women sit.'

Inside the building, Süreyya scanned the walls.

'The Turks covered the Christian mosaics,' Perihan said. 'There must be no human images in a mosque. We must think only of the one God.'

They walked up the uneven cobblestones to the galleries on the first floor. Süreyya still felt weak and leaned on Perihan's arm. Light poured in from the windows, illuminating the circular space beneath them. Below the wide balcony where the women sat, men stood waiting on the rich prayer rugs that covered the stone floor.

'Remember that niche in the wall is called the *mihrab*,' Perihan murmured. 'It faces Mecca, the holy city of Islam. We must face that way when we pray.'

Abdul Agha hissed at Perihan to be quiet and stay back out of sight. The congregation fell silent. There was a slight rustling as the royal women took their place behind a curtained area at the end of the balcony. The sultan, his son, ministers, and high-ranking soldiers would pray in the main area of the mosque with the men, surrounded by armed guards, according to Perihan.

After prayers, Abdul Agha led the heavily veiled women across the deserted street toward the ancient Hippodrome of Constantinople.

'I saw the army march out from here to their victory in Baghdad,' Perihan said. 'The Turks call it the *At Meydanı*—Horse Square. Each time I see the Janissary soldiers, I look for my brother.'

They followed a passageway behind a raised dais, then climbed up two steps onto a long platform. Abdul beckoned them forward, and they took their places in the front row of cushioned benches.

'You have a brother in the Ottoman army, Perihan?' Süreyya said as they sat down.

'Yes, Süreyya Jariye, my older brother. When the Turks captured part of the Crimea from the Tartars, they levied families. They took a boy from every household in our village for their army,' Perihan whispered. 'They call it the *devshirme*. They train the boys as Janissaries—Ottoman soldiers. My brother would be sixteen now. I squeezed up my eyes really hard last time while I looked, but I couldn't find him. *Inshallah*, I'll see him today.' She looked up at Süreyya. 'I *will* see him one day, madam. I'm sure of it!'

Süreyya squeezed the girl's hand. *I'm not alone*, she thought. *Everyone in the harem has been torn from their family or lost someone.* She looked around their seating area. Heavy brocade drapes, their tassels moving gently in the breeze, separated the women's section from the men. To her right, the sultan would take his place on the empty platform with his imperial guard and the *Divan*, his ministers of state.

She squinted through one of the lattice panels of the silk curtains that shielded the royal women from the crowds opposite and around them, and watched as servants brushed sand from the large empty parade ground in front of her.

'It's a great honour to sit here in the royal section; only a member of the royal family can order it.' Perihan moved forward and pointed. Through the silk curtains Süreyya could just make out a few bejewelled figures. 'That's the sultan's mother, Dilber Sultan, the prince's grandmother. She's the *Valide Sultan*, in charge of the sultan's harem. Emira Sultan is next to her because she's the mother of the sultan's son, Prince Orhan. The prince knows where everyone is sitting by the different coloured tassels on the outside of the curtains.'

Süreyya could discern Emira Sultan sitting very straight, surrounded by her waiting ladies, who were the same age as her. The eunuchs in her service, including Zeki, stood a few paces back.

'Prince Orhan's mission is extremely dangerous,' Perihan said. 'Emira Sultan didn't want him to go.'

Süreyya fingered the gold crescent that she'd pinned over her heart. She didn't want him to go either.

Then a roar erupted from the throng as the sultan rode into the *At Meydanı* on a white horse, flanked by his personal bodyguard. Behind him on foot were his other ministers of state. The mass of people in the square moved forward as one, and the military guards pushed them back. Two Janissaries held the sultan's horse as he dismounted. The ruler of the Ottoman Empire wore an elaborate green bejewelled coat over a dark kaftan. The upright feather in his green turban swayed in the gentle breeze, and the emerald at its centre glowed in the morning sun. He walked up to the carpeted dais, then turned to face his subjects. His richly dressed ministers followed, fanning out to stand on either side and behind him.

Only months ago, I was a captive slave. I was force-marched and hustled onto a ship. And now, I'm sitting close to the royal family of the Ottoman Empire!

She imagined Orhan standing on the dais to inspect his troops when he was sultan. Orhan, the man who had saved her. The man who had made tender love to her last night.

The raucous music of a military band drowned out the shouts of the people. Hundreds of men dressed in red uniforms, edged in gold brocade, their red hats bobbing, marched into the *At Meydanı*. Their gold sashes flashed in the sunlight and they sang in unison. Others carried poles topped with bells, which they hit on the ground. Harsh wind instruments competed with drums and cymbals as the soldier-musicians marched past the sultan's platform.

As the music faded, the crowd roared again when three horsemen rode into the arena. Their green flags with a white crescent fluttered in the breeze from the Bosphorus. Next came three mounted soldiers riding side by side, carrying curved swords raised above their heads.

Behind them, flanked by two flag bearers, was Prince Orhan. Süreyya leaned forward, desperate to get a clearer look at him through the silk curtains. He sat tall and straight in the saddle astride his black horse. His pointed gold helmet glowed in the sun, and he steered his mount forward in time to the beating drums. Orhan, soldier-prince, was dressed for battle. Under his gold-embellished leather vest, he wore a silver-sleeved jerkin. His long cape swept his thighs over sturdy black pants and polished leather riding boots. Behind him stretched columns of Janissary soldiers in red and gold uniforms, their hats startling white.

Süreyya put her hand on her chest to still her pounding heart, hardly able to believe that this powerful Ottoman prince was her lover. Next to her, Perihan moved forward, scanning the rows of troops. The column of soldiers stopped, the music faded, and Orhan halted his horse in front of his father. He touched his hand to his forehead and to his heart. The sultan bowed his head and repeated the gesture. In the silence, Süreyya risked a glance at Emira Sultan and saw her brush away a tear.

Orhan walked his horse forward and pulled on the jewelled reins. He was now directly opposite the covered area of the women of the imperial household. Although the drapes hid his grandmother and his mother from his view, he repeated the homage he'd paid to the sultan. Guided by the coloured jewelled tassels on the outside of the tents, he urged his horse forward until he was opposite the enclosure where Süreyya sat. He was so close that she could see the crescent brooch clearly. Curls escaped from beneath his helmet, and he focused his dark brown eyes directly on where she sat. Süreyya fixed her eyes on him. Would he acknowledge her—his concubine?

Holding his horse steady with one hand, Orhan touched his cloak where he'd fastened the gold crescent, the twin of hers. His eyes searched for her as he held his fingers against it. She repeated the secret gesture, although she knew she was invisible to him. Her eyes searched his face, trying to remember every detail as he inclined his head. With a smile, he raised his fingers to his lips, pulled his cloak back in place, and rode on. Her eyes followed the curve of the turah, his personal seal, that was embroidered on the back of his cloak. The prince turned his head right and left, acknowledging the cheers of the crowd.

As she watched him ride away, a chill gripped her heart. What if he were killed in battle?

Would the palace force her to stay in Constantinople forever? She'd heard that on the death of a sultan or a prince, the harem odalisques were either married off to high-ranking soldiers or lived out their lives in the old palace. Would this be her fate? If they never set her free, she might live in the old palace for the rest of her life—a miserable, unwilling captive.

The parade wound its way toward the exit of the *At Meydanı*. Süreyya strained her eyes, still hoping for one more glimpse of Orhan's gold helmet, or that he might turn his head and look back. But he didn't, and she knew his mind was now focused elsewhere. The ancient space rang with cheers and shouts as the army marched onto the wide street that Perihan told her led through the city to the Edirne Gate. From here, the column would head northwest to Edirne, at least three days' march away.

The small group of chattering women returned to the palace, their buoyant mood ebbing with every step. Perihan walked silently next to her mistress.

'Did you see your brother, Perihan?' Süreyya asked.

The girl shook her head and looked down. 'Maybe next time, madam.'

Like all the others, Süreyya removed her outdoor leather shoes and slid her feet into a pair of embroidered satin slippers. She longed to return to her chamber and lie down, but after midday prayers, Emira Sultan had other ideas. The palace eunuchs ushered them all into the salon. Servants were putting the finishing touches to an elaborate lunch, ready to serve it on the long low tables they had already set up. The mood of the harem women changed immediately as they chattered and saved places for their friends, talking excitedly about the parade.

'I remember when the prince went to Baghdad,' Perihan said. 'Emira Sultan arranged a feast for us then.'

She led Süreyya to a divan and handed her a silver plate. Etched in the centre was an elaborate symbol in Arabic script.

'That's the prince's personal seal—his turah. Did you see it on the back of his cloak?' Perihan asked. Before Süreyya could reply, Perihan clapped her hands. 'Oh, they're bringing in the meze.'

Attendants served the food with gold spoons, the handles decorated with tiny diamonds and rubies. They put small amounts of humus, a mixed salad of tomatoes and cucumber, and some vine-wrapped rice on Süreyya's plate.

'You will become strong again when you eat.' Perihan smiled as they ate.

Süreyya took a piece of warm bread from a basket and ate the meze. A servant removed her plate and replaced it and the gold spoon with another. More entrees followed: eggplant in olive oil, capsicum stuffed with rice, white beans, and ground lamb in tomato sauce. When two servants placed a mountain of salt on the table, the other women screamed with delight. With great aplomb, one of the servants dug a knife into it. The salt mountain collapsed, revealing a perfectly cooked fish that he served onto their plates. Several courses followed: lamb, chicken kebabs, and more salads, followed by sweet rice cooked in milk.

Süreyya felt her eyes closing before the servants served sweet honey pastries with nuts that Perihan said was called baklava. Her servant helped Süreyya to her chamber, reminding her she was still recovering from her ordeal and needed plenty of sleep. Once there, she sank gratefully beneath the sheets. Before sleep claimed her, she thought of Prince Orhan on his three-day ride to Edirne. She touched her lips where he had kissed her, and her breasts, which he'd touched so tenderly. A wave of sadness engulfed her. She had wanted to leave the prince and his harem since she arrived. Now Orhan had left her.

CHAPTER 11

The following day, when she returned from prayers, Abdul Agha was waiting in her chamber. He dismissed Perihan and told Süreyya to sit on the divan under the window. He set up the round table, then pulled a small stool across for himself.

'The prince has granted you a gift,' he announced. He placed a purple velvet box and four leather pouches on the small table. He picked up one of them. 'Each pouch contains akçes, the currency of the Ottoman Empire,' he said. 'There are enough coins in these purses to buy a diamond necklace, if you wish. Every woman in the harem, as you know, receives a certain amount of akçes per day, according to her status. You will continue to receive your allowance, in addition to these gifts.'

Süreyya stared at him, too astonished to speak.

'The prince has left a document regarding you. He wrote it in Russian and Turkish. Davut Hodja is waiting outside; as you know, he speaks and reads the Russian language better than I. He will read it to you, in my presence, and I shall answer questions you may have.'

'The prince left a document about me?'

Abdul nodded. 'We will read it shortly,' he repeated. 'The hodja does not need to know about the akçes, which are for you to spend.

You might like to buy trinkets when the peddlers come from the city,' the agha continued. 'Emira Sultan permits a few women from the city to visit the harem: a fortune teller'—he tutted—'and a kira, a woman who sells silver trinkets, sewing silks'—he waved his hands—'and such ...'

'I can use this money to buy things from her?'

Abdul inclined his head. 'You will have more than enough for trinkets, but you must tell no one of this gift. The prince's odalisques receive a few akçes each week to spend as they wish. Emira Sultan has accepted you as an odalisque in the harem. And you are the first woman in this harem to receive such a generous gift from the prince.'

The chief eunuch opened the gem-encrusted lid of the purple box. Süreyya stared at the contents. 'These are gold nuggets, madam,' he said. They lay in neat rows like blocks of lokum sweets. Abdul stroked his hand over them and looked up at her.

'This is mine?' she asked.

The agha inclined his head and told her they would keep the gold in the imperial treasury. Only he and Emira Sultan had a key. Süreyya must make a request if she wished to access it.

'I have heard,' Abdul continued, 'that the sultan once gifted gold to a favourite, and she tried to bribe the eunuchs to help her escape. She was executed, of course.' He paused and rolled his large brown eyes, showing the whites. 'So, Emira Sultan will only permit you to keep one purse of coins in your chamber.'

'But what can I use this gold for?' Süreyya shivered when she heard of an odalisque being executed. Before she fell ill, she had considered bribing a eunuch to show her a way out, using the priest's silver cross that she'd hidden in the back of an alcove.

'How can I buy anything when I live here, locked in the harem?'

'His majesty, the pādishah, was very generous to Emira Sultan. She owns houses in Constantinople, and one in the countryside,' Abdul said.

'But how did she buy such property?' Süreyya asked.

'She has a personal kira, a Jewish woman called Maryam, who acts as an agent,' Abdul replied. 'The kira lives in the city and can enter and leave the harem at will. She transacts business for Emira Sultan. The kira's daughter, Ezter, visits the harem too.'

Süreyya said nothing, marvelling at the power—and wealth— Emira Sultan had gained by becoming the sultan's favourite *and* producing a son.

'Her majesty has also funded the construction of a mosque, which she has named for the sultan,' Abdul said, nodding his approval. 'Now, Davut Hodja is waiting outside,' he repeated. 'The hodja will read Prince Orhan's words to you in your own language. His Russian is perfect, of course. If you have any questions, I shall attempt to answer them. You will then be permitted to read the document yourself. Emira Sultan and I will then sequester it, with your gold, in the imperial treasury.'

Abdul packed away the gold and purses, and secreted them in an alcove. He opened the door and called Davut Hodja into the chamber.

The teacher was dressed, as usual, in the dark crimson robes and flat hat of his profession. Abdul slit the wax seal, unrolled the parchment, and handed it to the teacher, who cleared his throat. After reading the opening salutations on the document, Davut Hodja announced:

'The prince states that in the event of his death, you, Süreyya Jariye, are free to leave the harem and return to your own people. His highness has instructed his staff to help you with that. You may choose to marry. You may take with you any gifts given to you by the prince. This might consist of gold, jewellery, akçes or property.'

'Marry?'

'You have a generous dowry,' Abdul added quietly.

Süreyya shook her head and tears pricked her eyes. She didn't want to contemplate Orhan's death, but was grateful to him for making such a provision for her future.

'The prince also wishes you to study hard,' Davut continued. 'He sends his love to you and continued good health.'

He handed the parchment to Abdul who passed it to Süreyya.

'This is an official document, written in both Russian and Turkish, in the prince's own hand. It is signed by him and finished with his turah, his royal seal.' The agha turned to Davut Hodja. 'You understand that you must never speak of this to anyone.'

The teacher bowed his head. 'I understand, Abdul Agha.'

'Then go in peace. Our thanks,' the agha said.

He knocked on the inside of the door. It was opened silently by the eunuch who waited in the passageway, and Davut Hodja left the chamber.

Abdul turned to Süreyya and handed her the document. 'You may read it yourself, if you wish.'

Süreyya took the heavy manuscript and read it carefully. She understood why Davut Hodja had been called to read Orhan's Russian script. The hodja had summarised the legal script in which the document was written.

Abdul permitted himself a smile. 'His highness has made provision for you as if you were …' He hesitated. 'As if you were a wife.' His eyes met hers again for an instant. The agha gathered his yellow satin robes around his body and stood.

'How can I convey my thanks to his highness?' Süreyya asked.

'Your teacher, Davut Hodja, is also a scribe. He will write a letter for you.' Abdul bowed, walked across her chamber, and removed one of the decorated wall tiles. He took a sturdy box from the wall cavity and handed it to her. 'Keep your coins in here, and always return the box to its hiding place.' He put one of the purses inside, turned the key in the lock, and handed it to her. 'This must stay on your person at all times.'

Süreyya hung the key on its gold chain around her neck and felt it slither down her body and come to rest between her breasts.

'Speak of this gift to no one else, including Perihan Jariye.'

Süreyya inclined her head.

'Emira Sultan wishes to see you this morning. I will come for you when she's ready.' He picked up the box of gold and the three purses of silver coins, bowed, and departed.

Süreyya sat alone and fingered the gold chain. Orhan had treated her with kindness and generosity, yet she had deceived him and led him to believe she was a virgin. Pray God he never found out the truth.

~

Zeki admitted Süreyya to Emira Sultan's chambers and told her to stand with bowed head and wait for her highness to acknowledge her. Emira dismissed her women. They left the chamber quietly, their skirts rustling as they passed Süreyya, who kept her eyes fixed on the patterned carpet.

'*Hoş geldiniz,*' Emira said. Her long skirts, too, rustled as she walked toward her visitor.

'*Hoş bulduk,* your highness.'

'I trust you have recovered from your accident?'

'Yes, madam, but it was not an accident. I—'

Emira raised her hand. 'Enough! Abdul Agha and I have dealt with the incident. Come!' The precious stones on Emira's deep purple bodice glittered as she moved toward the latticed window and beckoned Süreyya to follow. 'The previous sultan's father built this palace on a peninsula, as you can see.' Emira indicated the view of the sun-dappled blue water with an elegant, jewelled hand. 'There's the Golden Horn waterway. In Turkish it's called *haliç*, which means an estuary. I often sit here and watch the ships come and go from the city.'

Süreyya doubted the reality of Emira's remark. The prince's mother appeared to be in the public areas of the palace most of the day, either praying in the women's mosque or sitting with her ladies in the salon.

'And from that window you can see the Bosphorus, which eventually spills into the Black Sea.' Emira glanced at her guest. 'It's the route the slave ships take from the Crimea,' she said. 'And over there'—she waved an elegant hand to the right—'is the Sea of Marmara.'

'Your chambers are exquisite, your highness.'

Emira Sultan smiled. 'Of course, I didn't request your presence to admire the view.' She sat down and pointed for Süreyya to take a seat opposite her. 'We will have some *kahve* now.'

She rang a small bell, and Zeki arrived almost immediately with coffee and set down a gold platter of small cakes.

'I asked you here to discuss your future,' Emira continued, adjusting the diamond pendant at her throat. 'I have organised a schedule for you for the next three months.'

Süreyya glanced at Zeki, who hovered, waiting to pour the coffee.

'My son wishes you to continue your studies in the Turkish language,' Emira said in her harsh Russian. 'And, like the odalisques, you will have lessons in lovemaking. You are still a slave of course, and I shall decide shortly on whether you can be called an odalisque, or lady of the salon. You must learn how to please the prince when—*if* —he takes you to his bed.' She tilted her head to one side, then leaned forward slightly.

She doesn't know. Süreyya remembered how discreet Abdul was each time he took her to the prince's chambers. How he used the same trusted eunuchs to escort her back to her own bed. Emira Sultan must have her suspicions; she knew about Orhan's gift. She had the other key to the strongbox in the treasury.

'A knowledge of how to please a man adds to an odalisque's value as a wife should she leave the harem.' Emira passed Süreyya a cup of coffee, which Zeki had poured with aplomb. 'Sometimes we gift odalisques, always virgins of course, to deserving men—army generals, pashas, and so forth.' Emira looked hard at her visitor over the rim of the cup. 'Zeynep Hatun, you may remember her, is now the first wife of an older, but very wealthy pasha. She has her own establishment in the city.'

Süreyya said nothing—so Emira Sultan, maybe on Abdul's recommendation, had removed Zeynep from the harem. She was relieved that she would not have to confront the redhead again. She wondered if the prince's mother was hinting that one day this might be her destiny, too: an arranged marriage to an older man, and removal from the harem.

The other woman handed Süreyya a parchment written both in Russian and Turkish.

'So, you have been in the harem now for about five weeks. I have spoken with Davut Hodja, your teacher.' She tapped the parchment. 'We have drawn up a study timetable for you.' Emira gave her a sharp look. 'The hodja thinks you have promise; you can read and write your own language. You will soon learn your new one. That is all.'

Süreyya scrambled to her feet.

Emira Sultan clicked her fingers, and Zeki emerged from the shadows. The prince's mother rose to her feet slowly.

'My eunuch, Zeki.' She paused and smiled. 'My eyes and ears in the harem, as much as Abdul, will escort you to your chamber. You may go now,' she said with a dismissive wave of her hand.

Süreyya followed Zeki from Emira's suite of chambers through the meandering marble passageways to her own smaller chamber. Once or twice, Zeki asked her leading questions about the prince, but she pretended not to understand, and to her relief, Zeki didn't speak Russian.

Inside her chamber, she opened the parchment and examined the timetable. It took her breath away. From tomorrow, she would have longer daily lessons in the Turkish language, Imam Mustafa would continue her instructions in the religion of Islam, and Emira expected her to pray regularly five times a day at the women's mosque, not in her own chamber. A few times a week, she must attend lessons in dancing, singing, and other necessary accomplishments. In addition, Emira had hinted that she would arrange lessons in lovemaking soon.

After Emira had dismissed the 'Russian girl', she stood at her window, deep in thought. Her son's devotion to this slave when she was sick, and now the financial gift, alarmed her. She knew about the matching crescent brooches, and she was certain the couple had made love. It irritated her that Abdul had refused to let her examine the *Book of Couchings* to see when and how many times it had happened, if at all.

He reminded her that the volume was for his eyes only, but Emira vowed to herself that she would see it one day.

'My young lion must *not* fall in love again,' she muttered aloud. 'Orhan needs sons—many sons—and he must take *several* women to his bed!' Emira stared out at the view, and a plan began to form in her mind.

'You are so lucky to have your own chamber, madam,' Perihan said the following day, as she helped Süreyya into her white dress and blue vest. 'I sleep in a large chamber with five other girls—we're all about the same age. But if you become ikbal, madam, the favourite, you will get a bigger chamber with lots of servants.'

'If that happens, then I will request that you share the larger chamber with me,' Süreyya said. 'I want you to stay with me, always, Perihan.' She patted the girl's hand.

After a cursory knock, Abdul Agha swept in the door. 'I believe you have a new routine,' he began. 'Roshan Kalfa will continue to monitor your progress. I have had excellent reports from her, and I have passed these on to Emira Sultan. And,' he added with a sideways smile, 'you will soon know enough Turkish to write to Prince Orhan.'

'*Inshallah*,' she replied.

Süreyya didn't need reminding of why she was keen to learn how to write in Turkish. She thought about the prince day and night, and slept with the diamond brooch under her pillow. But if they sent her away from the harem, like Zeynep, or if she escaped, which now seemed unlikely, she would need to know the language of this country to survive.

Orhan and his soldiers made good time on the road to Edirne. He had spent his evenings reading dispatches from his brother, Ahmet, and discussing battle tactics with his generals. This was the last night the servants would set up the elaborate tents and guards stand on watch. The news from the palace at Edirne was not good. According to the latest information, the Bulgars were getting close to the city. The prince ordered an early start before he retired to his tent to say his evening prayers. When he was alone, he took the gold crescent from an inner pocket and sighed again. He lay awake on his narrow bed, holding the crescent. Outside he could hear the guards shuffling in the dark as they patrolled the camp.

The brooch revived memories of Süreyya, and he sighed when he remembered her warm body under his. Other memories flooded his brain: the look of horror when she'd spilled coffee on him, and his relief when he'd found her alive in the Greek village. He threw back his bed cover and crossed to his small desk where a candle still burned. He picked up a pen and wrote in Russian:

Dearest Süreyya,

We will soon arrive in Edirne and have not yet encountered the enemy. The journey was arduous, and I apologise for not writing sooner. I miss you, but I assure you, my darling, that I am safe. I trust Abdul brought my gifts to you, and that you will buy yourself some trinkets with the akçes. Believe that I think of you constantly, and remember our last night together with joy and sadness. As soon as we have quelled the enemy in Edirne, I will send for you to join me at the Edirne Palace. I miss you and I cover your face with kisses.

Orhan

He rolled the parchment into a scroll and wrote Süreyya's name on it in Turkish. He sealed the letter with his personal seal and put it into a silver holder. Orhan threw back the brocade curtain and ordered the guard to bring the dispatch rider. When the man arrived, he gave him the missive and instructed him to deliver the message directly to Abdul Agha. The servant bowed and left, and as Orhan returned to his bed, he heard the rider's horse as he quit the camp. The prince rubbed his hands over his face. He knew that fierce fighting lay ahead. But now he had written to Süreyya, he could say the last prayer of the day —the *Isha*—and then sleep peacefully.

~

Emira sent for Abdul Agha and dismissed her servants and the eunuch, Zeki. When the chief eunuch arrived, Emira laid out her daring plan. The agha listened without comment. When he returned, he told her he had completed most of the task, but he warned his mistress that he did not approve. Emira shook her head. Nothing would change her mind. The day after tomorrow, she planned to leave the palace and visit the Constantinople slave market disguised as a kira.

'Now, Abdul, a couple of my ladies know about this plan. Tell no one else, *particularly* Zeki; he would want to accompany us. I will take Süreyya Jariye with me.'

Abdul could not hide his disapproval. 'Is that wise, madam?' He frowned.

'She needs to appreciate the fate my son spared her when he rescued her from the slave ship.'

'Madam, I beg you. Allow me to go as I always do,' the agha said.

'No! I wish to choose a couple of new girls myself. I am anxious for my son to have a choice. He must not give his heart to only one woman again.'

Abdul brought kira-style clothes to Emira's chambers after lunch.

'I *cannot* wear these!' she exclaimed.

'Highness, if you wish to disguise yourself as a kira, then you must wear a lower grade of material in either blue or black,' he replied. 'As you no doubt know, only Muslims may wear silks and furs in the city. Christians and Jews must wear other, inferior fabrics.'

Emira shrugged.

'Permit me to repeat, madam,' Abdul continued, 'I am totally opposed to this plan.'

'And *I* am determined to go,' Emira said. She dismissed the agha with a wave of her hand, then ran her fingers over the fabric. The quality was excellent, but it was still *cotton*.

'Your highness, is this not a dangerous mission?' the chief lady asked after Abdul Agha had departed.

'I shall not be alone,' Emira said. 'I have an armed escort dressed as servants, and I'm taking Süreyya Jariye, the Russian girl, with me.' Emira didn't miss the raised eyebrows and the look that passed between her ladies-in-waiting. 'Help me with this, Beyza,' she ordered.

Her waiting woman assisted her as Emira changed into the simple gown and wrapped a long blue cloak around her body. Another of her ladies fastened Spanish-style gold earrings in her earlobes, and Emira pulled a matching blue scarf over her dark hair.

'You are very brave, madam, and now you do resemble a kira.' Beyza, her chief lady-in-waiting, held up a gold mirror.

Emira nodded, shuffled off the clothes, and dropped them on the floor. Time enough tomorrow to wear those, she thought. After her ladies had put the clothes away, she called for Zeki.

'Tell Süreyya Jariye that I wish to see her before afternoon prayers,' she told him.

When she comes with me tomorrow, she will see what her fate might have been, and be grateful to my son for rescuing her.

Süreyya waited with her head bowed until Emira Sultan spoke to her. The prince's mother had dismissed her ladies and Zeki, and they were alone in her sitting room.

'Roshan Kalfa tells me your studies went well today,' Emira began.

'Yes madam, I ...'

'Well, you have earned a day away from classes. I wish you to accompany me on an errand.' Emira outlined her plan to Süreyya, who kept her eyes lowered, hoping Emira would not guess what she was thinking.

Had the prince's mother lost her mind? Süreyya thought. She planned to wear a disguise and walk from the palace to an area called Eminönü, near the wharves on the Golden Horn. She'd said it was the main harbour area of the city. Then Emira intended to visit the slave market.

Süreyya felt sick with apprehension—the slave market! She dreaded seeing it, but this would be a rare chance to see Constantinople and walk among its people.

'I have ordered an escort for us; they will blend in among the ordinary people,' Emira added. 'I will send a servant for you after breakfast tomorrow, and my women will help you into clothes suitable for a kira. Look at me, girl!'

Süreyya raised her eyes and met Emira's excited gaze.

'You must tell *no one* about this. Do you understand? Abdul Agha knows, but of course, he doesn't approve. He has insisted I take a young eunuch, Selim, to bargain for me in the slave market. Your teacher knows you will be absent, but not your whereabouts. Roshan Kalfa will keep your servant busy while you are away.'

'Yes, your highness.'

'Perhaps when you see the slave market, you will realise what my son rescued you from,' Emira said sharply. 'And,' she added, 'do *not* attempt to escape by thinking you can take a boat across to the Christian part of the city. I have instructed the escort to watch you—and *I* will keep my eye on you as well.'

CHAPTER 12

Süreyya's heart thudded with fear the following day when someone tapped on her door. She opened it, and the waiting eunuch bade her to follow him. As she walked behind the man, she felt apprehensive. She was to leave the harem in disguise and accompany Emira Sultan on a visit to the slave market in the city. By her own admission, the prince's mother had chosen *her* as a companion to teach her a lesson in gratitude.

After leading her through a maze of passageways, the eunuch stopped and ushered her into a small chamber where Abdul, his face an unreadable mask, waited with Emira Sultan. Süreyya glanced around quickly; was this the secret exit she'd searched for in vain? She knew she would never remember the meandering route they'd taken through marble-tiled corridors, past closed doors and under granite arches.

The prince's mother wore a plain blue cloak over a similarly coloured gown, and a headscarf covered her dark hair. Two of Emira's waiting women hovered around her, adjusting her clothes. Abdul motioned Süreyya to a small alcove, where she changed into the same blue clothes and matching leather slippers.

When Süreyya emerged, her blond hair hidden completely under her scarf, Emira nodded her approval.

'After we have been to the slave market, I will visit an old friend of mine, Gülbahar,' Emira said in Russian. 'Abdul dislikes her, because she was once the madam of an exclusive brothel in Constantinople.'

Emira looked at the agha and smiled mischievously. Abdul pulled back his shoulders and stared straight ahead.

Süreyya heard him tut, but he didn't move. How did the prince's mother know such a person?

Abdul opened a small wooden door, and a gust of warm scented air filled the small space. He stepped out and turned to them. 'The path is clear, madam,' he said. 'You may go.'

Emira swore her ladies to secrecy and dismissed them.

'Remember, I have arranged an armed guard of four men, dressed in plain clothes, and an assistant, Selim,' Abdul said as Emira swept past him. 'They will be with you at all times.'

'Good!' Emira replied.

Abdul touched her arm. 'Madam, I repeat, if any harm comes to either of you, the sultan will order my execution,' the agha said.

Emira paused on the path, and Süreyya wondered if she was going to change her mind. Instead, she turned to the agha. 'I prevented your execution after Kyrgios, Abdul Agha, remember? I would never allow that to happen.'

'*Inshallah*, madam,' Abdul replied. When he bowed his head, the sun caught the amber stone in the centre of his white turban. He beckoned to a young man waiting in the building's shade. 'This is Selim. He is a first-class student at the eunuch's school, and I can trust him.'

The young man wore the dark red kaftan, matching long vest, and the flat turban of a scholar. He bowed low to Emira and wished her a good morning.

'He speaks Turkish, Arabic, and Russian,' Abdul said. 'Allow him to speak for you. I insist that you or he send word via the escort if you are in danger.'

'Of course!' Emira shrugged, then turned to Süreyya. 'Come!' she beckoned.

Süreyya had understood some of Abdul's comments. She guessed from the expression on the agha's usually impassive face that he was both angry and concerned about Emira's sortie into the outside world.

Süreyya's heart raced as she followed their escort and Emira along the narrow track. Eventually she recognised the main pathway around the side of the palace. There was no longer a chill in the breeze which cooled the hot day, and fanned the edge of the scarf that Süreyya had drawn across the lower half of her face. She could smell flowers from the gardens on the other side of the wall. As they walked, she guessed they were now close to the second courtyard, which housed the palace kitchens.

Preparations for lunch had already begun. Cooking smells drifted toward them: baking bread, meat, and vegetables cooked in olive oil. A guard opened a heavy iron gate, and Süreyya followed Emira and the escort as they stepped from the sandy path onto the cobblestone one.

'We are outside the palace now,' Selim said. 'If you turn, you will see the Imperial Gate. It leads to the first courtyard and the Janissaries quarters.'

A wave of excitement replaced Süreyya's previous apprehension. She was outside the confines of the palace, free to walk around as she had done all her life. Turning quickly, she saw the long, low structure of the Imperial Gate. Several Janissaries, in their orange uniforms and white hats, stood to attention on either side of it and at intervals along the palace walls. They ignored the kiras and their retinue.

But after her initial euphoria, Süreyya felt uneasy again; they were outside the protection of the palace, even though they had a body-guard. Leaving the palace had been easy, but would they be able to return without being challenged? As if reading her thoughts, Emira turned to her.

'The Imperial Gate is open from dawn to dusk. This is where people who wish to petition the sultan must wait. It is also the quarters for the Janissaries,' she said. 'We have come on the imperial path around the back of the courtyards to avoid questions from the soldiers. I have arranged for you to come back by water, on a private caique, to the royal jetty. I will return later on the imperial caique.'

Süreyya followed Emira Sultan and the group, and slowed to gaze again at the Aya Sofia Mosque. Sunlight bathed the squat ochre-coloured building and flashed off the crescent on the apex of the dome. Its single minaret reached to the heavens. The city was alive with noise and bustle; a street vendor calling his wares nearby startled her. As they passed Aya Sofia, Süreyya noticed with surprise that shabby houses clustered in the shadow of the mosque. Dogs barked and scuffled among the rubbish, and children shouted and squealed as they chased each other. She had not seen this other side of the mosque when she visited it with the royal party.

'We are passing the *At Meydanı*, the ancient Hippodrome, madam,' Selim said in Russian. This was where Süreyya had seen Orhan for the last time. She glanced at Emira, wondering if she was thinking of the day of the march-out. How proud the prince had looked as he led his troops on the campaign to Edirne! Today, dust blew across the vast space, and only a few people walked past the remains of the antique columns. The young man pointed out a rundown building and told them that the sultan's harem was once housed there in the Old Palace.

'A few years since, the Valide Sultan ordered that it should be moved to the Topkapı Palace,' he remarked. 'Now the old building is called "The House of Tears",' he added. 'On the death of the sultan or a prince, as you know, madam,' he said to Emira, 'his harem must move there.'

Emira didn't reply, but Süreyya swallowed hard and prayed to God that would not happen to her. She glanced at Emira. It would be her fate too, she thought, to live out the rest of her life far from the seat of power. Unless, of course, her son became the next sultan.

Selim led them toward a steep thoroughfare, bordered on either side by stone and wooden houses. 'We must take the stairs to the quayside,' he said over his shoulder. He and two of the guards went ahead, then Selim beckoned the women to follow.

Süreyya and Emira steadied themselves on the rough wall as they descended the steps that had been cut out of the rockface. Men, women, and children pushed past on the slimy stairs and Süreyya glanced across the road where people were labouring up the hill. She felt overwhelmed by the barking of dogs and the braying of foul-smelling donkeys. The women stopped and held their scarves close to their noses when the donkey's owners urged the animals down the steep roadway, within a hairsbreadth of them.

As she edged her way down the steps, Süreyya wondered again what had possessed the prince's mother to leave the safety of the harem. And why had she chosen to bring her? When they got to the bottom, Emira turned and took her arm as she steadied herself on the slippery cobbles.

'Selim says we will arrive soon,' she said. Her eyes above her face covering were bright with excitement.

Ahead of Süreyya, people thronged the quayside as boats and a few sailing ships rocked against the wharves. The breeze blew the fresh salty air toward them, cleansing the city for a moment from the noxious odours of decaying fish and rubbish. Emira squeezed her arm.

'This area is Eminönü,' she said. 'Now, look over there.' She pointed to a brown brick tower with a conical red roof. 'That area is Galata, and the building is the Genoese Fire Tower. From there fire-watchers give early warning if they see a fire in the city.' She stepped carefully around a heap of rubbish. 'It was the first thing I saw when they herded me off the slave ship.'

Süreyya glanced at Emira; her eyes were defiant. But Süreyya couldn't bear to look at the sailing ships. She still had nightmares about the voyage. This is where she would have ended her journey, poked and prodded off a ship, if she hadn't jumped overboard.

A man carrying circles of seed-encrusted bread, threaded on a long rod, pushed past them, shouting, *'Simit! Simit!'* at the top of his voice.

Men ran everywhere, some bent double under enormous packs strapped to their backs. A clerk in flowing robes and turban held a wooden board in his hand. He used a finely honed quill to check off the carts that trundled past him. The smell of spices mingled with that of frying fish from the wharf. The stallholders wrapped the cooked fish in flat bread and handed it to customers.

The midday prayer call from several mosques hurt Süreyya's ears. Veiled women pulled children along, stepping around the faithful who had laid out their prayer mats on the ground. Selim led them toward a grey stone building, and Süreyya's heart lurched with fear. This must be the slave market.

Selim ignored the hawkers who pestered them as they walked through the arched entrance. Once inside, Süreyya felt faint. The vaulted space with its old arches and cobbled floor stank of body odour mingled with another smell she remembered: fear and despair. It was the stench that permeated her nightmares. Her earlier exuberance drained away, and terrifying memories of her humiliation assaulted her. Before she could dwell on them, a rough-looking man appeared from the gloom. He bowed and touched his forehead.

'*Hoş geldiniz, kira hatun*—welcome, madam kira,' he fawned with a low bow to Emira.

'*Hoş bulduk*—we found welcome,' Selim answered for her.

'Allow me to introduce myself. I am Fetullah, lately of Kalla in the Crimea.' He bowed again.

As the man continued to talk, Selim translated quickly for Süreyya. Fetullah said he could speak in Russian if they wished. Emira told him to continue in Turkish.

Selim led the women to benches covered with strips of carpet, and ordered *ayran* for them. The man continued to gabble and gesture with his hands, his sharp eyes flicking between the women and their escort.

'The lady is looking for two women, aged about eighteen,' Selim interrupted.

Süreyya stifled a gasp. This was not just an excursion to show Süreyya how lucky she was. Emira's intention was obvious. She wanted to buy women to tempt Orhan away from her.

'Only two?' the trader tutted. 'I could show her twenty!'

He insisted Selim take a seat, and a young boy handed everyone a glass of ayran perched on a decorated saucer. The yoghurt drink tasted sour, unlike the refined beverage served at the palace. The trader snapped his fingers, and another man led two girls into the centre of the paved circle. Süreyya couldn't bear to look at the frightened teenagers. One was a tall brunette, the other a white-skinned Caucasian, whose thick blond hair reached halfway down her back. With a swift movement, the man pulled open the tapes on their calico shifts and the garments fell to the ground. Each girl stood with head bowed, one hand over her private parts, her forearm shielding her breasts.

'God have mercy,' Selim muttered.

'What do you think?' the trader asked. He pulled the brunette's arm away from her breasts and cupped one in his hand. He pushed her to turn around and ran his calloused hands over her buttocks. 'Wide hips—good for childbearing!' he said over his shoulder. 'And both of them are virgins. I examined them myself,' he leered.

Süreyya felt nauseous and looked away. Orhan had rescued her from these odious people. She glanced at Emira Sultan, who was sitting bolt upright in her seat.

'Enough! I will have them.' Emira broke her silence. She told Selim her price and rose to go, clicking her fingers at Süreyya to follow.

'But wait, madam! I have more,' Fetullah shouted.

The trader slapped the blonde girl on the buttocks as she bent to retrieve her shift. He called out an order in his guttural voice, and Emira stopped. Another man led out four naked prepubescent girls and paraded them in front of the onlookers. Süreyya felt sick, desperate to escape from the stinking building into the fresh air. The youngest girl was about ten years old, and the oldest bore a strong resemblance to Perihan. They were all crying.

'Stop snivelling,' their owner shouted. 'All virgins, madam, and what do you think of that redhead!'

'I'll take them,' Emira said to Selim. 'For the love of God, they can't stay here!'

Emira, too, seemed desperate to leave. Despite the entreaties of the fawning traders, she signalled to Süreyya to follow. Selim took them to the door, where the bodyguard was waiting. Selim and an escort stayed behind to bargain the price.

As soon as she was outside, Süreyya gulped air into her lungs and swallowed the bile in her throat. She looked across at Emira, who was breathing deeply like herself. The prince's mother turned to Süreyya.

'Now you see what my son rescued you from, Süreyya Jariye. I hope you are grateful!'

Süreyya said nothing, but stood with her head bowed, her mind still full of the distressing images. Selim's voice broke the silence between the two women, his youthful face full of concern. He told Emira that he had completed the transaction and organised transport for the six slaves to be sent to the harem.

'Shall I send for someone to transport you to the palace, madam?' he asked.

'No, that is my next transport.' She pointed to a superior-looking vessel, then turned to Süreyya. 'I shall cross the Golden Horn and visit my friend in Galata,' she said in Russian. 'Three of the armed guards will stay with me. Selim and a guard will return with you to the palace in a private caique. Go!'

Emira's friend Gülbahar shook her head in disbelief and clicked her fingers to a servant to bring coffee and cakes.

'Emira, *Allah aşkına!* For the love of God, my friend! You've been to the *slave* market? It's a terrible place. Have you forgotten how we suffered?'

'I wanted to purchase some new women to tempt my son,' Emira answered defensively. 'He is paying too much attention to the Russian girl, Süreyya.' She smoothed her hand over the fresh clothes Gülbahar had provided for her. 'But the market was much worse than I remember.'

'I used to send someone else there to get the girls for the business,' Gülbahar said.

Both women sat back and waited while a servant poured the coffee.

'So, do you think your son has fallen in love?' Gülbahar asked.

'Maybe.' Emira sipped her drink. 'But,' she said, her voice rising, 'the dynasty needs more children! In the slave market, I chose a girl who looks like his old love from Kalla, and a blonde who looks like Süreyya.'

'Looks like?' Gülbahar raised her plucked eyebrows. 'Most men are stupid, darling, but not *that* stupid.'

The two women settled themselves in the sofa, a cushioned area set in the bay window. Emira smiled as she looked through the silk drapes to the thoroughfare below. Gülbahar's house was at the top of a winding cobbled street. It had a view down to the waters of the Golden Horn, where it joined the Bosphorus. She could see the Topkapı palace on the opposite shore. From here the two women watched the people negotiating the paths that led to the waterside. Gülbahar tapped Emira's hand and waved her arm in a circle at the elegant salon with its thick carpets, an Italian glass chandelier, and European chairs.

'Do you like it?'

'It's spectacular, *aferin*—congratulations. So, your lover, the Venetian ambassador, looked after you as he promised?' Emira said.

'Yes, he bought me this house, and sent to Venice for the furnishings. Then he returned to his country with his bitch of a wife.' She sighed. 'I was raised in the Roman church, before, you know, so I tried to understand.' She shook her head. 'But it was not easy.'

Emira regarded Gülbahar sympathetically. Several years ago, Abdul had discovered the whereabouts of her friend from the slave ship. She and Gülbahar had corresponded and met several times a year, either in the harem or in Gülbahar's residence.

'Well, neither of us has our own man,' Emira said.

'But at least you have your son,' her friend reminded her. 'I only have a daughter, Clara.' She smiled fondly. 'She's Giuseppe's daughter, as you know. I made sure she married well, here in Constantinople. At least he didn't take her away from me.' She clapped her hands. 'Now, how can I help you, Emira Sultan? Training for the odalisques?'

Emira nodded. 'I'd like you to send someone to the palace as soon as possible. The Russian girl needs training in lovemaking.'

'I'll send Şefika. She's young, but very experienced.' Gülbahar hesitated. 'But has your son not already sent for Süreyya?'

'I suspect he has, but Abdul will not say.' Emira frowned.

Gülbahar laughed. 'Come and see me again if you can, dearest Emira. I love to hear stories of your recalcitrant chief eunuch.'

'*Inshallah*—God willing—I will visit you again soon. I have to be careful; the sultan would not be happy if he knew about my excursions.' Emira shrugged. 'But I've passed as a kira a couple of times before, as you know.'

Eventually, she rose to leave and the two women embraced.

'Allah has smiled on us in Constantinople, the two former slave girls!' Gülbahar whispered with tears in her eyes.

Selim helped Süreyya onto a private caique. It eventually pulled into the dock, close to the beach where Orhan had rescued her. The guard who accompanied them saluted to his colleagues as they passed unchallenged through the gate. Selim led the way through the underground passage, and Süreyya emerged in the rose garden. The roses were in full bloom now, reminding her of the rose Orhan had given her. As she inhaled their heady scent, Süreyya's thoughts were again in turmoil—torn between her longing for freedom and her feelings for the prince.

Selim bade her goodbye, and she slipped through the side door of the harem and into the alcove area. She tore off her kira clothes, and a eunuch helped her into a towelling coat and led her through the dark passages toward the harem. Once again, she tried to remember the maze of passages they traversed, but it was impossible. She inhaled the familiar smells of rosewater, lemon cologne and fresh flowers, so different from the evil place she'd been this morning. Süreyya followed the eunuch along the marble-floored passage to the hamam, desperate to bathe and wash away the foul odours of the city. She relaxed as the hamam servants poured warm water over her naked body. If Emira Sultan had taken her to the slave market to make her grateful for her new life in the harem, she thought, then she had certainly succeeded.

CHAPTER 13

The day after her visit to the slave market, Süreyya re-read Orhan's letter several times. She smoothed her fingers over the parchment as she imagined him writing to her in his tent. He wanted her to join him in Edirne—but when? If they were still fighting in the region, she must wait, but she longed to see him.

She replied to his letter, writing in Russian, but signed her name carefully in the Turkish script. Next time, she would ask Davut Hodja to help her pen more of the missive in Turkish. Today she wanted to write to Orhan in her own language, and tell him how much she missed him. Now at last, she could thank him for his generous gift of gold and akçes, and for saving her from the slave market. But she would never tell him she had been there with his mother. She sent for Abdul, who poured red wax on the rolled parchment, pressing his personal seal into it.

'They will recognise my seal, and know that the letter is private,' he said.

When the wax was dry, he put the rolled document into a long silver scroll holder, and secured the silver top.

'I will make sure it goes with the daily dispatch rider,' he told her, tapping the top with his finger.

During the next couple of weeks, Süreyya continued her studies in the Muslim religion, Turkish language, and the accomplishments required of a harem odalisque: dancing, embroidery, and gracious behaviour. When she could show Emira Sultan that she had succeeded in mastering her new skills, the prince's mother might allow her free access to the salon.

Emira summoned her to her chambers after two weeks. 'I still do not think you are ready to have the title *Hatun*—Lady, and be referred to as an "odalisque" a lady of the chamber, not a slave,' Emira told her. 'You are, however, very close to achieving it.'

The two girls Emira had purchased in the slave market joined her class. They said they were from Poland, but spoke a little Russian. Perihan told her that the four younger girls were Armenian. They were being trained as servants and were in a different learning group.

On a sultry afternoon in July, Abdul approached Süreyya as she was walking back from her studies. 'You will have a visitor tomorrow, after lunch,' he said and curled his lip. 'She's a *gecenin kadını.*'

Süreyya frowned and shook her head.

'A woman of the night,' Abdul translated into his fractured Russian. 'She will train you in lovemaking. It is Emira Sultan's wish.'

Süreyya blushed. Abdul knew she and the prince had already made love. But maybe Emira did not...

In the drowsy hour after lunch the following day, Abdul knocked on the door and ushered Şefika over the threshold. 'Şefika Hatun.' He raised his shoulders, pursed his lips, and after giving the woman a disdainful look, he left.

'*Merhaba!*—Hello,' Şefika trilled.

Warmth and kindness exuded from Şefika, like the rays of the sun. To Süreyya's surprise, the other woman was not tall with a curvaceous body, like many of the harem women, but short. She wore a long, figure-revealing pale pink satin gown under a dark flowing mantle that she tossed onto a chair. Her large breasts strained against the jewelled bodice. Her body was all soft curves, her face suffused with a dimpled smile, and she wore several jewelled rings on her small hands. When she removed her headscarf, her auburn hair tumbled in ringlets over her shoulders. Her wide eyes were the colour of amber and edged with thick, dark lashes. She opened a bag and laid the contents on Süreyya's divan.

'So, I will teach you how to please a prince,' she said in slow Turkish. She smiled at Süreyya, who stared at the long cucumber, against the base of which Şefika had arranged two large ripe figs. 'My man.' Şefika laughed. 'We will thrill him.'

Şefika didn't spare Süreyya's blushes as she showed her the art of lovemaking, using the fruit and vegetable. When it was Süreyya's turn, Şefika nodded approval, sometimes saying, 'Not too fast … be gentle. Feel how soft the figs are? Don't hurt him!' She told Süreyya the other parts of a man's body to caress, how to kiss, and what to expect from him.

'Royal princes learn about lovemaking from an early age.' Şefika smiled. She put her head on one side and said, 'You must also let him be your teacher.' She patted Süreyya's hand. 'So—finished!' she announced. 'Now maybe we can have some sherbet?'

Süreyya tapped on the inside of the door, the signal for attention, and ordered their refreshment.

Şefika packed away her props, and patted Süreyya's face. Her eyes were warm and kind. '*Sen, çok, çok güzel!* You are exquisite.' She sat on the divan and sipped her lemon sherbet. 'I'm sure you will soon be ikbal—the favourite.'

Süreyya sighed. 'But he isn't here.'

'If he cares for you, he will send for you soon.' Şefika squeezed her hand.

Before she left, Şefika drew Süreyya into a warm embrace.

'I wish us to be friends one day,' Süreyya said in halting Turkish.

'*Inshallah*—God willing. Study hard, my dear.' Şefika threw her light cloak over her shoulders and fastened her headscarf in place. She pulled it across her face so that only her eyes, amused and bright, showed above the silk. 'Goodbye, and good luck!'

Süreyya tapped on the door, and this time Abdul opened it.

'Ready?' he asked Şefika.

'For you, darling Abdul? Always!' she replied. 'Good luck, my dear.'

Şefika winked as her eyes met Süreyya's, then she waved and swept out of the door, leaving a faint perfume in her wake.

After Şefika had gone, Süreyya closed her eyes. She recalled Orhan's naked body against hers as he covered her in urgent kisses. She threw herself on the bed and lay on her stomach. Her body ached with an unquenchable need for him. Şefika's instructions had stirred a longing deep within her.

Constantinople sweltered in a heatwave as July slid into August. A haze that shimmered over the water and engulfed the city muffled the dawn prayer call from the city mosques. By midday, the haze burned off, and then the unforgiving sun irradiated everywhere until sunset.

In the late afternoon, Abdul received an urgent summons from Emira Sultan. The agha was sitting cross-legged on the floor of his chamber, reading his copy of the Holy Koran that was open on a wooden stand in front of him. He didn't respond; few things were urgent in Emira's life, and for him, the words of the Prophet took precedence over the whims of a woman.

When she sent the message a second time, he rose to his feet with a sigh, and marked his place in the holy book. He straightened his yellow satin robe and white turban, and made his way up the familiar stairs to her chambers. Zeki admitted him to Emira's salon, where she dismissed the women who always accompanied her. The agha waited with a bowed head. Emira clicked her fingers at Zeki and ordered some refreshments. After he had closed the door behind him, she addressed Abdul.

'At *last*, where have you been?'

Before the agha could answer, she said, 'I have another important and confidential task for you.'

Abdul waited. Emira Sultan often became agitated, but today she appeared more nervous than usual.

'I have something I want you to do. It's the ultimate test for the Russian girl, Süreyya, to see if she's worthy of becoming my son's favourite. It's a test of her ingenuity,' she finished with an arch look at Abdul. She paused as Zeki entered and poured sherbet very slowly into elegant glasses.

The eunuch bowed to Emira and Abdul, then left the chamber.

Emira sipped her drink, replaced the glass on the table, and smiled at Abdul. 'This is my plan ...'

When she'd finished, Abdul regarded her silently.

'Well?' she asked.

'Madam, Emira Sultan, *haseki* and favourite of the grand pādishah, he who is the shadow of God on earth. You, who are the mother of a future sultan ...' he began. He heard her sharp intake of breath when he enunciated her dearest wish: to become the Valide Sultan. 'I have known you from when you caught the sultan's eye to when you became Haseki Sultan—a chief royal lady, a princess. The mother of a son, a prince...'

'Abdul, will you do what I ask—yes or no?' Emira interrupted.

The eunuch touched his forehead, then put his hand on his heart. 'Madam, as you know, I was born in Africa. In my village, there was witchcraft and no mercy. I have embraced the religion of Islam. *Inshallah*, I am a good Muslim. It is contrary to the teachings of the prophet, peace be upon him, to steal or to lie.'

'No one ...' Emira began, but he interrupted.

'I regret ...' He bowed his head. 'What you ask is against the will of Allah.'

Emira leaped to her feet, almost upending her small table. 'What! It is not a *request*, it's an *order*. How dare you refuse?'

Abdul stood motionless, towering over his angry mistress. 'I will find someone to do your bidding, your highness, but I will not, *cannot*, do it myself.'

'But you're the only person I trust!'

'There is someone whom *I* trust.'

Emira glowered at him. 'Just get it done.'

Abdul left the chamber feeling injured. Emira had never respected his devotion to Allah. Sometimes her scheming and intrigues wearied him. He liked the girl Süreyya, and wished her no harm, but Emira had given him a task, and he had no choice but to obey.

The gossip in the harem was that there was ferocious fighting near the border. Süreyya dreaded hearing that Orhan might be injured—or dead. She shivered at the thought. Early the following morning, someone tapped on her door. She opened it, still in her blue satin shift, expecting Perihan's bright face, but Abdul stood on the threshold. She stepped aside, and he walked into the chamber commenting about the heat and hoping she was well.

'Another letter from his highness.' Abdul handed her a roll of parchment. 'The seal is unbroken, of course, madam.' He cleared his throat. 'Do not mention his highness's personal correspondence to anyone, except your teacher, Davut Hodja,' he added, glancing toward Emira Sultan's chambers.

Süreyya ran her fingers over the turah, the prince's personal signature, embedded in the wax seal of the document. Abdul handed her a knife, and watched as she slit the seal with its sharp blade.

'Is it true that there is fierce fighting near the border?' she asked.

'Maybe the prince's missive will answer your question,' Abdul replied.

'Perihan should be here by now.' She looked at Abdul enquiringly. The agha gave a slight shrug. 'No matter, when she arrives, I will dress and leave for class.'

'Of course, madam.'

She detected an odd tone in the agha's voice and glanced up at him. He bowed and bade her good day, his face its usual blank mask.

Süreyya waited until he closed the door before she unrolled the parchment. The prince had written the first half in Turkish. She would ask Davut Hodja to read it, as Abdul had suggested. Orhan had written the second page in the Russian Cyrillic script, and she smiled, admiring his penmanship and grasp of her language. She ran her fingers over the text, once again imagining him sitting in a tent somewhere, writing to her—thinking of her. She read the Russian script, relishing each word.

My dearest love,

We have been fighting for over six weeks now. I have had no rest—and little time to write, my darling. You may get your teacher to read the Turkish to you, because it describes the battles we've fought against our ever-present enemy, the Bulgars.

But these words are for you alone, to say how much I miss you. You are always in my thoughts, dear one. Sometimes I hold the crescent brooch in my hand late at night. I feel closer to you, knowing you have the other half. How I yearn to have your body next to mine, to kiss your sweet lips and run my hands through your beautiful hair.

Dearest Süreyya, since I began this letter, the tide in the battle against the Bulgars has turned, and I believe it is safer here now. I am writing to my mother today and I want you to accompany her to Edirne to be with me soon. It is a tedious journey of four days, but how I long to see you again, my own, my one true love. I want to rain kisses over your body, and for us to become one again, sevgilim, my darling.

Orhan

Süreyya re-read the letter and hugged it to her chest, longing to be reunited with him in Edirne. She moved away from the window, wondering why Perihan had not yet arrived. She opened the door just as a young maid was about to knock.

'Good morning, madam, my name is Nehir,' the girl said.

Startled, Süreyya returned her greeting. 'Where's Perihan?'

The girl shrugged. 'I don't know.'

'Is she sick?'

The young woman shrugged again. 'I am here to help you dress and arrange your hair before class,' Nehir repeated.

'Please find out why Perihan isn't here, as soon as you can.'

Nehir lowered her eyes. 'Of course, madam.'

After the girl had helped her dress, Süreyya sent her to wait outside. She put the Russian page of Orhan's letter in her safe, collected her bag of books, and slipped the Turkish page in a book. She joined Nehir, and following Roshan Kalfa's instructions, they walked sedately along the path to the school. Süreyya hugged her bag close to her body. Orhan's letter was the fourth she'd received from him and the most intimate. His second letter, also written in her own language, had been brief:

My darling,

We are in the heat of battle, and I cannot write what I want to say to you. Believe me, I think often of you. I miss you day and night, and kiss your eyes.

Orhan

The third had mentioned the intense fighting as they tried to control the rebels.

They are terrorising and burning Ottoman villages. Thank God we arrived in time to prevent them from overrunning the palace.

Kisses, Orhan

Süreyya's teacher helped her read the Turkish part of the latest letter concerning the campaign.

'I had the honour of instructing Prince Orhan when I was a young teacher,' he told Süreyya. 'See how beautifully he writes, even though he is fighting the infidel. *Mashallah!*—God protect him.'

'Davut Hodja, do you know anything about Perihan?' she asked hopefully. 'They have sent me a new servant, and she will not tell me anything.'

Her teacher looked away. 'I believe ...' he began, then appeared to change his mind. 'I believe you must address all such enquiries to Abdul Agha.'

Süreyya nodded, certain that the hodja had been about to tell her what had befallen her maid. She was sure something *had* happened to Perihan, but what? And why the secrecy? She knew there was one place she could find out—the hamam.

CHAPTER 14

Süreyya knew the hamam was where she would hear palace gossip and perhaps learn what had happened to Perihan. After midday prayers and lunch, she sent her new servant, Nehir, ahead to prepare her fresh clothes. While she was away, Süreyya replaced Orhan's letter behind the tile. But where was Perihan?

She had looked in vain for her at prayers, and in the salon while she had lunch. As she walked slowly along the cool corridors with their bright tiles, Süreyya thought of the prince and his recently hard-won battles. If only Perihan was there, she could talk to her about Orhan's bravery.

When the servants opened the door of the hamam and ushered her inside, she surrendered herself to their ministrations. Removing her thin cotton shift, she joined a small group of women. They sat on marble benches, murmuring quietly to each other, while servants poured warm water over them from large pitchers. Süreyya stretched her arms up, luxuriating in the steamy, soporific air. She watched it rise to the coloured glass dome above the mosaic massage tables in the centre of the hamam. She closed her eyes as the servants continued to pour warm water over her. The other women chatted among themselves. Süreyya listened as she usually did. Her Turkish was improving and she could understand most of the conversation.

'The kira, Ezter Hatun, can't come anymore,' an odalisque wailed.

'Why not?' another asked.

'Haven't you heard? There's a plague in the city. It happens every summer.'

'The authorities have closed some areas, and they've shut most of the gates in and out of Constantinople. Citizens and visitors can only enter and exit through the Edirne gate now.'

Süreyya opened her eyes and focused on the conversation. Did this mean she might not travel to Edirne, especially if they closed that gate too?

'Lots of people have died,' the first woman added as a servant poured water over her naked body. 'We're lucky we live in the palace.'

'I wanted the kira to bring me some things,' a second woman pouted. 'What about the fortune teller *and* the Armenian woman who sells ribbons?'

'All haram—forbidden.'

Süreyya slipped her feet into a pair of nalin, high wooden shoes, that the hamam servant gave her. She could hardly walk in the cumbersome footwear, and the servant guided her to a massage table, where she lay face down. Two servants kneaded her body with warm, scented oil and washed her hair. The soap from her hair ran down her face, temporarily blinding her. They rinsed her hair with warm water and combed the tangles out of it, exclaiming at the colour—like wild corn—and they laughed. In the steam area, the other odalisques, wrapped in towels like her, lounged on long benches, chatting.

'I wouldn't like to be in ... during the plague,' one of them remarked with a sideways look at Süreyya. She shook her head; she hadn't understood the word.

'*Hapis*,' the girl repeated, and crossed one wrist over the other. 'Hapis, like your maid, Perihan.'

'Hapis means prison. They've arrested your maid,' a Russian speaker translated.

Süreyya stared at her. 'Prison? Why?'

The Russian girl shrugged and replied in Turkish, 'They say she's *hırsız*—a thief. You should check your jewellery box.'

A couple of the others nodded their agreement.

Süreyya frowned at the gossiping women. 'Perihan is not a thief! She works for me.'

'She probably is …' another girl said.

Süreyya pulled her towel tighter around her body and walked over to the speaker. 'She *isn't!*'

A few of the group giggled. 'Shut up and sit down, *Russian.*'

One of Zeynep's former friends grabbed her arm. Süreyya, still wearing the high wooden clogs, tried to keep her balance.

The Russian speaker interrupted. 'Stop it! The servants will call Roshan Kalfa, and we'll all be in trouble.' She turned to Süreyya. 'The maids often steal things.'

'Where have they taken her?'

'The dungeons under the palace. They found some stolen things in her pillowcase.'

'They'll probably execute her soon,' a girl with a whining voice said.

'Execute?' Süreyya understood the Turkish word. 'But what if she's innocent?'

'The maids are *always* guilty. They're jealous of us.'

'She can appeal to Emira Sultan,' her Russian friend said. 'But *she* won't do anything.'

Süreyya was desperate to learn more, but the servants came for everyone. As they dried her with warm towels, Süreyya's mind was in turmoil—Perihan arrested for theft! What did they think she'd stolen? She had to see her, but how could she get into the dungeon?

Back in her chamber, she opened her safe and shook her head. Surely Perihan would not steal from her? She would not check her jewellery box. As she stood near the tile, someone knocked on the door. She rushed to open it, thinking it might be Perihan and everything she'd heard was harem gossip. Abdul walked past her into the chamber and closed the door.

'I expect you've heard about your servant,' he began, glancing at the open safe.

'They say she hid some stolen jewellery in her pillowcase,' Süreyya said. 'When did this happen?'

'Maybe early this morning when everyone was asleep.'

'Why didn't you tell me?'

'I checked your jewellery box.' Abdul walked across and closed the safe. 'Everything is there.'

Everything, including Orhan's private letters to her! She glared at Abdul, who turned to go. 'She is *not* a thief, Abdul. I want to see her!' Süreyya raised her voice.

The agha looked straight at her and spoke as if he were speaking to a child. 'You are a woman in Prince Orhan's harem. You do not have the authority to see a prisoner,' he said, his hand on the door handle. He told her that the girl had denied the theft, but they had proof of her guilt. 'They will execute Perihan tonight.'

Süreyya was aghast. 'Execute? But she's innocent. *Please* let me see her!'

'That is not possible,' Abdul replied. He hesitated, and turned to her. 'You have plenty of money. It can buy many things.' His eyes met hers, then he tapped on the door. A eunuch opened it quietly and it closed behind him.

Süreyya sat down on her divan, her mind in turmoil.

'You have plenty of money, it can buy many things,' Abdul had said. Did he mean she could buy Perihan's freedom?

She remembered the Kızlar Ağası telling her that in the past, odalisques had tried to bribe their way out of the sultan's palace. If she had enough akçes to buy a diamond necklace, could she use some as a bribe to release Perihan? But whom could she bribe? She didn't know.

Süreyya removed the wall tile and opened her strongbox with the key, spilling the coins out on her divan. She'd only spent a few akçes on ribbons from the Armenian woman, and silver hair ornaments from the kira. Then the palace authorities banished the visitors from the harem because of the plague.

If she visited the living quarters of the women she'd met in the hamam, she might find out more.

Süreyya opened her door and paused; but where were they? She beckoned to her eunuchs, who were chatting to each other further down the passageway. They hurried toward her.

'Where are the dormitories of the other odalisques and maids?' she asked. 'I wish to visit them.'

The eunuchs exchanged glances with each other. Were they going to refuse to answer? One of them muttered something to his companion under his breath.

'This way, madam,' he said. The other eunuch stood aside, and didn't accompany them.

Süreyya followed her guide down stone stairs and along a passage. She looked around; she had never been in this less opulent area of the harem quarters. Simple blue-flowered tiles decorated the walls, and the passageway underfoot was stone, not marble. The eunuch adjusted his flat turban and knocked on a door. He said something in rapid Turkish to the eunuch who opened it, and Süreyya saw him raise his eyebrows before he stood aside.

Süreyya stepped down into the narrow chamber. It was furnished with six beds that faced the door, each separated by a low cupboard. Some of the women Süreyya had seen in the hamam were moving around the crowded area, or sitting on their beds, getting ready for afternoon prayers. They looked up in surprise when they saw her in the doorway.

'What's *she* doing here? She's got her own chamber,' a dark-haired women said.

'I don't know,' her eunuch escort replied, backing out and closing the door.

'I want the truth about Perihan,' Süreyya said.

'She's guilty,' the other replied. 'The maids are always stealing from us. She's lucky she's in this dormitory with us too!'

'How do you know it was her?' Süreyya asked.

'She stole some silver jewellery from the next dormitory, then hid it in her pillowcase. Roshan Kalfa found it this morning.'

'She did it,' a younger woman called Ayla added. 'You can't change *kismet*.'

'They'll put her in a sack and drop her alive in the Bosphorus, at *Isha*, the night prayer call,' the first women commented. They all nodded their agreement and continued to get ready.

Süreyya rushed forward, got hold of Ayla's arm, and shook her.

'Ouch! You're hurting me!' she squealed.

'She's honest!' Süreyya said, angry tears welling in her throat. 'One of you must know the truth!' She raised her voice. 'Tell me!'

Ayla shook her off. 'Who do you think you are? You're a slave like us. Emira hasn't presented you in the salon as an odalisque *or* the prince's favourite,' she sneered. She stepped closer to Süreyya. 'Zeynep was right about you … you're rotten meat. You'll get tossed overboard tonight with your maid if you're not careful.'

Süreyya lunged at her and grabbed a handful of her hair.

'Enough!' Roshan Kalfa, the Mistress of the House, stood in the doorway. 'What's going on? And what are *you* doing here, Süreyya Jariye?' She glared at the small group of women. 'How *dare* you behave like this!'

'Roshan Kalfa, Perihan isn't guilty,' Süreyya began.

'Quiet! Süreyya Jariye, do *not* disrespect me, or Abdul,' Roshan Kalfa hissed. She looked over her shoulder at the agha, who stood behind her in the shadowy corridor. The kalfa turned back to Süreyya. 'You must stay in your own area of the palace. You know that.'

'She came in here to cause trouble!' Two of the women pointed at Süreyya.

'Quiet!' Roshan Kalfa snapped.

She turned to the agha. 'Süreyya Jariye is making a disturbance in here,' she said, stepping aside to allow him into the chamber.

'All women of Prince Orhan's harem,' the agha began, '*all* of you must behave with decorum *everywhere* in the palace.' He towered over Süreyya, who stood with her head bowed. 'Look at me, Süreyya Jariye! Your behaviour is *ayıp*—shameful. You may *not* roam the passageways or visit other areas of the harem without permission. Apologise to Roshan Kalfa, then come with me.'

Süreyya raised her head and apologised. She glanced at the other women. They were standing respectfully in a row, their hands clasped in front of them, heads bowed. Two of them were smirking.

'Come!' Abdul said to Süreyya.

As she followed the agha, she heard Roshan Kalfa upbraiding the other women.

When they got to her chamber, Abdul opened the door and ordered her to stand inside and keep her head bowed. He repeated the rules of the harem—respect, dignity, a calm manner of speaking, and politeness to everyone. 'You have disgraced yourself today. You had no permission to venture to that part of the harem, or disturb the others,' he said. 'I will inform Emira Sultan about the incident.'

He reminded her she had received more privileges than the other women. She had her own maid and chamber, *and* the attentions of the prince.

'The other women are well aware of the prince's regard for you,' the agha said. 'And they all know you will travel to Edirne tomorrow. But, when Emira Sultan hears of your unruly behaviour ...' Abdul paused. 'She may decide not to take you.'

Süreyya looked up. 'But Prince Orhan wrote to me. He wants me there! He said—'

'Silence!' Abdul interrupted. 'You will prepare for afternoon prayers in the harem mosque, then the servants will deliver supper to your chamber. You are to stay here and reflect on your behaviour. This evening, the servants will take your boxes for the journey—if you go.'

Süreyya opened her mouth to speak, but Abdul held up his large hand. She stopped, alarmed by the look of irritation on his usually impassive face.

'Your maid will stay in the dungeons until it is time for her execution tonight at *Isha*,' he said. Süreyya put her hand to her mouth and tears welled in her eyes. Perihan was so young!

The agha observed her for a second, his face again a blank mask, then he turned and left the chamber. A eunuch closed the door quietly behind him.

When she heard the afternoon prayer call, Süreyya hurried to pray in the women's mosque. A few of them looked sideways at her, but none spoke. To her surprise, Emira Sultan had joined the other women in their devotions. When the prayers finished, the prince's mother beckoned her to come forward.

'So, I believe you are to accompany me to Edirne tomorrow,' she began.

'Emira Sultan, I need …'

'The servants will provide you with everything you need,' Emira interrupted. 'Abdul has told me about your behaviour.' She stared hard at Süreyya. 'I have decided to overlook it. You are very fortunate.' She turned to go.

'But Perihan, my maid? She's going to be executed,' Süreyya said.

Emira was already walking away. Süreyya saw her stiffen. Emira paused and glanced over her shoulder, a slight smile on her lips.

'Maids are sometimes expensive. They cost as much as fifty akçes,' she said.

Her eyes met Süreyya's for a moment. Emira beckoned to her women and moved away, leaving a trail of rose-scented perfume in her wake. Süreyya's mind raced; had Emira suggested she could pay for Perihan's release? But whom would she pay?

CHAPTER 15

*O*rhan reined in his horse, Akkula, and looked around for his brother, Ahmet. He was enjoying his ride in the forest, hunting animals instead of humans. They had quashed the insurgency, and now it was time to relax and join his brother and some of his Janissary officers in one of his favourite pastimes—hunting.

He pulled off his leather hat and ran his hand through his hair. Orhan longed for Süreyya to be here in the countryside with him. He had sent a message to his mother that morning, asking that the caravan from the palace leave with all haste. He'd heard about the plague in Constantinople, and he worried that the gates of the city might be closed to travellers. A sudden shout roused him from his thoughts—someone had sighted a deer. He spurred his horse toward the sound, then pulled hard on the reins. Ahead of him, he saw his brother slump in the saddle, a spear lodged in his leg. How could Ahmet have been so careless and ride ahead of his bodyguard?

The prince saw a group of Bulgar horsemen, cloths tied around their foreheads, their rough smocks belted at the waist. Each of them brandished a sword, and some were firing arrows at him and his men.

'Protect Prince Ahmet. Fall in line. Fight them off. Send for reinforcements!' he yelled.

His brother had fallen forward onto the horse's neck. A soldier caught the reins of Ahmet's horse, and one of Ahmet's bodyguards mounted the prince's horse. Holding the injured prince and the reins, he rode toward the palace. Prince Orhan, flanked by six of his men, drew his sword and dashed through a hail of arrows toward the Bulgars.

After they had routed the small group of Bulgars, Orhan turned Akkula and galloped toward the palace. He was desperate to visit his wounded brother, Ahmet. He arrived in the inner courtyard, dismounted, and looked around. A small group of soldiers, their faces grave, greeted him. One of Prince Ahmet's generals stepped forward and bowed.

'Your highness.' The soldier cleared his throat. 'God grant you comfort.' He bowed his head. 'His highness, Prince Ahmet, has passed away. His mother requests your presence as soon as possible.'

Orhan could hardly believe that his brother was dead. Only an hour before, he had ridden alongside him, laughing and talking. He controlled his feelings and thanked the man.

'*Amin*,' he said.

He waved away the servants and ran up the stone stairs to his brother's chambers. Two armed guards stood to attention on either side of the entrance at his approach. Through the heavy door, he heard wailing and sobbing. He bowed his head and told the guard to knock, then open it.

In Prince Ahmet's bedchamber, his mother, Jihan Sultan, veiled and dressed in black, knelt by her son's bedside, weeping. Orhan put his hand to his throat. His dead brother lay pale and still on the dark-stained bedsheets where his life blood had soaked away.

Orhan knelt beside Jihan Sultan and took her hand. 'God grant you comfort.'

'My only son,' she sobbed. 'Allah be praised, my daughter is here to comfort me.'

'You must leave now,' he whispered. 'Allow me and some of his army officers to prepare him for burial tomorrow.'

He helped her to her feet, and she leaned on his arm as he escorted her to where her distraught daughter and maidservants waited in an adjoining chamber. Orhan said his condolences and took his leave with a heavy heart. He retired to his own chambers to think and pray, then called for three of Ahmet's soldiers to help with the painful task of washing and preparing his brother's body for burial the following day.

Thank God, my mother will be here soon, Orhan thought. He crossed to his worktable and composed several letters, including one to his mother. He knew they were setting off soon. The dispatch rider could intercept the travelling group, and the letter would forewarn his mother.

Orhan looked up from the parchments he was sorting on his brother's desk. 'Come!'

A servant entered and stood, head bowed, at a respectful distance.

'Yes?'

'Sire, Ersan Pasha, Prince Ahmet's chief counsellor, is here as you requested.'

'Tell him to come in.'

Ersan Pasha entered, bowed, and with lowered eyes, waited for the prince to speak. Orhan greeted him and asked if he knew when his brother Prince Murad would arrive to take over the governorship.

'Your highness, Prince Murad has refused the position of Prince Governor of Edirne,' the man said.

'Refused? But the pādishah ordered it!' Orhan jumped to his feet.

The man looked uncomfortable and said nothing.

'Does the sultan know this?'

'A fast rider has just arrived. He brings news that Prince Murad has heard of the death of his brother, Prince Ahmet. He intends to visit the pādishah in person, sire.'

Orhan, his hand on his forehead, stared at Ersan Pasha. 'You mean Prince Murad is going to Constantinople?'

'Yes, sire. Our informant tells us he is preparing to leave Manisa tomorrow.'

Orhan rubbed his temples with his fingers. Allah be praised, what were Murad's plans? He dismissed the man and sent a servant to find Hafız Pasha, his friend and chief commander. He needed to discuss the news with a tactician.

If Murad petitioned the sultan and asked to stay in the capital, he, Orhan, would have no choice but to stay in Edirne as Prince Governor. Both princes knew that when the sultan died, the first prince to arrive in the capital and lay claim to the Sword of Osman would become the next sultan. Despite Murad being *shezade*, crown prince and firstborn son of the sultan, he would not automatically succeed his father. Orhan knew that if Murad deposed the pādishah, Murad's supporters would then hunt him down and kill him. The sultan had only two surviving sons, himself and Murad. On the death of the pādishah, one of them had to die.

Prince Ahmet's chief general, Ali Pasha, had already shown Orhan the arrow that killed his brother. It was not an enemy arrow, but an Ottoman one. Murad's soldiers, disguised as Bulgars, had killed Ahmet. They were probably an advance cohort on their way to Constantinople.

Was he next? Orhan ran his fingers through his hair; he had to act swiftly.

A servant showed Hafız into the chamber, and Orhan felt relieved to see him.

'I am returning to Constantinople, Hafız Pasha. You must stay as interim governor. I expect you've heard that Murad is about to leave Manisa and ride to the capital?'

'Yes, sire.'

Hafız touched his forehead, bowed, and reassured the prince that he was a trustworthy and loyal subject. Orhan punched him lightly on the shoulder. 'And my best friend,' he said. 'When my mother arrives, she must oversee the domestic arrangements here.'

~

Süreyya knelt on her window seat and looked out over the Bosphorus; the water seemed to shimmer in the stifling late afternoon heat. Although the windows were fully open, the sultry air that fanned into the chamber did little to relieve the stuffiness. Servants had collected her boxes and the chamber was almost bare. She was desperate to go to Edirne, but she didn't want to travel without Perihan. Süreyya clenched her fists. There must be *something* she could do to prove the girl's innocence, and she had so little time left! She dreaded losing her only loyal friend in the harem, the only person she could trust.

Her thoughts wandered to Orhan as she scanned the waterway. If he were here, she was sure he would intercede and pardon Perihan. Süreyya looked down toward the small beach where Orhan had rescued her three months earlier. And he had saved her again when her enemies pushed her overboard from the imperial caique. She longed for the comfort of his arms around her, his warm lips on hers. When they met again in Edirne, she wanted to make love day and night. She hugged herself, delighting in her memories and longing to see him. But despair overwhelmed her. How could she save Perihan?

Orhan, she knew, was the most powerful person in the harem. But he was in Edirne, so the privilege now belonged to his mother, then Abdul Agha. Süreyya had tried to petition Emira Sultan without success. That left Abdul, who had ordered her to her chamber for the rest of the day. Time was trickling through her fingers. There was only one opportunity left for her. She opened her door and beckoned to the eunuch, who stood on duty outside.

'Yes, madam?' he asked.

'I want you to take a message to Abdul Agha.' She hesitated. 'Tell him I wish to see him.'

The eunuch looked startled; only Emira Sultan had the power to summon the agha. 'But madam …'

'Please, it's very important,' Süreyya said.

'I will try, madam.'

Süreyya closed the door on his retreating footsteps and took out the strong box, opening it with the key from around her neck. She counted out fifty akçes, emptied some earrings out of a small purse, slid the coins inside, and pulled it shut with the drawstrings.

The agha arrived sooner than she'd expected. He knocked, and as he entered, he touched his damp forehead in greeting. 'You have some concerns, madam, about your journey, maybe?' he asked.

'I am concerned about Perihan,' Süreyya said. 'I wish her to be released.' She held the purse out to Abdul. 'There are fifty akçes in there for you.' Her voice faltered when she looked up at him.

Abdul said nothing and made no move to take the purse.

'It is for you to gain Perihan's release.' Süreyya cleared her throat. Still the agha didn't speak. 'It is not *haram*—forbidden—to pay for what I want, is it Abdul Agha?'

'I have noted your request, madam,' he said. 'I will send a eunuch with some iced sherbet to cool your head.'

He departed, leaving her holding the purse of coins. Süreyya sat down on the window seat and put her hand over her thumping heart. She had tried to bribe the most powerful person in the harem after Emira Sultan. Had she made a grave error? And when Emira heard about it, would she send the guards to arrest her as well?

Day faded to night outside the window as Süreyya sat on her divan with hands clenched, wondering if she too was about to be arrested. She looked across the water at the dimly lit minaret of a mosque. She imagined the *muezzin* climbing the stairs to call the faithful to *Isha*, the last prayer call of the day. Süreyya knelt by her bed as *Isha* echoed over the city. She clutched the silver cross that the Greek priest had given her and prayed for Perihan's soul. Muezzins in other mosques repeated the call, and it hung on the sultry air. It was time for the execution boat, with Perihan on board, to leave on the night tide. Süreyya wept as she prayed.

Someone knocked sharply on her door, and Süreyya scrambled to her feet, pushing the cross into the pocket of her gown. 'Come!' she called, taking a step back. Abdul Agha towered over her in the doorway of her chamber. She clutched her throat with both hands.

'You are not under arrest,' Abdul said quietly.

Süreyya steadied herself on the door frame, unable to catch her breath.

'You have a visitor,' the agha said. He turned and ushered a weeping girl forward.

'Perihan! You're alive!' Süreyya gasped.

Abdul eased the door open wider and gently pushed the former prisoner across the threshold. He closed the door and stood with his back to it while the two women embraced.

'Oh madam, they …' Perihan sobbed, unable to get the words out as she clung to Süreyya.

The servants had dressed her in her usual white gown and a long-sleeved embroidered tunic. She wore no jewellery, befitting a lowlier status than before. Her thick tresses smelled clean, as if she'd been to the hamam. But when had they freed her? Süreyya wondered. While she calmed the girl, Süreyya looked across at Abdul in confusion.

'Why did no one tell me about Perihan's release earlier?'

'Madam, you must learn the ways of the harem,' Abdul said.

'The ways of the harem?' she repeated.

He raised his black hand, showing the dark lines etched in the pink skin of his palm.

'As the proverb says: "Eat the grape and do not ask where it comes from." The girl is free. *Allah'ya Şükür*—Give thanks to God.'

'But who did this?'

'Süreyya Jariye.' Abdul frowned. 'No questions. Speak to no one about your thoughts or your plans. Nor speak of Prince Orhan's actions, even to this jariye, Perihan.'

'But whom can I trust?'

'No one, madam,' he said. 'Even the highest in the harem may stoop to dishonourable actions to test others.' He paused and gave Süreyya a hard look. 'Your loyalty to this slave girl is admirable, but beware of being impulsive.'

'But it was unfair …'

Abdul's deep-set black eyes met hers for a moment. 'The harem can be a dangerous place. Learn from this.'

Süreyya opened her mouth to speak, but seeing the look on Abdul's face, she changed her mind.

'As you know, his highness, Prince Orhan, wishes you to travel to Edirne with his mother tomorrow.'

Perihan, standing next to Süreyya near the divan, squeezed her hand, but didn't dare look up.

'The jariye may sleep here tonight.' Abdul glanced at Perihan and pointed to the smaller divan. 'There is a box of clothes on the wagons for her. Just after dawn prayers tomorrow, I will accompany you to the carriages. The journey to Edirne will take four days. You and Perihan Jariye will be in the same carriage. At night you will sleep in tents under guard.' Abdul continued with his instructions. 'There will be four carriages. Emira Sultan is taking several of her own waiting women with her, and two other odalisques from the harem. Emira Sultan believes her son must have a choice.'

Süreyya stared at Abdul. Other women from the harem? Ignoring Abdul's warnings, she voiced her opinion. 'But the prince requested for *me* to come!'

The agha frowned and responded tersely. 'It is Emira Sultan's wish,' he said. 'I repeat, Süreyya Jariye, you must learn to accept the ways of the harem, not dispute them.'

Süreyya's skin prickled with alarm. So Emira was still trying to keep her son away from her. Which odalisques were going to Edirne? She didn't dare ask Abdul—she would find out tomorrow. Perhaps the prince had requested it; he wanted a different woman each night. As is his right, she reminded herself. Why then had he sent letters full of love to her?

The agha put his hand across his heart and bowed as the last phrases of *Isha* echoed around the palace.

'I must leave you and pray. Do the same and thank Allah for Perihan Jariye's deliverance. I will pray that Allah grants you a safe journey.'

Abdul walked along the stone passageway toward the Mosque of the Black Eunuchs and sighed. He had done everything in his power to aid both Süreyya Jariye and Emira Sultan. A grim smile played around his lips. True, the girl was brave, but in trying to manipulate her, Emira Sultan herself had played a dangerous game.

Süreyya had learned how to survive in the harem. As soon as she'd offered him the akçes as a bribe that he'd refused, he visited Emira Sultan and informed her. She ordered the immediate release of the girl. Süreyya, the Russian slave, had passed the test. He hoped Emira's son never found out what his mother had done. She had tested the girl who had caught the prince's eye, *and* put her in danger at the slave market. Abdul knew that Prince Orhan would be furious. He might banish his mother to a distant province. The agha vowed that the prince would never hear about his mother's behaviour from him.

He shook his head as he washed at the fountain in the mosque courtyard. 'We must all accept the ways of the harem,' he murmured.

He shuffled off his shoes and stepped into the holy building. Abdul held out his upturned palms to Allah and cleared his mind of everything but the divine.

As soon as the door closed, Perihan burst into a flood of thankful tears. 'They were going to drown me tonight!'

'Come, we must wash and pray and then give thanks for your escape from death.'

Süreyya laid out two small silk prayer mats in front of the mihrab, which was set in the wall. She whispered a prayer of thanks to the Virgin Mary before kneeling to thank Allah. After prayers, servants arrived and prepared the divans for sleeping. Perihan fell asleep at once, but sleep eluded Süreyya as she turned over Abdul's words in her mind: *You must learn to accept the ways of the harem* ... If the prince wished to sample the delights of other women as well, she could do nothing about it. A tear trickled down her cheek, then another, but she brushed them away and clenched her fists. She would fight for the prince's love if necessary.

Several servants woke Süreyya and Perihan for pre-dawn prayers and helped them dress. Perihan adjusted her plain thigh-length sleeveless vest over her cotton shift. Süreyya's shift was also white, but made from silk and fine wool, and her jewelled sleeveless vest was more elaborate than the one Perihan wore. The servants helped both women into warm cloaks to protect them from the slight chill and large scarves to cover their hair. Roshan Kalfa came into the chamber to check that Perihan had helped to dress her mistress correctly.

'It is a great honour for you, Perihan Jariye, to be included in the royal party. Remember your training. Speak only when spoken to by Emira Sultan or her ladies. And do not gossip with the servants in Edirne about your mistress or any of the other women.'

Perihan bowed her head. 'I will be silent, Roshan Kalfa,' she said. 'But will there be bandits on the road?'

'I doubt if common bandits will attack you,' Roshan Kalfa reassured her. 'You have an escort of outriders around the carriages. In addition, over one hundred Janissary soldiers are fronting and following the carriages. Remember, Perihan Jariye, when Abdul purchased you, you were a slave. Now you have been accepted into the imperial palace of the Ottoman sultan. You will be well protected on your journey.

Abdul Agha held a burning torch aloft as they walked down the stone stairs to the entrance area of the harem accompanied by Roshan Kalfa. Süreyya's step faltered—the two Polish odalisques were waiting with a couple of servants near the large door. Her heart clenched; both women, now transformed into odalisques since their purchase in the slave market, were outstandingly beautiful. Emira had chosen well.

'The prince's mother has allowed us to go to Edirne,' the dark-haired one said in her halting Turkish. Her excited eyes met Süreyya's above her face covering.

Roshan Kalfa grasped Süreyya's hands. 'God bless your journey,' she said. 'Perihan Jariye, I am glad that Allah saw fit to spare you.'

'There is still plague in the city,' Abdul announced. 'The servants have placed herbs around the inside of each carriage to ward off the foul air. Keep your faces covered at all times as you travel through the city. It will be safe to remove your face covering, but *only* inside the carriage, when you are on the Edirne Road and you can breathe the country air.'

Roshan Kalfa stood back as Abdul opened the door of the harem, and the women stepped outside. 'Allah give you a safe journey to Edirne, and a safe return,' she repeated.

The young boy, Sami, smiled and waved as he stood with the kalfa in front of the heavy door.

'The morning air is cool,' Abdul said as they stood on the path outside. 'But the day will be hot again. You will stop for refreshments.'

As they walked along the path, Süreyya thought about the Polish odalisques. Of course, Emira Sultan would bring these women with her. She had chosen them herself from the slave market and Süreyya, disguised as a kira, had been there. But the girls must never know she had witnessed their degradation. How different they were now. And how fickle was fate, that they were her rivals.

'We may have to share our tent with them,' Perihan muttered.

'No matter,' Süreyya replied.

'We are leaving the third courtyard—the imperial courtyard—through the Gate of Felicity,' Abdul said over his shoulder.

The dome over the grand gateway reflected the rays of the early morning sun as it emerged through the haze.

'It's beautiful, isn't it?' Süreyya whispered to Perihan.

'Madam, I did not know the palace was so large—or so magnificent!' The girl's rounded eyes met hers.

They followed Abdul through a door in the gateway's high arch. Süreyya looked around. The ornate doorway through which she'd just passed was huge. Above the door, masters of calligraphy had painted quotations from the Koran in gold. They were now in the second courtyard, which had a covered walkway all around it, supported by white marble columns embellished with gold at the top and at the base.

'It's magnificent!' she breathed.

Sequestered in the harem, Süreyya too had not appreciated the size or extent of the palace, or its appointed buildings. Orhan would inherit this splendid place when he became sultan! She walked with lowered eyes as instructed, but stole a glance at her surroundings. They were now passing through a large garden of lawns and shady trees. Five paths crossed the grass, and she risked a look to one side. She remembered the smell of fresh bread and cooking from before, as they passed the palace kitchens. She slowed and gazed at an elaborate building even more richly decorated in gold and marble than the gateway.

'What's that building, Abdul?' she asked.

'Don't stop, Süreyya Jariye!' the agha chided. 'That's the council building, where the sultan meets with his ministers. Your carriages are waiting in the first courtyard, outside the *Bâbüsselâm*—the Gate of Salutation.'

They walked through the gate. Several Janissaries, in their orange uniforms and white hats, stood to attention on either side of the door in the gateway. They bowed their heads as Abdul hurried his charges through to a wide courtyard with a beaten mud floor.

Her teacher had told her this was where the common people could send requests for consideration by the sultan. Six carriages were waiting, their horses shifting and snuffling. Süreyya felt a surge of excitement—she was about to leave the palace and follow the same route Orhan had taken to Edirne, almost three months since.

Servants helped the women into the vehicles, and Süreyya and Perihan arranged themselves on the velvet padded seats, moving the thick cushions around to make themselves more comfortable. After he'd spoken to them, Süreyya could hear Abdul giving the same instructions to the others as he went from carriage to carriage.

'Keep your faces covered until you leave the city. The plague has taken many people,' he warned.

He checked on Süreyya's comfort, and that the servants had delivered packages of food and drink to them for the first part of the journey. From the carriage behind her, Süreyya could hear the Polish odalisques chattering in their own language. She felt a wave of jealousy. Orhan had written to *her*. They had made love; surely he loved *her*. Was this another of Abdul's 'ways of the harem' that he insisted she must accept?

'You have an armed escort riding beside you, as have the other carriages,' Abdul said from where he stood at their carriage door. 'You are fortunate you do not have four persons to a carriage, like the other women,' he added.

He took a step back, and the large carriage wheels rolled forward slowly over the beaten mud surface of the first courtyard.

'Goodbye, Abdul Agha,' Süreyya said.

'*Güle güle!*—Go with smiles. God protect you on your journey.' He touched his hand to his forehead, then to his heart, and inclined his head.

With a jolt, their cumbersome, curtained carriage rumbled out the gates, and onto the streets of Constantinople. Through the narrow curtain panels of thin silk, Süreyya saw a few people lining the streets on either side of the main gate into the first courtyard, defying the plague order that everyone must stay home. Like many others in Constantinople, they had turned out after morning prayers to point and wave at the royal procession. Some hung out of windows and cheered as the long line of Janissary soldiers rode and marched ahead of the six imperial carriages.

Süreyya longed to see Orhan again after many months apart, but she had to accept that she was just one of the many women in his harem.

CHAPTER 16

$\mathcal{E}$arly in their journey, a cool breeze blew from the Sea of Marmara, but when the road led away from the water and the sun rose higher in the sky, the air inside the carriage became stuffy. After the excitement of the busy streets of Constantinople, they saw nothing but a tedious landscape of flat yellow land, scattered farms, villages, and distant hills.

Most of the road between the two important cities was paved, but the vehicle lurched frequently when it hit a pothole. Despite the padded seats, it was not a comfortable ride, and Süreyya's back and head ached from being bumped over the rough road. They stopped a few times for refreshments, and arrived at the first camp in the late afternoon.

Süreyya stepped into the vaulted interior of their blue silk-lined tent. It was big enough to house the Polish odalisques and herself as well as their servants. Emira Sultan and her retinue, she learned, were staying elsewhere each night. The servants from the palace busied themselves, making sure the plush divans around the silk walls were ready for sitting and sleeping.

'I can't believe we're in a tent!' Perihan whispered.

When the evening meal arrived, she was even more amazed. 'It's just like the food we have in the palace, madam!'

At night, despite the enclosure being guarded, a shared terror of the pitch-black terrain on the other side of the silk walls united the women and their servants.

'I heard something outside,' Perihan said.

The Polish girls, Ayşe and Oya, whispered and whimpered in their own language in the dark.

'It's only the guards patrolling the camp,' Süreyya said in slow Turkish to them. She, too, felt nervous when she heard creaking and shifting noises from the other side of the silk walls. During the night, the mournful screech of an owl startled them all awake. Süreyya didn't object when Perihan begged to squeeze into her divan with her.

The final day of the long journey, like the other three, was tedious and uncomfortable.

'Oh, madam, when are we ever going to get there?' Perihan wailed.

They spent their time shooing flies out of the carriage and fanning themselves as the cool morning turned to a sultry day. In the distance they heard the rumble of thunder.

Prince Orhan's secretary finally brought the news he'd been waiting for.

'Your highness.' The man bowed. 'The Edirne escort has met the Constantinople carriages. They're expected before afternoon prayers.'

Orhan opened the door and walked across the palace garden in the warm, late afternoon air. He pulled his shoulders back and inhaled the smell of the distant pine forests and the ripening fruit in the palace orchards. As he hurried across the grass, feeling happier than he had for weeks, he acknowledged the palace gardeners, who had stopped their work and stood with bowed heads.

He paused at one of the many ponds. On seeing him, the fish rose to the surface, rippling the water, their mouths opening in anticipation.

Orhan scattered fish food from an earthenware pot and observed them for a minute as they flicked their tails. The sunlight caught their golden backs, and he saw his own shadow reflected in the shimmering blue pool. His mind strayed to Süreyya, and he felt the familiar stirring in his body. He lingered by the water, yearning to see her and make love to her again.

Orhan ran up the stone steps to the top of the Prince's Tower. From this central palace building, he could see the multi-coloured expanse of the geometrical gardens below, as well as the surrounding countryside. He leaned on the rough wall and shaded his eyes against the sun. This was where his great-grandfather, the young sultan, Mehmed the Second, had stood when Edirne was the old capital. It was from here that he had gathered his troops for his successful assault and conquest of Constantinople.

The prince narrowed his eyes and saw a faint plume of dust on the horizon. The caravan from Constantinople was making its way toward him. At last, he would see Süreyya again. His mother had hinted at 'an early birthday gift'. But he would have everything he wanted when Süreyya arrived. What more could his mother give him? Orhan remained in the fresh air for as long as possible, then returned to his desk. He continued to sort his deceased brother's papers. But his mind kept wandering along erotic pathways.

'Oh, madam, I can't believe we're here!' Perihan clapped her small hands as the carriages trundled through an archway into an enclosed courtyard.

Feeling stiff and tired, the relieved travellers stepped down from the carriage, helped by the many servants who hovered around them. Süreyya breathed in the pine-scented air, and for a moment she felt a pang of homesickness for the pine forests of her homeland. A tall black man, dressed like Abdul, in flowing yellow robes and white turban, welcomed the veiled women and their ladies.

'Welcome ladies.' He bowed. 'I am Yusuf, the Kızlar Ağası. I am in charge of the women of the late prince's harem,' he announced, and with an elegant gesture, he indicated the kalfa. 'This is Zahra Kalfa, the Mistress of the House.'

The new arrivals gathered in a group behind Emira Sultan, who wore a splendid purple jewelled gown. Süreyya, still in her plain clothes, scanned the honey-coloured walls of the palace, wondering where Orhan's chambers were. She felt a glow of excitement—he was *here* and she would see him soon. Emira Sultan's voice rose above the buzz of the servants' chatter.

'Where is my son? Doesn't he know I've arrived?'

The words had barely left her lips when Orhan strode into the courtyard. Süreyya blushed when she saw him, remembering the intimate times they'd spent together. Behind him, Süreyya recognised Hafız Pasha, the pock-marked man she'd seen when the prince saved her from drowning. Now she knew he was the prince's closest friend and a general in the Ottoman army.

Orhan, dressed in a gold-threaded light beige kaftan, strode across the shaded courtyard to his mother, his hand on his heart. He wore a matching turban, and the diamond at its centre caught the last of the sunlight. She smiled to herself; his hair had escaped from under his turban in places, and he'd fastened the open neck of his kaftan with the crescent brooch. He knelt before his mother, kissed her hand, and raised it to his forehead. Süreyya watched the scene from behind her veil as a hush fell over the onlookers.

'*Hoş geldiniz, Annejim*—welcome, dearest mother.' He rose to his feet.

'*Hoş bulduk aslanım*—we found welcome, my lion.' She smiled, then cast a disdainful glance around the dusty courtyard. 'I see Edirne has not changed for the better.'

Süreyya, standing with the other women, searched the prince's face. Would he recognise her behind her veil? Prince Orhan stood back and bowed his head, then glanced around the small group behind his mother. Was he looking for her?

Süreyya had fastened her silk scarf across her face with her crescent brooch. When his eyes lighted on it, he smiled. He touched his own brooch, bowed his head slightly, then turned and escorted his mother through the arched entrance door of the harem.

Bathed and dressed, Süreyya smoothed her hands over her long, jewelled gown of rose-coloured satin. She adjusted her sapphire pendant and matching earrings. Accompanied by Perihan, she followed two eunuchs to meet the women of the Edirne harem. To Süreyya's surprise, there seemed to be only about sixteen young odalisques in the large salon. The first three days of mourning for the late prince were over, and they looked up, eager to meet the new arrivals. A little girl of about three years of age ran to greet them.

'This is Princess Banu, Prince Ahmet's daughter,' Yusuf said, materialising at her side. 'His late highness's other two daughters are yet babes.' He pointed to the young mothers sitting to one side, nursemaids holding their children.

After some initial shyness, the young women were full of questions about Constantinople and the fashionable ladies of Prince Orhan's harem.

'They say Prince Orhan's favourite has come from Constantinople,' one of them remarked. 'But we don't know who she is!'

Bathed and dressed, Süreyya smoothed her hands over her long,

After the evening meal, Süreyya and Perihan followed a female servant back along the meandering corridors. When they arrived at Süreyya's door, Yusuf, the agha in charge of the harem, was waiting.

'Süreyya Jariye—*Hoş geldiniz*—welcome, madam.'

'*Hoş bulduk*, we found welcome,' she replied automatically.

He opened the door for the two women and followed them inside. Glancing at Perihan, he asked Süreyya if he could trust her waiting woman.

'Of course!'

'His highness, Prince Orhan, desires your company. I will escort you when you are ready.'

He showed her some clothes that a servant had laid on the bed. They were the same ones she'd worn on her very first visit to the prince's chambers in Constantinople. Had Abdul, knowing the ways of the harem as he did, insisted they were included in her boxes?

'He orders that only your personal maidservant should help you dress. He chooses not to encourage harem gossip.' Yusuf shrugged, reminding her of Abdul.

'I will return after you have changed. Please be quick. The prince is impatient to see you.'

Süreyya blushed. The prince was *impatient* to see her.

'Thank you, Yusuf Agha,' she said. 'I will call you.'

The eunuch nodded and retreated from the chamber.

After Süreyya had bathed, Perihan helped her into the diaphanous sapphire-coloured gown. Memories of making love to Orhan over-whelmed her as Perihan deftly tied the silk cords of her gown at her throat. Süreyya remembered how apprehensive she had felt on her first and second visits to him, but now she knew what to expect.

'You look exquisite,' Perihan said as she smoothed the soft mate-rial in place. The evening was cool, and the maid arranged a long ermine-lined satin cloak around her mistress's body. Süreyya fastened it at the neck with her crescent brooch. She took Perihan's hand.

'I am so glad you are here,' she told her. The girl's eyes filled with tears and she nodded, unable to speak.

Yusuf Agha knocked and entered the chamber, carrying a leather-bound book under his arm. She recognised it at once: Abdul's *Book of Couchings* from the palace harem! Süreyya longed to look through it. The book would tell her everything she wanted to know about Orhan and his former partners, but the agha clutched it firmly to his body.

'Ready, madam?'

'Yes.'

She followed Yusuf along empty stone passageways, past closed doors, and up a flight of stairs. The agha knocked on a polished wooden door that swung open.

'Good evening, madam. I will take my leave.' The chief eunuch bowed his head and departed.

The large chamber was lit by flickering candles in onyx wall sconces, with furnishing as rich as the Constantinople palace. Heavy gold drapes closed out the night, and the silk carpet felt smooth under her feet. She was alone; both the eunuch who had opened the door and Yusuf had disappeared. She put her hands to her burning cheeks, trying to quell her racing heart.

'Süreyya, at last.' Orhan stepped out of the shadows.

Startled, she put her hand on the brooch at her throat and looked down at the ornate silk carpet. 'Your highness.' She bowed her head.

'Süreyya,' he said her name again quietly.

She heard the rustle of his clothes as he walked toward her. Süreyya made to kneel at his feet, ready to kiss the hem of his kaftan. He stopped her, and folding her in his arms, he held her close. She gazed up into his dark eyes, luminous in the low candlelight. His face was as handsome and kind as she remembered from her dreams of him. The light picked up gold streaks in his dark hair. He caressed her cheek with his fingers, stroking them down her skin, then encircling her mouth. She wrapped her arms around his neck, her knees weak.

'How I've missed you,' he murmured, his eyes liquid with desire.

'Your highness.'

'Call me by my name, beloved.'

'Orhan,' she said as their eyes locked.

The prince took her arms from around his neck. He ran his fingers over the crescent brooch, unpinned it, then removed her cloak, letting it fall to the floor. He tilted her head, and his lips met hers. All the weary days of travel melted away, and a flame of desire engulfed her body. She put her arms around his neck again, and her body dissolved into his kiss. He pressed her closer, his kiss more urgent, then released her and folded her hand in his.

'Come …' He led her to a second, inner chamber.

Candles in tall gold stands and smaller ones in wall sconces cast shadows on the walls. A large divan with a soft coverlet patterned with small red and yellow tulips stood in the middle. The strings of her gown loosened as he kissed her. It slithered to the floor when he slipped it off her shoulders. He removed his own clothes and pulled her close to his hard chest with its covering of soft hair.

'Do you remember the last time, sevgilim?' he murmured.

'Yes, it was wonderful,' she whispered.

'This time it will be even better, my darling.' He smiled.

The lovers lay exhausted in each other's arms. Süreyya returned to consciousness, aware of soft sounds from the flickering candles. She breathed in the heady perfume from a vase of flowers nearby.

Orhan stroked her damp hair, and she smiled up at him, her fingers tracing the line of his firm jaw. He smoothed her eyes closed, kissed the lids, then her cheeks and her mouth. This time, his kiss wasn't hungry and searching, but gentle.

'Darling Süreyya, we are one together again,' he breathed.

'Body and soul,' she whispered.

He kissed her again, and a wave of arousal swept over her.

'I must wash, then I'll return to you,' he said.

Süreyya got up from the bed and crossed to where a silver jug and basin stood on a polished wood table. She poured the scented water into the basin and washed herself in readiness for him.

They woke as *Fajr*, the pre-dawn prayer call, echoed around the palace. The candles in the prince's chamber had gutted and gone out. The sun had not yet risen, but early birdsong drifted into the open window on the fresh country air.

Orhan took her in his arms for a last kiss, and as his moist lips left hers, he whispered, 'I must bathe and pray. A eunuch is waiting in the passage. He will take you back to your chamber.' He hesitated. 'I will call for you again tonight, dearest Süreyya.'

She watched as he walked naked toward his bathing area. He

paused, turned, and swept his eyes over her body as she lay on the crumpled coverlet. He put his fingers to his lips and blew her a slow kiss. As soon as he closed the door, she eased herself off the divan and pulled the coverlet straight. Süreyya steadied herself against the ornate frame of his bed, washed, dressed, and pulled her warm cloak around her body with trembling hands. There would be no soft farewell, she realised.

She tapped on the outer door, and a eunuch opened it. He kept his eyes lowered as he spoke.

'Please follow me, madam,' he said. Perihan, the eunuch informed her as he led her to the hamam, was still asleep in the servants' area. He bowed and departed at the door of the hamam, where even at this early hour, servants were waiting for her.

'We have fresh clothes for you, madam,' one of them said.

So, she thought, news that she had left the prince's chambers had travelled ahead of her. *There are no secrets in the Edirne harem either. Only my own.*

A hamam servant quietly helped her bathe, gently pouring scented water over her body, then wrapped her in a soft towel before helping her to dress. Süreyya sighed as a languid joy washed over her. He had called for her on her first night in Edirne, a night of perfect lovemaking. Surely nothing and no one could come between them now?

CHAPTER 17

On her first working day at the Edirne Palace, Emira Sultan took charge, issuing orders and sending the servants scurrying throughout the palace passageways. She summoned Zahra Kalfa, the Mistress of the House, who organised the day-to-day running of the harem, together with Yusuf Agha, who was in charge of the harem women. When they arrived, Emira was pleased to see that the woman, at least, appeared deferential. The chief eunuch, like his counterpart, Abdul, in Constantinople, stood before her in his yellow satin robes and white turban, ready for orders, but also ready for arguments, she thought. He would need careful handling.

'Prince Ahmet's mother is in mourning,' Emira began as the pair raised their bowed heads. 'Now that the first three days of the mourning period have finished, I—'

'Madam, but there are yet the seventh and fortieth days …' Zahra Kalfa interrupted.

'—shall reorganise the household,' Emira continued, silencing the Mistress of the House. 'I also want to celebrate Prince Orhan's victory over the Bulgars.' She noticed Zahra bite her lip, but she said nothing. 'It will be a modest celebration, Zahra Kalfa.' Emira frowned at the woman.

Zahra inclined her head.

'I want the best food, of course,' Emira continued. 'And two of the Constantinople ladies, Ayşe and Oya, will dance for Prince Orhan's amusement.'

Emira ignored the shocked sideways look that passed between the servants at the mention of dancing during a period of mourning. *My son needs a choice of women*, Emira thought. She was determined to have her way. After all, she'd gone to the trouble of bringing them from Constantinople. She would not allow provincial piety to sway her decisions.

'And the women from Prince Ahmet's harem?' Yusuf asked. 'As your highness knows, they must stay secluded according to Koranic law for four-and-a-half months.'

'The mothers of Prince Ahmet's children will travel to the imperial palace harem, eventually, with their daughters,' Emira answered. The servants nodded as she continued. 'Please make some plans for that. I have chosen two others for my son's harem. I'll point them out to you. Please ensure the others leave for the House of Tears at the conclusion of the mourning period. Most of them are young, so we can discuss arranging marriages for them.'

Yusuf inclined his head, and Emira dismissed Zahra with a wave of her hand. She turned to the Kızlar Ağası.

'I believe Abdul Agha sent the *Book of Couchings* here from my son's harem,' she said.

'Yes, madam.'

Emira nodded and straightened her back. 'Bring it to me. I wish to see it.'

'I regret, madam,' the chief eunuch said, bowing low, 'I cannot allow such a privilege, even to your highness.'

'Of course not.' Emira laughed. 'I was testing you, Yusuf Agha. I know the book is for your and Abdul's eyes only. You may leave us now.'

She bestowed a distant smile on the eunuch as he bowed and left her chamber. When he'd gone, she picked up a large cushion and threw it so violently across the chamber that her braided hair came loose and fell over her shoulders.

'Stupid provincial *idiot*,' she hissed, pushing her hair out of the way. 'When I'm the Valide Sultan, I shall *demand* to be shown that book. Then I'll return to Edirne and *punish* Yusuf Agha.'

She threw another cushion, which sent a glass vase crashing to the floor. Two of her ladies ran into the chamber looking frightened.

'Clear that up!' Emira shouted, pointing to the scattered glass. 'Fix my hair, then send for my son.'

~

After they'd exchanged greetings, Orhan waited; his mother seemed eager to speak.

Emira glanced around her chamber with a deep sigh. 'My servants and I have settled into this inferior accommodation. Now, I wish to know when we may expect Prince Murad to arrive and take up his position as Prince Governor. Then we may all return to Constantinople.'

'Prince Murad is not coming to Edirne,' Orhan replied.

'What?' Emira sat down suddenly on a divan, and Orhan outlined what he knew about Prince Murad's movements. 'I am informed that he is about to set off for Constantinople. It means I may have to return sooner than I expected.'

'What a traitor!' Emira said. 'Just like his mother, Deniz, sly cat. I remember her from the pādishah's harem, she—'

Orhan interrupted her. 'I have appointed Hafız here as temporary governor, and I shall return to Constantinople almost immediately.'

'But I've only just arrived,' Emira replied. 'I can hardly make the return journey so soon.'

'Which is why I feel you should stay here and take charge of the household, Mother.'

'As you wish,' Emira said, giving him an irritated look. 'I have spoken to Yusuf Agha, the chief eunuch. He will arrange for the child princesses and their mothers to travel to Constantinople.'

Orhan nodded and thanked her.

'Fortunately, Prince Ahmet did not have any sons,' his mother added. Before Orhan could speak, she rushed on. 'I've arranged some entertainment for you this evening, after sunset prayers. If you're not busy elsewhere.' She raised her eyebrows.

Ignoring her comment, the prince thanked her, then got to his feet. At the doorway, he bowed his head briefly. She opened her mouth to speak, then appeared to change her mind.

Orhan returned to his work, moved a few papers around the desk, and sighed. Süreyya had been in his thoughts all morning. *Inshallah*—God willing—she would not be part of a public dancing display. She could dance for him—in private. He would send for her again, but he would not permit her to spend the night. He had to rise early.

Last night in his dim candlelit chamber, he had watched her face as she slept, marvelling at her unexpected arrival in his life. It was as if the sun had shone again through the darkness of his previous loss.

When he walked into the salon, Orhan heard nervous giggles from a few of the young women. He scanned the chamber, looking for Süreyya. Their eyes met, and her fair-skinned beauty again overwhelmed him. She was sitting on a divan at a distance from the main dais, where his mother stood waiting for him. Emira Sultan stood between her ladies and two young women, a blonde and a brunette. He greeted everyone, then took his place next to his mother. The other ladies arranged themselves on the divans. He accepted the seating arrangements she had chosen without comment, but shifted so that Süreyya was in his line of sight.

Servants moved around the salon, offering tantalising savoury snacks from large trays. Orhan helped himself to pickled olives and other delicacies from small bowls with a silver spoon.

'So, Mother,' he began as he dipped his fingers in a bowl of rose-water and wiped his hands on the napkin the servant handed him. 'What can I expect this evening?'

'Ayşe and Oya will dance for you,' his mother said. 'Look up, Ayşe.'

Orhan's heart skipped a beat; the girl bore a striking resemblance to Nesrin, his dead love.

She glanced boldly at him before lowering her hazel eyes, then rose and poured his coffee. The servants had threaded her heavy black hair with tiny diamonds and emeralds on a gold thread, and her light skin was almost translucent.

'And this is Oya,'

Orhan stared at the other young woman. She could have been Süreyya's twin sister, but for her straight hair. He knew what his mother was doing: she was offering him a choice of women. He didn't need it—the only woman he wanted was Süreyya. The prince looked around, his eyes seeking Süreyya's. He wanted to walk over to her, take her hand, and lead her to sit her next to him. But he understood the etiquette of the harem. He would keep her status as his chosen favourite a secret until they returned to Constantinople. He didn't want to be distracted by harem gossip here in Edirne. He had a job to do.

Emira clapped her hands. Ayşe and Oya rose gracefully from their seats and moved to the space in the middle of the large salon. Somewhere from the back of the chamber, a eunuch started playing a slow drumbeat. As the girls started to dance, Orhan glanced again to where Süreyya was sitting with lowered eyes. She knew what was happening. Everyone did.

'Don't lose your heart to the Russian girl, my darling,' Emira murmured to him. 'These two are your early birthday present—take one of them to your bed tonight.'

Süreyya reluctantly raised her eyes and watched the dancers click their cymbals and sway together. Their light clothes swirled around their bodies as they turned, gold bangles clinking on their wrists. Both had firm breasts encased in layers of silk. As they moved, they ran their hands under their breasts and across their undulating bellies, where a ruby flashed in each belly button.

No one spoke during the sexually charged dance, and Süreyya stole a look at Prince Orhan. He was smiling at the dancers as he clapped in time to the drumbeat. She felt humiliated—he'd made love to her, and now was he lusting after someone else.

The dancers finished, walked to the foot of the dais, and waited in front of the prince and his mother with lowered heads. Their bosoms heaved with the exertion of the dance. Emira Sultan slipped something into her son's hand, then Orhan rose to his feet from his cushioned divan with a smile and walked down the shallow step.

'Well done—exquisite.'

He took the blonde girl's delicate hand, opened her palm, and folded her fingers over a small silver mesh pouch.

'*Güle güle giy*—wear it with smiles,' he said.

Süreyya watched as the girl stepped back. She could see the sapphire he'd presented to the dancer through the transparent mesh purse. Orhan was rewarding another blue-eyed blonde with the same precious stone he'd given her. Feeling mortified, she looked down at the carpet. She was determined he wouldn't see how she felt.

He gave a gift to the second dancer and repeated the same words. Another sapphire in its mesh purse caught the light as the girl bowed her head and accepted it. Both girls tittered their thanks, and Süreyya felt miserable and rejected. If he sent for her tonight, she would refuse to go to his bed.

There was a brief silence as the prince resumed his seat. Emira beckoned the dancers to return to the dais. The other women applauded with little enthusiasm, it seemed to Süreyya. She watched as Emira Sultan patted the seat next to her and invited the smiling dancers to sit down.

'I think one of them is the prince's favourite,' a young woman next to her whispered. 'Oh, he's looking over here!'

Süreyya risked a look at him, and his eyes held hers. He moistened his lips and smiled briefly, making her heart lift for an instant. She looked down, then stole a covert look at him as he relaxed on the divan. She sighed, remembering how he'd pulled her against his hard body, how he'd pleasured her …

The doors flew open, and the salon came alive as a troop of dwarfs rushed in, tumbling and strutting. Emira Sultan clapped her hands and laughed, while the little people delighted the harem women with acrobatics and silly jokes. Emira shooed them away and stood up; the chattering and laughing stopped.

'This feast is to welcome my son to the Edirne Palace harem,' she began. 'He will be here for a short time.' She glanced at the startled listeners. 'Dilber Sultan, Prince Ahmet's mother, is grief stricken, of course. For a while, I will be in charge of this harem and the household, aided by Yusuf Agha and Zahra Kalfa. You will hear about the new arrangements in due course.'

The odalisques exchanged nervous glances, worried about what Emira's 'arrangements' might mean for each of them.

'Enjoy your meal. Let us enjoy it together,' she concluded.

Emira Sultan resumed her place next to her son, then nodded to the agha, who opened the salon doors. An army of servants marched in, carrying trays of food: stuffed vine leaves, pilav with pine nuts, lamb and chicken kebabs, savoury chicken with rice, green beans cooked in olive oil, eggplant salad, crispy green salads with fresh tomatoes, *börek*—pastry layered with savoury meat, and a large fish on a platter that was served piece by piece.

'Emira Sultan brought three of the best cooks from the Constantinople palace,' Perihan told their wide-eyed little group.

Süreyya watched as the *cesnici*—the food tasters—sampled each dish before serving it to the prince and his mother. Each time Süreyya looked across at him, she saw Oya and Ayşe tossing their hair and smiling at the prince. It appeared he wasn't averse to their charms. It was a miserable thought. Emira caught her eye and raised her shoulders in a faint shrug.

More servants arrived with plates of sweetened wild strawberries, baklava, and fresh figs. The prince caught her eye again and lifted half a ripe fig to his lips. As he sucked on it and consumed it, his eyes locked with hers. She felt a tingling sensation deep in her body. He finished the fig and wiped his mouth with a white napkin, still keeping his eyes on her. Could he still want her with those beauties to choose from? She felt weak with anticipation. Of course, she'd go to him tonight. How could she resist—or refuse?

The party ended on the call to evening prayers. The prince stood, and the women followed his lead. He turned to them and bowed, then left the salon arm-in-arm with his mother, followed by her personal retinue.

When she returned to her chamber from evening prayers, Yusuf Agha was setting out clothes for Süreyya on her divan.

'His highness wishes to see you again. I will call for your maid to assist you,' he said.

Süreyya nodded and turned away, trying to hide the delight she felt. Despite the other beautiful women who had been presented to him, Orhan had chosen her again. How could she have thought of refusing him, an Ottoman prince?

CHAPTER 18

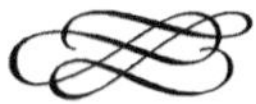

$\mathcal{O}$rhan followed his mother to her chambers. Emira Sultan sat on her divan and smiled at him.

'So,' she said. 'Which one is it to be? The blonde or the brunette? They will both be ready.'

'Thank you, Mother. I will make my decision, and inform the Kızlar Ağası, Yusuf.' He hesitated, then said. 'I must leave the day after tomorrow.'

'What? So soon!'

'I can't allow Prince Murad to arrive in Constantinople before me. He may usurp my father and claim the Sword of Osman as his.'

His mother stood and grasped his hands. '*You* must be the next sultan. Prince Murad is unworthy. It is your destiny, *aslanım,* my lion!'

Orhan thought it wise not to tell his mother that he planned to take Süreyya and her servant with him to Constantinople. He would inform her later. Now all he wanted was to see his beloved. He bid his mother goodnight and ran up the stone stairs to his own chambers in the round tower, his thoughts full of Süreyya. He sighed with pleasure, but on nearing the top of the stairway, he heard voices. A small group of soldiers and advisers was standing outside his door. His friend

Hafız Pasha bowed, and Orhan glanced at the rolled maps he was carrying.

'Good evening, sire. We need to speak with you,' Hafız said.

Orhan nodded, disquieted by the serious expressions on their faces.

Perihan waited with Süreyya for Yusuf Agha's knock and the summons to visit the prince's quarters. She had helped her mistress change into a long thin gown of deep red silk. Although there was an open fire piled with logs in the corner of the chamber, Süreyya shivered and asked Perihan to fetch her mantle as protection from the chilly night air.

'I'm so tired, madam.' Perihan yawned.

'You may go to bed here. I shall wait for the agha,' Süreyya said, pointing to a divan on the opposite side of the large chamber. The servants had turned back the covers on Süreyya's divan, and she sat down to wait as dusk turned slowly to night. The logs in the grate shifted and burned low. Outside the window, birds flew home to their nests, calling to each other.

Eventually, Perihan's breathing as she slept was the only sound in the chamber. Süreyya waited with mounting anguish for the chief eunuch to knock on her door with a summons from the prince. The light had now faded from the sky. The muezzin at the palace mosque called *Isha,* the last prayer of the day, and the other mosques in Edirne echoed the muezzin's voice. Süreyya tried to clear her mind. She finished her prayers, but there was still no word from the prince, and her thoughts turned dark again.

He would not send for her now! Had he taken another woman to his bed?

She recalled Abdul's words: 'You must learn to accept the ways of the harem …'

So, he had chosen one of the other girls. And he had probably already made love to either Oya or Ayşe. Yusuf would write a new name in the *Book of Couchings* below hers. And she would never know who it was. Süreyya sat on her bed, feeling heartbroken, still wearing the luxurious cloak. Of course, he had every right to make love to other women. He was not hers alone, but he had promised he would send for her! She slipped off her mantle, then her silk robe and gown, and pulled on the plain cotton shift that she used in the hamam. She despised silks and finery now.

She lay awake, torturing herself with thoughts of him. Had she not pleased him when they made love? Maybe when he'd seen her again, he no longer found her attractive compared with Ayşe and Oya, who had danced so seductively for him. Süreyya pulled the covers over her head as misery engulfed her. Not for the first time, she longed to escape from the harem and find a husband who loved her enough to marry her and stay faithful. But she wanted that man to be Prince Orhan.

Orhan looked up in surprise when he heard the *Isha*. He had no idea it was so late. All evening, he and his generals had bent over the maps and charts on the long table. For the third time, they traced various routes from Manisa to Constantinople and finally came to an agreement. Once again, Orhan turned his attention to the map. A fast rider had brought new intelligence about Prince Murad; he had now left the city of Manisa, and was making good progress toward the capital. Hafız Pasha had organised for one hundred of the best troops to accompany Prince Orhan on his return journey to the capital.

'Good! If we travel with fewer men, we will be quicker,' Orhan opined.

'I agree, sire.'

'I want Süreyya Jariye and her maid to travel with us as well.'

His friend frowned and seemed on the verge of querying the wisdom of the order. Then he bowed his head without comment.

'And Emira Sultan?'

'She must remain here with you, Hafız Pasha, as I said. I wish you to be the interim governor. I'll complete everything tomorrow and leave early the next day.'

The other man inclined his head again, but Orhan could see that Hafız would rather the prince left on the morrow. 'We will leave at dawn, after *Fajr*,' Orhan promised.

'Sire, everything—provisions, weapons, and men—will be ready.'

The sound of the prayer call died on the night air.

'It is time to pray now, and take action tomorrow, gentlemen,' Orhan said.

The soldiers and counsellors took their leave. After his prayers, Orhan sent for the agha. He wanted to see Süreyya, but it was very late. Was she still waiting for him?

Süreyya woke from a deep sleep and gasped. Yusuf Agha's face was close to hers, and he was shaking her shoulder gently.

'His highness wishes to see you,' he whispered, holding a candle aloft. 'I'll wake your maid to help you dress.'

'No, I can do it myself,' Süreyya said.

She dressed by the light of the candle Yusuf had left, then tapped on the inside of the door. He opened it and, holding a burning torch aloft, walked ahead of her. The air in the deserted stone passageways felt cold on her face, and she hugged her cloak to her body. Wide awake, she followed Yusuf's flickering torch, which lit up walls decorated with panels of marble interspersed with tiles in blue and red geometric designs.

As usual, two guards stood with heads bowed outside the prince's chambers. Yusuf knocked and waited. Under her fur-lined mantle, Süreyya wore her red silk shift. A shiver ran through her when she heard Orhan's deep voice calling them in. Yusuf swung open the door, stepped back, and closed it behind her. They were alone again, but Süreyya stood with her head bowed, her feet sinking into the soft carpet. She heard him move across toward her and saw his bare feet with their sprinkling of dark hair.

'Come this way, Süreyya Jariye. Keep your eyes down.' He sounded amused as he took her hand.

She did as he instructed, and let him lead her across the carpet, then he pushed open a door to the other chamber. Scented candles flickered in wall sconces, filling the warm bedchamber with an aromatic perfume.

'You can look up now.' He was naked except for a white towel he'd tied around his waist. He held out a box to her, smiling. 'Open it.'

'Oh ...' She raised the lid. *'Oh!'*

A heavy necklace of diamonds and sapphires lay on the blue velvet interior of the box.

'From now on, sapphires are only for you, sevgilim,' he whispered. 'But not trinkets like rings and earrings ... Do you like it?'

'Oh, I love it, Orhan,' she answered, touching the necklace with her fingertips.

He picked it up and fastened it around her neck, then brushed his lips along her skin. She walked with him to the wall mirror to admire it. She looked at their reflections in the glass as he drew her against his bare chest, and when she leaned back against his body and his soft pelt of chest hair, she felt something else.

Their eyes met in the mirror, and he smiled. His olive skin, high cheekbones, and dark eyes were a complete contrast to her rounded cheeks, fair hair, and white skin. He held her gaze and ran his hands gently through her hair. Süreyya touched the necklace and smiled at him. He bent his head, and she turned a little, seeing their reflections again in the mirror as he kissed her neck. He turned her around and kissed her.

'Güle güle giy—wear it with smiles and think of me, always,' he whispered. 'My beautiful Süreyya,' he said, pulling her closer. 'Yes, I'm ready.'

Orhan unhooked the necklace and returned it to its box. He took her hand and let the towel fall to the floor. She gazed at his firm, olive-skinned body, his chest with its soft hair, and his muscular legs.

'Orhan!' Her voice was shaky with desire.

She did everything Şefika had taught her. He covered her lips with his, locking their bodies together in tangled lust. Later, when she opened her eyes, the candles had sunk lower. He was watching her, his eyes luminous and deep.

'Süreyya, my soul,' he whispered.

Tracing her mouth with his finger, he whispered he was leaving for Constantinople the following day. She stared at him, speechless.

'I want to take you with me.' He smiled in the half-light. 'You will stay in comfort, at my hunting lodge and other country houses. It will take me three days; it may take you four in the carriage, but some nights we will be together. Now you must go, bathe, and get some sleep, dearest Süreyya.'

He stood at the end of the low divan and held his hand out for her. He embraced her tenderly.

'I couldn't bear to leave you, sevgilim,' he said.

He reached out for his silk robe and shrugged it over his naked body. 'Until tomorrow …' He turned and blew her a kiss before closing the door of his bathing chamber.

Süreyya scooped up her clothes from the floor, then washed and dressed with trembling hands. When she collected the jewel box from where he had left it below the mirror, she caught sight of her reflection. Her face was flushed, and she put up her hand to smooth her unruly blond hair. Her lips were pink and swollen from his kisses, but she didn't care.

She knocked on the inside of the door. The eunuch who was waiting in the passageway opened it and closed it behind her. He kept his eyes lowered as he led her past the ever-present guards and through the cold, silent passages. As she followed him, her mind was in a daze. She was returning to Constantinople only two days after arriving in Edirne! This time she would travel with Prince Orhan.

As she arrived at her chamber, she heard the muezzin calling *Fajr*, the pre-dawn prayer call, from the minaret of the palace mosque. It echoed across the city in the inky night. She spread her mat on the floor and prayed, but her mind wandered from her prayers. Was she the favourite? He had called her his soul and his sevgilim—his beloved, but not ikbal—favourite, so how would she know?

CHAPTER 19

Süreyya woke late to a day full of frantic activity in the Edirne palace. News of her departure had spread through the Edirne harem. During lunch, she saw some of the other women glancing covertly in her direction.

In the afternoon, Prince Orhan's mother summoned Süreyya to her chambers. 'It seems you are returning to Constantinople,' she said.

'Yes, madam.'

'You realise I could order that you remain here, don't you?'

Süreyya said nothing.

'However, my son was adamant that you should return with him, so …' She shrugged. Emira stood and walked in her slow, graceful way to an elaborately decorated alcove in a corner of her chamber. 'I wish you to take these letters and deliver them personally to the ladies who couldn't travel with me.' She passed several rolled and sealed parchments to Süreyya. 'You may give them to Abdul—he will distribute them. There is one for him too. I wish you a pleasant journey.' Emira Sultan reached forward and touched Süreyya's arm. 'My son,' she began, then paused as if choosing her words.

Süreyya waited nervously. Maybe Orhan had changed his mind.

'When my son's former favourite, Nesrin Hatun, died two years ago,' Emira continued, 'it broke his heart. She was the only woman he has ever loved. He seems to have recovered, but I don't believe he will ever love like that again. You must resign yourself to being the first of many.' She smiled, and without giving Süreyya the chance to reply, the prince's mother nodded to her servant, who opened the door with a bow.

Süreyya returned to her chamber, feeling dispirited as she turned Emira's words over in her brain: '… the first of many.' Orhan's own mother was warning her, and she knew her son better than anyone else. Süreyya tried to stay awake for him that evening, but he didn't send for her.

The pre-dawn prayer call vibrated on the cold air, waking Süreyya and Perihan. It was still dark as they washed, dressed, and prayed. A eunuch brought them breakfast, and when they were ready, Yusuf Agha escorted them to the courtyard, his torch flickering in the draughty passage as they followed him. Süreyya shivered and pulled her ermine-lined cloak closer to her body.

Emira Sultan was already in the courtyard, accompanied by two of her ladies. When Süreyya said good morning, Emira Sultan returned the greeting.

'You seem surprised to see me,' she remarked. 'It is the custom that the mother of a prince bid him goodbye.'

'Of course, madam.'

'It will be a dangerous journey, not really suitable for a woman,' Emira said curtly. She told Süreyya to stand at a distance.

Süreyya obeyed and glanced around the torch-lit courtyard. The vast square buzzed with sounds of snorting horses and servants calling in low voices. Beyond the arched entrance, she heard the clink of armour from the soldiers that waited outside. The men called to each other, and the horses snorted and shifted in the early morning air.

Only one man had permission to enter the harem courtyard, and the servants fell silent when Orhan rode through the archway on Akkula, his strong Turkoman horse, and dismounted. His long, grey cloak, with its fur collar, draped loosely over his thigh-length crimson wool tunic and black riding pants. Süreyya felt a twinge of fear when she saw the dark leather breastplate with gold studs beneath his cloak. Did he expect to encounter danger so soon on their journey? Once again, he was a soldier, with a clipped beard and regal bearing. Stray strands of his dark hair mingled with the fur of his Cossack-style leather hat. Embedded in the fur trim was a circle of diamonds set in gold, and in the centre, an artisan had fashioned the calligraphy of his personal turah in thick gold. Below his breastplate, Süreyya saw the glint of the sheathed dagger he was carrying, and she felt a wave of fear for his safety.

He passed his jewelled sword to the servant, who held the reins of his horse. Yusuf Agha emerged from behind the veiled women carrying a torch. With a brief glance at Süreyya, Orhan walked across to his mother. She bowed her head, and he took her hand, held it to his lips, his heart, and finally his forehead. They murmured together for a few minutes, then Emira Sultan turned and inclined her head in Süreyya's direction. She said something to her son. He glanced at Süreyya and nodded.

Was she telling her son not to take her? Süreyya wondered with a sinking heart.

Orhan took his mother's arm and led her to the door. Accompanied by her ladies and the agha, she walked back into the palace.

'I thought she might make us stay here.' Perihan echoed Süreyya's thoughts.

The prince strode across to where Süreyya stood with a bowed head. He nodded to Perihan, who stepped back several paces and stood with Zahra Kalfa.

'Süreyya Jariye, good morning,' Orhan said quietly.

She raised her head, and in the light of the flickering torches, her eyes met his.

'Our journey may be dangerous,' Orhan murmured, his eyes searching hers. 'Am I asking too much of you to come with me? You may stay if you wish.' He took Süreyya's hand and squeezed it gently, his eyes seeking hers.

'Sire, I want to come,' she answered. 'We have an escort,' she added. 'I'm brave, sire! Let me prove it to you again.'

'Dearest Süreyya.' A half-smile hovered on his lips, then he raised her hand to his mouth and kissed it. 'May Allah cast his light upon you, my beloved.'

'May Allah grant you a safe journey. I await your pleasure, sire,' she whispered as the prince released her hand.

'And you, sevgilim.' Orhan smiled. 'You are wearing the crescent brooch.'

In the torchlight, the diamonds of his own brooch flashed against the dark fabric of his cloak. He touched it with his hand, his eyes troubled, then moved away.

'Yusuf Agha!' he said as the chief eunuch returned to the courtyard. 'See that these ladies are comfortable in the carriage. And take care of those I've had to leave behind.'

'Of course, sire. Allah grant you a safe journey, your highness.' The agha bowed.

Orhan mounted Akkula, wheeled the animal around, and adjusted his cloak. Its folds ruffled in the morning breeze as it settled over his dark tunic. He rode through the arched exit without a backward glance. Süreyya watched him go, heard him shout an order and, with hooves clattering, the prince and his company of men set off on the road to Constantinople. As the sun rose, birds called and swooped over the castle walls and servants scurried with last-minute preparations.

Yusuf Agha gave a signal, and a carriage pulled by four powerful horses came through the gateway. The carriage horses snorted, their breath clearly visible in the sharp morning air.

'It is time. May Allah protect you on your journey,' Yusuf repeated as he took Süreyya's elbow and assisted her into the carriage. 'Your escort is waiting beyond the gate.'

When she had settled into the plush seat, others helped Perihan into the velvet-lined interior of their vehicle. The servants handed each of them a small box of food and stoppered flasks of honey-sweet lemon juice. They closed the polished wooden doors of the carriage and bowed. Perihan rolled her eyes in amazement at her mistress.

They were in Emira Sultan's carriage, drawn by four strong fast horses. Süreyya nodded, wondering how Emira Sultan would receive the news that Prince Orhan had purloined her vehicle for another woman.

The driver shouted a command, the horses' harnesses jingled and rattled, and the carriage moved forward through the gateway. Once again, a mounted guard of six soldiers rode alongside them. Süreyya felt a quiver of alarm as they set off.

Would someone attack them? And was she still the same brave woman who had jumped off the slave ship?

Yes, I am.

Perihan's voice broke across her thoughts. 'Yusuf Agha says we're staying at the prince's hunting lodge tonight.'

'Yes,' Süreyya said, thinking of the prince's promise that he'd send for her that evening. 'We'll be staying in konaks in villages, after that, and arrive in Constantinople in four days' time,' she added.

'Villages?' Perihan wrinkled her nose.

'Konaks are large country houses. Be thankful you will not be in in a tent like the soldiers, Perihan!' Lulled by the rocking of the carriage, they slept and woke when the sun was high in the sky.

A worrying message had arrived for Orhan shortly before he left Edirne. Prince Murad had made good time on the road from Manisa. It seemed he intended to save a day of his journey by sailing across the Sea of Marmara. Orhan frowned; his half-brother would arrive before him in Constantinople. As the prince rode, he turned the news over in his mind, and touched the dagger at his waist. Murad would know that he, too, was riding toward the capital. Would he need his soldiers to help him fight his brother on the outskirts of Constantinople? Did Murad intend to depose their father and seize the sultanate? If he did, then he, Orhan, would ride into a trap.

He decided to send a fast rider to the palace and warn them of his brother's plans. His father could mobilise extra troops to meet Murad's men on the Edirne Road. Maybe he should not have exposed Süreyya and her young maid to such danger. But life is brief, he reflected, and he couldn't bear to be separated from her. He would never leave a beloved woman again.

~

The coach, with its outriders, passed a village as *Asr*, the late afternoon call to prayer, echoed across the fields. At Perihan's suggestion, they prayed in the carriage, while the drivers and escort stopped to pray at the side of the road.

When they set off again, Süreyya yawned and stretched. The journey seemed interminable. Eventually, the driver clicked and encouraged the horses off the main road. The ground felt bumpy under the wheels, and some minutes later, the vehicle slowed and stopped. The women exchanged excited glances.

A servant opened the door. Süreyya and Perihan stepped down from the carriage and looked around. They were in a clearing surrounded by pine trees. After the sultry heat of the day, Süreyya patted her cheeks and lifted her veil slightly to let the cool air fan her face. A eunuch from the lodge ran to help them. Süreyya took a few tentative steps, feeling soft pine needles underfoot, then Perihan grasped her arm.

'Look madam, there it is—the royal hunting lodge. It's beautiful!'

Süreyya looked up; the rays of the setting sun fanned across a shingled roof and turned the windows into mirrors. The lower floor was of rough stone, and the two wooden upper storeys, supported by strong timber beams, projected out over the stonework. Boxes of red geraniums hung from windowsills over honey-coloured walls. Honeysuckle trailed in scented profusion over a lattice-covered terrace on the top floor.

The soldiers were setting up camp behind the lodge, and armed sentries stood at intervals around the lower level of the building.

Süreyya felt apprehensive. Surely Prince Orhan didn't expect the hunting lodge to come under attack? It was in the middle of a pine forest—but someone had killed Prince Ahmet while he was hunting. She shuddered, relieved that Orhan, soldier and prince, was leaving nothing to chance.

An old servant hurried forward to welcome them and led them up steep wooden stairs, past an open area with divans, then to an identical space on the top floor. 'The *selamlık*—the gentlemen's chambers— are to the left. This is the ladies' side.' She pointed.

They followed the servant along a passageway with sweet-smelling wooden walls. The lodge was intimate and homely, unlike the tiled passages and vast chambers of the palace. But this was no ordinary house, Süreyya realised, when the servant, Hava Hatun, opened the door to a sumptuously furnished chamber.

'Madam,' Perihan whispered. 'This is fit for a princess!'

'A servant will take you to the hamam, Süreyya Jariye. After the evening prayer, Prince Orhan wishes you to join him on the terrace for supper, madam.' The housekeeper turned to Perihan. 'Your chamber is this way, then your mistress will need you to help her bathe and dress.'

Prince Orhan leaned on the rail of the terrace. He looked across the scented pine forest and breathed in the fresh evening air. A servant approached him and told him quietly that 'the lady' had arrived and was waiting in his chamber. He nodded a dismissal, hiding his feeling of joy at being alone with Süreyya again.

'Süreyya!' He drew her into an embrace. She smiled as their eyes met. 'How was your journey, sevgilim?' he murmured.

'It was long, sire, but not too uncomfortable.'

He kissed her lips. 'Brave Süreyya, come.' He took her hand and led her through the open doors and onto the wooden terrace. 'The evening air is fresh after such a hot day.' He smiled, watching her as she breathed in the fresh scent of the forest.

'It's lovely here,' Süreyya said, touching the honeysuckle he wound in her hair. 'How green the forest looks against the blue sky. It reminds me of home,' she said.

He slipped his arm around her waist and pulled her closer to his body. 'You must feel homesick sometimes,' he murmured. 'Tell me about your life in Russia.'

She bit her lip and looked away from him.

'I know so little about you,' he added.

She sighed. 'I was once a carefree young woman,' she said. 'In one terrible day, I became a captive slave. You might find it hard to understand what it was like …'

'I am an army commander, Süreyya. I have seen many terrible things.' Orhan led her to a seat and sat beside her, still holding her hand. 'You told my mother your uncle and aunt raised you,' he reminded her.

'Yes, after my parents died, my Uncle Andrei and Aunt Ludmilla took me and my brothers to live with them. Aunt Ludmilla is my uncle's sister—she kept house for him. They lived next to the church in our town of Slavo,' she began. 'I was alone with the servants; my brothers were away with my aunt and uncle on church business.' She looked up at Orhan and he took her hand, encouraging her to continue. 'The Tartars invaded early in the morning. They galloped down the main street, two abreast, on enormous horses. They blocked every street at either end. There was no escape, nowhere to hide. They are wild, savage people—they dragged everyone out of their houses and took them captive or killed them. They ransacked our town and set it on fire.'

Süreyya took a breath and hesitated. Should she mention Stefan? After all, he was dead. She decided not to.

'I hid in the back of my uncle's church, then ran into the forest, but the Tartars found me. They killed anyone who resisted them.' Süreyya looked up into Prince Orhan's eyes, and he clasped both her hands in his.

'You must have been terrified …'

'No one could fight them; they were too strong.' Süreyya slipped her hands out of his, then walked to the terrace. She leaned on the rail of the terrace, gripping it with both hands. 'The Tartars dragged me out of the ditch where I was hiding.' She lowered her head, aware of him next to her, but she didn't want him to see her pain. 'They tied a rope around my neck and secured my hands to a stick down my back. They made us walk in groups: walk and walk and walk across the plains toward the Crimean Khanate and the port of Kalla.' The memories were painful. She wanted to be honest, but she could never tell him about her lost maidenhood. 'I don't know how long it took. At night, we ate horse meat stew and slept on the ground. It was the first raid of spring, and it was freezing at night.' Süreyya gripped the rail with both hands, close to tears. 'In Kalla, the slave traders herded us on a ship. They separated me from the others and locked me in a rope store. When the lock broke, I escaped—and you saved me.' She looked at him, her hands across her mouth. Silent tears coursed down her face.

He put his arms around her and she sobbed against his chest. 'And your aunt and uncle, what happened to them?' he asked.

'They must have received the news on their return. They probably thought I was dead. The Tartars ...' She paused. 'The Tartars killed our servants. I escaped from the house, but they captured me in the end.'

'I'll take care of you, Süreyya, sevgilim,' he whispered. 'You're safe here. We are the Ottomans; we're much stronger than the Tartars. And my soldiers are on guard here throughout the night. If an enemy approaches the house, we will kill them.'

Cooking smells and laughter drifted toward them from the military camp at the rear of the lodge. His words and the sounds from the soldier's camp reassured her. After they had taken supper together, he continued to question her.

'Did you ever ride?' He paused. 'Forgive me, Süreyya. That was a thoughtless question. You told me the Tartars arrived on fast horses.'

Süreyya smiled, shook her head slightly, and undid the top button of her gown. 'I learned to ride.'

She looked at him, her eyes challenging. He continued to undo the small buttons as she spoke, a smile curving the corners of his mouth.

'I love horses. I know it's unusual for a girl, but my father bought me a pony. We all feared a Tartar raid. He thought it might save my life one day.' She sighed as he undid the last button and eased the garment open.

'Go on,' he murmured.

'I learned to swim as well, as you know …'

He stood, helped her to her feet, and kissed her neck.

'I used to disguise myself as a boy and ride through the forests with my brothers,' she whispered.

'You don't look like a boy to me,' he muttered.

'I expect you think that's not ladylike?'

'It's exciting,' he said. 'But then, only one lady in my harem …' he added softly as her shift slithered to the floor and she stepped out of it. 'Only one is brave enough to jump off a ship and into the Bosphorus.' He tilted her face upward and kissed her, holding her naked body against his soft kaftan. 'I love your brave spirit,' he whispered. 'It arouses me.' His dark eyes met hers as he took her hand and led her toward the bedchamber. 'And now it's time to make love …'

Much later, Süreyya, still dizzy with desire, allowed a eunuch with lowered eyes to escort her back to her own chamber. She bathed and fell into a deep sleep in the comfortable divan.

She woke suddenly; someone was shaking her hard.

'Madam, madam, wake up. We're under attack!'

Süreyya's eyes shot open. She looked around, feeling confused, then frightened. Pale morning light filtered through the shutters, and she saw Perihan's terrified face close to hers.

'Someone's firing burning arrows at the hunting lodge, madam. Get up, get dressed! We've got to leave,' the girl shrieked. 'Now, madam, now!'

Süreyya scrambled off her divan, bleary-eyed. She heard a thump against the outside wall and grabbed Perihan's arm. 'What's that?'

Servants banged on their door, flung it open, and rushed in.

'An arrow! I told you, we're being attacked,' Perihan shouted.

'Dress in these!' The panicked servants threw a jumble of clothes on the divans.

'Men's clothes?' Perihan shouted.

'Prince's orders. Dress as boys!'

'Where is he?'

'Outside fighting. Be quick!' Perihan dragged Süreyya's nightshift off her sleepy body, and with fumbling fingers, helped her into under-garments, shirt, leather vest, and a warm padded jacket. Other servants helped Süreyya and Perihan struggle into pants and riding boots.

'Hat!' Perihan gasped. She rammed a man's leather hat over Süreyya's hair. She stuffed the curls under it with trembling hands and tied a scarf around Süreyya's neck, then ordered her to turn up her collar. Her terrified eyes met Süreyya's. 'Quickly, madam, we must go!'

Still half asleep, Süreyya's thoughts tumbled over each other as the servants helped her run down the stairs in her cumbersome clothes. Was this a Tartar raid? Would they kill her this time?

CHAPTER 20

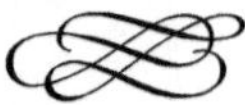

*P*rince Orhan woke when the first burning arrow hit the building. He leaped out of bed and pulled on his clothes. The prince had expected his brother, Prince Murad, to attack them either on the road or when they neared Constantinople, but not pin them down here. He shouted orders to the frightened servants who hovered in the passageways, then ran down the stairs and outside. Adjusting his leather breastplate against his chest, he mounted Akkula, who shifted with fear when he smelled the smoke. Orhan yelled commands to his men and joined them as they returned enemy fire with their bows and arrows.

The sun slid from behind the clouds, revealing the enemy, dressed in Murad's colours and firing from horseback. They were advancing on the hunting lodge from all sides. Orhan castigated himself for not bringing a larger contingent of Janissaries. He had only a hundred, and Murad's men outnumbered them at least two to one. Six mounted soldiers joined him as a second tent caught fire. He'd handpicked them, and they were excellent archers and swordsmen. They continued to return fire, but still Prince Murad's men got closer.

'Sire, you must leave! Get to higher ground,' his captain shouted.

'No!'

'Prince Murad is not with them; he's riding to Constantinople with the rest of his men.'

Six of Orhan's soldiers hemmed him in. 'Your life is in danger here, sire. The throne is in danger.'

The enemy fanned out, surrounding them. Orhan was furious with his brother. How dare he force Turks to fight one another?

'Where are the women?' he yelled.

'Over there, sire.'

Orhan's heart sank when he saw Süreyya and her maid huddled under a tree.

'Cover me,' he ordered. He wheeled his horse around and walked Akkula over to them. Because of him, the women were in terrible danger. What if the enemy captured them and held them for ransom? Or worse.

'Süreyya Jariye!'

His horse shifted from side to side and Süreyya's blue eyes, wide with fear, met his.

He should never have endangered her like this. Orhan called to a couple of servants to take the reins as he dismounted.

'We must get out of here, Süreyya. Can you ride behind me?' He grasped her hand.

'And Perihan?'

'They'll look after her. Watch me,' he said. He gathered his reins, stood on a high flat step, steadied his horse, put his left foot into the stirrup, and hoisted himself into the saddle. 'It's a long saddle—can you do it?'

'I think so.'

Servants helped her onto the step. The large horse moved as she put her foot in the stirrup, and she almost fell backward.

'Lean forward when you mount,' Orhan said. 'Put your arm around my chest and pull yourself up.'

He steadied Akkula, and she tried again. Time was running out. He leaned down, swept his arm around her back and, holding her firmly, helped her up. She gasped as she threw her leg over the horse. She squeezed in behind him and locked her arms around his waist. The horse shifted when a hot arrow hit the ground close by. Orhan patted the animal's neck as six Janissaries formed a protective shield around them.

'We must head for that ridge, sire,' one of them said, spurring his mount forward.

Süreyya clung to Orhan as he pulled Akkula's reins and guided him toward the rough path. As they ascended, the noise from below became fainter. In the east, streaks of pink lit up the long grey clouds. He stopped halfway up the ridge and turned his horse to observe the battle below.

He looked over his shoulder at Süreyya. 'How are you?'

Süreyya nodded as she clung to him, unable to speak.

'I should be there!' he called to his guard.

'Sire, Ali Pasha is leading them. He's a good soldier,' one of them replied. 'It is our duty to protect you, our next sultan.' The riders spurred the horses further up the steep ridge.

Orhan called over his shoulder again to Süreyya as she leaned on his back. 'Still well?' He pressed her hands against his body.

'Yes, sire.'

'God save us.' Orhan glanced down at his ruined camp and burning house as he reined in his horse. They reached the top of the ridge and stopped near a flat rock.

Two soldiers held the horse as Süreyya dismounted with Orhan's help.

'I should have left you in Edirne, Süreyya.' He shook his head and sighed.

'Orhan, I want to be with you.'

'You'll be safe here, sevgilim,' he said. 'We will fight our way out of this.'

Süreyya watched as he walked toward his men, leading Akkula by the jewelled reins.

～

Perihan, who had ridden behind a soldier, joined her, and they sat on a flat rock under a tree. Neither woman spoke, but each flinched when she heard the swish of arrows, the shouts of the soldiers below, and the clash of metal on metal. From there, they could see flames rising from the hunting lodge, and yet the enemy was still pounding the area with burning arrows.

Süreyya pulled her scarf tighter across her nose and mouth as clouds of smoke rose to the ridge. She glanced down only once. Several soldiers lay unmoving on the ground, their uniforms streaked with mud and blood.

Perihan broke the silence between them. 'What if the enemy overrun our soldiers, madam, and ride up here to the ridge?'

'Prince Orhan and his men will protect us,' Süreyya reassured the girl, trying to sound confident. In her heart, she doubted their small group could fight off the enemy if they rode up the ridge. She shivered, remembering the Tartar raid and how they'd captured her. She had hidden in a ditch, but they had still found her. That could happen here, even though a belt of trees obscured them from the enemy below.

Orhan, a veteran of many battles, was desperate to be involved. He was angry that they had forced him to watch the destruction below from the ridge, the burned-out hunting lodge, his men fighting and falling.

In the distance, he heard a sound he'd dreaded: the thud of hooves coming through the forest. Had Murad sent reinforcements to finish him? Orhan mounted his horse, drew his sword, and eased the animal onto the rough path. He readied Akkula to ride down the rugged slope and into the battle.

'Sire, it's too dangerous,' one of his men remonstrated, reaching for the horse's reins.

Orhan shook him off. 'Just get them to safety.' He pointed to Süreyya and Perihan. 'I'll fight to the death with my men.' He fingered his collar where his servant had pinned a *nazar boncuğu*, a blue eye amulet to ward off danger. 'Allah protect us,' he prayed.

He spurred his horse down the slope, followed by four bodyguards, and launched himself into the battle. Finally, the tide of the battle turned and the enemy galloped away into the forest, pursued by his men and others he didn't recognise. Some of the new arrivals rode out of the woodlands carrying their weapons aloft. Their leader raised his palm and signalled for them to stop. As one, they sheathed their swords in their wide red cummerbunds.

One of his guards turned to him. 'Zeybek sire.'

Zeybek! he thought with relief. These fierce horsemen and devoted subjects of the sultan had saved him and his men from annihilation. Orhan rode forward to greet the Zeybek commander.

A burly man dressed in black from head to foot detached himself from the group. Like the others with him, he had sheathed his sword in his cummerbund. He rode up to the prince, touched his forehead beneath his embroidered cap, then with a hand on his heart, he bowed.

'*Hoş geldiniz*—Welcome, your highness,' the man said in a powerful voice. 'I am Seljuk Efe, leader of the Zeybek of Rum.'

'*Hoş bulduk*, Seljuk Efe, my thanks and that of my father, the sultan. You have saved our lives.'

Following their leader's cue, the Zeybek horsemen bowed their heads in deference to the son of the sultan.

'We are your loyal subjects, sire,' Seljuk said. 'We heard Prince Murad's men were coming north to attack you, and we have routed many more of them.'

'My grateful thanks again to you, Seljuk Efe. When I return to Constantinople, I will inform the pādishah of your bravery.' Orhan signalled to a soldier, who tossed a large purse of coins to the leader. 'Our thanks.'

'It was our great honour, your highness.' Seljuk caught the leather purse, a grin lighting his sunburned face. 'May Allah grant you a safe journey to the capital. We will join your soldiers and defend you as you travel through Rum.'

Süreyya and Perihan watched the exchange from their vantage point on the ridge.

Perihan touched her mistress's arm. 'They're the Zeybek tribe, fierce and loyal fighters, madam,' she whispered. 'Some time ago, they came to the capital to declare allegiance to his majesty, the sultan. The kira told us she saw them waiting in the first courtyard of the palace. See that long flap on their sleeves? It's the symbol of their totem, the eagle. The servants at the hunting lodge told me the Zeybek despise Prince Murad, because he demands high rents from them for their own lands further south.'

Süreyya watched Orhan speak to his subjects. He was a natural leader who inspired confidence and loyalty.

Orhan rode among his men, ordering them into ranks and praising their bravery. He dismounted and walked to where the bodies of the dead awaited burial. He bowed his head, said a prayer, and gave orders for their swift internment.

'The fire has destroyed the carriage,' he said when he returned to Süreyya's side, a servant leading his horse. His brown eyes met hers above her scarf. 'Do you have strength for the next part of the journey on horseback?'

'Yes, sire.'

'My escort will protect us, and Ali Pasha will lead the men ahead of us,' he told her.

After she'd mounted the horse, she slid her arms around his waist.

'Sevgilim,' he whispered.

She leaned against him; her protector smelled of smoke and the lush forest.

'Are you ready?' He turned his head, and when she nodded, he urged Akkula forward.

Süreyya glanced back to where Perihan sat on a large horse, clinging to a soldier.

Orhan's strength helped Süreyya endure the long journey. She leaned on his broad back and felt his firm body close to hers. When they stopped to rest the horses near fresh streams, the two women sat at a distance in the shade. A soldier brought them water, hard bread, and tough mutton. Perihan pulled her face when she tasted the food.

'Soldier's rations, Perihan! I'm sure there will be a good meal for us at the next village,' Süreyya reassured her.

In the late afternoon, spent and weary, she heard the welcome sound of a prayer call from a nearby mosque.

'We've reached our destination,' Orhan said over his shoulder, squeezing her hands. 'You'll be safe in the village headman's house, my darling.'

The headman's home sat on a rise above the well-appointed village. The headman and his wife, Nermin Hatun, greeted them at the door. After they had bathed and changed from their boys' clothes, Nermin entertained Süreyya in her salon with a sumptuous meal. She was full of questions about Edirne and Constantinople, but seeing Süreyya was tired, she called a servant to take her to her chamber.

The prince didn't send for her that night. After a deep sleep, Süreyya bathed, prayed, and took an early breakfast with her hostess. Nermin told her that the prince and the Janissaries had already left for the next stage of their journey.

'A new carriage has arrived for you and your maid,' she said, smiling. 'Ah, here's Aisha.'

The young woman, Aisha, served their breakfast without speaking.

'Aisha is my husband's new wife,' Nermin said.

Süreyya couldn't help staring; she'd thought the girl was Nermin's daughter.

'*Afiyet olsun*—enjoy your meal,' her hostess offered.

'*Sizede afiyet*—and you,' Süreyya replied.

The young woman poured two cups of coffee, then offered them fruit, cheese, and black olives. Aisha left the chamber silently.

'I am teaching her how to entertain guests.' Nermin's eyes suddenly welled with tears that she struggled to control. 'My husband married her two months ago,' she said. She poured some water for Süreyya with a shaking hand. 'He can take four wives if he wishes, of course ...' She paused, then the words tumbled out. 'He and I married twenty-three years ago. We were so devoted, I never expected it, and she's so young.' A tear ran down Nermin's face. 'Please excuse me,' she begged. 'I should never have spoken of it.' She brushed away her tear with an embroidered handkerchief.

Süreyya leaned over and patted her hostess's hand. She was about to speak when Nermin rushed on.

'Aisha's chamber is opposite mine.' Her voice broke. 'When he visits her, I hear ...' She sniffed. 'I hear *everything*.'

'I'm so sorry,' Süreyya said. The words seemed inadequate and trite. A chill ran through her body—would this be her future?

Nermin pushed a streak of greying hair under her headscarf. '*Please*, speak to no one about this, Süreyya Jariye. My husband has every right to take a second wife.'

Süreyya assured her that she would say nothing, but when Aisha returned, Süreyya observed the young woman more closely. How would she feel if Orhan took another to his bed when she became older? It could happen even sooner. He had so many women to choose from. But, she reflected, Nermin is a legal wife, something she would never be. Ottoman sultans and princes have favourite concubines, she reminded herself, but they rarely marry. Even Emira Sultan, despite her power and money, was not a wife.

CHAPTER 21

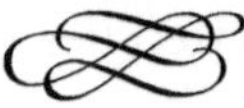

The replacement carriage was as fast and comfortable as
Emira's. At the end of another long day, Süreyya pushed the
window curtains aside. They were rattling down a narrow, cobbled
street with three-storey houses on either side. Bright flowers spilled in
profusion from window boxes.

So, this is Orhanköy, she thought as their coach rumbled through a
set of open gates in a high stone wall.

'Oh, madam!' Perihan squinted her eyes and craned her neck.
'What a spectacular house. Who lives here?'

'I don't know,' Süreyya answered. 'But I think it's our lodging for
the night.'

A guard opened the carriage door, and another helped her down
the small wooden steps. She heard heavy iron gates grind shut behind
them. Süreyya scanned the painted white walls of the residence. Like
Nermin's house, this was on several levels. It was traditionally built:
two upper storeys jutted out over the lower stone one. But the house
was not on a street. A large courtyard, enclosed by iron gates and high
walls, surrounded it. Servants hurried across the wide dusty space to
assist them.

Süreyya inhaled the heady perfume of jasmine from the elaborate creeper that wound its way around the painted shutters of the upper floors.

The housekeeper helped them change into leather house slippers, then led them through a carved wooden door into the luxurious home. Süreyya looked around in amazement as they climbed the wooden stairs to the first storey. Was she in a village? She marvelled as she walked across the silk rugs. Gold bowls and ewers with long spouts sat in alcoves in the wall. Unlike Nermin's house, this smelled of fresh flowers, not cooking. And there was no sound of animals from the lower storey. Instead, the sun filtered through the silver lattice, casting dappled shapes on the wooden floors.

'Welcome, Süreyya Jariye!' A cheery voice startled her.

'I found welcome,' she replied. 'Is that *you*, Zeki?'

She recognised him immediately, the eunuch who served Emira Sultan in the harem. Perihan had told Süreyya that he was originally from Macedonia. She had heard, too, that his ambition was to be chief of the white eunuchs in the Imperial Harem, if Orhan became sultan.

'And,' Perihan had whispered, 'he is Emira Sultan's spy! He reports everything he hears to her. Everyone calls him *dedicoduju*—gossip monger. Be careful what you say to him.'

Zeki's light-brown brocade kaftan complemented his startling green eyes and olive skin. He fussed around Süreyya and told her she was in Emira's country house, called a konak in Turkish.

'Emira Sultan stayed here on her outward journey,' he told the two women. 'The house and the entire village was gifted to her by the sultan on the birth of her son, his highness, Prince Orhan. That's why it's called Orhanköy.' He nodded and patted his small, close-fitting turban. 'It means "the village of Orhan".'

'She owns this village?' Perihan gasped from where she stood behind her mistress.

The eunuch ignored her and addressed Süreyya. 'The revenues have made her a rich and powerful woman,' Zeki said. 'Orhanköy is not a rundown village, like some. This is her house, and she supervised all the designs and furnishings herself. Her next project is to build a mosque in Constantinople to honour the sultan.'

Süreyya stared at him, speechless. A mosque!

Seeing her expression, Zeki nodded. 'Yes, pretty one, a mosque. Imagine how much that will cost! Now, you must visit the hamam.'

When they returned, Zeki waved his hand and dismissed Perihan. He helped Süreyya into a dress of ivory silk. The dressmakers had sewn diamonds and rubies down the pin-tucked bodice and on the edges of the wide sleeves. Süreyya smoothed the skirt, where it fell in pleats from the pin tucks.

'As it's still warm, the silk isn't too heavy.' Zeki adjusted the gown and stood back, looking satisfied. 'The prince ordered these for you.' He picked up a box from a low table and opened it with a flourish. 'Diamond and ruby earrings, dear. Worth a fortune, Russian girl, and a matching bracelet.' The eunuch attached the earrings in her earlobes, and the bracelet on her wrist, and stood back. 'Lovely!' he said, holding a mirror up for her. 'You're ready for the prince. He'll send for you soon.'

Süreyya looked at her flushed face in the glass and bit her lip. Had the sun caused this pink glow on her cheeks during the last few days? She decided not to ask Zeki if she looked too pink. She didn't want him brushing white powder over her face.

Sitting alone after Zeki left, Süreyya reflected on the eunuch's words. Emira Sultan had once been a slave, like her. Süreyya knew Emira was a powerful woman, but she hadn't realised the extent of Emira's wealth.

Zeki returned after a short time and told her that the prince had requested to see her. He chivvied her out of the chamber.

'This way, this way,' he said, hurrying her up the creaking stairs to the top floor of the house. 'Now,' he said, turning to her, 'this part of the house is the *selamlık*, reserved for male visitors only, and'—he gave her a coy look—'*special* ladies, of course.'

Süreyya, holding up the hem of her gown, hurried up the stairs behind the eunuch.

'Here we are, Russian girl.' Zeki extended a hand toward a polished door. He nodded at the two guards, who stood motionless and unblinking on either side of it. Zeki knocked and waited, then knocked again. A breathless servant appeared behind them at the top of the stairs.

'What?' Zeki snapped.

'Prince Orhan bids the lady to enter and wait. He has been delayed.'

Zeki tutted and murmured under his breath, 'Very irregular.' He waved away the servant and opened the door. He took Süreyya's hand and led her into a small alcove, then tapped on a second door. 'His highness might have come back. We have to be sure.'

They waited in silence for a few seconds, then he opened the second door.

'Come in,' he beckoned to Süreyya.

She did as she was bid, and looked around the large chamber. A bright carpet with a flower pattern at its centre covered the floor.

'Silk on silk, made especially for the royal family,' Zeki commented, following her gaze. 'The prince will have to bathe again if he's been to the soldier's camp!' The eunuch raised his eyebrows, wrinkled his nose, and crossed to the bathing chamber. 'I'm sure he'd rather bathe here than the hamam.' He nodded at Süreyya. 'So, I expected this, not the delay of course, but I ordered water brought up. I'll fill the bath,' he called over his shoulder as he opened the door.

Süreyya stood irresolute in the chamber, listening to Zeki sloshing water into a tub. She half-expected him to suggest she should wait in the bath for the prince. He emerged breathless from his exertions and told her the water was extremely hot. He instructed her to stand opposite the door when she heard the prince, and bow her head when he entered.

'Look at that while you're waiting.' Zeki pointed to a chess set. 'It's our Ottoman soldiers lined up for battle.'

Süreyya glanced at the board on a low circular table. On either side, plush padded seats waited for the players.

'I'll be outside in the passageway waiting for his highness.' Zeki bowed and left.

After he'd gone, a deep silence descended on the chamber. Süreyya walked across the silk carpet to the window, then stopped and listened for sounds beyond the door. All was silent. Above the windows, little birds rustled in the eves and a crow screeched, startling her. She knelt on the window seat and looked down. Beyond a high wall, she could see the village houses. As Zeki said, they were well cared for; the streets were clean, and fertile farmland spread out around the village.

A group of village women was coming home from working in the fields, their hair wrapped in white scarves. Their laughter carried up to where Süreyya kneeled on the window seat. She smiled when she saw the bags of produce they carried: fresh peaches, plums, and vine leaves. They reminded her of the Russian countrywomen who had come into the Slavo market to sell their wares.

Süreyya turned away from the window. *I'm a concubine. In my own country, I would be a fallen woman. Damaged goods.* A tear pricked her eyes, and she felt overwhelmed with homesickness. She didn't belong here in Türkiye, among the people her uncle called 'the infidel'. But even if Prince Orhan released her one day, she could never go home and marry. Would she be doomed to live in the harem for the rest of her life? Or married off to a compliant army officer as 'spoiled meat'?

She looked around. The chess set intrigued her, and she crossed the chamber to examine it. She'd played chess with her father when she was a child, but this set was very different. Süreyya picked up the piece representing the king; it was the figure of a sultan in a large turban. Standing next to him, in place of the queen, was an older female. His mother! Süreyya sighed, and her thoughts strayed to Emira Sultan, and how Orhan's mother attempted to wield power over her son.

The other figures wore the uniforms of the Ottoman army, and the pieces representing the bishops were dressed as Muslim clergy. The artist had decorated the richly coloured clothes of the royal figures with precious stones. Süreyya shivered and glanced at the window. The sun was lower in the sky now, and a cool breeze blew through the lattice. The door to Orhan's bedchamber stood half open. She tiptoed across to it and slid into the chamber.

The furnishings were simple: a large cushioned divan with a carved awning, shelves in decorated wall alcoves, and a long table. A polished wooden box in one of the alcoves caught her eye. On its lid was the intricate flourish of the prince's personal seal, painted in gold leaf. Süreyya looked over her shoulder and hurried across the carpet, her ears alert for the slightest sound.

What did he keep in there? She knew so little about him …

After another quick glance at the door, she opened the box. A gold-backed hairbrush and comb, engraved, like the lid, with the prince's turah, lay on the crimson lining. In a corner of the box was a small green satin purse. When she picked it up, it opened like a book. There were two pockets. With a thumping heart, Süreyya slid her fingers into one of them. They closed around a lock of hair, which she withdrew carefully. The curled hair was a rich chestnut colour, held together by tiny diamonds on a silver thread. Süreyya frowned; it was much lighter than Emira's. Whose was it? As she held it in her palm, her breath caught in her throat. It was Nesrin's hair; Nesrin, the mother of Orhan's only child, who had died giving birth to their son.

Süreyya carefully replaced the soft tresses. There was something else; another small lock of hair, much finer and softer. She eased out the dark baby hair, but pushed it back quickly. She put her hand to her mouth. These were Orhan's mementoes of Nesrin and their dead child. Süreyya felt overwhelmed with sadness, and a sick feeling of guilt for touching his personal tokens. Unable to stop herself, she slid her finger into the other pocket and pulled out a lock of her own golden hair. It was the curl he had cut off in the imperial caique, after he'd found her in the Greek village. He had a keepsake of her too! Süreyya felt ashamed that she'd pried into her lover's personal belongings. She crammed the curl back, replaced the purse on the velvet lining, and shut the box.

Süreyya hurried out of the chamber, half-closing the door as it had been before, then sat on the window seat, her heart thumping in her chest. She regretted giving in to her curiosity, but, Süreyya reflected, she knew so little about Orhan's nature. For an instant, she thought of Stefan, killed by the Tartars. She had no mementoes of him or her family. They belonged to her other life. The one she had lost and would never regain.

She heard Orhan's voice and quickly took up her position in the middle of the chamber, standing with her head bowed. The inner door swung open, and the floorboards creaked as he walked over to her.

'Süreyya, my love,' he said quietly.

Süreyya was glad that custom dictated she keep her eyes lowered. She concentrated on his diamond-studded slippers as a blush rose to her cheeks. How could she have invaded his privacy like that? He stroked her face, then put his fingers under her chin. On an impulse, she took his hand and kissed the soft skin of his inside wrist, where the blue veins ran through his olive skin.

'Look up, Süreyya, and let me see your beautiful eyes,' he murmured.

Would he see her guilt mirrored there?

Their eyes met, and his distracted expression alarmed her. For a minute, she wondered if he'd been in the first chamber and seen what she'd done. But of course, he hadn't.

'Darling Süreyya,' he said. 'You look flushed. Are you well?'

Without waiting for an answer, he pulled her into his arms and kissed her mouth. He smelled of wood smoke from the soldier's camp, and his face was firm and soft against her cheek as he held her.

'I'm so sorry I kept you waiting, sevgilim. My captain needed to see me on an urgent matter.'

She smiled, not trusting herself to reply.

'They were expecting a message from an express rider, but he hasn't arrived,' Orhan added. He released her and ran his hands through his hair. 'I must bathe again now. It's dusty in the camp.'

'Zeki has filled the bath with hot water.' She glanced at the bathing chamber.

He took her hand and kissed it. 'I am glad you are here, Süreyya.' He smiled slowly. 'Maybe you would like to bathe me, then I'll relax. I'll call you when I'm ready.'

Süreyya watched as he walked to the bathing chamber. A tide of guilt engulfed her again. She'd invaded his privacy and touched something personal. Why would he not keep something of his dead love? She chastised herself for her curiosity and prayed that she'd returned everything to the same place.

In her heart, she was sure he would never know. It was another secret, like her lost virginity, that she would keep from him. She hated what she'd done. Orhan had treated her, an escaped slave, like a princess. And she was repaying him with lies and deceit. He called her name, interrupting her thoughts.

'Süreyya, my angel. I'm ready.'

She took a deep breath, smiled, and pushed the door open. Orhan sat in the spacious bath, leaning his elbows on either side. The scented water ran in rivulets over his broad chest and curled the damp hairs. His eyes, liquid with desire, met hers. She lowered her gaze, then met his again and smiled. He was ready for her.

'Undress for me.'

She slipped her clothes and jewellery off, until she was naked. 'Thank you for these,' she whispered, putting the rubies to one side.

Her eyes locked with his and he sat up higher in the deep bath.

'Especially for you, my love. Now …' His lips curved into a slow smile, and he passed her a cloth. 'Wash me! Then join me in here. There's space enough for two!'

Later, they laid on his divan, her head on his chest. He turned to her, his face serious.

'I love you, Süreyya, I love you. Say you love me!'

She felt tears welling in her eyes—he'd said he loved her! She was safe at last.

'I love you too, Orhan.' She kissed his mouth.

He brushed away a tear from her cheek and circled his arm around her. She fell asleep against his firm body.

When she woke, he had bathed and changed into a black and blue patterned robe, tied at his waist over his loose black pants.

'Let us have supper together,' he said. 'You may use the bathing chamber. There is fresh water and a robe for you as well.'

After she'd bathed, she dressed in a long white robe. She joined him at a small table, where the servants had laid supper. As they ate, Orhan discussed the skirmish at the hunting lodge.

'I wanted to fight with my men, but as you know, my officers insisted I watch the battle from the hill. But then I had to join my soldiers. You were very brave, Süreyya.' He touched her hand. 'I must leave tomorrow for the capital. I have just received word that the sultan has sent Janissary troops to meet me. Hopefully, we will not encounter Prince Murad on the Edirne Road, but we can trap him between my men and the Janissaries from the palace.'

'Are we far from the city, sire?' His words had alarmed her. Had he put himself and his men in danger because of her?

'A half day's ride for me, a whole day in the carriage for you,' he replied. 'I wanted to stay with you tonight, sevgilim!'

Should he not have left today? But it was not her place to query his decisions. Instead, she glanced at the chess set.

'My father taught me to play. It's a strategic game of battle.' She looked across at the prince and smiled.

'Then after supper, we clash swords!' he said.

Once the servants had cleared away the remains of their meal, Orhan sat down in one of the upholstered seats at the table with the chess set.

'So, master tactician,' he said, 'how should I plan my battles in the future? Did I do the right thing yesterday by watching the battle from the hill?'

'Permit me, Orhan.' She met his eyes, then pointed to a piece that represented the sultan. 'You were in a safe place. The duty of your *pashas*—your generals—here and here, was to protect you. The sultan, or the prince,' she said, extending her hand to him, 'can only move a little way on the board, when it is safe and he is well protected. If the opposing side captures the sultan or the prince, the battle is lost.'

'So, you *are* a master tactician?' he said, shifting forward in his seat, his face alive with interest.

She shook her head, sat down, and moved a soldier-pawn two paces forward.

'Ah!' He rubbed his hands together. 'Let the battle commence!'

They were so engrossed in the game, with first Süreyya's sultan, then Orhan's, under threat, that a loud knock on the outer door startled them.

'*Allah Aşkına!* For the love of God!' he sighed. 'They know I'm with you.' He turned to her. 'Wait in the bedchamber, sevgilim—and touch nothing on the board.' He smiled and raised his eyebrows, then strode to the door.

Süreyya ran across to the bedchamber and smoothed the bedclothes that were still rumpled from their recent lovemaking. She heard him open the outer door, then the murmur of voices.

'I don't believe it!' he exclaimed. After more mumbling, she heard him say, 'Yes, yes, I'll meet them now in the main salon.'

She heard the door close, and he returned to where she stood irresolute next to the divan. He took her hand, his face serious.

'Terrible news, Süreyya,' he said, ashen-faced. 'Prince Murad's ship sank in the Sea of Marmara, several hours ago. They have saved no one.' He put his hand to his forehead. 'May Allah protect me. I am now shezade: Crown Prince of the Ottoman Empire. I'm the last living son of the sultan!'

'My condolences on the loss of your brother, Shezade Orhan,' Süreyya replied, bowing her head.

He took her hand, and his eyes met hers. 'I must leave for Constantinople at first light,' he said, his face anguished. He kissed her, holding her body close against his. 'I shall miss you, Süreyya. I must see my generals now. Zeki will take you back to your chamber. There is nothing to fear,' he whispered. 'You will have an armed escort during your return to Constantinople.'

He released her, took her hands in his, and kissed them. He turned once at the door and looked at her, then he was gone.

CHAPTER 22

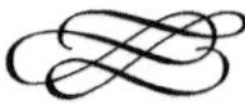

The sun was yet a sliver of gold in the sky when the pre-dawn prayer call woke Süreyya. She shrugged on her ermine-lined robe, ran to the window, and pushed the shutters open. The ranks of Orhan's mounted soldiers waited in the courtyard and beyond the open gates. The horses shifted, impatient to move, their breath like mist on the cool air. Servants stood at a distance; some held torches, and others walked among the riders and foot soldiers distributing cups of steaming liquid.

Süreyya saw Orhan astride Akkula and flanked by four officers. She wanted to call out to him. Instead, she pressed her white handkerchief through the lattice just as he glanced up. He put his hand on his heart and smiled, then turned his horse and joined his officers. The prince raised his fist, and keeping his eyes straight ahead, led his company forward. With a heavy heart, Süreyya watched him ride out of the courtyard. The iron gates clanged shut behind him.

'God give you a safe journey,' she whispered as the sound of the horses' hooves receded in the morning air.

Perihan arrived to help her bathe, dress and pray but her thoughts kept straying to Orhan, wondering when she'd see him again.

'I'm glad we're going back to Constantinople,' Perihan said cheerfully as their carriage left Orhanköy with its military escort. 'The housekeeper said Zeki told her Prince Murad was dead. Is that true, madam? How did it happen?'

'His ship sank, that's all I know,' Süreyya replied.

When she thought of Orhan's journey to Constantinople, she felt fearful for him. Would the remnants of Prince Murad's army attack him on the country roads? But then, he was travelling with a large group of soldiers. She knew her lover would only be out of danger when he entered the city and the Edirne Gate closed behind him. He would then make his way to the safety of the fortified Topkapı Palace.

'Oh madam, I will have to share a chamber with five others again!' Perihan said.

Süreyya nodded. Perihan would have plenty of exciting stories from the outside world to tell her friends. Her own thoughts were still with Shezade Orhan, the son and successor to the Sultan of the Ottoman empire. His mother would pressure him even more to create plenty of heirs for the imperial throne. Süreyya sighed. Even though he had professed his love for her, his obligation would always be to his imperial family and the Ottoman throne.

By late afternoon, the roads became busier. They passed horses, donkeys, carts, and people on foot. Süreyya was relieved that they had four armed soldiers riding alongside the coach. When she raised the curtain, she saw they were passing larger villages. Across the fields, the minarets of mosques rose above the brown shingle roofs of simple wooden houses.

'We'll be in Constantinople by nightfall,' she said to Perihan, but the young woman had fallen asleep.

Süreyya felt her own eyes closing. The evening prayer call from a mosque woke her with a start. The carriage was travelling faster now on smoother roads, and she peered around the curtain. They must be close to the capital. She smiled to herself—she would soon be reunited with Orhan.

Wooden houses clustered together along the Edirne Road. Süreyya moved the curtain on the opposite side of the carriage and caught glimpses of the Sea of Marmara in the evening light. She smelled the tang of the salt air that mingled with the aroma of roasting chestnuts. It reminded her of autumn in Russia. Once again, she felt the stab of homesickness she'd experienced when she'd seen the home-going villagers in Orhanköy.

The carriage halted, and she heard voices as they passed through the Edirne Gate. As it trundled along the road to the palace, Süreyya peered with delight at the busy city. Everywhere braziers lit up the streets, where hawkers sold their hot roasted chestnuts and corn cobs. In the cool of the late autumn evening, people huddled their clothes to their bodies. Several women, their hair and faces covered with large woollen shawls, haggled with street vendors. A servant woman passed, carrying two dead chickens by their legs. She looked up at the carriage, smiled, and nodded when she saw the imperial symbol on the doors.

A sudden longing for freedom overwhelmed Süreyya. But freedom for a woman meant marriage. She knew that the sultan and princes permitted some of the harem women to leave and marry army officers or officials from the palace. But that would not be her fate, and she pondered her future again. She was no longer a virgin. What would her fate be when the prince tired of her?

Perihan woke and interrupted her musings. 'We're home!' she said in her high-pitched voice. She pulled the drapery aside, wiped the window glass with her small hand, and both women watched as the darkening streets of Constantinople passed by.

Orhan arrived in the early afternoon and went straight to the hamam. He undressed, and with a thick white towel around his waist, he sat on the marble bench in the steam area. In the quiet, steamy atmosphere, he tried to make sense of the events of the past few days. His half-brother, Murad, would never arrive in Constantinople. Prince Murad, his soldiers, and their ship were at the bottom of the Sea of Marmara. Murad's other followers had disbanded, and Orhan and his men had had an uneventful passage into the city.

Other thoughts pressed on his mind. He was the sole heir to the throne, and it was imperative that he produce a male heir. He sighed when he remembered his dead son—how different everything would be now if the child had lived. He had cherished the child's mother, Nesrin, and he would have stayed true to her. Orhan shook his head. Süreyya had come into his life like a star dropped from the sky. Allah had smiled on him, and he would cherish and care for her. Perhaps after their lovemaking, she might be with child.

During his father's reign and when the sultan passed away, Orhan knew he must ensure that their diverse empire did not splinter. They could not afford to lose the countries they'd conquered. His father ruled millions of people from the Arabian Peninsula almost to the gates of Vienna.

He thought of Süreyya again and sighed. Maybe his mother was right: it was a luxury for a prince to have only one favourite. It was his duty to make love to several of the beauties in his harem and ensure the succession. Orhan remembered his childhood when he lived in the imperial harem of the sultan with his mother and his half-brothers and sisters until he was twelve years old. As he got older, he had often longed for a family life, one wife, several sons, and a house where they would all live together.

Orhan's thoughts wandered to his half-brothers, Ahmet and Murad. They had played together as children, but it was their destiny to become enemies in later life. The rules of succession dictated that they must kill each other on the death of their father. The survivor became the next sultan—and even though fate had spared him from organising the execution of his half-brothers, *he* was that survivor.

His hamam servant, Mohammed, dressed in his usual loincloth, interrupted his thoughts and greeted him affectionately. As well as being a masseuse, Mohammed was a talented wrestler and had a finger-crushing handshake.

'Welcome, your highness. I believe you've just returned from my land of Rum,' he said.

Orhan smiled as he got up. 'I met your people, the Zeybek, Mohammed. They're brave fighters.'

Mohammed grunted his agreement. 'This way, sire.' He held up a dry towel.

Orhan lay on a warm marble slab while Mohammed soaped his body, then poured warm water over him.

'Sage and olive oil soap, your highness,' Mohammed said as he rinsed the prince's hair and body. 'Made by my wife, Makbule.'

'Your first wife?' Orhan turned his face to the side so he could see the man more clearly.

'First and only, as you know, sire. Many families come to my house, wanting me to marry their daughters, your highness. I say no every time.' Mohammed tutted as he rubbed a rolled cloth down the prince's back. 'Makbule Hatun, the wife, sire, she's given me four sons and two daughters, as you know. Even though the Prophet, peace be upon him, sanctioned four wives, one wife is enough for me, your highness.'

'She wouldn't be pleased if you took a second spouse?'

Orhan knew the answer, but he loved teasing Mohammed and hearing about the antics in the masseuse's household. 'No, sire, she's quite an opponent. She's a large woman, as big as many wrestlers I've been in combat with, your highness.'

He tapped the prince's back hard, from shoulder to ankles, with the sides of his hands. Although it was excruciating, the prince felt his muscles relaxing with each blow.

'She's Zeybek too, if I remember?'

'She's a healthy woman, your highness, with many brothers,' Mohammed answered as he stretched the prince's arms and legs. 'She's a wonderful cook too, sire. She makes *kuru fasulye* better than anything you'd eat from the palace kitchens.'

Orhan doubted he would ever see cooked dried beans in tomatoes and oil on the imperial table.

During Orhan's adolescence, Mohammed had been his surrogate teacher. In his matter-of-fact way, the man had taught the prince everything he knew about lovemaking, especially how to please a woman in bed. No wonder Makbule objected to the idea of her husband taking a second wife.

'Makbule Hatun, sire. She wouldn't have another woman in her kitchen. I'd have no peace, that I wouldn't, your highness.' Mohammed sighed and changed the subject. 'It's a long ride from Edirne, sire, a long ride. Allah be thanked that you are home safely,' he said as he massaged the prince's torso with oil. He rubbed a large rough cloth over him to remove the surplus oil and gave the prince another towel to wrap around his waist. Mohammed escorted Orhan to where his servants waited with his clothes. The masseuse stood back with a deferential bow.

'My thanks and my *selams* to Makbule Hatun.' The prince nodded to a servant, who handed Mohammed a purse of silver coins.

'Bless you, sire.'

Still smiling about Mohammed's wife, Orhan stood while his attendants helped him into clean clothes. As he walked back to his chambers, the late afternoon prayer call echoed from the Aya Sofia mosque. *Inshallah*, Süreyya would arrive shortly from her journey. He sighed with contentment as he made his way along the palace corridors. Guards and eunuchs lowered their heads as he passed.

I can't wait to see her. How delighted she'll be with her gift!

Orhan turned his mind to state affairs; the pādishah had summoned him to report on the situation in Edirne later the following day.

When Süreyya stepped down from the carriage, she was surprised to see Abdul waiting to escort them along their usual route to the harem. She sensed a subtle change in his attitude toward her.

'Maybe you would like to visit the hamam, madam?' Abdul said.

'Yes, of course.'

'Later I will take you to your new chambers.'

'New chambers?'

'Yes, madam,' Abdul replied.

He snapped his fingers and the little boy, Sami, ran forward. He helped them wash their feet, chattering and smiling as usual. The hamam servants then took them to bathe after their long journey.

Roshan Kalfa was waiting for Süreyya and her maid at the door of her chamber when they returned. She bowed her head slightly and asked them to follow.

Perihan rolled her eyes at Süreyya. The Mistress of the House led them along a corridor, through an area Süreyya had never visited before.

'Where are we going, madam?' Perihan whispered. Before she could utter another word, Abdul appeared at the top of a flight of stairs.

'Welcome to your new chambers,' he announced, throwing open a door with a flourish.

'Prince Orhan wishes you to live here from now on. This is a dwelling for the ikbal, the chosen favourite.' Abdul permitted himself a smile. 'There is a divan in the second chamber for your maid as well, if you choose for her to stay the night.'

'Oh madam, it's lovely!' Perihan exclaimed. She stood on tiptoe and looked over her mistress's shoulder.

Süreyya hesitated on the threshold of the exotic chambers, hardly able to believe that this was her new home. She walked slowly into the first chamber, touched the rose-pink furnishings, and rubbed her foot on the silk carpets. Exquisite gold ornaments and gold-framed mirrors reflected her astonished face in the light from wall sconces and candles.

'The next chamber, madam,' Abdul said, standing aside and pointing, 'is your bedchamber and private bathing area. You have excellent views. This way …'

She gazed at the windows as Roshan Kalfa straightened the covers of the cushioned seats.

'You can sit here and watch the ships sailing by,' Abdul said. 'Emira Sultan has approved your title. You are now Süreyya Hatun, and you may also be referred to as Ikbal Süreyya.' Abdul pushed the outer window shutters wide and turned to her. 'The titles mean the Lady Süreyya and Süreyya the Favourite.'

Süreyya looked across to where the Golden Horn flowed into the Bosphorus. On the opposite shore, spots of light lit up the lanes and a mosque glowed warmly. Servants were lighting lamps in the distant wooden houses of Galata, and further up the hill in the suburb of Pera. The waters of the Golden Horn mirrored a rippling reflection of the darkening city that clustered along the shoreline.

Prince Orhan's capital was now her adopted one. He had gifted her a beautiful place of her own. She wondered how she could ever thank him.

Abdul cleared his throat and spoke carefully. 'The prince may take other favourites. Their accommodation will be separate to yours, of course. The size of the chambers indicates the status of a favourite.'

Süreyya turned to him, feeling alarmed.

'At the moment, there are no other favourites,' he added hastily. 'Madam, you may choose your ladies-in-waiting from the servant women.'

Süreyya swallowed and took a breath.

'Perihan.' She smiled at the delighted young girl. 'And Galina—Melek—from my country.'

'Roshan Kalfa will see to it, and you will, of course, have several other attendants,' Abdul said. He nodded to Roshan Kalfa, who took her leave.

Süreyya asked Abdul the question that was uppermost in her mind. 'Does Emira Sultan know about this?'

'Yes, she does, madam. She will return from Edirne shortly,' Abdul replied. 'Her highness will then present you formally in the salon.' He told her there would always be two eunuchs outside her door, who would run errands for her.

'If the prince sends for you, they will be your escort.'

'And can I still visit the harem salon and the hamam?'

'You are not a prisoner, madam.' The agha glanced at Perihan, who looked frightened. 'If you wish to contact the prince, then you may write. A eunuch will deliver your note.'

Abdul Agha asked her if she needed help to prepare for bed, and she shook her head; she wanted to be alone. Abdul pushed Perihan ahead of him and closed the door quietly. Süreyya stood in the centre of the silk carpet, then on impulse she threw her arms out wide and twirled around, delighted by Orhan's wonderful gift.

'I love you, Prince Orhan!' she said out loud, and stretched her arms to the ceiling. She pushed the agha's remarks about 'other favourites' to the back of her mind. Orhan had taken the time to send a message to Abdul to arrange this. He had gifted her a personal space in the palace! And now she had a larger haven than her previous chamber. Süreyya was relieved she might be able to avoid the intrigues and gossip of the harem salon. She could read and study here, or watch the ships as they sailed along the Bosphorus.

There was even a more elaborate mihrab, a niche toward which she could pray privately. Süreyya heaved a great sigh of joy and shook her head in disbelief. Orhan had singled her out; Rusalka, the former captive, was now Süreyya, the beloved favourite of Shezade Prince Orhan.

When Süreyya walked into the salon the following day with Perihan, she felt everyone's eyes on her.

'Madam,' Perihan whispered, 'Abdul is beckoning to us from near Emira Sultan's divan.'

Süreyya looked toward Abdul Agha, who pointed to the seat close to the one where Prince Orhan's mother usually sat.

'You must sit here from now on,' the agha told her. 'Emira Sultan will expect it. This is your area of the salon now. But,' he added, 'on her return, you must wait until she invites you.'

Süreyya walked up the two shallow steps to the long dais, feeling as if many eyes were watching her. 'Thank you, Abdul.' She sat down with Perihan and the three other women she'd chosen as her attendants.

~

Shortly after refreshments, Ezter the kira arrived, carrying her large bag of embroidery silks, ribbons, and trinkets. She had also included small packets of hot roasted chestnuts, a gift from beyond the palace walls. The kira handed them out to the excited women who gathered around her. Instead of silk garments that were only permitted for Muslims, Ezter wore a gown of blue cotton material, similar to the one Süreyya had worn on her visit to the slave market. The kira had combed her thick dark hair off her face and pulled it neatly into a silver mesh. Süreyya fancied she saw a resemblance between Doctor Rebeka and Ezter. Maybe the kira was a relative—a younger cousin? On her right hand, Ezter wore a heavy gold wedding band.

Ezter looked around the salon, as if she were seeking someone in particular. Her large brown eyes met Süreyya's, and she smiled. Ezter spoke to Abdul, picked up her tapestry bag, and walked across to where Süreyya was sitting. After the formal greetings and responses, Ezter smiled and sat next to her.

'Süreyya Hatun, congratulations, I believe you are ikbal, Prince Orhan's favourite!' Unlike Doctor Rebeka, Ezter spoke perfect Turkish. 'Someone told me you're from Slavo in Russia,' Ezter went on.

'Yes,' Süreyya answered, surprised by the other woman's directness. 'Who told you?'

'Harem gossip.' The other woman laughed lightly and took out ribbons and silver trinkets to show Süreyya and her ladies. While the novelties distracted the others, Ezter tapped Süreyya's hand. 'They tell me that once a girl arrives in the harem, they give her a new name.' She handed Süreyya a pair of silver earrings in the shape of tiny bells. 'They suit you, Süreyya Hatun. Süreyya is such a pretty name! What was your Russian one?'

'Rusalka,' Süreyya answered as she tried the earrings against her ears, and looked in the mirror that Perihan held up for her.

'Rusalka, who?' the other woman asked with a friendly smile.

Süreyya put the earrings down and turned to Ezter with a slight frown. 'Rusalka Maria Ivanova. Why do you ask?'

'No matter.' The kira smiled and patted her hand. 'Please accept the earrings as a gift, Süreyya Hatun.'

Ezter collected her bag and moved away to another group. Süreyya watched her go; she didn't know why, but the woman's questions had made her feel uneasy.

CHAPTER 23

After midday prayers, Prince Orhan, accompanied by two imperial guards, walked from his chambers in the third courtyard toward the first courtyard. Today he planned to visit the Janissary soldiers' barracks in the first courtyard before he had his audience with his father, the sultan. The grand vizier, his father's chief minister, would know where to find him when the pādishah was ready to see him.

The prince paused when he saw two men coming out of the ornate throne room, where the pādishah received foreign ambassadors and important visitors. Orhan recognised one man: His All Holiness, George, the Ecumenical Patriarch of Constantinople. He was the spiritual leader of the Greek and Eastern Orthodox Church. When Orhan's great-grandfather, Mehmet II, had conquered the city sixty-five years previously, he had permitted the patriarch to continue living in his residence, close to Topkapı palace.

The Patriarch's robes were plain black, but the other man was richly dressed. Orhan recognised the robes of a bishop of the Russian Orthodox Church. During his time as Prince Governor in Kalla in the Ottoman provinces of the Crimea, he had received plenty of princes of the church in the smaller Ottoman palace there. He frowned, curious to know the reason these high-ranking churchmen had visited the sultan. Was this why his father wished to see him later that day? A feeling of apprehension trickled down the prince's spine. Süreyya had told him her uncle was a bishop. An alarming thought crossed Orhan's mind. Could this man be the Bishop of Slavo? Was he in the palace looking for his niece? Surely not. How could her uncle know she was here?

Even though the morning wasn't cold, Orhan shivered. The churchmen were deep in conversation and hadn't noticed him. He watched as they paused next to one of the marble columns of the throne room. He couldn't see their faces clearly as they stood in the shadows under the wide overhanging eves of the building. What were they discussing so intently? Orhan continued to watch from a distance as the two men conferred for a while. Eventually, a high-ranking official arrived to escort them from the third courtyard. He followed them through the Gate of Felicity, toward the Gate of Salutation, then to the first courtyard and the city gate.

Prince Orhan remained behind them at a discrete distance. He was still curious; why had the bishops attended an audience with the sultan? And a Russian bishop especially. *Like Süreyya's uncle!* He took a breath—surely this had nothing to do with Süreyya? The churchmen could be here to petition the sultan because there was trouble again between the Muslims and the Christian community in Pera. He frowned, remembering that there was a Russian community in addition to a Greek community in Pera.

The churchmen walked across the first courtyard together, deep in conversation. The first courtyard housed the Janissaries' barracks, and it was Orhan's destination. This morning, the prince was going to congratulate the soldiers who had recently fought alongside him. He arrived in the first courtyard at the same time as the patriarch and the bishop. Orhan turned quickly when he heard hasty footsteps behind him.

'Halt! Do not run in the presence of his royal highness.'

One of his officers stepped forward. He seized the arm of a woman in a blue robe and head covering. Her brown eyes widened when she realised he was the prince.

'My apologies, sire.' She bowed her head, pulling her scarf more tightly across the lower half of her face.

'Release her,' the prince ordered. 'Where have you come from, madam?'

Orhan was used to deference when subjects met him, so the look of fear in the woman's eyes startled him.

'From your harem, your highness,' she said breathlessly, lowering her gaze. 'I am Ezter, a kira. I sell ribbons and jewellery to your ladies.'

Orhan laughed. 'Haven't my ladies got ribbons and jewellery enough?'

She raised her eyes, still looking fearful.

Orhan smiled at her. 'Go on your way, ribbon seller.'

Still smiling, he strode into the Janissaries' barracks, where the men greeted him warmly. On an impulse, he crossed to a small window and looked into the courtyard. The woman had caught up with the churchmen and walked alongside them, talking earnestly. All three stopped. The kira, after nodding vigorously, wished them goodbye and hurried quickly to the gate that led from the Topkapı Palace to the street. As Orhan watched, the churchmen turned and headed back in the opposite direction toward the second courtyard. Were they going to revisit the pādishah? If so, was it because of something the kira had told them? Something about a woman in his harem—about Süreyya?

'Ready for your inspection, sire,' the captain's voice cut across Orhan's thoughts.

Orhan turned away from the window, trying to shake off an ominous feeling of disquiet.

On Süreyya's way back from morning prayers the following day, Abdul motioned to her to step aside from the group. 'The doctor wishes to see you after breakfast,' he said.

'Why? I'm not sick.'

Abdul glanced around to make sure no one was listening. 'It is customary for the ikbal to see the doctor monthly,' he said quietly.

Would the doctor check her every month to see if she was with child? The agha's eyes met hers and he nodded as if reading her thoughts.

Süreyya hadn't seen Doctor Rebeka since her clever stitching had restored her virginity. The October day was sunny but cool. She clutched her cloak close to her body as she walked along the path to the hospital. Süreyya approached the white building with its shiny black window frames and door, and reflected on her first visit to the doctor. She had known only a few words of Turkish, and she'd entered the building with a sick feeling of dread. Now, six months later, she was nearly fluent in Turkish. Her status had changed from harem slave to ikbal—the favourite. Just as Doctor Rebeka had predicted. A servant helped her to change, then ushered her into the doctor's surgery.

The doctor's appearance shocked Süreyya. The robust, friendly woman whom Süreyya had met months ago was now a shadow of her former self. Doctor Rebeka looked exhausted. Her face was gaunt and sallow, and she had dark shadows under her eyes.

Süreyya searched the other woman's face as they exchanged greetings. 'Doctor Rebeka, excuse me, are you sick?'

'I hear you are the favourite of the prince now,' the doctor commented, ignoring Süreyya's question. 'Maybe you wish to have a child soon?'

She told Süreyya to lie on the examination table. She pressed various parts of her patient's abdomen, then asked her to sit up. When Süreyya told her that her courses had not come because she had been travelling, the doctor nodded distractedly.

'I ask Abdul to look in the *Book of Couchings*,' the doctor said vaguely.

'Doctor Rebeka, I'm sorry to pry, but are you unwell?'

The doctor helped her from the table, led her to a seat, and sat opposite her patient.

'Three days ago, my husband was arrested for embezzlement. They say he stole money from the prince's Treasury. Prince Orhan has agreed to his execution.' Doctor Rebeka covered her face with her hands. 'It will be in two days, by the sword!'

'Prince Orhan ordered an execution?' Süreyya felt faint.

'My husband's enemies forced his hand. But the prince can stop it.' The doctor stifled a sob. 'My husband is innocent.'

'I'm so sorry!' The words seemed inadequate. Süreyya knew only too well that punishment in the palace was swift and merciless.

The doctor leaned forward and seized her hand. 'You must get a pardon for him. Abdul tells me you are ikbal now. Prince Orhan will listen to you. He will give you anything you want.'

Süreyya stared at the doctor. She couldn't do this again. Hadn't she nearly lost everything when she saved Perihan?

'Doctor Hatun, I can't ask ...'

'You *must*.' The doctor's eyes darkened. She squeezed Süreyya's hand hard and lowered her voice. 'If you don't, I will tell the prince that his ikbal was not a virgin when she came to his bed.'

Süreyya clutched her throat with her other hand, feeling sick with dread. 'He won't believe you!' She snatched her hand away from the doctor.

'Who will Prince Orhan believe?' Doctor Rebeka snapped. 'Me, a respectable doctor, or you, an odalisque—a slave girl?'

'But they will punish you for lying, for stitching me,' Süreyya said weakly.

'My life is worthless now.'

Süreyya was aghast; it was clear Doctor Rebeka felt she had nothing to lose. She was making a desperate last bid to save her husband's life.

'You ask, you get a pardon. Or I tell about you!' the other woman repeated.

'But ...'

'If you do not, my husband will die!' The doctor stood up. She leaned forward and grasped Süreyya's shoulders, then shook her hard.

'Your prince—he is a proud Ottoman.' She released her grip. '*You* have made a fool of him.'

'What if he refuses?' Süreyya felt as if someone was squeezing the breath from her body.

'If you fail, and my husband dies, I will inform Emira Sultan of your secret. She will tell her son. After they execute my husband, I will kill myself. Now go!'

Süreyya hurried out, her mind in a turmoil. Surely Orhan loved her enough to forgive her? But in her heart, she knew that his mother could overrule any of his wishes. The doctor knew who had the power in the harem: Emira Sultan. She was due to return from Edirne shortly, and again her powerful presence would radiate throughout the harem.

Perihan was waiting to help Süreyya into her clothes. She moved Süreyya's trembling hands away and tied the cords of her outdoor cloak for her mistress. In answer to the girl's concern, Süreyya shook her head and told her everything was all right. But that was far from the truth. What if Orhan was too busy to see her? Then, if the doctor told Emira her secret, Süreyya knew what Emira would do. She would order her son's favourite be put in a sack and dumped alive into the Bosphorus. It would be the ultimate irony. Orhan had rescued her from the water, and his mother would send her back to it.

Every fibre in her body screamed at her to run back to her chambers and bar the door, but custom forced her to walk sedately through the deserted gardens. A eunuch opened the harem door as they approached. Feeling dazed, she entered the washing area, where he helped her rinse her hands and feet and change into satin slippers. Süreyya dismissed Perihan with the excuse that she wanted to be alone and rest.

'But, madam, you don't look well. Let me bring some refreshment for you.'

'Thank you, yes, but I need to be alone.'

She had to think, to clear her mind. Perihan brought the drink and left, looking worried. As she drank, Süreyya paced the floor. If the doctor carried out her threat, then she, the prince's favourite, might be sleeping on a straw mattress in the dungeon tonight. Maybe because she was the favourite, they would kill her here in her own bed, she thought, shivering. Perihan had told her that they trained deaf mutes to do that. The men came at night and strangled their victims with a silken cord. Süreyya clutched her neck.

For the first time in months, she remembered the slave ship, the seasickness, her rough treatment at the hands of the sailors and slave traders. Evil memories tortured her as she paced her new chambers: the sailors exposing their genitals to her at every opportunity; the Tartar men who squeezed and sucked her breasts.

Süreyya had jumped off the vessel because she wasn't a virgin, and the slave traders would have sold her to a brothel. Instead, because of the lie she and the doctor shared, she was Prince Orhan's favourite. She might eventually give birth to an Ottoman prince. Or Emira Sultan might order her execution within days.

When they had made love the previous night, Orhan had promised to send for her as soon as possible after her return.

'I must see you,' he'd whispered. 'You are the only woman I ever want in my life and my bed.' He had stroked her face and kissed her eyes. 'Say you love me too, darling Süreyya.'

'I adore you, my prince.'

He had gathered her to him, and they made love again. For her, the world didn't exist when they were together. Her lost virginity was a thing of the past. But that was before. Now her life might crash down around her, like buildings in an earthquake. If he wanted to see her tonight, she must plead the doctor's case and invent a convincing reason for her request. She had to choose her words carefully, otherwise he might query why she was championing the doctor's husband.

Holy Virgin and all the saints! She made the sign of the cross secretly on her palm. Despite the luxury, the jewels, the gifts, she might have only days to live. How could she prevent this? To her relief, Abdul knocked on her door in the late afternoon. The prince wished to dine with her that evening in his chambers.

Süreyya kissed Orhan's hand, still feeling terribly afraid. But when he held her close and stroked her hair and face, she felt somewhat reassured.

'Every time I see you, I love you more,' he said.

'Oh!' Something dug into her flesh, and she stepped back. 'You're armed!' She touched the jewelled dagger in its scabbard on his belt.

Did he know already? Was he going to kill her himself … tonight? She shook her head slightly to dispel the terrible notion.

'I'm so sorry, sevgilim. I may have to go on an errand for my father, but I couldn't wait to see you,' he said. He unbuckled his belt and laid it and the dagger on a small table. He turned and smiled at her. 'I heard you visited the doctor this morning?'

She looked up at him, startled. 'How did you know?'

He patted her face. 'There are no secrets in the harem.'

Secrets and the doctor! Süreyya felt as if an icy hand was clutching her heart. She bit her lip.

'What is it, my darling?' His concerned brown eyes met hers. He led her to a cushioned seat and took his place opposite her.

'When I visited the doctor today …' she began.

'Do you have some news for me?' His eyes were bright with expectation.

'Oh, no, I'm sorry.' She shook her head. Was he hoping she was with child?

'No matter,' he said with a smile. He picked up a small silver bell from the table and summoned the servants. They bowed to him and to Süreyya, then prepared the table between them to serve the food. She must ask soon! But she remained silent.

'Let us eat together and talk,' he said, supervising the attendants as they served dishes of green beans in olive oil, artichoke hearts, creamy humous, and thinly sliced lamb between layers of warm bread. He picked up his glass of ayran in its silver holder and smiled at her across the table.

This was the moment.

'Orhan.' She tried to speak slowly, but the words came out in a rush. 'When I saw the doctor today, she was very distressed.'

He nodded to a servant to put some sliced lamb and vegetables on his plate and hers, and looked up. 'Distressed?'

She met his eyes and said in Russian. 'Could we speak in private?'

'Of course.' He dismissed the attendants. 'You said the doctor was distressed?' He reached out and took her hand and, smiling, he squeezed it lightly with his cool fingers.

She must ask *now*.

'It shouldn't distress the doctor that you are not with child.'

'It is my dearest wish to bear your son,' she replied honestly. 'But the doctor was very upset about her husband ...'

The prince released her hand and leaned back against the divan cushions. 'Her husband?'

'He's in prison, about to be executed. Doctor Rebeka is devastated.' The words tumbled out. 'She told me that only you can save his life.'

The prince looked at her and sighed. Would he tell her not to get involved in politics?

'So now they know you are the favourite, people are already petitioning you to help them.' He shook his head. 'What's the man's name?'

Süreyya's heart sank; she didn't know. 'I only know that the doctor is a Jewish lady originally from Spain. Someone has accused her husband of embezzling money.' She met his eyes, trying to gauge his reaction. To her relief, Orhan nodded slowly.

'His name in Turkish is Ibrahim,' he said. 'It surprised me to hear of the arrest. He seemed such an honest, hard-working man.'

'Could he be ... could you order his release?'

The prince leaned across the table and patted her face. 'Now, why is that so important to you?' He smiled. 'You have such a kind heart.'

Süreyya had prepared her answer carefully. She had even practised saying it out loud. 'The Doctor Hatun is indispensable for the women in your harem. If I were ever to be with child, I could trust her to deliver him safely. If they execute her husband, the palace will banish her.'

'You make an excellent case, my advocate.' He took her hand and kissed it.

'Thank you, dearest Orhan. We need her. Will you do this for me?' She feared there was an edge of desperation in her voice.

The prince hesitated. 'I must find out some facts first,' he said.

Please, please don't say no!

'Let me look at the case. Embezzlement—stealing money—is a very serious crime.'

'They will execute him in two days.' She tried to keep her voice steady.

'Then I will order a stay of execution immediately, if that makes you happy. I'll send the guard from outside the door.'

Süreyya stifled a sigh. She'd hoped her lover would order an immediate release. She should have known better. Of course, there would be documents to sign, even if the prince ordered a pardon. But suppose he forgot? Would he get suspicious if she reminded him on the morrow?

Orhan stood up, walked to the door, and stepped out into the passage, closing the door behind him. Süreyya scrambled to her feet and, following in his footsteps, pressed her ear against the wood. She heard him talking to the guard, but she couldn't hear his words clearly.

The soldier replied loudly: 'At once, your highness.'

She ran back and sat down in her seat just as he closed the outer door. He walked across to her, took her in his arms, and pulled her close. He kissed her, and she sighed.

'There, it's done, they will not execute him yet,' he said. 'I have asked for the papers to be brought to me so that I can sign his release. I will have to study them carefully. You have made a good case, dearest Süreyya. Ibrahim may lose his position, but the doctor can stay.'

Her hands shook in her lap as Orhan resumed his seat opposite her and smiled. *Pray God he never discovers that he has saved me from ruin. And himself from general ridicule.*

Her secret was safe—for the time being.

Orhan rang the bell again and servants arrived with more food: tiny peppers stuffed with savoury meat and rice, and large black olives in a silver bowl that the attendants served to them with silver spoons.

'Do you like your new chambers?' he asked when the servants had left.

'Oh, I do, dear Orhan. I love them.'

'And how are your religious studies going?'

'Very well, I am making progress reading the holy Koran in Arabic.' She met his eyes, and felt surprised when he looked away.

'Süreyya,' he began, 'it must have been hard for you to give up your own religion.'

'We share the same God,' she answered.

'True.' He nodded and reached inside the pocket of his kaftan, extracting a small bound volume. He came around the table and joined her on the low seat. 'I want you to have this copy of the Holy Koran. I've had it since I was a child. The script is in gold leaf.' He opened the book from the back and smiled at her. 'Are you used to opening your books this way yet?'

She laughed, leaned forward, and touched the small volume. 'This is yours?'

'It is yours now,' he said. 'I have written a message for you inside it.' His eyes were serious when they met hers. 'Can you read it?'

She traced the calligraphy with her fingertip, and he read the words with her: 'To dearest Süreyya, my one true love. Orhan.'

'It's beautiful, thank you.' Tears pricked her eyes.

He took her in his arms and kissed her cheeks. 'Süreyya, I would hate to lose you,' he whispered.

She looked up into his eyes. Did he know? Had he been humouring her?

'Why would you lose me?' she asked unsteadily.

He kissed her again then stroked her face. 'I'm being foolish.' He said. 'When Nesrin ... when I lost her ... I never expected to love anyone else again. And now I have found you.'

Despite being held in his comforting arms, Süreyya shivered.

～

After Süreyya had returned to her chambers, Orhan requested to see the papers regarding Ibrahim Efendi. When they arrived, he sent an official stay of execution, signed and sealed by himself, to the jail. He put the papers on one side to study later, then called his servant.

'I believe the pādishah wishes to see me?' he said.

'The sultan has retired, sire,' the man replied. 'He has just sent word that the shezade must present himself tomorrow, after midday prayers.'

The servants cleared away the remains of their meal. Orhan prepared for the final prayer of the day. As he washed, he wondered why his father had summoned him to the throne room. This was the place where the sultan received foreign ambassadors and delegations from the provinces. Why had his father not chosen to talk to him in his private chambers, as he often did? Orhan felt slightly uneasy. His father must want to speak with him on a formal matter.

He finished his ablutions and sighed. His mother had returned from Edirne and retired to her chambers to rest. Emira, too, wanted to see him tomorrow, but *he* wanted to see Süreyya.

CHAPTER 24

After she'd helped her mistress dress, Perihan looked enquiringly at her. 'You look very pale, madam. Maybe you should not go to the salon this morning.'

'I must—Emira Sultan has returned from Edirne, and expects everyone to attend.'

The prince's mother was not there when they arrived, but was due shortly, according to Abdul. The agha reminded Süreyya to wait until Emira Sultan invited her to the dais. Several women plied Süreyya and Perihan with questions about the odalisques whom Emira Sultan would eventually bring from Edirne.

'They may go to sultan's harem,' Süreyya ventured.

A hush fell over the women when Abdul announced the imminent arrival of Emira Sultan. The prince's mother entered the salon with the aplomb of a queen and took her place on her divan. Emira nodded to Abdul, who motioned Süreyya to come forward.

After exchanging greetings, Emira smiled faintly. 'I believe you are now my son's favourite, so you may sit here.' She patted the thick cushions next to her.

Because of the October chill, Emira sat at the far end of the dais, away from the windows and close to the wood fire that burned in the large grate. The older woman glanced at Süreyya with her sharp eyes as she sat down. After exchanging greetings, she asked, 'Are you well, dear?'

'Very well, madam.'

'You look pale, and I believe you visited the doctor yesterday?' Emira queried, but before Süreyya could answer, she continued. 'Within a few days, I will make an announcement about your new status as ikbal. You will be officially presented to the harem, and we will have another celebratory lunch. However, my son will not be here today. He has an audience with the pādishah.' Emira turned away and clapped her hands. 'Here they are!'

The Polish odalisques, Oya and Ayşe, who had accompanied the prince's mother to Edirne, also made a grand entrance. The Polish girls chattered and squealed, but although Emira frowned at them, she invited them to sit with her.

Süreyya moved further along the divan, away from Emira's penetrating gaze. The doctor's words haunted her. A nagging question hammered in her brain: had Orhan signed the release document for the doctor's condemned husband? How could she find out? Could she ask Abdul? Would the agha, and the prince, become suspicious? Süreyya desperately wanted to leave the salon, but she would need permission from Emira Sultan. And leaving early would cause comment.

The morning passed slowly, and Süreyya was relieved when she heard the call for midday prayers. After the ritual, she was obliged to stay for the sumptuous lunch that had been arranged to celebrate Emira Sultan's homecoming. Süreyya wanted to return to her chambers and assemble her scattered thoughts. What had Orhan meant when he'd talked about losing her?

Süreyya returned from lunch through the marble passageways of the harem, half listening to Perihan's chatter about the women in Edirne. The doctor's threat pulsated through Süreyya's brain at every step.

How could she find out if they had released Doctor Rebeka's husband? Maybe Abdul knew. She decided to call for him when she returned to her new chambers.

Süreyya breathed more easily. Abdul *would* know; he knew everything. She turned the corner, with Perihan still chattering beside her. They both stopped suddenly when they reached their destination. The door of her chambers was wide open, and Abdul stood in the middle of the sitting area. Someone had stripped bare every part of her new living quarters! She steadied herself on Perihan's arm.

'Abdul, what's happening? Am I … am I no longer the favourite?' The words stuck in her throat.

So, the doctor had told Orhan the truth! Süreyya looked around fearfully. Was someone waiting to take her to the dungeons? Abdul?

Abdul Agha turned toward her, his face an unreadable mask. 'You are to leave the palace immediately, Süreyya Hatun, by order of the sultan,' he said. 'Perihan Jariye will help you dress in your outdoor clothes.'

'I am to go to the dungeons?' Her voice cracked.

'No, the sultan has ordered that you must leave Prince Orhan's harem.'

Perihan clutched her arm. Süreyya stood on the threshold of the empty chamber, unable to believe what Abdul had just said.

'Leave? By order of his majesty? Why?'

'I am informed that your uncle, the Bishop of Slavo, received a letter from you. In it, you related where you were, and begged him to come and save you. I believe you sent it from a Greek village, via a priest? Maybe you have forgotten, madam.'

Of course, she hadn't forgotten. When she wrote it, she'd been obsessed with leaving the harem. But now her life had changed completely.

Abdul's voice cut across her thoughts. 'The bishop is here in Constantinople. He visited the pādishah recently and showed him your letter. He related how Tartars captured and enslaved you, and now he wishes you to be reunited with your family. Your uncle will take you to Pera, where he and your aunt are staying. Eventually you will return to your own country, and your people.'

'But what are Prince Orhan's wishes?' she asked.

'The shezade is also a subject of the sultan. He must abide by the pādishah's orders,' Abdul said. He looked around the empty chambers, then at her. 'The servants have packed all your possessions. The jewellery, coins, and gold that Prince Orhan gifted to you have been sent to your uncle's house in Pera,' the agha continued. 'You will have an excellent dowry.'

'A dowry?'

'When foreign families claim an odalisque from the harem, they arrange for her to be married before she returns to her own country,' Abdul replied, his voice empty of emotion.

'But I do not wish to marry!'

'You are a woman, Süreyya Hatun. You have no choice. It is the custom, madam.' The agha lowered his eyes. 'I have heard the Christian communities believe the harem is …' He hesitated. 'They think it is like a whorehouse. You will become respectable when you marry.'

Süreyya stared at him and grasped the chief eunuch's arm. Her knees felt weak. 'Please don't let them take me, Abdul Agha! Call for Prince Orhan. Make him stop this!'

The Kızlar Ağası sighed and shook his head. 'You will never see the prince again, Süreyya Hatun. He is dead to you from now on.'

'Never see him again? No! Prince Orhan won't let this happen!'

'He, too, must obey the sultan,' Abdul repeated.

'Oh madam, what will I do without you?' Perihan started to cry.

Ignoring the girl, Abdul pointed to the crescent brooch that Süreyya always wore. 'You must keep the brooch out of sight in the Christian community—the crescent is a Muslim symbol. They will take it from you.' He retrieved the prince's copy of the Koran from within the folds of his kaftan. 'Maybe you would like to keep this out of sight too,' he said quietly.

Still sniffing, Perihan helped Süreyya fasten the precious jewel inside her bodice. Süreyya slipped the small Koran into the pocket of her gown. The brooch and the Koran were her only links with the prince. Her throat tightened with unshed tears. She vowed to keep them for as long as she lived.

'Abdul, I beg you, call for the prince! I do not want to leave,' she said desperately.

'Think of what I have told you many times, Süreyya Hatun: do not question the ways of the harem. You have no choice.' Abdul pointed to her desk. 'I have prepared parchment and ink. You have time to pen a brief note to his highness. I will make sure he receives it. Quickly, madam.'

Süreyya hastily scratched a few words on the parchment, rolled it, and gave it to the agha. 'Thank you, thank you, Abdul.'

The servants adjusted a black ermine-lined cape around her shoulders, and Süreyya, feeling dazed, slipped her feet out of her satin shoes and into leather ones. She arranged a wide blue scarf over her hair and tied the ends across the lower part of her face. The group of servants and the Kızlar Ağası paused as the muezzin began the call to afternoon prayers.

'It is time for me and the servants to pray,' Abdul said. *'Allah size korusun*, Süreyya Hatun—God bless you.'

'Oh madam!' Perihan sobbed.

Süreyya pulled the weeping girl to her breast and hugged her. 'Goodbye, my dearest friend. I will miss you more than I can say.'

She wiped the tears from the young woman's face with her fingers. She pulled on her calf skin gloves and clutched Abdul's hands in both of hers.

'Please tell him goodbye, ask him to remember me, and give him the note,' she said as tears flowed freely down her face.

Abdul slowly lowered then lifted his head. 'This way, madam.'

Süreyya looked at her chambers for a last time and stifled a sob. How long would it be before another favourite would occupy them?

Prince Orhan could not attend his mother's homecoming lunch. A messenger came to tell him he must join the sultan for midday worship. After that, the pādishah wished his son to take a meal with him and discuss the situation in Edirne and Manisa.

When the sultan embraced him, Orhan felt the pādishah was holding back something; maybe a topic his father would not raise before entering the mosque. They washed in silence before the ritual. Orhan knew better than to disobey the rule that prohibited anyone, even a prince, from opening a conversation with the pādishah. After prayers, the sultan led the way to throne room.

As he walked three steps behind his father, Orhan observed the sultan closely. Although he was well over fifty, the sultan appeared as fit and young as a man half his age. He had a soldier's bearing and held his head high and his back ramrod straight. He looked directly ahead as he strode in front of his son, flanked as ever, by several bodyguards. Orhan followed him into the elaborately furnished space. The only sound was the swish of the sultan's gold brocade kaftan as he walked across the large silk carpet, then took his place on a cushioned divan.

Prince Orhan stood waiting with bowed head until his father bade him look up, then motioned him to sit. Orhan sat opposite his father. Two of the bodyguards, who stood at intervals against the blue-tiled walls of the chamber, closed the doors. The sultan's food taster hovered close to the low pearl and gold inlaid table that separated prince and sultan.

The pādishah nodded to the waiting servants, and they piled food onto the gold plates: rice-filled dolmas, small peppers stuffed with savoury meat and rice in a rich tomato sauce, eggplant in olive oil, and warm bread.

'It is with regret we learned of the death of two of our sons,' the sultan began. 'You, my last son, now crown prince, fought bravely but not wisely.'

Orhan said nothing. The sultan rarely praised anyone, but even this faint praise had a sting of criticism.

'Had it not been for our fearless Zeybek subjects, you might have been killed. You are now my only son,' the pādishah continued.

Orhan touched his heart with his fingertips. 'I am beholden to them.'

'It is not wise for the offspring of the sultan to be obligated to anyone.' His father raised his voice. 'You showed poor judgement. You did not have enough Janissaries with you. We are extremely displeased; we understand you had other distractions in your life.' The sultan looked directly at him.

'I assure you, my mind was on the battle, sire, I—'

His father held up his hand, and Orhan stopped speaking.

'I saw your mother, Emira Sultan, earlier today. She tells me you have no children yet.'

The prince tried to hide his astonishment. The pādishah had granted his mother an audience!

'At twenty-six years of age, only a little older than you,' the sultan continued, 'I had two daughters, two sons, and another of my women was with child.'

'I had a son, sire, but he died.' Prince Orhan spoke quietly, not wishing to appear contradictory or raise his father's ire.

'I believe you have a new favourite?'

'Yes, sire, her name is Süreyya.'

His father regarded him before he spoke. 'This favourite ...' The sultan nodded to a servant, who piled slivers of lamb on his plate, then added a spoonful of rice. 'A Russian girl, yes?'

'Yes, sire.'

Why had his mother discussed Süreyya with the sultan?

'Do you know what her Russian name was?'

The prince hesitated before he answered. 'Rusalka Maria Ivanova, I believe. Now she is Süreyya.'

The sultan signalled to a servant, who brought gold beakers of ayran for them. The two men ate and drank in silence, then Orhan's father spoke again.

'You know we have had trouble with the Christians in the city,' the pādishah stated.

'Yes, sire, I negotiated with them recently, if you remember.' Where was this conversation leading? He wondered.

Orhan had the same sense of foreboding he'd felt when he saw the churchmen. His heart raced, but the next pronouncement from his father took his breath away. Even though he had half-expected bad news, this was worse than he'd imagined.

'His All Holiness, George, the Ecumenical Patriarch of Constantinople, came to see us,' the sultan began, giving the patriarch his full title. 'The Russian girl's uncle accompanied him. I am told the uncle is the bishop of Slavo, a town in southern Russia.'

Orhan opened his mouth to speak, but his father raised his hand and stopped him.

'The odalisque's uncle wishes her to be returned to her family. We have sent word to Abdul, your Kızlar Ağası. The bishop will collect his niece before afternoon prayers today. We have made arrangements for their journey to Pera.'

Orhan felt as if an earthquake had rolled beneath his feet. 'Sire, she is in *my* harem. Should not the decision to return her be mine?'

'It is a political decision, and only the sultan can make it.' His father's steely eyes met his son's. 'The girl will leave.'

'It is not what I want, sire!'

Orhan stood up, knocking the table in his haste to leave and stop Abdul. Dishes of food crashed to the floor. The sultan jumped to his feet and put his hand on his dagger. Several imperial guards rushed forward and grabbed the prince's arms.

'Sit down and be silent, sir!' his father barked.

Orhan shook off the guards and obeyed his father.

'We will continue our meal.'

The sultan dismissed the attendants, who were clearing up the scattered food. The guards returned to their positions against the wall. Father and son continued their meal in silence. Orhan obeyed the custom and waited for the sultan to speak again.

How could he stop this? Did Süreyya really want to leave? She had vowed she loved him.

His father changed the subject and spoke about matters of state. He raised his eyebrows for a response.

'Your majesty, I will pay them for the girl, if that is what they want,' the prince ventured.

'*Allah Aşkına!* For the love of God! Do you know nothing?' his father shouted. 'This goes deeper than money. Her uncle had a letter from the girl, begging for his help. She sent it via a Greek priest.'

'When?' In all their conversations, Süreyya had never mentioned it to him.

The sultan glared at his son and ignored the question. He leaned forward and waved a gold spoon in his son's face. 'We do not want agitation in the Christian community—or the Jewish community. We want peace here and war elsewhere.' The pādishah angrily dismissed a hovering attendant. He looked up at his son. 'The matter of the Russian odalisque is *closed*. Do you understand?'

Orhan bowed his head. The sultan of the Ottoman Empire had spoken; he had no choice but to obey.

His father's voice broke across his thoughts. 'It is your duty, my son, to conquer new territories, defeat our enemies, and produce many sons.' A faint smile crossed the sultan's face and he met his son's eyes. 'I have many beautiful women in the imperial harem, and I am still a vigorous man. You may yet have more half-brothers, other claimants for the Sword of Osman,' he said slyly.

'Yes, sire.' Orhan looked down, fearing that the dislike he felt for his manipulative father might be visible on his face.

They finished their food in silence, then the sultan rose to his feet. It was a signal that the audience and the meal were over. Orhan bowed and took three steps back. He was about to turn and leave when the door opened. The grand vizier and members of the Divan, the sultan's ministers of state, walked in.

'We have matters of state to discuss, and your presence is required.' The sultan looked steadily at his son, walked across the room and sat down on his canopied throne. He signalled to his son and his ministers to move closer.

Orhan grew increasingly impatient as the discussions continued late into the afternoon. Finally, the pādishah stood as *Asr*, the call to afternoon prayers, began. The meeting was finally over.

Orhan's father turned to him. 'Join me for prayers. We are yet in mourning for our sons Murad and Ahmet. You must pray with me for their souls.'

After prayers, the sultan laid his hand on his son's shoulder. 'Go in peace, my son,' he said.

Orhan felt furious; he was certain the sultan had delayed him deliberately, perhaps at his mother's suggestion, while they hustled Süreyya out of the palace. He vowed he would find her and bring her back. His heart pumped in his chest as he hurried toward her chambers. Maybe he was wrong and she hadn't gone. Maybe he could see her for a last time.

CHAPTER 25

*A*n armed escort took Süreyya via the side path to the first courtyard. A curtained carriage was waiting, and standing next to it was her Uncle Andrei, wearing his bishop's robes. He stepped forward and took both of her hands in his.

'At last, my dearest Rusalka. God bless you—you are alive and free!'

He helped her into the carriage and sat opposite her on the padded bench. The vehicle moved through the main gate and passed the Aya Sofia mosque. On the steep descent to Eminönü and the Golden Horn, her uncle talked continually. The motion of the carriage made Süreyya feel sick, and she found it hard to follow what he was saying. Place names and people's names meant little to her. When they alighted, her uncle told her that the palace had organised a royal caique to take them across the waterway.

With a terrible sense of finality, Süreyya saw the shoreline of Eminönü recede as the royal vessel took her across the Golden Horn to the opposite side of the city. She stared miserably at the outline of the Topkapı palace on the distant shore. At Galata, she stepped into another coach. It hauled them up the steep hill, past the Genoese fire tower, then along the flat road to Pera. She moved the curtain aside and looked at the darkening streets. Women in long cloaks, their hoods pulled up against the chill, walked arm-in-arm, and black-robed priests scurried by. The entire world was in Pera—Muslims, Jews, and Christians all mingling together.

She had demanded that Prince Orhan take her to this place when he'd rescued her. Now she had her wish, and she would give anything not to be here.

Orhan nearly collided with Abdul at the top of the stairs that led to Süreyya's former chambers. He grabbed the agha by the arm and shook him.

'Is she here?'

'No, sire. She left with her uncle at the afternoon prayer call.'

'Did she leave word?'

'She insisted on wearing the crescent brooch, sire, and she took the Koran. She said to tell you goodbye and asked you to remember her.'

The prince looked down, not wanting Abdul to see his anguish.

'Ikbal Süreyya left you a note,' Abdul said and handed it to him.

Orhan took the small parchment. The agha had sealed it with his own seal. The prince thanked him. He touched the closed door of Süreyya's former residence. 'Open it please. I wish to be alone.'

Abdul bowed and turned the key in the lock. 'Sire, excuse me, Emira Sultan wishes to see you.'

'Of course. I will see my mother shortly.'

The agha bowed and left. Orhan stepped across the threshold, closed the door, and stood in the middle of the quiet chamber. He fancied he could hear Süreyya's excited voice when he'd asked if she liked it:

'Oh, I do, dear Orhan. I love it!'

He walked to her small desk, slit the seal on the parchment, and unrolled it. It was not her usual careful script, but a hasty scrawl in her own language.

'I love you, Orhan. Please find me and save me! Süreyya.'

He read and re-read her message, then crossed to the window, grasping the note in his hand. Across the Courtyard of the Favourites, the waters of the Golden Horn were grey under a sombre sky. Orhan scanned the opposite bank where the Genoese fire tower rose above the houses.

'I *will* find you, Süreyya!' he said aloud.

Orhan remembered seeing the kira talking earnestly to the priests. This, and the letter she had sent from the Greek village, was how they found her! Had Süreyya told the kira her real identity? If she hadn't written that last desperate note, he might have doubted her and thought she had sent a message via the kira. When she wrote from the Greek village, she was afraid and had wanted to escape. Abdul informed the prince someone had tried to kill her.

But that was many months ago. That she had changed her mind was clear from this desperate last message to him. Süreyya had taken the brooch, a matching half to his, and his Koran with her, and begged him to save her. But he would have to defy the sultan and palace protocol to do it.

The prince returned to his chambers, feeling weary and defeated. The final release document for Ibrahim, the doctor's husband, was on his desk. He hesitated before signing it. Was there any point in saving the man's life now that Süreyya was no longer here? The man was guilty. He deserved to be punished.

Orhan sighed. Süreyya had wanted to save Ibrahim so that the doctor could help the harem women. She petitioned for the doctor to stay, not for herself, but to help the other women in his harem. Orhan signed the release, poured wax on the document, and impressed his seal on it, then rolled and sealed it again. He called for a servant to take it to the jail. They would release Ibrahim immediately. Orhan would make sure the doctor stayed. It was a favour he could do for Süreyya. He clenched his fists. He *would* save her.

~

As the carriage trundled along through Pera, Süreyya's uncle told her how, when he had received her letter, he'd petitioned the sultan's envoy in Russia and contacted the Patriarch of Constantinople to enlist his help in gaining her freedom.

'It took a long time, Rusalka, but now you are here, released from your bondage in the infidel's harem.'

Süreyya nodded, not trusting herself to speak. She reminded herself she must hide the 'infidel' items the prince had given her.

The carriage stopped outside a set of high black gates, and she peered out of the carriage window. The gates swung open with a loud creak, and the carriage lumbered through into a wide courtyard. Telling her to wait, Uncle Andrei stepped down with the help of a servant. He supported his niece as she alighted and carefully put first one foot, then the other, on the uneven ground.

'Welcome to our Constantinople home, Rusalka,' he said. 'My sister, your Aunt Ludmilla, is expecting you.'

Süreyya glanced up at the large brick house constructed in the Turkish style, with wide eves overhanging the outer walls. She noticed a curtain move at a window on the second floor. Maybe the servants were ogling her: Rusalka, the whore from the harem.

The housekeeper, dressed in a long black gown, a white kerchief over her dark hair, was waiting on the doorstep. She glanced at Süreyya's ermine-lined coat and seemed to calculate its worth before she greeted her master and his niece.

'The mistress is waiting in the salon, sir and madam.' She ushered them inside and took their outdoor clothes.

Süreyya followed her uncle along a wide chilly passage, furnished only with a long table covered in an embroidered cloth. In the centre of the table, a gold crucifix reflected the light from the dim candles. A framed icon in gold and blue, of the Virgin Mary with the Child Jesus, looked down on Süreyya from a plain wall.

'Rusalka! My darling niece, thank God you're alive!' Aunt Ludmilla rushed forward and embraced her. 'The Holy Virgin and all the Saints protected you and you survived. I prayed for you every day,' she said, holding Süreyya close to her bosom, then at arm's length. 'How different you look in all your finery.' She beamed. 'But I would recognise your halo of curls anywhere.'

'I am still your same Rusalka,' Süreyya said. But even as the words left her lips, she knew in her heart they weren't true.

Her aunt ushered her into a warm salon, heated by an open fire. The carpets on the wooden floor were wool mixed with cotton, and not the silk she'd become accustomed to. More Christian icons and a plain cross hung on the white walls. Aunt Ludmilla led her to an upholstered bench with a high back. Her aunt and uncle sat down opposite her, looking relieved.

'We didn't know if the sultan would release you,' her aunt said. 'Then your uncle showed the letter you had written. It took the palace a few days to decide. But your uncle says the sultan, God bless him, is a good man.' She exchanged a look with her brother.

'We will return to Russia within a few weeks,' Bishop Andrei said. 'Until then, we are guests of His All Holiness, the Patriarch of Constantinople. This is a house for visiting clergy. But first—'

'First,' Ludmilla interrupted with a frown, 'Rusalka must see her chamber.'

Anna, the housekeeper, showed Süreyya to a sparsely furnished chamber with a small window. A crucifix and an icon of the Virgin Mary and Child hung above a narrow bed. Süreyya glanced around; her clothes from the harem were still in their boxes—no one had unpacked them for her.

'Your aunt wishes you to rest for a while. I will call you before the evening meal. You must wear this gown.' The housekeeper pointed to a plain dark gown that lay spread on a chair. 'No one in Pera dresses in silk,' the woman added, glancing at the gem-encrusted bodice of Süreyya's gown. 'You must dress modestly from now on.'

Süreyya said nothing.

'I expect you're used to help,' the housekeeper continued, 'but there is only me, a cook, and two serving maids. You will have to manage alone most of the time.' The woman gave her a tight smile and left, closing the door behind her.

Süreyya lay on the hard bed and fell into a sleep full of jumbled images of the palace and the Russian house. Waking before she was called, she fingered the rough material, then changed into the gown. She was glad to be alone; it meant she could pin the crescent brooch inside the folds of her bodice, where it nudged her heart.

Süreyya sighed. Unlike the palace, there was no mirror in the chamber. She missed Perihan's excited attentions as she'd brushed powder on Süreyya's cheeks and held up jewels for her to choose. Everything in this house was austere and cold. She splashed her face with water from a white ceramic bowl set on a scrubbed table and readied herself for the evening meal.

As she descended the stairs, she heard men's voices coming from the salon. Maybe her uncle had invited one of the Russian Orthodox clergy for dinner. Süreyya opened the door slowly and stopped on the threshold.

'Stefan!'

Her dead fiancé was sitting near the open fire, talking to her uncle! A spark spluttered in the grate as he turned toward her.

'Dearest Rusalka, it's been such a long time,' he said.

'Oh, my dear, you look as if you've seen a ghost,' her aunt cried and hurried toward her. 'We should have warned you.'

Süreyya felt faint, truly believing she *was* looking at a ghost, and leaned on her aunt's arm. She remembered seeing her fiancé's body after the Tartars had killed him. Yet here he was, sitting beside the fire in this house in Constantinople.

He got to his feet and walked toward her, hands outstretched. 'Rusalka Maria Ivanova,' he said.

She stood frozen, clinging to her aunt.

'Rusalka, don't you recognise me? I'm Stefan's older brother, Vasily. We met once.'

She recognised him as soon as he spoke, but in profile he closely resembled his brother, Stefan. An image of her fiancé's blood-spattered lifeless body flashed across her inward eye, and she remembered the Tartars dragging her away screaming. Her breath came in gasps, and she put her hands over her face.

Vasily pulled her hands away and fastened his rough ones around them. She tried to take a step back, but he held her in an iron grip. Süreyya remembered him clearly now. She had never liked him; he was as rough as Stefan was refined.

Her aunt led her to a chair near the fire and brought her some hot lemon-flavoured water. As she drank, Süreyya was aware of Vasily's eyes on her. He was looking at her with a mixture of lust and curiosity on his broad ruddy face. She remembered Abdul's words: 'They think the harem is a whorehouse.'

Her uncle plied her with questions about Stefan, the journey, and the palace. Süreyya found it hard to observe the horror in their eyes when she told them about the raid. She told them of the terror she and the servants felt, how the Tartars set the town on fire, and how Stefan had died trying to defend her. She didn't dwell on her experience on the slave ship.

'I fell overboard in a storm,' she told them. 'The prince rescued me and took me to the palace. He and his mother gave me a home.'

Her uncle tutted and frowned. 'You are back with your own people now. You must forget the infidel Muslims.'

Before she could answer, her aunt interrupted. 'And now we will break bread together and take our evening meal.'

Aunt Ludmilla led her to the long wooden table. She sat in an uncomfortable upright chair as her uncle said grace. They ate the plain boiled meat and watery vegetables that the servants laid before them.

'We need to discuss your future ...' Her uncle's voice seemed to come from far away.

'We can do that tomorrow,' her aunt interrupted. 'Rusalka must sleep now.'

Aunt Ludmilla took a candle and gave one to her niece. Together, they negotiated the dark, narrow stairs to her bedchamber. Despite being tired, Süreyya lay awake in her hard bed, thinking about the events of the day. Were they going to make her marry someone?

Vasily? Is that why he was here? She started to cry, muffling her sobs into the hard pillow. She could not, *would* not, marry Vasily Ljubov. Surely when he read her note, Orhan would come and find her. He was a powerful prince. He'd said he loved her! She fell asleep clutching the crescent brooch in her hand.

CHAPTER 26

The dawn prayer call woke Süreyya with a start. She sat up and swung her legs over the side of the bed, ready to join the other women for morning prayers. When her feet touched the bare floor, she remembered she wasn't in the Topkapı Palace. Süreyya remembered she was in a house next to the Russian Church, in Constantinople's Christian district of Pera. She'd cried herself to sleep, muffling her sobs into the pillow. She must accept that she would never hear Orhan's voice again, never see his face or kiss his lips.

Standing in the cold chamber, a wave of desolation and grief washed over her. Süreyya could still hear Perihan's sobs, then Abdul had hurried her from the Topkapı Palace to join her Uncle Andrei. No one had permitted her to see Prince Orhan.

Had he tried to intervene? Had he even known she was leaving? Did he care? Or had he accepted that it was 'the way of the harem'?

She steadied herself on the wooden rail at the end of the narrow bed and stumbled to the small window set in the white wall. She pulled it open and breathed in the chilly air. Squinting through the window bars, she could see a steep street that led down to the Golden Horn.

The city was waking up, and below her window, people were hurrying up and down the hill. Stray cats perched on walls, and ragged children shouted to each other. At the end of the street, she could see the waters of the Golden Horn, and on the opposite shore, the Topkapı Palace appeared to be floating as mist and clouds shrouded its turrets and grey walls. Life was continuing there without her. She imagined Perihan joining the other sleepy women for their morning prayer ritual, chivvied through the chilly passageways by Abdul.

They had probably forgotten her already. Süreyya, the former favourite.

She shivered, closed the window, and looked around the chamber. She fixed her gaze on the crucifix and the icon of the Virgin and Child above where she'd slept. She knelt next to her bed and whispered a prayer.

'Holy Virgin, please help me, let me return to the prince.'

A sharp knock on the door interrupted her prayers. She got to her feet and threw her woollen shawl around her shoulders and over her silk nightdress.

'Come,' she called in Russian. Her own language felt strange on her tongue.

'Good morning, madam. It's Anna, the housekeeper.' Anna shut the door behind her. She was carrying a grey gown and laid it on the chair. 'Are you feeling unwell, madam? You seem very pale.' The woman's piercing dark eyes met Süreyya's.

'I'm well, thank you. May I trouble you for some ayran and a pastry?'

The housekeeper raised her eyebrows. 'Ayran and a *pastry*?' she said. 'The family takes breakfast downstairs, but if madam wishes ...' She paused. 'I'll see what I can arrange. First, let me show you the privy and ablutions area.'

'Thank you.' Süreyya smiled at Anna.

'Are you sure you are well?' The woman's dark eyes narrowed.

'Yesterday was very difficult for me,' Süreyya replied.

'Your aunt has sent another plain gown for you.' The housekeeper pointed. 'As I mentioned yesterday, I advised madam that the dresses you brought from the palace were too elaborate for the niece of a bishop.'

'Of course.' Süreyya glanced at the plain dress the woman had laid out.

The housekeeper said nothing, stood back, and waved Süreyya into the cold passage. She pointed to the privy and promised to send a maid with a drink. 'And bread. We don't have pastries.' With a faint smile and a straight back, Anna walked down the stairs to the lower floor.

When Süreyya returned from the bathing area, a maid was waiting for her with a glass of hot water flavoured with lemon and a hunk of black bread. She was a wide-eyed, fair-skinned creature. She told Süreyya that her mother was from the Caucasus Mountains in Southern Russia, and her father was Greek. He had lived in Constantinople all his life. She continued to talk while she helped Süreyya dress.

'My father won't call the city *Konstantiniye*, as the Turks often do,' the maid remarked. Süreyya sipped her hot water and nibbled the heavy black bread without comment. 'Everyone in Pera calls it Constantinople.'

'The old name for the city,' Süreyya answered.

'The *correct* name of the city,' the maid responded sharply. She helped Süreyya into the plain gown.

Süreyya sighed—did it matter what anyone called the city? She had never heard Orhan say Konstantiniye, but her teacher had shown her how to write it. Davut Hodja explained that the scribes used it in official documents. She sighed when she thought of her patient teacher and all the other people she hadn't bade goodbye.

After the maid left, Süreyya slipped her hand under her pillow and retrieved her crescent brooch. She kissed it and pinned the gold and diamond gift from the prince inside the folds of her plain dress. *At least they let me keep my shawl*, she thought as she pulled it around her shoulders. She fingered the gold strands that ran through the dark crimson wool and shivered. Unlike the palace, her bedchamber had no heating.

At breakfast, Süreyya's aunt plied her with dark rye bread, cheese, honey and yoghurt. They ate in silence for a while. When a carriage rattled past in the street, both women started.

'I haven't heard street noises for a long time,' Süreyya said as she sipped her hot water. It tasted bland and acidic, unlike the refined beverages of the palace.

'Yes,' Aunt Ludmilla replied. 'I don't know my way around the city —it's very busy.'

'It was silent in the palace, except for the prayer calls,' Süreyya said. Her aunt raised her eyebrows slightly.

She strained her ears and listened to the ordinary sounds—a horse snorting, wheels rattling over cobblestones, and a street vendor calling his wares. Noises like these hadn't penetrated the palace walls. Süreyya suspected it would be strange and a little frightening to walk along busy streets—if her uncle permitted it. The first and last time she had visited the city had been to the slave market with Emira Sultan, but that seemed as if it had happened in a bygone age, *and* Emira had taken an armed escort with her.

'Could we go out in the fresh air?'

'Yes, of course,' her aunt replied with a smile. 'We will take a walk, but after breakfast your uncle wishes to speak with you.'

Uncle Andrei rose from behind his desk when she was ushered into his study. He made the sign of the cross over her, then returned to his seat, leaving her standing in front of him.

'Vasily has agreed to take you as a wife,' he said without preamble.

She opened her mouth to speak, but the bishop raised his hand.

'When we return home, we will say you escaped from the slave ship and lived with a respectable Russian family in Constantinople until we found you.' Her uncle put his fingertips together and nodded. 'You are fortunate, Rusalka.'

'Uncle, I do not want to marry.'

'Vasily,' her uncle interrupted, 'will accept you as you are. You have a sizeable dowry.'

But I love Orhan, she thought desperately. *I will not marry Vasily!* She protested, but her uncle raised his hand.

'You must have a husband quickly, Rusalka,' her uncle said.

Süreyya turned to her aunt, who had followed her into the study. 'I am to be married?'

'Of course,' her aunt said. 'Vasily has agreed to take you.'

'The wedding will be next week,' her uncle concluded. 'The wedding must be before the Great Christmas Fast begins.'

In less than two weeks! But she was Süreyya; she was no longer the Rusalka they had known.

'After your marriage to Vasily, we will return to our homeland. That is all, Rusalka, you may leave.' Her uncle picked up a document from his desk and began to read it.

Aunt Ludmilla hurried Süreyya from her uncle's study and took her to the salon.

'*Please* Aunt,' she begged. 'I cannot marry Vasily.'

Her aunt, who was usually kind and understanding, shook her head. 'This is how it must be, Rusalka. He is a good man.' She looked embarrassed. 'And he hasn't asked for proof that you are still a maid,' she whispered.

Of course not! Süreyya thought angrily. *He wants my dowry. The gold and jewellery Orhan gave me—his gift of love to me.* 'But I don't know him. I have not been engaged to him!'

Her aunt patted her arm. 'Very few brides know their husbands before their marriage, Rusalka. Yours is the lot of many women. As you know, I have never married, but have devoted my life to caring for your uncle, my brother, in his service of our holy church. You must care for Vasily as a wife.'

Süreyya burst into tears. When would this misery end, and where was Orhan? Why hadn't he come for her? Had he forgotten her already?

Aunt Ludmilla took her hands. 'No good will come of this weeping,' she chided. 'We must begin the preparations for your wedding.

Anna knows a dressmaker who can fashion a wedding gown for you. We can walk there today, and you can show me how well you speak Turkish!'

On the day they took Süreyya from him, Prince Orhan returned to the salon after evening prayers. He removed his silver-soled shoes and was greeted with the usual buzz of expectation when he walked in the door. He glanced across to the place where Süreyya used to sit, the place where he'd first seen her in the salon. The only person there was her little servant. A wave of grief and loss swept over him when he saw the girl's red-rimmed eyes.

He had eventually recovered from the death of his first love, Nesrin, but this was worse. Süreyya was alive. She was just across the water in his own city. He took a deep breath and caught his mother's eye. Emira was standing waiting for him, and she beckoned him to join her.

'Good evening, my lion.' She patted the divan.

When he sat down, she took her own place and laid her cool hand on his.

'I have organised some dancing and a wonderful supper. You missed my welcome home lunch,' she said, smiling. 'Remember the beautiful women who danced for you in Edirne? One of them will dance for you again this evening, and I suggest that Abdul should bring her to your chambers tonight.'

Prince Orhan sighed. 'No, mother.'

She gave him a steady look. 'The pādishah wishes that you forget this business with the Russian odalisque.' She leaned forward. 'It is imperative that you produce heirs, and *quickly*.'

'The new woman may come tomorrow, and not before.'

His mother nodded and pursed her lips.

Later that evening, Abdul tapped on Orhan's door after the final prayer call of the day.

'Come!'

Abdul entered, holding the *Book of Couchings* under his arm.

'I told my mother I would see the woman tomorrow.'

'She is exquisite, sire,' Abdul replied. 'She would be a distraction from the events of today.'

'I do not need a distraction!'

'The girl will lose face if she is returned,' the agha said.

Prince Orhan glared at the eunuch. He knew this was his mother's manoeuvrings; he would have words with her tomorrow. He sighed and nodded to Abdul.

'Send my servant to help me prepare, then I will see her.'

Abdul led the young woman into the prince's chamber. Under her cloak, Orhan glimpsed white diaphanous silk robes. She walked forward with her head bowed. The agha stopped with his charge in the middle of the salon where the prince waited. On a signal from Abdul, the woman removed her cloak and slipped her scarf away, revealing a cascade of bright blond hair. Orhan caught his breath. This was the woman whom his mother had suggested resembled Süreyya. He was furious with Emira for sending this particular odalisque. He wasn't stupid. This woman was nothing like Süreyya.

The girl sank to her knees and kissed the hem of the prince's kaftan. Orhan placed his hand beneath her chin and asked her to stand. She glanced at the prince with her blue eyes, a faint blush illuminating her fair skin, then whispered, 'Good evening, your highness.'

Orhan met Abdul's eyes over the woman's head. The agha's face was impassive as he stood near the door holding the *Book of Couchings* under his arm.

'Thank you, Abdul, you may leave us.' Orhan sighed. It had to happen eventually, why not now? He waited until he heard the door close, then put his fingers under the girl's chin and turned her face up to his. 'What is your name?'

'Oya, sire,' she said.

'Haven't I seen you before?'

'I danced for you in Edirne, sire,' the girl replied in accented Turkish.

Prince Orhan took the girl's hand and led her to his bedchamber. 'Don't be nervous,' he said.

'I have received training, sire,' she replied hesitantly.

He bent forward to kiss her lips. She raised her face to him and put her slender arms around his neck. He felt aroused when he put his mouth on hers, but her enthusiastic response took him aback. She pressed her body against his, then went down on her knees. Fumbling under his kaftan, she pushed away the fabric so that she could pleasure him as she'd been trained to do. A sudden feeling of revulsion overwhelmed him. This was not what he wanted. He might as well visit a whorehouse!

'Get up,' he said, helping her to her feet. He struggled to steady his voice—it wasn't the woman's fault. 'Oya Jariye, my apologies,' he said. 'We will not be together tonight. Wait here in the bedchamber.'

He strode through the salon and threw the door open. Abdul Agha was outside conversing with the eunuch escort for the girl.

The agha started with surprise. 'Your highness!'

Orhan signalled for Abdul Agha to approach. 'Take her back.'

'But ...'

'You.' Orhan pointed to the other eunuchs. 'Take ... her ... back ... now! I want to speak with you, Abdul.'

'With your permission.' The eunuchs moved toward the prince's door.

When they opened it, Orhan winced. They could all hear the woman sobbing loudly in his bedchamber. He raised his hand and ordered them to wait. The prince went into his chambers and shut the door on their astonished faces. He walked across to the girl and sat next to her on his divan. He put his arm around her shoulders, and she leaned on him, gulping back her tears.

'You're a beautiful young woman and I'm sure you are very skilled in lovemaking,' he said. 'But tonight, I wish to be alone.'

The girl sniffed, and looked up at him.

'This is *our* secret, do you understand?' Prince Orhan met the girl's eyes. 'I'll instruct Abdul to enter your visit in the book.'

'Thank you, sire,' she whispered.

'You must tell no one what happened this evening,' he repeated.

She bit her lip and nodded.

Orhan helped her to her feet and walked her to his door, furious with his mother for engineering this awkward situation. Outside in the passageway, he made sure the eunuchs wrapped Oya warmly in her cloak. He signalled Abdul to come into his chamber.

'Enter her visit in the book,' he said. 'Make sure she receives a gift of gold earrings.'

'Yes, sire.'

Prince Orhan frowned at Abdul Agha. At least he didn't question why the odalisque was with him for such a short time.

'Abdul, the only woman I wish to see is Süreyya, whom I chose as my favourite.' He looked straight at the chief eunuch.

The agha's expression didn't change, but his ebony face glistened with perspiration. 'Her removal was a political decision, your highness.'

'I'm aware of that, Abdul. I care nothing for the politics of the situation. I just want her returned to the harem,' Orhan said. He lowered his voice. 'There are plenty of palace spies in Pera. Tell them to find her. I want to know where she's living, and what plans her family has for her. Understand? I will make it worth your while.' He walked to his desk and took a purse of coins from a drawer. 'Tell no one, and report what you find directly to me,' he ordered, handing the purse to Abdul. 'There will be more. Now go!'

CHAPTER 27

bdul continued to bring the prince news of his former favourite. Orhan was sure that his mother knew nothing of the activity. Five long days had passed since Süreyya had been removed from the harem. The prince filled them with work, but she was always on his mind. The spies saw her, two days ago, Abdul informed him. Süreyya was walking in the street with her aunt, her face half-covered by the hood of her cloak. She visited a dressmaker several times, that's all he knew.

Why would Süreyya go to a dressmaker? Hadn't the palace provided enough clothes for her?

Frowning, he returned to work in his large chamber. He had daily dispatches from Edirne and Manisa that required his attention. A servant approached and told him that the Kızlar Ağası was waiting to see him. Orhan pushed his work aside.

'I'll see him in private,' he said, dismissing the servants. He rose from his ornate desk as the agha entered.

'So, Abdul?' he said as the agha closed the door.

'As you know, sire, she is staying in a house next to the Russian Orthodox Church.' Abdul hesitated. 'She was seen with a young man, your highness …'

The prince walked around the desk and grabbed Abdul's arm. 'Who?'

'He's Russian. I'm told he's a coarse-looking man, with brown hair. My informant followed them to a goldsmith, where he purchased two plain gold rings.'

'Wedding bands?'

'It would seem so, sire.'

'She is to marry?'

Abdul nodded.

'*Allah!*'

Abdul cleared his throat. 'Sire, no one can stop it …'

'I want to know when,' Orhan interrupted. 'Do you understand? Don't fail me!'

'Yes, sire.'

Orhan slipped a heavy purse of coins into Abdul's grateful hand.

The following day, Abdul Agha was waiting in the passageway when the prince returned to his chambers.

'Inside!' Orhan ordered. 'What news?'

Abdul stood with his head bowed. 'The informants in Pera tell me, Süreyya Hatun …' Abdul paused, '… will marry on Friday to a Russian merchant, Vasily Ljubov. He is a friend of the family.'

Orhan stared at Abdul's bland face and clenched his fists at his side. 'Friday?' he repeated.

Abdul inclined his head.

Orhan closed his eyes; Friday was the holiest day of the Muslim week. He was the Crown Prince of the Ottoman Empire. He had attended Friday prayers with his father, the sultan, every Friday at midday since he had learned to walk. It was impossible to be excused. It was his royal obligation, a duty he must perform.

'Find out what time, and anything else they can glean.'

'Sire.' Abdul looked up. 'But …'

'I know about Friday prayers!' the prince raised his voice. 'Just find out *when*. Do you have more information?'

Orhan clenched and unclenched his fists as Abdul related how Süreyya's family had taken her money and her jewellery as expected. They were going to use it as her dowry.

Another man would touch her. He would not permit it. Orhan loved her, and *he* would free her!

There was no hope of reclaiming her through diplomatic means. His father would reject the idea outright. Whatever happened, Orhan vowed, no one would force Süreyya to marry against her will.

After he'd dismissed Abdul, the prince stared out the window at the Golden Horn. Heavy rain blew in, sweeping clouds across the water. He knew that if he stopped a Christian wedding, his father would be furious. And the Christian community would be outraged. But he could face that if it meant he could save Süreyya from marrying this Russian peasant, Vasily Ljubov.

He paced the floor. While he'd lived in the Crimea, he had learned the customs of the Russian Orthodox church. The couple would be declared man and wife when the priest placed wedding crowns on their heads. After that, not even he, an Ottoman prince, could separate them. Unless he had Vasily Ljubov killed. But again, if his father discovered he was involved in the murder of a Russian Christian, the sultan would order his execution. It would be a gesture of peace, and his father would sacrifice him, whether he was shezade or not. That plan would not bring he and Süreyya together.

One evening, close to the wedding day, Aunt Ludmilla arranged for Süreyya and Vasily to sit together in the salon, where she would chaperone them. Soon her aunt was dozing near the warm fire and Vasily, after checking that her aunt was asleep, joined his fiancée on the settle.

'So …' He took Süreyya's hand. 'Did you enjoy your time in the harem?'

She looked at him, wondering where the question was leading. 'It was an interesting life,' she said.

'I'm sure it was. You little *whore*.'

He dragged her hand and pulled it to his crotch, then pressed her fingers on his swollen penis. She tried to pull her hand away, but he held it tight, pressing it and moving it against him.

'Stop! Let me go,' she shouted.

'You should be used to doing this!' he hissed.

He released her hand, then grabbing her hair, he pushed her face between his legs, pulling aside the rough cloth of his pants. She struggled, half-suffocated by the disgusting smell of his crotch and his hand pushing against the back of her head.

'Put your mouth around it, whore! Wait until I get you into our marriage bed. I'll show you what a nice prick can do. And you can show me what you learned from the Turk.'

Aunt Ludmilla snorted in her sleep and moved. Vasily yanked Süreyya's head up and pulled his jerkin across to cover himself. He stood up, put his hand over her mouth, and dragged her, struggling and angry, to her feet. He pushed her into the corner, behind where her aunt slept. She struggled and tried to bite his hand, but he threw her against the wall. As he fumbled with his clothes and her skirt, she felt him shudder and gasp. He released her and crumpled to his knees, his hand over his leaking crotch. He tried to pull her with him as he lost control of himself. She kicked his shoulder hard and knocked him sideways onto the floor.

'Animal!' she spat and fled from the chamber, leaving Vasily in a desperate, gasping heap.

Süreyya didn't care if her aunt woke and saw him, but she knew she had to leave before they forced her into a marriage with this brutish man. Seizing a candle, she ran up to her bedchamber. Once inside, she pulled the table across to bar the door. She dragged a bag from under her bed and threw some clothes into it. There were bars on the window, but she knew how to get out of the house, and how to get to the waterside. She moved the table aside and turned the handle of her door. But someone had locked it. Vasily—he had followed her up the stairs and imprisoned her.

'You will stay there till our wedding day, bitch,' he hissed through the keyhole.

She shook the door handle. 'Open this door! How dare you lock me in?'

His mocking laugh enraged her. 'Stay in there, whore!'

She hit the door with her bag. 'I will not be a prisoner in my uncle's house!' she shouted. 'Open the door or I'll tell him what you did!'

She heard the key grate in the lock. Enraged, she flung the door open and hit Vasily hard in the crotch with her travel bag. He doubled over and fell to his knees. She grabbed the key from the lock and ran to the stairs. But Vasily staggered to his feet and seized her when she was halfway down. The commotion had disturbed the servants and woken her aunt.

'What is going on here?' she demanded.

'I caught her trying to escape,' Vasily gasped.

'Oh no, no, no, Rusalka.' She took the bag from her niece's hand and hurried her back up the stairs. 'Go, Vasily!' she said firmly over her shoulder as she led Süreyya back to her bare chamber. 'Calm yourself, niece, and lie down.' Her aunt smoothed the bedclothes and, shaking her head, she left the chamber.

Süreyya rushed to the door and locked it, then threw herself on the bed.

'Where are you, Orhan?' she said out loud, a sob catching in her throat. 'Come and save your sevgili!'

To the prince's surprise, the grand vizier himself visited Orhan with a personal message from the sultan. 'His Highness wishes to speak with you after midday prayers on Friday,' the chief minister said. 'He has sent you a missive.'

The statesman handed the prince a scroll, bowed, and left. Orhan closed the door, sat at his desk, and slit the wax seal. He unrolled the thick paper and read his father's words with mounting irritation:

My dearest and only son, Shezade Orhan,

    I remind you that I, Sultan of all the Ottomans, shadow of God on earth, commander of the faithful and successor of the Prophet, custodian of the holy cities of Mecca and Medina … Pādishah of the three cities of Constantinople, Edirne and Bursa, I, your father, am also the Caliph, the religious leader of all Muslims. You will inherit this duty on my death. It is therefore imperative that you show your piety. Nothing_must prevent you from attending tomorrow's worship with me, your sultan, at the Aya Sofia Mosque.'

Orhan threw the scroll down. Did his father know about the wedding in Pera? Were spies reporting to him as well? This was an order, not a reminder, of his duty. Orhan was frantic; he was being controlled by palace protocol. It was already Thursday morning, and he desperately needed a plan of action that didn't involve force and bloodshed in Pera. Another directive from his father instructed the prince to finish Prince Ahmet's Edirne papers today. The sultan would discuss them with his heir tomorrow after prayers. In addition, his mother had sent a message about a celebratory meal, starting early Friday evening. Orhan didn't know what she was celebrating, and he didn't care. He suspected his parents were conspiring to keep him in the palace, to prevent him from causing trouble. He must keep his arrangements secret. The sultan might decide to put a guard on his door and confine his son to his chambers.

Orhan's servant responded to a gentle tap on the door.

'Sire, Abdul Agha wishes to speak with you, on a matter of some urgency, he says.'

'Show him in.'

To Orhan's surprise, the agha had the *Book of Couchings* under his arm. He waited with bowed head until Orhan, after seeing the volume, dismissed the servants.

'Abdul?'

'Sire,' Abdul said. 'I have had a visit from Doctor Rebeka.'

'Is she happy her husband is not to be executed?'

'Relieved, sire, yes. But she came on a different matter, which concerns you and Ikbal Süreyya ...'

'Don't cry, darling Rusalka,' Aunt Ludmilla chided her. 'This is your wedding day!' She brushed the tears off Süreyya's blue gown and dabbed her niece's eyes. 'Your gown is beautiful, and you will be a beautiful bride.' She hugged Süreyya. 'I'm sorry you can't marry your prince, but Ottoman princes and sultans don't marry—you know that. You would always be a slave.'

Süreyya sipped the ayran the maid brought her, trying to quell the nausea she'd felt every morning since arriving at her aunt and uncle's house.

'Do you have my sapphire pendant, Aunt? I must wear it.'

'I have it. Vasily took your jewellery and the gold as a dowry, but I set the pendant aside as you requested.'

Süreyya held out her hand.

'Is it wise to wear it?' her aunt asked. 'Vasily knows your jewellery was a gift from the prince.'

'It is very special to me, Aunt. Vasily will not see it.'

Her aunt sighed and helped her fasten the gold chain around her neck. The sapphire nestled between Süreyya's breasts. She slipped the crescent brooch into her pocket without her aunt noticing. Even though the fateful ceremony was drawing closer, she still hoped there might be a chance for her to escape Vasily's clutches. She had escaped from the slave ship—surely she could escape from him?

Shezade, Crown Prince Orhan, flanked by his guards, walked several steps behind the pādishah on their way to the mosque. He heard the call to prayer as it echoed from Aya Sofia to the smaller mosques in the district. He nodded to the townsfolk, who stood on either side of the path, eager to glimpse the royal family, but he couldn't stop thinking of Süreyya. Only one thought thudded in his brain—she was to be married today. After what Abdul had told him, Orhan felt he would be justified in going ahead with his plan.

Cheers and shouts of 'Allah save the sultan!' roused him from his reverie as Prince Orhan followed his father into the courtyard of the Aya Sofia mosque. Two guards went ahead and two stayed as Orhan washed in the separate area set aside for the royal household. It was a ritual he had performed a thousand times: he splashed cold water from the running fountain on his face, washed his hands, arms and feet, and rinsed his mouth. He extended his hand to a servant for a towel.

'Here, sire,' a familiar voice said.

Orhan blinked and wiped his eyes with the back of his hand. Instead of his usual servant, Abdul Agha handed him the white cloth.

'News?' Orhan dried his hands and face quickly.

'Sire.' Abdul glanced around, and the prince waved away his guards.

'Is she married?' He wanted to grab the agha's arm, but controlled himself.

'No sire. The wedding is late this afternoon, in the Church of St Michael in Pera.'

Orhan dried his feet and returned the cloth. He stared at the ground, trying to assemble his scattered thoughts. He was conscious of the water emptying into the fountain, the muezzin calling the faithful to prayer, and the shifting feet of his guards, who were waiting at a distance to escort him inside the mosque.

'At *Maghreb*—sunset prayers?'

Abdul nodded, but said nothing, and Orhan clenched his fists.

'I must stop it, Abdul.'

Orhan signalled to his chief guard.

'Have the royal caique ready for me at the dock between afternoon and sunset prayers,' he said quietly. 'I will cross to Galata. On the Galata side, I need a saddled horse. I also want a royal coach to follow me to Pera, and I will take four guards with me. No one must know of this plan, except those who are involved.'

The man bowed his head. 'Yes, sire. I will have everything in place.'

Abdul stepped forward. 'Sire, is it wise?' he ventured.

'Maybe not, Abdul, but I shall still do it,' the prince answered. 'Have the chambers ready for the return of Ikbal Süreyya this evening.'

Abdul bowed his head and moved away.

Orhan clenched his fists. He would stop this wedding, even if he died in the attempt. He chafed at his present duty to his father and to Allah.

It seemed most of the city had crammed into the Aya Sofia mosque, all straining to look at the royal family. Prince Orhan took his place alongside his father in the secluded imperial area and joined in the prayer ritual. He was too preoccupied to listen to the sermon. He went over and over his plan as he kneeled on his prayer rug.

CHAPTER 28

Süreyya's aunt and uncle walked with her from the house to the nearby church. When they got close to the open door, she heard the congregation singing the wedding hymn. The sound rose on the damp, windswept air, and Süreyya stopped. She covered her mouth, wanting to shout 'NO!' at the top of her voice. Her aunt and uncle held her tightly as she swayed on her feet.

'It's for the best, believe me, Rusalka,' Aunt Ludmilla said as she adjusted the fine lace veil over Süreyya's blank face and nudged her toward the open door. 'You look beautiful and respectable in your blue dress,' she added.

Süreyya didn't reply. Her closed-up throat ached with unshed tears.

Why were they doing this to her? Everyone in the house knew Vasily had tried to lock her in the bedchamber. Her aunt must have seen his stained crotch when she'd woken suddenly the previous evening. If only her father were here, she thought, he would stop this.

Her uncle left her with her aunt and walked to the narthex: the entrance porch of the small Russian Orthodox Church. Süreyya heard him greet Vasily Ljubov, who had arrived ahead of them. When she entered the church, Vasily was standing to the left of the bishop. He wore the elaborate dark clothes of a successful merchant. They were in stark contrast to Uncle Andrei's splendid bishop's crown and vestments. The bishop's gold-embroidered cream satin robes shimmered in the sombre church.

Vasily paid for his clothes with my gold—a gift from Prince Orhan to me. Süreyya clenched her fists. The bishop took her hand and joined it with Vasily's hard, calloused one. She flinched when he squeezed her fingers tightly. In his other hand, Vasily held a lit candle, and a priest handed one to Süreyya; the flame flickered as she grasped it with trembling fingers.

Through her veil, she glimpsed curious eyes following the passage of the bride and groom. The bishop led the couple toward a table covered with an ivory cloth on which a gold crucifix glowed in the dimness. From every wall, paintings of saints of the church watched her slow progress.

Everything was so familiar to her. She looked up at the iconostasis, the elaborate wooden wall that separated the congregation from the sanctuary. Icons of gold-haloed saints looked down on her: the Holy Virgin with her Child, and then Christ, the ruler of the world.

As they neared the wedding table, the congregation, who stood in silence, moved with them until a semi-circle of strangers surrounded her. She looked at the icon of the Virgin Mary in its arched silver frame and said a silent prayer:

You saved me once, Holy Virgin. Save me again, I beg you!

Her step faltered when she saw the two wedding crowns on a low table. As soon as her uncle fixed the crowns on their heads, she would be Vasily's wife. She loathed him, and she knew he despised everything about her except her dowry.

Why had Orhan not come for her? He was a rich and powerful prince; he must know what would happen to her. Surely Abdul had told him? Didn't he love her enough to save her from this terrible fate?

The church door creaked shut behind her. It muffled the sound of *Maghreb*, the call to evening prayers that floated across the Golden Horn and over the buildings of Pera. Her heart sank and tears rose in her throat. She had to accept her fate; Prince Orhan would not come on this Muslim holy day.

The bishop released the bride's and groom's hands and took his place in front of them.

Süreyya swayed, and her future husband took her arm to steady her, as the flame of her candle flickered. *It's over*, she thought. *He isn't coming.*

Her uncle read from the bible in Russian, his voice resonating around the small church. He sang the liturgy and paused as the congregation answered. Süreyya felt them pressing forward, hemming her in. She longed to hear Orhan's deep voice, see his dark eyes meeting hers, his lips seeking her lips.

Vasily took her hand and slipped the ring on her finger. Her uncle looked at his niece and told her she should do the same for her fiancé. Through her veil, she watched as the priest readied the crowns for the irrevocable part of the marriage ceremony. She felt her throat closing up again with unshed tears. The bishop folded the bride and groom's hands in his and walked the couple around the altar table three times. He turned to Vasily.

'Vasily Ljubov, do you know of any reason you should not marry this woman?' The bishop's voice rang out in the silent church.

'I know of none,' Vasily replied.

'And you, Rusalka Maria Ivanova, do you know of any reason you should not marry this man?' her uncle intoned.

The congregation murmured; people were pressing closer to her now, eager to hear her response. Süreyya kept her eyes fixed on the bare marble floor of the church. *There is a very good reason,* she thought. *I am not a virgin, and Vasily revolts me.* She felt nauseous—this odious man would touch every part of her body with his calloused hands and force himself inside her.

Her uncle's voice cut across her thoughts. 'Rusalka Maria Ivanova.' He frowned and repeated the question. 'Do you know of any reason you should not marry this man?'

Before she could answer, Süreyya heard a voice say her name and felt a flutter of cold air sweep through the church. She turned her head; the outer door of the church was wide open. She could hardly believe her eyes. Prince Orhan was standing in the doorway. The persistent rain swept through the open door and his cloak, fastened at the neck with the crescent brooch, swirled around his thighs.

Orhan's breath caught in his throat as he looked intently at her. She wasn't wearing the wedding crown. She hadn't married Vasily yet. He had taken a boat across the treacherous, windswept waters of the Golden Horn, rode up the hill to Pera, and it had not been in vain.

The congregation turned as one and stared at the tall stranger. They parted as he walked toward the altar table. The diamond at the centre of his black turban glowed in the sombre church. He glanced at the startled gaping faces, knowing that few of them had ever seen an Ottoman prince. He caught his breath.

'Süreyya!' he said.

Hearing his voice, she turned, swayed, and dropped her candle. A priest caught her arm and stamped out the candle flame.

'*I* know a reason Rusalka Maria Ivanova should not marry him!' Prince Orhan announced in Russian. 'She is engaged to me, Prince Orhan, the next sultan of the Ottoman Empire.'

The onlookers gasped as he strode past them, cleaving his way through the circle of people surrounding the couple.

'Take your hand off your dagger, Vasily Ljubov!' he said. 'I am armed, and so are my guards. Step back!'

When Orhan reached the frozen tableau of churchmen at the altar, he put his hand on his heart and bowed.

'My apologies, Your Grace. I am Prince Orhan, son of the Ottoman Sultan. I wish to marry your niece.'

Süreyya clutched her throat. A deep silence had descended on the stunned congregation. After a few seconds, Bishop Andrei looked around, then turned to Orhan.

'Your highness, this is …' But he couldn't find the words.

Orhan took Süreyya's arm. 'Of course, I would come for you, sevgilim,' he whispered in Turkish. 'I love you.'

Vasily Ljubov moved for the first time. 'You tricked me,' he hissed at the bishop. 'You said he did not defile her!'

Prince Orhan reached out and shook the man's arm. Still speaking in Russian, he said, 'I did not *defile* her. I will break with Ottoman tradition, and forsake all others. She will become my wife, and I believe she is carrying my child.'

Several people in the congregation gasped.

'My *wife*,' Orhan repeated.

Vasily shrugged off Orhan's hand and stepped back. The bishop regained his composure.

'This is outrageous!' Bishop Andrei said. 'You have disturbed the sanctity of a Christian church and interrupted a Christian wedding!'

'Your Grace.' The prince bowed again. 'Please accept my deepest apologies for entering your church in this manner. As she will be my wife, my only wife, this is an affair of state as much as of the heart. So, to show my gratitude to you and your people, I will make a generous gift to the parish here in Constantinople, and to your diocese in Russia.'

He turned to Süreyya and brought her hand to his lips, then looked from uncle to niece. 'My dearest Süreyya, I will love you and care for you all my life.'

'Orhan,' Süreyya whispered his name.

'If you come with me and be my only one, my *only* one, you must bid your family farewell,' he said. He leaned toward her. 'Doctor Rebeka told me the good news. You are with child. She is certain of it.'

Süreyya searched his face and looked deep into his eyes through her veil. 'A child?'

Orhan nodded and watched her as she turned to her aunt.

Was she wavering? Would she come with him, or would she choose her own people and religion? She might not believe him about the child. He might yet still lose her.

Süreyya kissed first her aunt's cheek, then bowed her head to her uncle.

'I beg your blessing and forgiveness,' she said to her family. 'I love Prince Orhan. He is God's gift to me, and I know in my heart and my head that he will take care of me.'

Orhan released his pent-up breath as Süreyya's uncle fixed her with a stern expression. He looked to Orhan and back to Süreyya.

'Rusalka, the sultan himself signed a paper releasing you into our care ...' the bishop began.

'Into *your* care, Uncle, not Vasily's,' she countered, and turned to Orhan.

'Your Grace,' Orhan said. 'I repeat, I shall marry your niece. She will be my wife, not an odalisque. I will take care of her.'

Bishop Andrei bowed his head and murmured a prayer asking for God's guidance. His deep sigh echoed around the silent church as he raised his head.

'Then God bless you and protect you, Rusalka. You have rejected your own people, but go in peace.' He made the sign of the cross over her bowed head. 'Christians of Constantinople, and his All Holiness, George, the Patriarch, must accept the rule of the infidel.' He gave Orhan a hard look. 'If the sultan's son desires your hand, then so be it.'

Süreyya held Orhan's arm, and they turned away from the group at the wedding table. The congregation parted. Through her veil, she saw Vasily's furious expression and the stunned faces of the crowd. Some prayed for her soul; others crossed themselves and whispered comments.

'He's the son of the sultan.'

'How could she dishonour her family? She's a fallen woman. She has consorted with the infidel.'

Outside the church door, the imperial guard stood with bowed heads. Orhan turned to her and took her hand.

'Are you certain? You *do* want to return with me to the palace?' he asked. 'We will marry and be a family. You will always be my ikbal, my favourite.'

Süreyya smiled and took his other hand. She placed the crescent brooch in his palm.

'The circle is complete, Orhan … sevgilim … my love.'

ACKNOWLEDGMENTS

Several people have read, corrected, and commented on the manuscript of *The Favourite of the Harem*. Many thanks to my husband Harvey Broadbent, whose knowledge of Ottoman history and Turkish has been invaluable to me while writing this novel. In addition, he's kept the domestic wheels turning while I've edited and re-edited the text. Thank you Jane Cameron, Louise Cox, and Frances Lyon for reading an early draft of the novel. Your comments helped me reshape the manuscript. I'm also grateful for the input from members of my two writing groups. Thanks to Vivien Wilson, Helen Lyne, Felicity Pulman, Bea Yell, Rita Shaw, and Margaret Zanardo for letting me know when things didn't work. Many thanks also to the 'Turramurra Writers': Isolde Martyn, Kandy Shepherd, Cathleen Ross, Penny Janu, Cynthia Scott, and Melinda Seed, whose combined writing experience was extremely helpful.

Thank you Deb Lewis-Bizley and Tim Brook for drawing the excellent maps of the palace and Istanbul at the beginning of the book.

I'd also like to thank my publisher, Michelle Lovi of Odyssey Books, for her careful final edit of this work. I'm indebted to Dr Leslie Pierce, the American academic, for her detailed scholarly works about the imperial harem of the Ottoman sultans. Thanks also to Dr Colin Imber, formerly lecturer in Turkish studies at Manchester University, UK, for his contributions and comments about various aspects of harem life.

ABOUT THE AUTHOR

Cindy Davies lives in Sydney, Australia with husband Harvey Broadbent. Her previous novels, also published by Odyssey Books, *The Afghan Wife* and *The Revolutionary's Cousin,* are set in Iran, USA, and Australia. Both novels have won awards. Cindy wanted to write a story set in Turkey because she lived there for two years. She has studied the history of the country, and returned many times as a visitor and tour guide. *The Favourite of the Harem* is the result.

Cindy has worked as an English language teacher, freelance writer, and tour guide in Sydney and Turkey. In between writing, she spends her time giving talks about Iran, the Brontë sisters (a personal passion), and the harems of the Ottoman sultans. She's also a member of a choir, which serves to keep her brain sharp. In 2020, she was awarded a writer's residency in Devon, UK. She took this up in 2023 to research her fourth novel, set in both Australia and the UK. Its working title is *Unaccompanied Baggage.*

www.cindydavies.com.au